For John -

Happy
Birthday!

Your friend,

Mike

↑

APPLES

AND PEARS

AND OTHER STORIES
BY GUY DAVENPORT

NORTH POINT PRESS · SAN FRANCISCO · 1984

"The Bowmen of Shu" has been published before in *Blast 3* and in a finely printed limited edition by The Grenfell Press; "Fifty-Seven Views of Fuji-yama" was first published in *Granta*, in England, and later in the United States by *The Hudson Review*; parts of "Apples and Pears" have appeared before, in early drafts: "Joop Zoetemelk Gagne le Maillot Jaune" in *Antaeus*, and a section provisionally titled "Apples and Pears" in *Conjunctions*.

The drawings on pp. 8 and 10 are by Henri Gaudier-Brzeska; all other drawings are by Guy Davenport.

To the Memory of
FRANÇOIS MARIE CHARLES FOURIER [1772–1837]

Stories

since Eden gardens labor, For
series distributes harmonies, attraction Governs
destinies.
  Louis Zukofsky, "A"–23

The Bowmen of Shu

27 DECEMBER 1914

Here we are picking the first fern shoots and saying when shall we get back to our country, away from *das Trommelfeuer*, the gunners spent like winded dogs, white smoke and drizzle of sparks blowing across barbed wire in coils, the stink of cordite. 27 December 1914. Avalanches of shrapnel from field guns firing point-blank with fuses set at zero spray down in gusts, an iron windy rain. Here we are because we have the huns for our foemen. It's with pleasure, dear Cournos, that I've received news from you. We have no comfort because of these Mongols. You must have heard of my whereabouts from Ezra to whom I wrote some time ago. Since then nothing new except that the weather has had a change for the better. We grub the soft fern shoots, the rain has stopped for several days and with it keeping the watch in a foot deep of liquid mud, the crazy duckwalks, hack and spit of point guns.

HOOGE RICHEBOURG GIVENCHY

The smell of the dead out on the wire is all of barbarity in one essence. Also sleeping on sodden ground. The frost having set it, we have the pleasure of a firm if not warm bed, and when you have turned to a warrior you become hardened to many evils. When anyone says *return* the others are full of sorrow. Anyway we leave the marshes on the fifth January for a rest behind the lines, and we cannot but look forward to the long forgotten luxury of a bundle of straw in a warm barn or loft, also to that of hot food, for we are so near the enemy and they behave so badly with their guns that we dare not light kitchen fire within two or three miles, so that when we get the daily meal at one in the morning it is necessarily cold, but alike the chinese bowmen in Ezra's poem we had rather eat fern shoots than go back now, and whatever the suffering may be it is soon forgotten and we want the victory.

SCULPTURAL ENERGY IS THE MOUNTAIN

Sculptural feeling is the appreciation of masses in relation. Sculptural ability is the defining of these masses by planes. The Paleolithic Vortex resulted in the decoration of the Dordogne caverns. Early stone-age man disputed the earth with animals.

LES FALLACIEUX DÉTOURS DU LABYRINTHE

The rifles, *crack! thuck!* whip at the bob of helmets of the *boches* in the trenches across the desolation of an orchard. If they stir too busily at a point, our *mitrailleuses* rattle at them, their tracers bright as bees in a garden even in this dead light. With my knife I have carved the stock of a German rifle into a woman with her arms as interlocked rounded triangles over her head, her breasts are triangles, her sex, her thighs. Like the Africans I am constrained by the volume of my material, the figure to be found wholly within a section of trunk. De Launay handles the piece with understanding eyes and hands. He is an anthropologist working on labyrinths, and has a major paper prepared for the *Revue Archéologique*. I am, I tell him, a sculptor, descended from the masons who built Chartres. We have seen a cathedral burn, its lead roof melting in on its ruin. De Launay sees a pattern in this hell. We are the generation to understand the world, the accelerations of the turn of vortices, how their energy spent itself, all the way back to the Paleolithic (he tells me about Cartailhac and Teilhard and Breuil). But our knowledge, which must come from contemplation and careful inspection, has collided with a storm, a vortex of stupidity and idiocy. His tracing of the labyrinth from prehistory forward has

put him in a real labyrinth of trenches, its Minotaur the Germans, that cretin-
ous monster of pedantic dullness. Yet, Henri, he says, we are learning the
Paleolithic in a way that was closed to us as *savant* and *sculpteur*. His smile is
deliciously ironic in a face freckled with mud spatter, his eyes lively under the
brim of his helmet.

MAÇON
How veddy interesting, Miss Mansfield said, sipping tea, when I told her I
was descended from the craftsmen who carved Chartres. *I could have died of
shame*, Sophie screeched at me as soon as we were outside. These people, she
said, will have no respect for you. I am of the Polish gentry, which is hard
enough to get them to understand. Very much the *pusinka*.

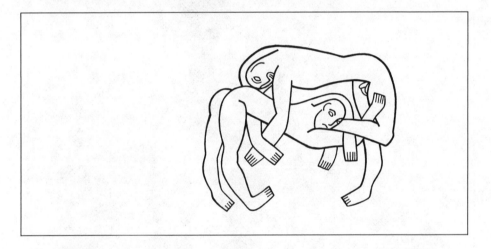

SMOKING RIVERS OF MUD
We say will we be let to go back in October. There is no ease in royal affairs.
We have no comfort. Our sorrow is bitter. But we would not return to our
country. What flower has come into blossom. We have time to busy ourselves
with art, reading poems, so that intellectually we are not yet dead nor degenerate. Whose chariot, the General's horses, his horses even, are tired. They
were strong. We have no rest. Three battles a month. By heaven, his horses are
tired. The generals are on them, the soldiers are by them. If you can write me
all about the Kensington colony, the neo-greeks and neo-chinese. Does the
Egoist still appear? What does it contain? My best wishes for a prosperous
and happy 1915. Yours Sincerely Henri Gaudierbrzeska.

THE NORTH BORDER. BLUE MOUNTAINS. BARBARIANS.

The horses are well trained. The generals have ivory arrows and quivers ornamented with fishskin. The enemy is swift. We must be careful. When we set out, the willows were drooping with spring. We come back in the snow. We are hungry and thirsty, our mind is full of sorrow. Who will know of our grief? The newspapers say that our trench labyrinths are comfortable, that the British throw grenades with the ease of men accustomed to games of sport from their infancy. Tiger in the bamboo. Thunder from beyond the mountain. How and when we shall survive who knows? Stink of cordite. Rain of ash.

THE IMP

Stands in mischief, knees flexed to scoot.

DAS LABYRINTH

Between Neuville-St.-Vaast to the north and Arras to the south, and Mt. St.-Eloi and Vimy east and west, lay the underground maze of tunnels, mines, fortresses in slant caves, some as deep as fifty feet, which the Germans called The Labyrinth, as insane a nest of armaments and men as military strategy ever conceived. Its approaches were seeded with deathtraps and mine fields. It was invisible to aerial observation. Even its designers had forgotten all the corridors, an *Irrgarten* lit with pale battery-powered lights. Foch himself came to oversee its siege. The British hacked their way toward Lille, the French toward Lens, past The Labyrinth. The offensive began 9 May 1915. Out from Arras, past Ste.-Catherine, 7ᵉ Compagnie, 129ᵉ Infanterie, IIIᵉ Corps, Capitaine Ménager the Commandant, marched on the road to Vimy Ridge, Corporal Henri Gaudier at the head of his squad. Except for mad wildflowers in sudden patches, their tricolor was the only alleviation in the grey desert of craters, burnt farms, a blistered sky.

THE SOLDAT'S REMARK TO GENERAL APPLAUSE

Fuck all starters of wars up the arse with a handspike dipped in tetanus.

BRANCUSI TO GAUDIER

Les hommes nus dans la plastique ne sont pas si beaux que les crapauds.

THE WOLF

Is my brother, the tiger my sister. They think *eat*, they think grass, bamboo, forest, plain, river. Their regal indifference to my drawing them, on my knees outside their cages, is the indifference of the stars. I feel abased, ashamed, worthless in their presence. But I close, a little, the gap between me and them, in catching some of their grace. And afterwards, they will say, *He drew the wolf, the deer, the cat. His sculpture was of stag and birds, of men and women in whom there was animal grace.*

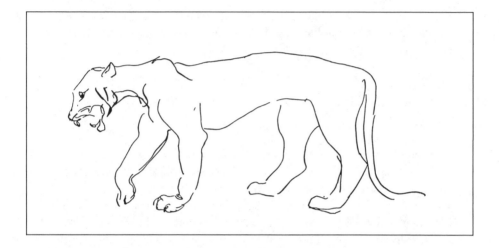

THE CATHEDRAL BURNT IN FRONT OF MY EYES
Rheims. My Lieutenant sent me to repair some barbed wire between our trenches and the enemy's. I went through the mist with two fellows. I was on my back under the wire when *zut!* out comes the moon. The *boches* could see me *et alors! pan pan pan!* Their fire cut through the tangle above me, which came down and snared me. I sawed it with my knife in a dozen places. The detail got back to the trench, said I was done for, and with the lieutenant's concurrence they blasted away at the *boches*, who returned the volleys, and then the artillery joined in, with me smack between them. I crawled flat on my stomach back to our trench, and brought the repair coil of barbed wire and my piece with me. The lieutenant could not believe his eyes. When the ruckus quieted down, I went back out, finished the job, and got back at 5 a.m. I have a gash, from the wire, in my right leg, and a bullet nick in my right heel.

LA ROSALIE
The bayonet, so called because we draw it red from the round guts of pig-eyed Germans.

FONT DE GAUME

A hundred and fifty meters of blind cave drilled a million years ago by a river underground into the soft green hills at Les Eyzies de Tayac in the Val Dordogne, in which, some forty thousand years ago, hunters of Magdalenian times painted and engraved the immediate reaches with a grammar of horses and bison, and deeper up the bore, mammoths, reindeer, cougars, human fetuses, human hands, a red rhinoceros, palings of lines recording the recurrence of some event, masks or faces, perhaps of the wind god, the rain god, the god of the wolves, and at the utmost back depth, horse and mountain cat.

NIGHT ATTACK

We crept through a wood as dark as pitch, fixed bayonets, and pushed some 500 yards amid fields until we came to a wood. There we opened fire and in a bound we were along the bank of the road where the Prussians stood. We shot at each other some quarter of an hour at a distance of 12 to 15 yards and the work was deadly. I brought down two great giants who stood against a burning heap of straw.

SOLDAT

I have been fighting for two months and I can now gauge the intensity of life.

DOGFIGHT

Enid Bagnold, horse-necked, square-jawed, nymph-eyed, finally came to sit, after weeks of postponing, Sophie sniffy with jealousy, suspicion, fright. The day was damp and cold. Gaudier lumped the clay on its armature and set to, nimble-fingered, eyes from the Bagnold to the clay. His nose began to bleed. He worked on. The Bagnold said, Your nose is bleeding. I know, said Gaudier. In that sack on the wall behind you there's something to stop it. She looked in the bag: clothes. Some male and dirty, some female and dirty. Rancid shirts, mildewed stockings. She chose a pair of Sophie's drawers and tied them around Gaudier's face, to soak up, at least, some of the blood, which had reddened his neck and smock. Lower, he said, I can't see. Take your pose again, quickly, quickly. She dared not look at him, wild hair, bright black eyes ajiggle above a ruin of bloody rags. The light was going swiftly, the room dark and cold. He worked on, as if by touch. And then a barrage of roars pierced the air. A dogfight outside. My God, she said. Tilt your chin, he said. Keep your neck tall. She tried the pose, wondering how he could see her in the dark. The dogfight raged the louder. Gaudier went to the window. The streetlamp at that moment came on, and she watched him with the fascination of horror, masked as he was in bloody cloth, staring out at the dogfight. He watched it with dark, interested eyes, his hands white with clay against the dirty window. Monsieur Gaudier! she said, are you quite in command of yourself? You may go, he said.

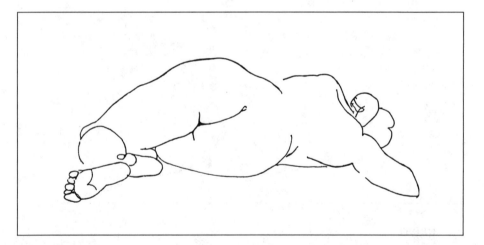

PARTRIDGES

Horses are worn out in three weeks, die by the roadside. Dogs wander, are destroyed, and others come along. With all the destruction that works around us, nothing is changed, even superficially. Life is the same strength, the moving agent that permits the small individual to assert himself. The bursting shells, the volleys, wire entanglements, projectors, motors, the chaos of battle do not alter in the least the outlines of the hill we are besieging. A company of partridges scuttles along before our very trench.

FRITH STREET

Sat on the floor at Hulme's widow's while he talked bolt upright in his North Country farmer's body and stuttered through his admiration and phlegmatic defense of Epstein's flenite pieces, so African as to be more Soninke made than Soninke derived, *feck undity in all its so to speak milky bovinity* (and Marsh clasping his hands, as if in prayer, and giving responses, *teddibly vital isn't it I mean to say* and *the phallic note*, with Ezra cutting his wicked eye at me from his Villon face). Sat with the godlike poet Brooke and the catatonically seriousMiddleton Murray, and the devout, Tancred, Flint, FitzGerald, and the fair-minded skeptics, Wadsworth and Nevinson. The ale was good and Hulme chose his words with booming precision and attack.

RODIN

Conceive form in depth. Under all the planes there is a center in the stone. All things alive swell out from a center. Observe relief, not outline: relief determines the contour. Let emotion stream to your center as water up a root, as sunlight into a leaf. Love, hope, tremble, live.

PARIS 1910

The chisel does not cut the stone, but crushes it. It bites. You brush away, blow away the dust the fine blade has crumbled. The mind drifts free as you work, and memories play at their richest when the attention is engaged with the stone. There was Paris, there was the decision, there was Zosik. England and Germany have nothing like the Parisian café where of a spring evening you sit

outside making a glass of red wine last and last. It was at the Café Cujas that he met another stranger to the city, a poet, a Czech poet—Hlaváček? Svobodová? Bezruč? Dyk?—who, talking of Neruda, of Rimbaud, sorted out Gaudier's array of ambitions and focused them upon sculpture. Rodin! Phidias! Michelangelo! It was the one art that involved the heroic, the bringing of a talent to its fullest maturity to do anything at all. It was an art that demanded the flawless hand, a sense of perfection in the whole, a pitiless and totally demanding art. But it had not been to the Czech that he had announced his commitment, but to the woman Sophie, not as an intention or experiment but as a road he was upon, boldly striding out. *Moi? Je suis sculpteur.* She, for her part, was a writer, a novelist. She had never shown anyone her work, it was too personal, too vulnerable before an unfeeling and uncomprehending world. Night after night he heard her story, not really listening, as it was her face, her eyes, her spirit that he loved, coveting her her maturity—she was thirty-nine, he a green and raw seventeen—and her story was a kind of badly constructed Russian novel. She was a Pole, from near Cracow. Her father threw away a considerable inheritance on gaming and shameless girls. She was the only daughter of nine children, and she was made to feel the disgrace of it, as she was useless as a worker, would have to be provided with a dowry in time. Her brothers called her names, and reproached her with her inferior gender. At sixteen she was put out to work, as her family was tired of supporting her as a burden. They found an old man, a Jew, and offered her to him as a wife. But he, like any other, demanded a dowry with her. This threw Papa Brzesky into a fit. A Jew want a dowry! There were three other attempts to marry her off. Two were likely business for the undertaker. The other was a sensitive young man of broken health whom she loved, the apple of his mother's eye. He came courting and played cards with Mama Brzeska, who one day accused him of cheating and chased him out of the house. Then her father went bankrupt. Sophie made her way to Cracow, hoping to study at the university, but she was neither qualified to enter it nor able to pay the tuition it asked. She came to Paris, took a nursemaid's job, and was driven away by the snide remarks of the other servants, who were ill-bred. She went from menial job to menial job until her health, never robust, gave way. Then she was taken on as a nurse to a rich American family about to return to Philadelphia. She was to look after a ten-year-old boy and his sister. The boy died soon after. The sister begged to hear dirty stories, and when Sophie refused to tell her any, complained to her parents that the nurse bored her to tears. Entertain the child, commanded the parents, so Sophie told her dirty stories, and was promptly fired for moral turpitude and kicked out without a reference. She found refuge in an orphanage in New York run by nuns. They farmed her out as a nanny. Fathers made advances to her, which she could have accepted and gotten rich. But all this time she kept her body pure and virgin. What money

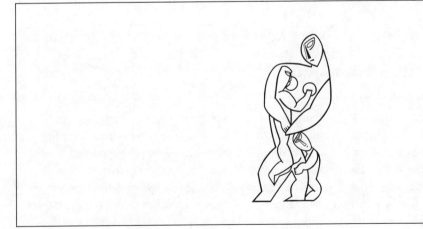

she could manage to save she sent to her youngest brother in Poland, enabling him to emigrate to America. He came, was disappointed, worked as a garbage boy for a hotel, accused Sophie of having tricked him, and would not speak to her ever afterward. A nursing job came along that took her to Paris again. Here she was destitute, and returned to Poland, where she was taken in by a rich uncle. This uncle was a widower and lived in sin with her cousin, whom he had enticed into his bed by telling her that Sophie had often done so. The shock of this lie unstrung her nerves and made a wreck of her composure for the rest of her life. Her brothers taunted her with having gone to America and failed to come back rich. She took up a life of dissipation. If no one believed in her virtue, why keep it? But dissipation undermined her constitution, and she had to recuperate at Baden, little as she could afford it. She then fell in love with a wealthy manufacturer aged fifty-three. He was witty, bright, kind, and in possession of a keen appreciation of the beauties of Nature. He courted her for a year without asking for her hand. When she tried to bring matters to a head, they had a fight that nearly sent them both to the hospital and thence to their graves. In this fracas he disclosed to her that he loved another, by whom

he already had a son, and wished to remain free in case the other ever agreed to be his wife. She felt that her sanity was going. Her rich lover paid for her recuperation at a home in the country. She wrote him daily; he answered none of her letters. She would contemplate for hours the most painless means of doing away with herself. She returned to her family in Poland, where they taunted her with her failure, her age, her pretensions, her ugliness. She made her way to Paris again, and began to observe with fascination the faun-like young man who came every evening to the Bibliothèque Ste.-Geneviève to read books of anatomy. They met on the steps one evening at closing time, and walked along the Seine. She could scarcely believe it when he said he was in love with her.

THE BRITISH MUSEUM
Out of the past, out of Assyria, China, Egypt, the new.

EPSTEIN, BRANCUSI, MODIGLIANI, ZADKINE
Out of the new, a past.

VORTEX
From Rodin, passion. From John Cournos, courage. From Alfred Wolmark, spontaneity of execution. From Epstein, the stone, direct cutting. From Brancusi, purity of form. From Modigliani, the irony of grace. From Africa, the compression of form into minimal volume. From Lewis, the geometric. From Horace Brodsky, *camaraderie de la caserne*. From Ezra Pound, archaic China, the medieval, Dante, recognition. From Sophie, love, abrasion, doubt, the sweetness of an hour.

THE BRONZES OF BENIN
The Calf Bearer, T'ang sacrificial vessels, the shields of New South Wales, Soninke masks, the Egypt of *The Scribe* and *The Pharaoh Hunting Duck in the Papyrus Marsh*, Hokusai, Font de Gaume, Les Combarelles.

JE REVIENS D'UN ENFER

The young anthropologist Robert de Launay, the student of mazes whose paper on labyrinths has been accepted for publication, has been shot through the neck outside the Labyrinth at Neuville-St.-Vaast, drowned in his own blood before the medics could see to the wound. *Je t'écris, cher Ezra, du fond d'une tranchée que nous avons creusée hier pour se protéger des obus qui nous arrivent sur la tête regulièrement toutes les cinq minutes, je suis ici depuis une semaine et nous couchons en plein air, les nuits sont humides et froides et nous en souffrons beaucoup plus que du feu de l'ennemi nous avons du repos aujourd'hui et ça fait bien plaisir.*

ST.-JEAN DE BRAYE

In the dry, brown October of 1891 there was born to Joseph Gaudier of St.-Jean de Braye, maker of fine doors and cabinets, descendant of one of the sculptors of Chartres, a son whom he baptized Henri.

CHARLEVILLE

Far to the south the one-legged Rimbaud lay dying in Marseilles, which he imagined to be Abyssinia. He was anxious that his caravan of camels laden with rifles and ammo should get off to a start before dawn, for the march was to Aden. *Armed with the fierceness of our patience,* he once wrote, *we shall reach the splendid cities at daybreak.*

TARGU JIU

In Craiova the fourteen-year-old Constantin Brancusi was learning to carve wood with chisel and maul. He was a peasant from Pestisani Gori across a larch forest from Targu Jiu, which he left when he was eleven, in the manner of the Rumanians, to master a trade. He would enter the national school for sculptors, and then walk from Rumania to Paris.

L'ENFANT DIFFICILE

He did not spank well, the child Henri. He doubled his fists, held his breath, and arched his back in an agony of stubbornness, until at an early age his parents began to reason with him before whacking his behind. He reasoned back. As he grew older, he kicked them when he was punished, and they reasoned the harder. *A very philosopher*, his father said, and his mother put her head to one side, crossed her hands over her apron, and looked at her son with complacent disappointment. *The rogue*, she said, *the darling little rogue*. He drew, like all children. His mother taught him to draw rabbits, and to surround them with grass and flowers. With his father's marking pencil, carefully sharpened for him with a penknife, he drew ships, igloos, medieval trees, the cathedral at Orléans, and American Indians in their eagle-feather bonnets. At six he turned to insects. At first he drew gay fritillaries and gaudy moths. Only flowers had their absolute design and economy of form, which he thought of as *sitting right*. A roseleaf hopper was tucked into its abrupt parabola as if it were a creature all hat, and yet if you looked it had feet and eyes and chest and belly just like the great dragonflies and damsels of the

Loiret, or the mason wasps that built their combs under the eaves of the shed. But it was the grasshoppers and crickets that he drew most. From the forelegs of the grasshopper he learned the stark clarity of a bold design one half of which was mirror image of the other half. The wings of moths were like that, but the principle was different. Wings worked together, the grasshopper's forelegs worked in opposition to the hindlegs, and yet the effort of the one complemented the effort of the other, like two beings jumping into each other, both going straight up. Earwigs, ants: nothing could be added, nothing subtracted. Who could draw a mosquito? In profile it was an elegance of lines, each at a perfect angle to the others. *Bugs*, his sisters said. Uncle Pierre gave him a box of colored pencils, and he drew pages of ladybirds and shieldbugs and speckled moths.

ARTILLERY BARRAGE. THE LABYRINTH. JUNE 1915.
Smoke boiling black, white underbelly, blooming sulphur, falling dirt and splinters. The daytime moon. Larks.

HENRI LE PETIT
The first day of school, his new oilcloth satchel in his lap, his new pencil box in his hands, he breathed the strange new smell of floor polish and washed slate blackboards in numb expectation. The upper half of the classroom door was glass, through which a bald gentleman in a celluloid collar came and peered from time to time. The teacher was a woman who handled books as he had never seen them handled before, with professional delicacy, grace, smart deliberateness. Down the front of her polka-dot dress she wore a necktie, like a man on Sunday, and a purple ribbon ran from her glasses to her bosom, anchored there by a brooch. The letter A was a moth, B was a butterfly, C was a caterpillar, D was a beetle, E an ant, F a mantis. G and H he knew: he had learned them the other way round, with a dot after each, to indicate who drew his drawings.

RAILWAY ARCH 25
His Font de Gaume. Planes, the surfaces of mass, meet at lines, each tilted at a different angle to light. The mass is energy. The harmony of its surfaces the emotion forever contained and forever released. Here he drank and roared with Brodsky, here he sculpted the phallus, the menhir, the totem called *Hieratic Bust of Ezra Pound. It will not look like you, you know.* It will look like your energy.

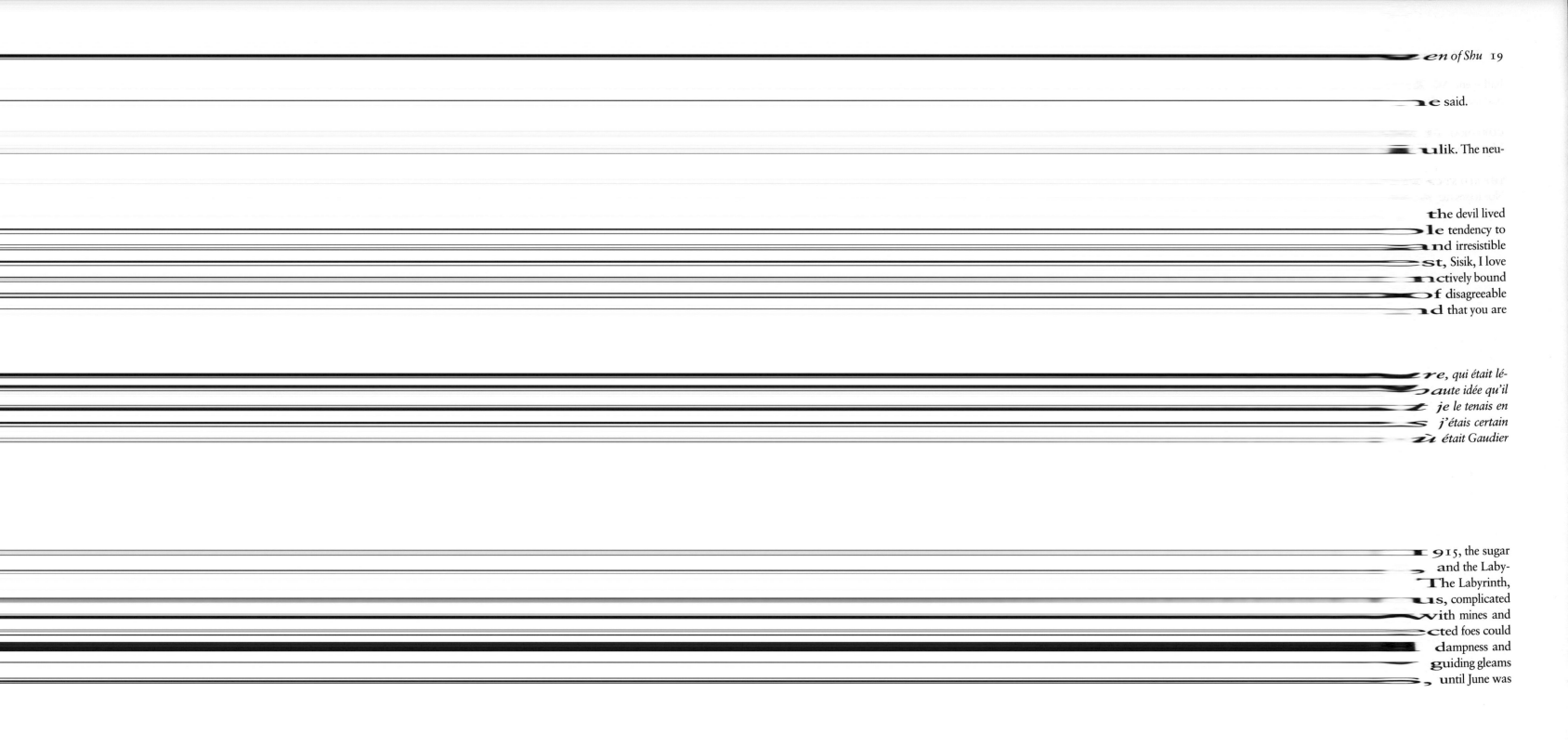

e said.

ulik. The neu-

the devil lived
le tendency to
nd irresistible
st, Sisik, I love
ctively bound
f disagreeable
d that you are

re, qui était lé-
aute idée qu'il
je le tenais en
j'étais certain
était Gaudier

915, the sugar
and the Laby-
The Labyrinth,
s, complicated
ith mines and
cted foes could
dampness and
guiding gleams
until June was

TARGU JIU

In Craiova the fourteen-year-old Constantin Brancusi was learning to carve wood with chisel and maul. He was a peasant from Pestisani Gori across a larch forest from Targu Jiu, which he left when he was eleven, in the manner of the Rumanians, to master a trade. He would enter the national school for sculptors, and then walk from Rumania to Paris.

L'ENFANT DIFFICILE

He did not spank well, the child Henri. He doubled his fists, held his breath, and arched his back in an agony of stubbornness, until at an early age his parents began to reason with him before whacking his behind. He reasoned back. As he grew older, he kicked them when he was punished, and they reasoned the harder. *A very philosopher*, his father said, and his mother put her head to one side, crossed her hands over her apron, and looked at her son with complacent disappointment. *The rogue*, she said, *the darling little rogue.* He drew, like all children. His mother taught him to draw rabbits, and to surround them with grass and flowers. With his father's marking pencil, carefully sharpened for him with a penknife, he drew ships, igloos, medieval trees, the cathedral at Orléans, and American Indians in their eagle-feather bonnets. At six he turned to insects. At first he drew gay fritillaries and gaudy moths. Only flowers had their absolute design and economy of form, which he thought of as *sitting right*. A roseleaf hopper was tucked into its abrupt parabola as if it were a creature all hat, and yet if you looked it had feet and eyes and chest and belly just like the great dragonflies and damsels of the

Loiret, or the mason wasps that built their combs under the eaves of the shed. But it was the grasshoppers and crickets that he drew most. From the forelegs of the grasshopper he learned the stark clarity of a bold design one half of which was mirror image of the other half. The wings of moths were like that, but the principle was different. Wings worked together, the grasshopper's forelegs worked in opposition to the hindlegs, and yet the effort of the one complemented the effort of the other, like two beings jumping into each other, both going straight up. Earwigs, ants: nothing could be added, nothing subtracted. Who could draw a mosquito? In profile it was an elegance of lines, each at a perfect angle to the others. *Bugs*, his sisters said. Uncle Pierre gave him a box of colored pencils, and he drew pages of ladybirds and shieldbugs and speckled moths.

ARTILLERY BARRAGE. THE LABYRINTH. JUNE 1915.
Smoke boiling black, white underbelly, blooming sulphur, falling dirt and splinters. The daytime moon. Larks.

HENRI LE PETIT
The first day of school, his new oilcloth satchel in his lap, his new pencil box in his hands, he breathed the strange new smell of floor polish and washed slate blackboards in numb expectation. The upper half of the classroom door was glass, through which a bald gentleman in a celluloid collar came and peered from time to time. The teacher was a woman who handled books as he had never seen them handled before, with professional delicacy, grace, smart deliberateness. Down the front of her polka-dot dress she wore a necktie, like a man on Sunday, and a purple ribbon ran from her glasses to her bosom, anchored there by a brooch. The letter A was a moth, B was a butterfly, C was a caterpillar, D was a beetle, E an ant, F a mantis. G and H he knew: he had learned them the other way round, with a dot after each, to indicate who drew his drawings.

RAILWAY ARCH 25
His Font de Gaume. Planes, the surfaces of mass, meet at lines, each tilted at a different angle to light. The mass is energy. The harmony of its surfaces the emotion forever contained and forever released. Here he drank and roared with Brodsky, here he sculpted the phallus, the menhir, the totem called *Hieratic Bust of Ezra Pound. It will not look like you, you know.* It will look like your energy.

SOPHIE
All night by her bed, imploring her. It is revolting, unspiritual, she said.

PIK AND ZOSIK
Brother and sister. Even Mr. Pound believed it. Pikus and Zosiulik. The neurotic Pole and her sly fawn of a lover.

MON BON DZIECKO UKOCHANY
According to the little book which I am reading about Dante, the devil lived on very good terms with very few people, because of his terrible tendency to invective and reproach, and his extraordinary gift for irony and irresistible sarcasm—just like my own funny little Sisik. To be quite honest, Sisik, I love you passionately, from the depth of all my being, and I feel instinctively bound to you; what may often make me seem nasty to you is a kind of disagreeable horror that you don't love me nearly so much as I love you, and that you are always on the point of leaving me.

CAPITAINE MÉNAGER
Nous admirions tous Gaudier, non seulement pour sa bravoure, qui était légendaire, mais aussi et surtout pour sa vive intelligence et la haute idée qu'il avait de ses devoirs. A ma compagnie il était aimé de tous, et je le tenais en particulière estime car à cette époque de guerre de tranchées j'étais certain que—grâce à l'exemple qu'il donnerait à ses camarades—là où était Gaudier les Boches ne passeraient pas.

THE OLD WOMAN TO PASSERSBY
J'ai perdu mon fils. L'avez-vous trouvé? Il s'appelle Henri.

CHARGEZ!
One after another in those weeks of May and early June of 1915, the sugar refinery at Souchez, the cemetery of Ablain, the White Road, and the Labyrinth yielded to the fierce, unremitting blows of the French. The Labyrinth, all but impregnable, was a fortification contrived with tortuous, complicated tunnels, sometimes as deep as fifty feet below the surface, with mines and fortresses, deathtraps, caves and shelters, from which unexpected foes could attack with liquid fire or gas or knives. In the darkness and dampness and foulness of those Stygian vaults where in some places the only guiding gleams were from electric flashlights, men battled for days, for weeks, until June was

half spent. What wonder that the Germans could scarcely believe the enemy had made it their own?

CORPORAL HENRI GAUDIER
Mort pour la Patrie. 4 Octobre 1891–5 Juin 1915.

THE RED STONE DANCER
Nos fesses ne sont pas les leurs. Il faut être absolument moderne.

FIFTY-SEVEN VIEWS OF FUJIYAMA

Months, days, eternity's sojourners. Years that unfold from the cherry in flower to rice thick in the flat fields to the gingko suddenly gold the first day of frost to the red fox across the snow. The sampan pilot from Shiogama to Ishinomaki, the postman galloping from Kyoto to Ogaki, what do they travel but time? Our great journey is through the years, even when we doze by the brazier. Clouds move on the winds. We long to travel with them. For I, Bashō, am a traveler. No sooner, last autumn, did I get home from a fine journey along the coast, take the broom to the cobwebs in my neglected house on the Sumida River, see the New Year in, watch the wolves slinking down from the hills shoulder-deep in white drifts, look in wonder all over again, as every spring, at the mist on the marshes, than I was ready to set out through the gates at Shirakawa. I stitched up the slits and rips in my trousers, hitched a new chinstrap to my hat, rubbed my legs with burnt wormwood leaves (which puts vigor into the muscles), and thought all the while of the moon rising full over Matsushima, what a sight that would be when I got there and could gaze on it.

•

We set out, she and I, a fine late summer day, happy in the heft and chink of our gear. We had provender for a fortnight in the wilderness along the Vermont Trail, which we took up on a path through an orchard abandoned years ago, where in generous morning light busy with cabbage butterflies and the green blink of grasshoppers an old pear tree still as frisky and crisp as a girl stood with authority among dark unpruned winesaps gone wild, and prodigal sprawling zinnias, sweetpeas, and hollyhocks that had once been some honest farmwife's flowers and garden grown from seeds that came in Shaker packets from upstate New York or even Ohio, now blooming tall and profuse in sedge and thistle all the way to the tamaracks of the forest edge, all in that elective

concert by which the lion's fellowship makes the mimosa spread. This trail was
blazed back in the century's teens by a knickerbockered and tweed-capped
comitatus from Yale, carrying on a tradition from Raphael Pumpelly and
Percy Wallace and Steele MacKaye, from Thoreau and Burroughs: a journey
with no purpose but to be in the wilderness, to be in its silence, to be together
deep among its trees and valleys and heights.

•

Having, with great luck, sold my house by the river, thereby casting myself
adrift, so to speak, from obligations and responsibilities, I moved in for a while
with my friend and patron, the merchant Sampu, himself a poet. *Bright flash
makes me blink: spring field, farmer's spade.* But before I went I brushed a
poem for my old doorpost. *Others now will sing high in peach blossom time
behind this door wild grass blocks.* And at dawn I set out, more of night still
in the sky than day, as much by moonlight fading as by sunlight arriving, the
twenty-seventh of March. I could just make out the dim outline of Fuji and
the thin white cherry blossoms of Ueno and Yanaka. Farewell, Fuji! Farewell,
cherry blossoms! Friends had got up early to see me off, indeed to go with me
for the first leg of the journey by boat, as far as Senju. It was not until they left
me that I felt, with a jump of my heart, the three hundred miles I was propos-
ing to go. Water stood in my eyes. I looked at my friends and the neat clusters
of houses at Senju as if through rain. *Fish and bird regret that springtime is so
brief.* This was my parting poem. My friends took copies, and watched till I
was out of sight.

•

On the beach at Sounion. Tar and seaweed shift in the spent collapse and slide
of shirred green water just beyond our toes. We had been to see Byron's name
carved with a penknife on a column of Poseidon's temple. Homer mentions
this cape in the *Iliad*, perhaps all of Attika that he knew. It was here that the
redstone *kouros* was excavated who stands in Athens by the javelin-hurling
Zeus. We lie in Greek light. The silence is musical: the restlessness of the Ionian, the click of pebbles pushed by the seawash. There is no other sound. *I am
Hermes. I stand by the grey sea-shingle and wait in the windy wood where
three roads meet.* A poem? From the *Anthology*. Wet eyelashes, lens of water
in navel. Another. *To Priapos, god of gardens and friend to travelers, Damon*

the farmer laid on this altar, with a prayer that his trees and body be hale of limb for yet a while, a pomegranate glossy bright, a skippet of figs dried in the sun, a cluster of grapes, half red, half green, a mellow quince, a walnut splitting from its husk, a cucumber wrapped in flowers and leaves, and a jar of olives golden ripe.

•

All that March day I walked with a wondering sadness. I would see the north, but would I, at my age, ever return? My hair would grow whiter on the long journey. It was already Genroku, the second year thereof, and I would turn forty-five on the way. My shoulders were sore with my pack when I came to Soka, a village, at the end of the day. Travel light! I have always intended to, and my pack with its paper overcoat, cotton bathrobe (neither of which was much in a heavy rain), my notebook, inkblock, and brushes, would have been light enough except for gifts my friends loaded me with at parting, and my own unessential one thing and another which I cannot throw away because my heart is silly. We went, Sora and I, to see the sacred place of Muro-no-Yashima, Ko-no-Hana Sakuya Hime, the goddess of flowering trees. There is another shrine to her on the lower slopes of Fuji. When she was with child, Ninigi-no-Mikoto, her husband, would not believe that she was pregnant by a god. She locked herself into a room, set fire to it, and in the flames gave birth to Hohodemi-no-Mikoto, the fire-born noble. Here poets write of the smoke, and the peasants do not eat a speckled fish called *konoshiro*.

•

We set out, she and I, like Bashō on the narrow road to the deep north from his house on the Sumida where he could not stay for thinking of the road, of the red gate at Shirakawa, of the full moon over the islands of Matsushina, he and Kawai Sogoro in their paper coats, journey proud in *wabi zumai*, thinking of wasps in the cedar close of an inn, chrysanthemums touched by the first mountain frost. A few years before Minoru Hara and I had climbed Chocorua to find a single lady slipper on a carpet of pine needles, to which he bowed, Chocorua that Ezra Pound remembered in the concentration camp at Pisa, fusing it with Tai Shan in his imagination, Chocorua where Jessie Whitehead lived with her pet porcupines and bear, Chocorua where William James died, Thoreau's Chocorua that he strolled up laughing that people used the word *climb* of its easy slopes. We set out into the deuteronomical mountains Charles Ives rings against *The Rockstrewn Hills Join in the People's Outdoor Meeting* with the chime of iron on iron, sabre, bell, and hammer, bugle and messkit, ramrod and spur, remembering how congenial and incantatory music led the caissons over the Potomac to Shiloh.

•

I spent the night of March thirtieth at Gozaemon the Honest's Inn at Nikko Mountain. Such was my landlord's name, which he made much of, assuring me that I would sleep out of harm's way on his grass pillows. When a stranger so advertises his honesty, you take more care than ever, but this innkeeper was as good as his name. There was no more guile in him than in Buddha the merciful, and Confucius would have approved of his scrupulousness and manners. Next day, April first, we climbed Nikko, Mountain of the Sun's Brilliance. The sainted Kobo Daishi named it and built the temple on it a thousand years ago. Its holiness is beyond words. You can see its benevolence in every field round about. In it I wrote: *New leaves, with what holy wonder do I watch the sunlight on your green.* Through the mist we could just make out Mount Kurokami from the temple on Nikko. The snow on its slopes belies its name, Black-Haired Mountain. Sora wrote: *I arrived at Kurokami with my hair shorn, in new clean summer clothes.* Sora, whose name is Kawai Sogoro, used to chop wood and draw water for me. We were neighbors. I aroused his curiosity and made him a student of scenery. He too wanted to travel to see Matsushima in its beauty, and serene Kisagata.

•

Crickets creaking trills so loud we had to raise our voices, even on the beach down from the cycladic wall under the yellow spongy dry scrub with spiky stars of flowers. It is, he said, as if the light were noisy, all of it Heraclitus' little fine particles cheeping away, madly counting each other. *Thotheka! entheka! thekaksi! ikosieksi! khilioi! Ena thio tris tessera!* Hair of the family of hay, torso of the family of dog, testicles of the family of Ionian pebbles, glans of the family of plum. Give us another poem, here by the fountain-pen-blue-ink sea. *To Apollo of the Lykoreans Evnomos of Lokris gives this cricket of bronze. Know that, matched against Parthis in the finals for the harp, his strings rang keen under the pick until one of them snapped. But the prancing melody missed never a beat: a cricket sprang onto the harp and sounded the missing note in a perfection of harmony. For this sweet miracle, O godly son of Leto, Evnomos places this little singer on your altar.* From the *Anthology*. So it's Apollo and not Heraclitus running these nattering hoppergrasses and their katydid aunts and crickcrack uncles? And salty-kneed old Poseidon singing along from the sea.

•

So Sora, to be worthy of the beauty of the world, shaved his head the day we departed, and donned a wandering priest's black robe, and took yet a third name, Sogo, which means Enlightened, for the road. When he wrote his haiku for Mount Kurokami, he was not merely describing his visit but dedicating himself to the sacredness of perception. We climbed higher above the shrine. We found the waterfall. It is a hundred feet high, splashing into a pool of darkest green. Urami-no-Taki is its name, See from Inside, for you can climb among the rocks and get in behind it. I wrote: *From a silent cave I saw the waterfall, summer's first grand sight for me.* I had a friend at Kurobane in Nasu County. To get there you cross a wide grassy moor for many's the mile, following a path. We kept our eyes on a village in the distance as a landmark, but night came on and rain began to pelt down before we could get there. We spent the night at a farmer's hut along the way. Next day we saw a farmer with a horse, which we asked the loan of. The paths over the moor, he said, are like a great net. You will soon get lost at the crossroads. But the horse will know the way. Let him decide which path to take.

•

These were the hills whose elegiac autumns Ives summons with bronze Brahms as a ground for Lee standing in his stirrups as he crossed the Mason and Dixon Line while a band of Moravian cornets alto, tenor, and baritone, an E-flat helicon bass horn, drums battle and snare, strutted out the cakewalk dash of *Dixie*. The rebels danced in rank and gave a loud *huzzah!* These are the everlasting hills that stand from dawn time to red men to French hunter to Calvinist boot to rumors from farm to village that the bands played waltzes and polkas under the guns at Gettysburg when the cannonade was at its fiercest. We trod these hills because we loved them and because we loved each other, and because in them we might feel that consonance of hazard and intent which was the way Ives heard and Cézanne saw, the *moiré* of sound in the studio at West Redding where a Yale baseball cap sat on a bust of Wagner, the *moiré* of light in the quarries and pines at Bibémus. What tone of things might we not involve ourselves in the gathering of in these hills? With each step we left one world and walked into another.

•

I mounted the farmer's horse. Sora walked beside us. Two little children ran behind us. One was a girl named Kasane. Sora was delighted with her name, which means *many petalled*. He wrote: *Your name fits you, O Kasane, and fits the double carnation in its richness of petals!* When we reached the village, we sent the horse back by itself, with a tip knotted into the saddle sash. My friend the samurai Joboji Takakatsu, the steward of a lord, was surprised to see me, and we renewed our friendship and we could not have enough of each other's talk. Our happy conversations saw the sun across the country sky and wore the lantern dim way past moonrise. We walked in the outskirts of the town, saw an old academy for dog hunters—that cruel and unseemly sport was of short duration in ancient times—and paid our respects to the tomb of the lady Tamamo, a fox who took human shape. It was on this grave that the samurai archer Yoichi prayed before he shot a fan, at a great distance, from the mast of a drifting boat. Her grave is far out on the moor of grass, and is as lonely a place as you can imagine. The wind traveling through the grass! The silence! It was dark when we returned.

•

Leaves not opposite on a stem arrange themselves in two, five, eight, or thirteen rows. If the leaves in order of height up the stem be connected by a thread wound round the stem, then between any two successive leaves in a row the thread winds round the stem once if the leaves are in two or three rows, twice if in five rows, thrice if in eight, five if in thirteen. That is, two successive leaves on the stem will be at such a distance that if there are two rows, the second leaf will be halfway round the stem, if three rows, the second leaf will be one-third of the way around, if five, the second will be two-fifths of the way around; if eight, three-eighths; if thirteen, five-thirteenths. These are Fibonacci progressions in phyllotaxic arrangement. The organic law of vegetable growth is the surd towards which the series one-half, one-third, two-fifths, three-eighths, and so on, approximates. Professor T. C. Hilgard sought for the germ of phyllotaxis in the numerical genesis of cells, the computation of which demonstrates Fibonacci progressions in time.

•

The tomb of En-no-Gyoja, founder of the Shugen sect, who nine hundred years ago used to preach everywhere in humble clogs, is in Komyoji Temple. My friend Joboji took me to visit it. In full summer, in the mountains, I bowed before the clog-shod saint's tall image to be blessed in my travels. Unganji the Zen temple is nearby. Here the hermit Buccho, my old Zen master at Edo, lived out his life in solitude. I remember that he once wrote a poem in pine charcoal on a rock in front of his hut. *I would leave this little place, with its five foot of grass this way, five foot of grass that way, except that it keeps me dry when it rains.* We were joined by some young worshipers on the way. Their bright chatter made the climb seem no time at all. The temple is in a wood of cedars and pine, and the way there is narrow, mossy, and wet. There is a gate and a bridge. Though it was April, the air was very cold. Buccho's hut is behind the temple, a small box of a house under a big rock. I sensed the holiness of the place. I might have been at Yuan-miao's cave or Fa-yun's cliff. I made up this poem and left it there on a post: *Even the woodpeckers have not dared touch this little house.*

•

The first thing to go when you walk into the wilderness is time. You eat when you are hungry, rest when you are tired. You fill a moment to its brim. At a ford shoaling over rocks we doffed our packs, took off our boots and jeans, and waded in our shirttails for the childishness of it. Creek-washed feet, she said, as God intended. We dried in the sun on a boulder as warm as a dying stove, and fribbled and monkeyed with each other, priming for later. Jim Dandy! she said, and purred, but we geared up and pushed on, through Winslow Homer glades and dapple and tones that rose as if horn-heralded across sunny fields and greendark woods and tonalities now lost except for the stubborn masks of their autochthony, Ives imitating a trumpet on the piano for Nikolai Slonimsky and hearing at Waterbury gavottes his father had played during the artillery barrage at Chancellorsville, Apollinaire hanging a N'tomo mask of the Bambara on his wall beside Picassos and Laurencins, Gaudier drawing Siberian wolves in the London Zoo, tonalities with lost coordinates, for essences survive by chance allegiances and griefs: the harness chains on the caissons moving toward Seven Pines, dissonance and valence.

•

We ended our visit at Kurobane. I had asked of my host that he show me the way to Sessho-seki, the famous killing stone which slew birds and bugs that lit on it. He lent me a horse and guide. The guide shyly asked me, once we were out on the road, to compose a poem for him, and so delighted was I with the surprise of his request, that I wrote: *Let us leave the road and go across the moors, the better to hear that cuckoo.* The killing stone was no mystery. It is beside a hot spring that gives off a deadly gas. Around it the ground was covered with dead butterflies and bees. Then I found the very willow about which Saigyo wrote in his *Shin Kokin Shu*: *In the shade of this willow lying kindly on the grass and on the stream as clear as glass, we rest awhile on the way to the far north.* The willow is near the village Ashino, where I had been told I would find it, and we too, like Saigyo, rested in its shade. *Only when the girls nearby had finished planting rice in a square of their paddy did I leave the famous willow's shade.* Then, after many days of walking without seeing a soul, we reached the Shirakawa boundary gate, the true beginning of the road north. I felt a peace come over me, felt anxiety drop away. I remembered the sweet excitement of travelers before me.

•

All of that again, he said, I long to see all of that again, the villages of the Pyrenees, Pau, the roads. O Lord, to smell French coffee again all mixed in with the smell of the earth, brandy, hay. Some of it will have changed, not all. The French peasant goes on forever. I asked if indeed there was any chance, any likelihood, that he could go. His smile was a resigned irony. Who knows, he said, that Saint Anthony didn't take the streetcar into Alexandria? There hasn't been a desert father in centuries and centuries, and there's considerable confusion as to the rules of the game. He indicated a field to our left, beyond the wood of white oak and sweet gum where we were walking, a field of wheat stubble. That's where I asked Joan Baez to take off her shoes and stockings so that I could see a woman's feet again. She was so lovely against the spring wheat. Back in the hermitage we ate goat's cheese and salted peanuts, and sipped whiskey from jelly glasses. On his table lay letters from Nicanor Parrá and Marguerite Yourcenar. He held the whiskey bottle up to the cold bright Kentucky sunlight blazing through the window. And then out to the privy, where he kicked the door with his hobnail boot, to shoo off the black snake who was usually inside. *Out! Out! You old son of a bitch! You can come back later.*

•

The great gate at Shirakawa, where the North begins, is one of the three largest checkpoints in all the kingdom. All poets who have passed through it have made a poem of the event. I approached it along a road overhung with dark trees. It was already autumn here, and winds troubled the branches above me. The unohana were still in bloom beside the road, and their profuse white blossoms met those of the blackberry brambles in the ditch. You would think an early snow had speckled all the underwood. Kiyosuke tells us in the *Fukuro Zoshi* that in ancient times no one went through this gate except in his finest clothes. Because of this Sora wrote: *A garland of white unohana flowers around my head, I passed through Shirakawa Gate, the only finery I could command.* We crossed the Abukuma River and walked north with the Aizu cliffs on our right, and villages on our left, Iwaki, Soma, Miharu. Over the mountains beyond them, we knew, were the counties Hitachi and Shimotsuke. We found the Shadow Pond, where all shadows cast on it are exact of outline. The day was overcast, however, and we saw only the grey sky mirrored in it. At Sukagawa I visited the poet Tokyu, who holds a government post there.

•

Dissonance chiming with order, strict physical law in its dance with hazard, valences as weightless as light bonding an *aperitif à la gentiane* Suze, a newspaper, carafe, ace of clubs, stummel. And in a shatter and jig of scialytic prismfall quiet women, Hortense Cézanne among her geraniums, Gertrude Stein resting her elbows on her knees like a washerwoman, Madame Ginoux, of Arles, reader of novels, sitting in a black dress against a yellow wall, a portrait painted by Vincent in three quarters of an hour, quiet women at the centers of houses, and by the pipe, carafe, and newspaper on the tabletop men with a new inwardness of mind, an inwardness for listening to green silence, to watch

tones and brilliances and subtleties of light, dawn, noon, and dusk, Etienne
Louis Malus walking at sunset in the gardens of the Palais du Luxembourg,
seeing how twice refracted level light was polarized by the palace windows,
alert to remember what we would see and hold and share. From fields of
yellow sedge to undergrowth of wild ferns tall as our shoulders, from slippery
paths Indian file through trees to bear walks along black beaver ponds we set
out to see the great rocks rolled into Vermont by glaciers ten thousand years
ago.

•

Tokyu, once we were at the tea bowl, asked with what emotion I had passed
through the great gate at Shirakawa. So taken had I been by the landscape, I
admitted, and with memories of former poets and their emotions, that I composed few *haiku* of my own. The only one I would keep was: *The first poetry
I found in the far north was the worksongs of the rice farmers.* We made three
books of linked *haiku* beginning with this poem. Outside this provincial town
on the post road there was a venerable chestnut tree under which a priest lived.
In the presence of that tree I could feel that I was in the mountain forests where
the poet Saigyo gathered nuts. I wrote these words then and there: *O holy
chestnut tree, the Chinese write your name with the character for* tree *below
that of* west, *the direction of all things holy.* Gyoki the priest of the common
people in the Nara period had a chestnut walking stick, and the ridgepole of
his house was chestnut. And I wrote this *haiku*: *Worldly men pass by the
chestnut in bloom by the roof.* We ended our visit with Tokyu. We came to the
renowned Asaka Hills and their many lakes. The *katsumi* iris, I knew, would
be in bloom, and we left the high road to go see them.

•

Sequoia Langsdorfii is found in the Cretaceous of both British Columbia and
Greenland, and *Gingko polymorpha* in the former of these localities. *Cinna-
momum Scheuchzeri* occurs in the Dakota group of Western Kansas as well as
at Fort Ellis. Sir William Dawson detects in strata regarded as Laramie by
Professor G. M. Dawson, of the Geological Survey of Canada, a form which
he considers to be allied to *Quercus antiqua*, Newby., from Rio Dolores,
Utah, in strata positively declared to be the equivalent of the Dakota group.
Besides these cases there are several in which the same species occurs in the

Eocene and the Cretaceous, though wanting in the Laramie. _Cinnamomum Sezannense_, of the Paleocene of Sézanne and Gelinden, was found by Heer, not only in the upper Cretaceous of Patoot, but in the Cenomanian of Atane, in Greenland. _Myrtophyllum cryptoneuron_ is common to the Paleocene of Gelinden and the Senonian of Westphalia, and the same is true of _Dewalquea Gelindensis. Sterculia variabilis_ is another case of a Sézanne species occurring in the upper Cretaceous of Greenland, and Heer rediscovers in this same Senonian bed the Eocene plant _Sapotacites reticulatus_, which he described in the Sachs-Thüringen lignite beds.

•

But not a single _katsumi_ iris could we find. No one we asked, moreover, had ever heard of them. Night was coming on, and we made haste to have a quick look at the urozuka cave by taking a shortcut at Nihonmatsu. We spent the night at Fukushima. Next day I stopped at Shinobu village to see the stone where _shinobu-zuri_ cloth used to be dyed. It is a composite stone with an amazing facet smooth as glass of many different minerals and quartz. The stone used to be far up the mountain, I was told by a child, but the many tourists who came to see it trampled the crops on the way, so the villagers brought it down to the square. I wrote: _Now only the nimble hands of girls planting rice give us an idea of the ancient dyers at their work_. We crossed by ferry at Tsuki-no-wa—Ring around the Moon!—and came to Se-no-ue, a post town. There is a field nearby, with a hill named Maruyama in it: on this hill are the ruins of the warrior Sato's house. I wept to see the broken gate at the foot of the hill. A temple stands in the neighborhood with the graves of the Sato family in its grounds. I felt that I was in China at the tombstone of Yang Hu, which no person of cultivation has ever visited without weeping.

•

Through forests of sweet gum and hickory rising to larch, meadows of fern and thistle, we came toward the end of a day to an old mill of the kind I had known at Price's Shoals in South Carolina, wagons and mules under its elms, dogs asleep in the shade beneath the wagons, chickens and ducks maundering about. This New England country mill was, however, of brick, with tall windows, but with the same wide doors and ample loading platforms. It was a day in which we had lost time. I interrupted our singing along a logging road to say that my watch had stopped. So had hers, she said, or the map was cockeyed, or night comes earlier in this part of New Hampshire than any-where else in the Republic. Clouds and a long rain had kept most of the day in twilight. A new rain was setting in for the night. But there was the mill, and we were saved from another night of wet such as we had endured the second night out. Tentless, we had slept in our bedrolls zipped together into one on a slope of deep ferns and waked to find ourselves as wet as if we had slept in a creek. The map showed shelter ahead, which we had expected to reach. But there had been the strange advancement of the day in defiance of my watch, which had stopped hours ago and started up again. What luck, to chance on this old mill.

•

In the temple I saw, after tea with the priests, the sword of Yoshitsune and the haversack of his loyal servant Benkei. It was the Feast Day of Boys and the Iris. *Show with pride*, I wrote of the arms in the temple, *the warrior's sword, his companion's pack on the first of May.* We went on and spent the night at Iisuka, having had a bath in a hot spring beforehand. Our inn was dirty, lampless, and the beds were pallets of straw on an earthen floor. There were fleas in the pallets, mosquitoes in the room. A fierce storm came up in the night. The roof leaked. All of this brought on an attack of fever and chills, and I was miserable and afraid of dying next day. I rode awhile and walked awhile, weak and in pain. We got as far as the gate into County Okido. I passed the castles at Abumizuri and Shiroishi. I'd wanted to see the tomb of Sanekata, one of the Fujiwara, a poet and exile, but the road there was all mud after the rains, and the tomb was overgrown with grass, I was told, and hard to find. We spent the night at Iwanuma. *How far to Kasajima and is this river of mud the road to take?*

•

Our packs off, the sleeping bags laid out and zipped together, supper in the pan, we could listen to the rain in that windy old mill, hugging our luck and each other. Packrats in little white pants, and spiders, and lizards, no doubt, I said, and we will make friends with them all. Her hair had lost the spring of its curls and stuck rakishly to her forehead and cheeks, the way I had first seen it as she climbed from a swimming pool in the Poconos. What are you talking about? she asked. She searched my eyes with a smiling and questioning look. I thought by such comic inquisitiveness that our luck was hard to believe. The mill there, Sweetheart, I repeated, pointing. A grand old New England water mill, dry as a chip and as substantial as Calvin's *Institutes*. She looked at the mill, at me again, and her mouth fell open. The stone steps to the door rose from a thicket of bramble we would have to climb across with care. There was something of the Florentine in all these old brick mills. Their Tuscan flavor came from architectural manuals issued by Scotch engineering firms that had listened to Ruskin and believed him when he said there was truth in Italian proportions and justice in Italian windows.

•

With what joy I found the Takekuma pine, double-trunked, just as the olden poets said. When Noin made his second visit to this tree, it had been cut down for bridge pilings by some upstart of a government official. It has been re-planted over the years, it always grows back the same, always the most beau-tiful of pines. I was seeing it in its thousandth year. When I set out on my journey the poet Kyohaku had written: *Do not neglect to see the pine at Takekuma amid late spring cherry blossoms in the far north.* And for him, as an answer, I wrote: *We saw cherry blossoms together, you and I, three months ago. Now I have come to the double pine in all its grandeur.* On the fourth of May we arrived at Sendai across the Natori River, the day one throws iris leaves on the roof for good health. We put up at an inn. I sought out the painter Kaemon, who showed me the clover fields of Miyagino, the hills of Tamada, Yokono, and Tsutsuji-ga-oka, all white with rhododendron in bloom, the pine wood of Konoshita, where at noon it seems to be night, and where it is so damp you feel the need of an umbrella. He also showed me the shrines of Yakushido and Tenjin. A painter is the best of guides.

•

The Bay of Spezia, mulberry groves, sheds where the silkworms fatten, but here, the sun in golden sheets and slats on the floor, young Revely's study was all Archimedes and Sicily, or a tabletop by Holbein with instruments in brass and walnut, calipers, rules, maps, calculations in silverpoint and red ink. Un-der a map in French colors, slate blues and provincial yellows, poppy reds, cabbage greens, a sepia line from Genua across the Lunae Portus to Pisa, there sat in harmonic disarray a wooden bowl of quicksilver (a cup of Tuscan moonlight, a dish for gnomes to sip down in the iron roots of mountains where the earthquake demons swill lava and munch gold), cogged wheels, a screw propeller, drawings of frigates, steamboats, a machinery of gears and levers colored blue and yellow, lighthouses with cyclopean lamps, plans of harbors and moorings, a heap of rosin, a china cup full of ink, a half-burnt match, a box of watercolors, a block of ivory, a volume of Laplace, a book of conic sections, spherics, logarithms, Saunderson's *Algebra*, Simms' *Trigonometry*, and most beautiful of all this Archimagian gear, the newly unpacked theodolite, tilted in its fine calibrations, gleaming index and glass.

•

When we parted, the painter Kaemon gave me drawings of Matsushima and Shiogama and two pairs of sandals of straw with iris-purple straps. *I walk in iris blossoms, it seems, so rich the blue of my sandal laces.* He also gave me drawings to guide my way along the Narrow Road to the Deep North. At Ichikawa I found the tall inscribed stone of Tsubo-no-ishibumi. The characters were legible through lichen and moss. Taga Castle was built on this site the first year of Jinki by order of General Ono-no-Azumabito, Governor of the Far North by decree of the Emperor, rebuilt in the sixth year of Tempyo-hoji by Emi-no-Asakari, Governor General of the Provinces East and North. This stone is 965 years old. Mountains break and fall, rivers shift their beds, highways grow up in grass, rocks sink into the earth, trees wither with age, and yet this stone has stood from ancient times. I wept to see it, and knelt before its presence, very happy and very sad. We went on across the Noda-no-tamagawa River to the pine forest of Sue-no-matsuyama, where there is a temple and graveyard that gave me melancholy thoughts of the death that must end all our lives, whatever be our love of the world.

•

I could imagine the inside: spiderwebs and dog droppings, the inevitable Mason jar and flattened crump of overalls that one always found in abandoned buildings, a newspaper gone brown and some enigma of a utensil that turned out to be the handle of a meat grinder or meal sifter or mangle gearing. I anticipated rills of ancient flour in the seams of sills, the flat smell of mildewed wheat, the quick smell of wet brick. Mill? she said. Her smile was strangely goofy. She took me by the sleeve. What mill? Then I stood dumb and cold. There was no mill. Ahead of us was the edge of a wood, nothing more. The dusk thickened as we looked at each other in the rain. We went on, stubbornly. We knew better than to follow a blazed trail by dark. We hoped that the campsite with shelter marked on the map was just on the other side of the wood before us. It was not yet wholly dark. Were it not a rainy day, we might plausibly have an hour's half-light yet: plenty of time to nip through the wood, get to the shelter, and be dry for the night. You say you saw an old mill? Underfoot there were rocks and roots again. We longed for the easy tread of the logging road.

•

We came to Shiogama just as the curfew bell was tolling, the darkening sky completely cloudless, the island of Magaki-gashima already but a shadow in a sea that was white with moonlight. We could hear the fishermen counting their take. How lonely it is to enter a town at dusk! We heard a blind singer chanting the rustic folksongs of the north. Next day, we worshiped at the Myojin Shrine of Shiogama, a handsome building. The way to it is paved, the fence around it is painted vermilion. It pleased me that the powers of the gods are so honored here in the Deep North, and I made a sincere obeisance at the altar. An ancient lantern burns near the altar to keep alive the memory of Izumi-no-Saburo, that gallant warrior of five hundred years ago. In the afternoon we took a boat to Matsushima, two miles out. Everyone knows that these are the most beautiful islands in all Japan. I would add that they rival Tungting Hu in Hunan and Si Hu in Chekiang. These islands are our China. Every pine branch is perfect. They have the grace of women walking, and so perfectly are the islands placed that Heaven's serenity is apparent everywhere.

•

Ezra Pound came down the *salita* through the olive grove, white mane jouncing as he stepped his cane with precision stride by long stride. He wore a cream sports jacket, a blue shirt with open collar, pleated white slacks, brown socks, and espadrilles. The speckled bony fingers of his left hand pinched a panama by the brim. The way was strewn with hard green olives torn from their branches by a storm the week before. *Shocking waste*, Miss Rudge said, *and yet it seems to happen year after year, and somehow there's always an olive crop, isn't there, Ezra?* Then, over her shoulder, she asked me if I knew the Spanish for *romance.* Ezra wants to know, and can't remember. *As in* medieval romance? I ask, startled. *Romanthé, I think.* Novela *would be a later word.* Relato, *perhaps. Ezra,* she called ahead, *would that be right? No!* he said, a quiver of doubt in his voice. Romancero, I said, *is a word Mr. Pound himself has used of Spanish balladry.* Romancero, *Ezra?* Miss Rudge said cheerfully. Single file was the rule on the *salita.* He always went first, up or down, steep and rough as it was. *Not the word,* he said, without looking back.

•

Ojima, though called an island, is a narrow strip of land. Ungo, the Shinto priest, lived here in his retirement. We were shown the rock where he liked to sit for hours. We saw small houses among the pines, blue smoke from their chimneys, the red moon rising beyond them. My room at the inn overlooked the bay and the islands. A great wind howled, and clouds scudded at a gallop across the moon; nevertheless, I kept my windows open, for I had that wonderful feeling that only travelers know: that this was a different world from any I had known before. Different winds, a different moon, an alien sea. Sora, too, felt the peculiarity of the place and the moment, and wrote: *Flute-tongued cuckoo, you must long for the heron's wings of silver to fly from island to island at Matsushima.* So fine was my emotion that I could not sleep. I got out my notebook and read again the poems my friends gave me when I set out, about these islands: a poem by Sodo in Chinese, a *waka* by Dr. Hara Anteki, *haiku* by the samurai Dakushi and Sampu. Being at Matsushima made the poems much richer, and the poems made Matsushima a finer experience.

•

We juggled in debate whether we should doss down then and there in leaf-muck and boulder rubble, or, heartened by the thin light we found in clearings, suppose that the failure of the day was more raindusk than the beginning of night, and push on. We found at least an arm of the lake on the map in a quarter of an hour. It was a spillway which we had to cross on a footlog. Rabbitfoot, I said, and don't look down. We got across more in dismay at the unfairness of a footlog to deal with in failing light and drizzle than with any skill with footlogs. What a miserable mean thing to do, she said, putting a blithering log to balance across with both of us winded and wet and you seeing hotels. The rain had settled in to stay. We had fair going for a while and then we came upon swamp. There was no question of camping in water that came over our shoe tops. I broke out a flashlight, she held onto my pack so as not to get lost from me, and we nosed our way through ferns and huckleberries, sinking up to our shins in mud. I think I'm scared, she said. Of what? Nothing in particular. Of everything. I'm scared, I said, if for no other reason than that I don't know where we are.

•

We set out for Hiraizumi on the twelfth, our immediate plans being to visit the Aneha Pine and Odae Bridge. Our way was along a woodcutter's path in the mountains, as lonely and quiet a trail as I have ever trod. By some inattention to my instructions I lost my way and came instead to Ishinomaki, a port in a bay where we saw a hundred ships. The air was thick with smoke from chimneys. What a busy place! They seemed to know nothing of putting up foot travelers, or of the art of looking at scenery. So we had to make do with shoddy quarters for the night. We left next day by a road that went I knew not whither. It took us past a ford on the Sode, the meadows of Obuchi, and the grasslands of Mano. We followed the river and came at last to Hiraizumi, having wandered a good twenty miles out of our way. We looked with melancholy on the ruins of the Fujiwara estate, now so many rice paddies. We found Yasuhira's abandoned house to the north of the Koromo-ga-seki Gate. Though the grandeur of the Fujiwara lasted three generations only, their achievements will be remembered forever, and looking on the ruins of their castles and lands I wept that such glory has come to nothing, and covered my face with my hat.

•

In July I saw several cuckoos skimming over a large pond; and found, after some observation, that they were feeding on the *libellulae*, or dragonflies, some of which they caught as they settled on the weeds, and some as they were on the wing. Notwithstanding what Linnaeus says, I cannot be induced to believe that they are birds of prey. A countryman told me that he had found a young fern-owl in the nest of a small bird on the ground; and that it was fed by the little bird. I went to see this extraordinary phenomenon, and found that it was a young cuckoo hatched in the nest of a titlark; it was become vastly too big for its nest. The dupe of a dam appeared at a distance, hovering about with meat in its mouth, and expressing the greatest solicitude. Ray remarks, that birds of the *gallinae* order, as cocks and hens, partridges and pheasants, are *pulveratrices*, such as dust themselves, using that method of cleansing their feathers, and ridding themselves of their vermin. As far as I can observe, many birds that wash themselves would never dust; but here I find myself mistaken; for common house sparrows are great *pulveratrices*, being frequently seen groveling and wallowing in dusty roads; and yet they are great washers. Does not the skylark dust?

•

Tall grass grows over the dreams of an ancient aristocracy. Look there! Did I not see Yoshitsune's servant Kanefusa in the white blur of the unohana flowers? But not all was gone. The temples remain, with their statues and tombs and sutras. *Dry in the rains of May, the Hikari Do keeps its gold and gloom for a thousand years.* We reached Cape Ogoru next day, and the little island of Mizu in the river. Onward, we came to the Dewa border, where the guards questioned us so long and so suspiciously (they rarely see foot travelers even in the best of weather) that we got a late start. Dusk caught us on the mountain road and we had to stay the night with a tollkeeper, and were lucky to find even this hut in so desolate a place. *Fleas and lice bit us, and all night a horse pissed beside my mat.* The tollkeeper said that many mountains lay between us and Dewa. I was most surely apt to get lost and perish. He knew a stout young man who would consent to be our guide, a strapping fellow with a sword and oak staff. He was indeed necessary: the way was an overgrown wilderness. Black clouds just above our heads darkened the thick underwood of bamboo.

•

Where we are, she said, is slogging our way by flashlight through a New England swamp up to our butts in goo and I'm so tired I could give up and howl. The important thing to understand, I said, is that we aren't on the trail. We were, I think, she said, when we got off into this. We couldn't be far off it. Off the trail, she said in something of a snit, is off the trail. And there's something wrong with my knees. They're shaking. We're probably walking into the lake that stupid log back there went over an outlet of. I turned and gave her as thorough an inspection as I could under the circumstances. She was dead tired, she was wet, and her knees did indeed shake. Lovely knees, but they were cold and splashed with mud. I slipped her pack off and fitted it across my chest, accoutred front and back like a paratrooper. We went on, the flashlight beam finding nothing ahead but bushes in water, a swamp of ferns. There was a rudimentary trail, it seemed. At least someone had put down logs in the more succulent places. It is the trail, I insisted. A yelp from behind, a disgusted and slowly articulated *Jiminy!* and while I was helping her up, sobs. Don't cry, Sweetheart! It rolled. The motherless log rolled when I stepped on it.

•

In Obanazawa I visited the merchant poet Seifu, who had often stopped on business trips to see me in Edo. He was full of sympathy for our hard way across the mountains, and made up for it with splendid hospitality. Sora was entranced by the silkworm nurseries, and wrote: *Come out, toad, and let me see you: I hear your got-a-duck got-a-duck under the silkworm house.* And: *The silkworm workers are dressed like ancient gods.* We climbed to the quiet temple of Ryushakuji, famous for being in so remote and peaceful a site. The late afternoon sun was still on it, and on the great rocks around it, when we arrived, and shone golden in the oaks and pines that have stood there for hundreds of years. The very ground seemed to be eternity, a velvet of moss. I felt the holiness of the place in my bones; my spirit partook of it with each bow that I made to the shrines in the silent rocks. *Silence as whole as time. The only sound is crickets.* Our next plan was to go down the Mogami River by boat, and while we were waiting for one to take us, the local poets at Oishida sought me out and asked me to show them how to make linked verses, of which they had heard but did not know the technique. With great pleasure I made a whole book for them.

•

Could she stand? She thought so. It hurt, but she could stand. I shone the flashlight as far as I could ahead. Treetops! Treetops ahead, Samwise. Higher ground, don't you think that means? She limped frighteningly. We sloshed on. I could tell how miserable she was from her silence. We were slowly getting onto firmer ground. I studied her again by flashlight. She was a very tired girl with a sprained ankle or the nearest thing to it. I was getting my second wind, and put it to good use by heaving her onto my hip. She held to my neck, kissing my ear in gratitude. By coupling my hands under her behind, I could carry her to high ground if it was near enough. We reached forest, with roots to slip on and rocks to stumble over. The flashlight found a reasonably level place. I cleared trash from it while she held the light. We spread our tarpaulin, unrolled and zipped together the sleeping bags. It was our pride that we were hiking without a tent, though at that moment we longed for one. We undressed in the rain, stuffing our damp clothes into our packs. At least they wouldn't get any wetter. We slipped naked into the sleeping bag. Too tired to shiver, she said. She got dried peaches and apples from her pack, and we chewed them, lying on our elbows, looking out into the dark.

•

The Mogami River flows down from the mountains through Yamagata Province, with many treacherous rapids along the way, and enters the sea at Sakata. We went down the river in a farmer's old-timey rice boat, our hearts in our mouths. We saw Shiraito-no-take, the Silver-Stringed Waterfall, half-hidden by thick bamboo, and the temple of Sennindo. Because the river was high and rough, I wrote: *On all the rains of May in one river, I tossed along down the swift Mogami.* I was glad to get ashore. On the third of June we climbed Haguro Mountain and were granted an audience with Egaku the high priest, who treated us with civility and put us up in a cabin. Next day, in the Great Hall with the high priest, I wrote: *This valley is sacred. The sweet wind smells of snow.* On the fifth we saw the Gongen Shrine, of uncertain date. It may be the shrine Fujiwara-no-Tokihira in the *Rites and Ceremonies* says is on Mount Sato in Dewa, confusing the Chinese for *Sato* and *Kuro, Haguro* being a variant of *Kuro.* Here they teach Total Meditation as the Tendai sect understands it, and the Freedom of the Spirit and Enlightenment, teaching as pure as moonlight and as sweet as a single lantern in pitch dark.

•

He and Bruni, the watercolor painter, you know, they were the closest of friends, used to argue God something terrible. He was an atheist, Tatlin, and Bruni was a very Russian believer. It terrified me as a child. Tatlin would take us to swim in the river in the spring, and he wore no icon around his neck and didn't cross himself before diving in. He was wonderful with children, a grown-up who knew how to play with us without condescending, but with other people he was self-centered, vain about his singing voice. Pasternak, now, had no way with children at all. He didn't even see them. Tatlin made his own lute, a replica of a traditional Slavic lute such as blind singers had, strolling from village to village. Especially in the south. What did Tatlin look like? O, he was lanky, as you say, skinny. He had slate-grey eyes, very jolly eyes that had a way of going dead and silvery when he fell into a brown study. His hair was, how shall I put it, a grey blond. When he sang the blind singers' songs he made his eyes look blind, rolled back, unseeing. The voice was between baritone and bass. He was not educated, you know. He lived in the bell tower of a monastery.

•

On Haguro Mountain there are hundreds of small houses where priests meditate in strictest discipline, and will meditate, to keep this place holy, as long as there are people on the earth. On the eighth we climbed Mount Gassan. I had a paper rope around my shoulders, and a shawl of white cotton on my head. For eight miles we strove upward, through the clouds, which were like a fog around us, over rocks slick with ice, through snow. When we came to the top, in full sunlight, I was out of breath and frozen. How glorious the sight! We spent the night there, on beds of leaves. On the way down next day we came to the smithy where Gassan used to make his famous swords, tempering them in the cold mountain stream. His swords were made of his devotion to his craft and of the divine power latent in the mountain. Near here I saw a late-blooming cherry in the snow. I cannot speak of all I saw, but this cherry will stand for all, determined as it was, however late, however unseasonable, to bring its beauty into the world. Egaku, when I returned, asked me to make poems of my pilgrimage to this sacred mountain.

•

Bedded down in dark and rain, we felt both a wonderful security, warm and dry in our bed, and a sharp awareness that we didn't know where in the world we were. That swamp grew there since they printed the map, she said. I feel, I said, as if we were all alone in the middle of a wood as big as Vermont. We could be six feet from the lake, or on the merest island of trees in the world's biggest swamp. I don't care where we are, she said. We're here, we're dry, we're not in that swamp. We hugged awhile, and then lay on our backs to distribute the rock weight of our exhaustion, a hand on each other's tummy for sympathy and fellowship. You saw a mill? she said. A fine old water mill, of red brick, about a hundred years old, I suppose. As plain as day. I said that I was both glad and a bit frightened to have seen it, a superimposition of desire on reality. The first ghost I'd ever seen, if a mill can be a ghost. If it had been real, we would have had a hot supper, with coffee, and could have set up house, and got laid, twice running, after a wonderful long time of toning things up beforehand, with porcupines standing on their hind legs and looking through the windows. But she was asleep.

•

How cold the white sickle moon above the dark valleys of Mount Haguro. How many clouds had gathered and broken apart before we could see the silent moon above Mount Gassan. Because I could not speak of Mount Yudono, I wet my sleeves with tears. *Tears stood in my eyes*, Sora wrote, *as I walked over the coins at Yudono, along the sacred way.* Next day we came to Tsuru-ga-oka Castle, where the warrior Nagayama Shigeyuki welcomed me and Zushi Sakichi, who had accompanied us from Haguro. We wrote a book of linked verse together. We returned to our boat and went down the river Sakata. Here we were the guests of Dr. Fugyoku. I wrote: *Cool of the evening in the winds crisscrossing the beach at Fukuura, and twilight: but the tip of Mount Atsumi was still bright with the sun. Deep into the estuary of Mogami River the summer sun has quenched its fire.* By now my fund of natural beauty was bountiful, yet I could not rest until I had seen Lake Kisagata. To get there I walked ten miles along a path, over rocky hills, down to sandy beaches and up again. The sun was touching the horizon when I arrived. Mount Chokai was hidden in fog.

•

We woke next morning to find that we were no more than twenty yards from the campsite we were trying to reach. Golly, she said, looking out of the sleeping bag. A black lake lay in a cedar wood whose greenish dark made its shores seem noonbright in early morning. We rose naked and put our clothes on bushes in the sun. She spied blueberries for our mush. I managed to get wood ash in our coffee, and we had to eat with the one spoon, as mine had got lost. The lake was too brackish to swim in, so we stood in the shallows and soaped each other, dancing from the chill of the water. I was rinsing her back with handsful of water poured over her shoulders when I saw a pop-eyed man gaping at us from beyond our breakfast fire. His face was scholarly and bespectacled and he wore a Boy Scout uniform. The staff in his hand gave him a biblical air. He was warning away his troop with a backward hand. Hi! she hailed him. We're just getting off some grime from the trail. We got lost in the rain last night and came here through the swamp. We'll give you time, he said with a grin. Oh for Pete's sake, said she, proceeding to soap up my back. We're just people. They've seen people, haven't they?

●

If the halflight and the rain were so beautiful at Kisagata, how lovely the lake would be in good weather. Next day was indeed brilliant, I sailed across the lake, stopping at the mere rock of an island where the monk Noin once meditated. On the far shore we found the ancient cherry tree of Saigyo's poem, in which he compares its blossoms to the froth on waves. From the large hall of the temple Kanmanjuji you can see the whole lake, and beyond it Mount Chokai like a pillar supporting Heaven, and the gate of Muyamuya faintly in the west, the highway to Akita in the east, and Shiogoshi in the north, where the lake meets the breakers of the ocean. Only two lakes are so beautiful: Matsushima is the other. But whereas Matsushima is gay and joyful, Kisagata is grave and religious, as if some sorrow underlay its charm. *Silk tree blossoming in the monotonous rain at Kisagata, you are like the Lady Seishi in her sorrow. On the wet beach at Shiogoshi the herons strut in the sea's edge. Some sweetmeat not known elsewhere is probably sold at Kisagata on the feast days.* Teiji has a poem about Kisagata: *In the evening the fishermen sit and rest in their doorways.* Sora wrote of the ospreys: *Does God tell them how to build their nests higher than the tide?*

●

I loved her for her brashness. Her seventeen-year-old body, in all the larger and speculative senses aesthetic and biological, was something to see. It was Spartan, it was Corinthian: hale of limb, firmnesses continuing into softnesses, softnesses into firmnesses. There was a little boy's stance in the clean porpoise curve of calf, a tummy flat and grooved. Corinth asserted itself in hips and breasts, in the denim blue of her eyes, the ruck of her upper lip, in the pert girlishness of her nose. We aren't proud, she said. I can't recommend the pond here, as it's full of leaf trash from several geological epochs back. The blueberries over there on that spit are delicious. By this time there were Boy Scout eyes over the scoutmaster's shoulders. We went back to our stretch of the beach, dried in the sun while making more coffee, and fished shirts from our packs in deference to our neighbors. It was further along the trail that day that we found in a lean-to a pair of Jockey shorts, size small, stuck full of porcupine quills. One of our Boy Scouts', she said. Do you suppose he was in or out of them when Brother Porky took a rolling dive?

•

Leaving Sakata, we set out on the hundred-and-thirty-mile road to the county seat of Kaga Province. Clouds gathered over the mountains on the Hokuriku Road, down which we had to go, and clouds gathered in my heart at the thought of the distance. We walked through the Nezu Gate into Echigo, we walked through the Ichiburi Gate into Ecchu. We were nine days on the road. The weather was wet and hot all the way, and my malaria acted up and made the going harder. *The sixth of July, the nights are changing, and tomorrow the Weaver Star and the Shepherd Star cross the Milky Way together.* At Ichiburi I was kept awake by two Geisha in the next room. They had been visiting the Ise Shrine with an old man, who was going home the next day, and they were plying him with silly things to say to all their friends. How frivolous and empty their lives! And next day they tried to attach themselves to us, pleading that they were pilgrims. I was stern with them, for they were making a mock of religion, but as soon as I had shooed them away my heart welled with pity. Beyond the forty-eight shoals of the Kurobe, we came to the village of Nago and asked to see the famous wisteria of Tako.

•

Hephaistiskos, our Renault bought in Paris, who had slept in a stable in Ville-franche, kicked a spring outside Tarbes, and spent the night under the great chestnut tree in the square at Montignac, under palms at Menton, and under pines at Ravenna, was hoisted onto the foredeck of the *Kriti* at Venice for a voyage down the Adriatic to Athens. We had no such firm arrangements for a berth. Along with two Parisian typists of witty comeliness; two German cyclists blond, brown, and obsequious; a trio of English consisting of a psychiatrist and her two lovers, the one an Oxford undergraduate, the other the Liberal Member from Bath; and a seasoned traveler from Alton, Illinois, a Mrs. Brown, we were billeted on the aft deck, in the open air, with cots to sleep on. All the cabins were taken by Aztecs. _Mexican Rotary and their wives_, explained the lady psychiatrist, who had Greek and who had interviewed the Captain, leaving a flea in his ear. The sporting bartender had shouted to us over the Greek band, in a kind of English, that it was ever the way of the pirate who owned this ship to sell all the tickets he could, let the passengers survive by their wits. _It's only a week. No say drachma, say thrakmé._

•

The wisteria of Tako, I was told, was five lonely miles up the coast, with no house of any sort nearby or along the way. Discouraged, I went on into Kaga Province. _Mist over the rice fields, below me the mutinous waves._ I crossed the Unohanayama Mountains, the Kurikara-dani Valley, and came on the fifteenth of July to Kanazawa. Here the merchant Kasho from Osaka asked me to stay with him at his inn. There used to live in Kanazawa a poet named Issho, whose verse was known over all Japan. He had died the year before. I went to his grave with his brother, and wrote there: _Give some sign, O silent tomb of my friend, if you can hear my lament and the gusts of autumn wind joining my grief._ At a hermit's house: _This autumn day is cold, let us slice cucumbers and mad-apples and call them dinner._ On the road: _The sun is red and heedless of time, but the wind knows how cold it is, O red is the sun!_ At Komtasu, Dwarf Pine: _The right name for this place, Dwarf Pine, wind combs the clover and makes waves in the grass._ At the shrine at Tada I saw the samurai Sanemori's helmet and the embroidered shirt he wore under his armor.

•

The Liberal Member from Bath, the Oxford undergraduate name of Gerald, and the lady British psychiatrist demonstrated the Greek folk dances played by the band. _A Crimean Field Hospital_, I said of our cots and thin blankets set up as our dormitory on the fantail of the _Kriti_. _Exactly!_ said the Liberal Member from Bath, accepting us thereby. _Rather jolly, don't you think?_ The Parisian typists chittered and giggled. _Pas de la retraite! Que nous soyons en fam-_

ille. Mrs. Brown of Alton tucked a blanket under her chin and undressed with her back to the Adriatic. The Parisian typists came to her aid, and they became a trio, with their cots together, like the English. They stripped to lace bras and panties, causing the Liberal Member from Bath to say, *O well, there's nothing else for it, is there?* The German boys undressed pedantically to pissburnt briefs of ultracontemporary conciseness. We followed suit, nothing daunted, and the Liberal Member from Bath did everybody one better, and took off every stitch, a magnified infant, chubby of knee, paunchy, with random swirls and tufts of ginger hair. The Parisian typists squealed. The Germans looked at him with keen slit eyes. He was surely overstepping a bound.

●

Sanemori's helmet was decorated with swirls of chrysanthemums across the visor and earflaps; a vermilion dragon formed the crest, between two great horns. When Sanemori died and the helmet was enshrined, Kiso Yoshinaka wrote a poem and sent it by Higuchi-no-Jiro: *With what wonder do I hear a cricket chirping inside an empty helmet.* The snowy summit of Shirane Mountain was visible all the way to the Nata Shrine, which the Emperor Kazan built to Kannon, the Goddess of Mercy. The garden here was of rocks and pines. *The rocks are white at the Rock Temple, but the autumn wind is whiter.* At the hot spring nearby, where I bathed: *Washed in the steaming waters at Yamanaka, do I need also to pick chrysanthemums?* I was told by the innkeeper that it was here that Teishitsu realized his humiliating deficiencies as a poet, and began to study under Teitoku when he returned to Kyoto. Alas, while we were here, my companion Sora began to have a pain in his stomach, and left to go to his kinpeople in Nagashima. He wrote a farewell poem: *No matter if I fall on the road, I will fall among flowers.*

●

The Liberal Member from Bath had indeed overstepped a bound in taking off all his clothes on the fantail of the *Kriti.* Just as the lady psychiatrist was urging her other lover, the Oxford undergraduate, to join him in cheeking these outrageous foreigners for booking us passages and then deploying us out here under the sky in what the American archaeologists so aptly dub The Crimean Field Hospital, the Captain of the ship, together with the Steward, made their way through a tumult of pointing Mexican Rotarians and arrived in our midst whirling their arms. The Liberal Member stared at them pop-eyed. _What's the Pirate King saying? Who can understand the blighter?_ He says you must put on your clothes, I offered. He says you are an affront to morals and an insult to decency. _He does, does he?_ said the lady psychiatrist. _Gerald dear! Off with your undershorts._ She then, with help from Gerald dear and the Liberal Member, set out on a speech in Greek which we realized with an exchange of glances was a patchwork of Homeric phrases, more or less syntactical on the psychiatrist's part, but formulaic from her chorus, so that her _what an overweening hatefulness has crossed the barrier of thy teeth_ was seconded by Gerald dear's _when that rosyfingered dawn had shed her beams over mortals and immortals together._

•

When Sora left me, because of his illness, I felt both his sadness and mine, and wrote: _Let the dew fade the words on my hat, Two Pilgrims Traveling Together._ When I stayed at the Zenshoji Temple, they gave me a poem of Sora's that he had left there for me: _All night I heard the autumn wind in the hills above the shrine._ I too listened to the wind that night, grieving for my companion. Next morning I attended services, ate with the priests, and was leaving when a young monk ran after me with inkblock, brush, and paper, begging for a poem. I wrote: _For your kindness I should have swept the willow leaves from the garden._ Such was my sweet confusion at being asked for a poem that I left with my sandals untied. I rented a boat at Yoshizaki and rowed out to see the pine of Shiogoshi. The beauty of its setting is best caught in Saigyo's poem: _Urging the wind against the salt sea, the Shiogoshi pine sheds moonlight from its branches._ At Kanazawa I had been joined by the poet Hokushi, who walked with me as far as the Tenryuji Temple in Matsuoka, far further than he had meant to go.

•

We notice the ugliness of the Hellenistic and Roman style of Greek lettering as compared to the Archaic. Small columns of marble lying about that look as if they might have been grave markers. The Tower of the Winds with its curious figures that look Baroque: a few columns left standing, forming a corner of the street. This sort of ruin is actually what is most prevalent, especially at the theatres and at Eleusis, dismantled Roman ruins built on top of the Greek. An excavation trench near the church with a large urn only half dug out, under an olive tree. More piles of marble, looking very unorderly and as if the archaeologist had never been there: no attempt to order, classify, straighten. Little indication of street levels, except around the standing columns, these being straight shafts of marble, rather than sections fitted together. The Greek snails. We photographed a snailshell in your hand held beside a piece of marble ornament. What a motif. The pattern on the snails much more closely resembling the Geometric and Cycladic jars. The snails are caught by the sun as they climb a column and cooked there in their shells, which cling to the stone. Their spiral design is a chestnut brown band separated from a charcoal band by a thin white line.

•

It was only three miles to Fukui. The way, however, was dark, as I had started thither after supper. The poet Tosai lived there, whom I had known in Edo ten years before. As soon as I arrived I asked for him. A citizen directed me, and as soon as I found a house charmingly neglected, fenced around by a profusion of gourd vines, moonflowers, wild cockscomb kneedeep, and goosefoot blocking the way to the front door, I knew this was Tosai's home and no other's. I knocked. A woman answered, saying that Tosai was downtown somewhere. I was delighted that he had taken a wife, and told him so with glee when I routed him out of a wineshop later. I stayed with him for three days. When I departed, saying that I wanted to see the full moon over Tsuruga, he decided to come with me, tucking up his house kimono as his only concession to the road. The peak of Shirane gave way to that of Hina. At Asamuzu Bridge we saw the reeds of Tamae in bloom. With the first migrating geese in the sky above me. I entered Tsuruga on the fourteenth. The moon was to be full the next night. We went to the Myojin Shrine of Kei, which honors the soul of the Emperor Chuai, bringing, as is the custom, a handful of white sand for the courtyard.

•

Most of them are plants that are abundantly represented in nearly all the more recent deposits, such as *Taxodium Europaeum*, found all the way from the Middle Bagshot of Bournemouth to the Pliocene of Meximieux, *Ficus liliaefolia*, *Laurus primigenia*, and *Cinnamomum lanceolatum*, abundant in nearly all the Oligocene and Miocene beds of Europe. _Quercus chlorophylla_ occurs in the Mississippi Tertiary as well as at Skopau in Sachs-Thüringen, and is also abundant in the Miocene, and _Ficus tiliaefolia_ is found in the Green River formation at Florrisant, Colorado. The two species of hazel, and also the sensitive fern from the Fort Union deposits regarded by Dr. Newberry as identical with the living forms, must be specifically so referred until fruits or other parts are found to show the contrary. Forms of the Gingko tree occur not only in the Fort Union beds, but in the lower Laramie beds at Point of Rocks, Wyoming Territory, which differ inappreciably except in size of leaf from the living species. A few Laramie forms occur in Cretaceous strata.

•

This was a custom begun by the priest Yugyo, so that at the full of the moon the area before the shrine would be as white as frost. _The pure full moon shone on Yugyo the Bishop's sand._ But on the night of the fifteenth it rained. _But for the fickle weather of the north I would have seen the full moon in autumn._ The sixteenth, however, was fine, and I went shell-gathering on the beach. A man named Tenya came with me, and his servants with a picnic. We savored the loneliness of the long beaches. _Autumn comes to the sea, and the beach is more desolate than that at Suma. Clover petals blown into the sea roll up with fine pink shells in the waves._ I asked Tosai to write an account of our day's excursion and to deposit it at the temple for other pilgrims. My friend Rotsu met me when I returned, and went with me to Mino Province. We rode into Ogaki on horseback, and we were met by Sora. At Joko's house we were welcomed by Zensen, Keiko, and many other friends who acted as if I had returned from the dead. On the sixth of September I left for the shrine at Ise, though I was still tired from my journey to the far north. _Tight clam shells fall open in the autumn, just as I, no sooner made comfortable than I feel the call of the road._ Friends, goodbye!

THE CHAIR

The Rebbe from Belz is taking his evening walk at Marienbad. Behind him, at a respectful distance, walks a courtier carrying a chair by its hind legs. This is for the Rebbe to sit on, should he want to sit.

The square seat of this upraised chair, its oval back upholstered with a sturdy cloth embroidered in a rich design of flowers and leaves, its carved, chastely bowed legs, and the tasteful scrollwork of its walnut frame, give it a French air. Like all furniture out of context it seems distressed in its displacement. It belongs in the company of capacious Russian teacups and deep saucers, string quartets by Schumann, polite conversations, and books with gilt leather bindings.

One of the Rebbe's disciples, a lanky young man with long sidelocks beautifully curled and oiled, hastens from the Hotel National. He has a bottle cradled in his arms. He is taking it to a mineral spring to have it filled. The Rebbe wants soda water. He hums as he walks, this disciple, the lively tune *Uforatzto*, a happy march that expresses his joy in being sent for a bottle of soda water for the Rebbe.

The Rebbe's carriage with its tasseled red velvet window curtains comes for him at half past seven every evening, when the shadows have gone blue. He drives to the forest. His court walks behind. One of them carries his silver cane, another an open umbrella, out to his side. It is not for him, but for the Rebbe, should it rain. Another carries a shawl folded on a cushion, in case the Rebbe feels a chill. And one carries the wellbred chair.

It is, by the common reckoning, the year 1916. The armies of the gentiles are slaughtering each other all over the world.

Somewhere along the leafy road the Rebbe will stop the carriage and get out. His court will assemble behind him. He is going to observe, and meditate upon, the beauty of nature, which, created by the Master of the Universe and Lord of All, is full of instruction.

On this particular July evening a fellow guest at the Hotel National has asked and been given permission to walk in the Rebbe's following. He is a young lawyer in the insurance business in Prague, Herr Doktor Franz Kafka. Like all the rest, he must keep his distance, and always be behind the Rebbe. Should the Rebbe suddenly turn and face them, they must quickly run around so as to be behind him. And back around again should he turn again.

The Rebbe, a man of great learning, is neither short nor tall, neither fat nor thin. Wide in the hips, he yet moves with a liquid grace, like a seal in water. He will overflow the slender chair if with a vague ripple of fingers he commands it to be placed so that he can sit on it. Then his followers will range themselves behind him, the secretary leaning a little to catch his every word, the shawl bearer at the ready, should the Rebbe raise his hands toward his shoulders. The secretary takes down what he says in a ledger. These remarks will be studied, later. They will question him about them. The Rebbe means great things by remarks which seem at first to be casual. He asks questions which are traps for their ignorance. The entourage does not always read his gestures correctly. If he has to put into words what he means by an open hand, or raised eyes, or an abrupt halt, he will add a reprimand. *Hasidim is it you call your-selves?* he will say. *Or is it oafs maybe? For brains I'm thinking it's noodles you have.*

If he asks for the soda water, they've had it. The one chosen to fetch it had gone to the Rudolph Spring. It was the opinion of everyone he asked that it was further along this road, that road, another road. And it never was. He'd passed it, or it was another three minutes just around to the left. Around to the right. The Rudolph Spring, the Rudolph Spring, could that be its name? Some answers as to its whereabouts were in foreign languages and a waste of time. Some, sad to say, paid no attention at all to the frantic disciple of the Rebbe from Belz, hard to believe, but true. Moreover, it began to rain. Finally, a man told the disciple that all the mineral springs close at seven. How could a spring be closed? he asked, running off in the direction pointed out. The Rudolph Spring was indeed closed, as he could see long before he got there. The green latticed doors were shut, and a sign reading CLOSED hung on them. *Oi veh!* He rattled the doors, and knocked, and shouted that the Rebbe from Belz had sent him for soda water. All they had to do was fill his bottle and take his money, the work of a moment. All of life, it occurred to him, is one disappoint-ment after another, and he was about to weep when a stroller suggested that he make haste and run to the Ambrosius Spring, which closed a little later than the others. This he did. The Ambrosius was open, by the mercy of God. There were women inside washing glasses. But when he asked them to fill his bottle, the women said that they were through with their work for the day. They should stay open for everybody who can't remember the long hours they were there filling bottles yet? Is the Rebbe from Belz different already? He should learn better how business is conducted in Marienbad.

Who will write the history of despair?

Dr Kafka waits at the steps of the Hotel National for the Rebbe and his following. In Prague Dr Kafka was famous among his friends for the oxlike patience with which he waited. Once, waiting in the street outside a small Parisian theatre Dr Kafka and a donkey had made friends. He was waiting to buy a ticket to *Carmen*, the donkey was waiting to go on in Act II. They both had big ears, Dr Kafka and the donkey. They were both patient by nature, both shy. Waiting is an act of great purity. Something is being accomplished, in a regular and steady way, by doing nothing at all.

First the Rebbe arrived, and then the carriage. So the Rebbe had to wait a little, too. He had a long beard, beautifully white, and very long sidelocks. These are symbols of sound doctrine and piety. The longer your locks, it is said, the greater the respect you get from the Rebbe. All boys with long side-locks he called handsome and smart. One of his eyes, blind, was as blank as if it had been of glass. One side of his mouth was paralyzed, so that at his most solemn he seemed to be smiling ironically, with a witty and forgiving under-standing of the world. His silk kaftan was worn open, held in place by a broad oriental belt. His hat was tall, and of fur. His stockings and knee britches were white, like his beard.

The Rebbe, walking at a plump pace, savors nature in the woods. So Chinese dukes must walk of an evening, stopping to smell an hibiscus, casually reciting a couplet that sounds like notes on a zither, about another hibiscus centuries before, an hibiscus in a classical poem which had made the poet think of a noble woman, a jade owl, and a warrior's ghost on the frontiers maintained against the barbarian hordes.

One of the Rebbe's legs is gimp, perhaps only sore from sitting all day at the Torah. When he gets down from his carriage he has a good cough. Then he sets out, looking. When he stops, the entourage stops, and Dr Kafka behind them. If he turns, they swing with him, like a school of fish behind their pilot. He points out things, such as details of buildings in the woods, which they all strain to see. Is that a tile roof? he asks. They consult. Yes, one says, we think you are right, O Rebbe. It is a tile roof. Where does that path go? No one knows. What kind of tree is that? One thinks that it is a pine, another a fir, another a spruce.

They come to the Zander Institute high on a stone embankment and with a garden in front of it, and an iron fence around it. The Rebbe is interested in the Institute, and in its garden. What kind of garden, he asks, is it? One of the entourage, whose name Dr Kafka catches as Schlesinger, runs up to the fence, elbows out, head thrown back. He really does not look at the garden, but turns as soon as he has reached its gate, and runs down again, knees high, feet plopping. It is, he says breathlessly, the garden of the Zander Institute. Just so, says the Rebbe. Is it a private garden? They consult in whispers. Yes, says their spokesman, it is a private garden. The Rebbe stares at the garden, rocking on his heels. It is, he says, an attractive garden, and the secretary takes this remark down in his ledger.

Their walk brings them to the New Bath House. The Rebbe has someone read the name of it. He strolls behind it, and finds a ditch into which the water from the bathhouse drains. He traces the pipes with his silver cane. The water must come from there, he says, pointing high, and run down to here, and then into here. They all follow his gestures, nodding. They try to make sense of pipes which connect with other pipes. The New Bath House is in a modern style of architecture, and obviously looks strange to the Rebbe. He notices that the ground floor has its windows in the arches of an arcade. At the top of each arch is an animal's head in painted porcelain. What, he asks, is the meaning of that? No one knows. It is, one ventures, a custom. Why? asks the Rebbe. It is the opinion that the animal heads are a whim of the designer, and have no meaning. Mere ornament. This makes the Rebbe say, *Ah!* He walks from window to window along the arcade, giving each his full attention. He comes around to the front of the building. Looking up at the golden lettering in an Art Nouveau alphabet, he reads again *New Bath House*. Why, he asks, is it so named? Because, someone says, it is a new bathhouse. The Rebbe pays no attention to this remark. It is, he says instead, a handsome, a fine, an admirable building. Good lines it has, and well-pondered proportions. The secretary writes this down. Look! he cries. When the rain falls on the roof, it flows into the gutter along the edge there, do you see, and then into the pipes that come down the corners of the building, and then into this stone gutter all around, from which it goes to the same ditch in back where all the pipes are from the baths. They walk around the building, discovering the complete system of the drainpipes. The Rebbe is delighted, he rubs his hands together. He makes one of the entourage repeat the plan of the pipes, as if he were examining him. He gets it right, with some correction along the way, and the Rebbe gives him a kind of blessing with his hands. Wonderful! he says. These pipes are wonderful.

Who will write the history of affection?

They come to an apple orchard, which the Rebbe admires, and to a pear orchard, which he also admires. O the goodness of the Master of the Universe, he says, to have created apples and pears.

The chair held aloft by its bearer, Dr Kafka notices, has now defined what art is as distinct from nature, for its pattern of flowers and leaves looks tawdry and artificial and seriously out of place against the green and rustling leaves of apple and pear trees. He is tempted to put this into words, as a casual remark which one of the entourage just might pass on to the Rebbe, but he reconsiders how whimsical and perhaps mad it would sound. Besides, no word must be spoken except at the command of the Rebbe.

Instead, he prays. Have mercy on me, O God. I am sinful in every corner of my being. The gifts thou has given me are not contemptible. My talent is a small one, and even that I have wasted. It is precisely when a work is about to mature, to fulfill its promise, that we mortals realize that we have thrown our time away, have squandered our energies. It is absurd, I know, for one insignificant creature to cry that it is alive, and does not want to be hurled into the dark along with the lost. It is the life in me that speaks, not me, though I speak with it, selfishly, in its ridiculous longing to stay alive, and partake of its presumptuous joy in being.

.

Apples and Pears:

HET EREWHONISCH SCHETSBOEK

MESSIDOR–VENDÉMIAIRE 1981

Joop Zoetemelk Gagne
le Maillot Jaune

12 MESSIDOR

The mountain ash, or rowan, Virgil's *ornus* but not Ovid's *fraxinus*, is by family a rose and by ancient rumor a birch.

•

It all goes back, this complex friendship, to the year Picasso died, while I was finishing *De Boventonen van Stilleven* and beginning the commentary on Fourier, and to Paris the July Joop Zoetemelk won the Tour de France. Its plangencies cross philosophy at angles one might, with luck, trace. Fourier thought that our dream of a golden age that never was is a vision of his *Période Amphiharmonique*. In our time we long not for a lost past but for a lost future.

•

Mimes on the Plateau Beaubourg. Two trim boys in jeans and sweaters, barefoot, surrounded by a ring of international *uitschot*. Very exclusive, this unwashed sect of wanderers who call themselves students and are called students by a world that has long ago given up calling things by their names. Have heard that diseases turn up amongst them that have not been diagnosed since the thirteenth century. The Nazis were less arrogant than this *meesterras*. The mimes acted to the music of a guitar and harmonica. Faces covered by blind white masks held on at the chin, male, as regular and general of feature as a department-store mannequin. They mimed some *agon* of challenge and rivalry, circling each other with menacing and boasting gestures, two samurai in a sword dance. They leaned toward each other, wide-legged, nose to nose. Leapt back. Drew hands up thighs from knees to hips. One smoothed a cupped hand over a feigned protrusion of fly. The other snapped his legs together, bounced on his toes three steps back, flowed into a stance with his feet wide apart, unbuttoned his jeans, drew their zipper down. Foxred pubic clump, no underwear. Antagonist stalked toward him. Zipped up as he drew close. Antagonist in turn unzipped, *ook onderbroekjeloos.* Moved their masks away from their faces to meet nose to nose. Then back on their faces again, slowly. Padded around each other like wrestlers crouched to grapple. The first unzipped his jeans again, dreamily, as if absentmindedly, in slow motion. They danced a seesaw jig, as the guitar had changed over to a jouncing peasant quickstep. A wonderful strangeness in the conjunction of the white expressionless masks, the *joligheid* of the music, the bared pelvic nakedness. God knows what the mime meant to the spooky faces watching it warily, as expressionless as the masks, flat handsome eyes looking through wire-rim specs and from under barbarian hair, faces from Stuttgart, Ohio, Liverpool, San Francisco, Stockholm. Suddenly the mimes fell apart, shed their jeans in a swift agile gesture, tossed them to each other, and drew them on again, all in the shaking of a sheep's tail except for zipping up, which they did with dreamlike slowness. Finale. Masks off, they were simply sullen French youngsters *knap, modern, wereldwijs.*

.

The nineteenth century disappeared along the road beyond Orly to Choisy-le-Roi. It passed through Paris on a bicycle, Zola in knickerbockers, panama, pince-nez. It rode on a sealed train across Germany, Lenin at the window. It marched through Doncières at dawn as a military band. It painted hayricks at Giverny. It was Röntgen looking at a black skeleton standing inside the living body, it was Proust wrapped in blankets watching a frieze of girls on a beach in Brittany, Semmelweis urging us to wash our hands. It sent children into the mines, it sang gorgeous hymns in church. It blossomed, rang like a telephone, danced the Chicken Reel in the camps at Ladysmith, turned Europe black. Rossini cried that Mozart was very God. It loaded every possibility with promise for the new century. It danced the tango, screamed at Sarajevo, and died at Passchendaele.

.

Naderhand, what could there be? Walking in the Cimitière Montparnasse this morning, among the graves of the Jews of the Deportation, I came across the phrase *la barbarie nazie* on a tombstone. I took a sprig of privet blossom, in an aspirin bottle, and put it on Sartre's grave: which would seem to be the style for votive offerings there, flowers snitched from other graves by international riffraff, a child's drawing in a jam jar, a dornick inscribed in Chinese. No stone as yet, many faded wreaths. *Der Heer hebbe zijn ziel.*

.

French boy about nineteen reading Proust in the seat across from me on the train into Paris, pale blond hair in feathery disarray. Scruffy jeans, the crotch of which he fondled with attentive fingers every so often, wrinkled shirt, handsome large eyes as alert as a sailor's on watch. He read awhile, watched awhile the villages and fields streaming past the window. A big smile for me whenever our eyes met.

•

Coffee at the Balzac on the Friedland. The mimes at the Beaubourg were Piet and me after the war, in the woods hollow back of the park, having kicked a ball around to our satisfaction, and talked our fill on a ramble, busily idle, retreating and advancing in the one strategy. The broad tip of his snub nose stippled orange and brown, irides the same strong blue of his pupils, upper lip ridged into a prowlet beneath the philtrum: I didn't know that I thought him beautiful. What dried the roof of my mouth was the spirited way he disregarded tacitly sanctioned distances. Forearms on my shoulders, he'd talk forehead touching forehead. Green of the woods hollow, the smell of leafmold and water, Piet's speculative *bel guardo*, my timid scrootch of shoulders, foot dragged in the grass.

•

Een quaggaridder, twelve, the yellow rundle of his hair runched and flopping, is the imp of Fourier's imagination, a *peuter* whose breezy good nature is fused with his body as synergetically as water and light in a leaf. He and his kind, tomboy and ardent friend, bonded with difficult animals and with each other, were to be, how tragic the tense, the radiant source of the community's energy. His counterpart, sister or *anima*, was the spunky saucy little girl whose type was organized into the Bands, mounted on ponies, policing manners, gardens, and grammar.

13 MESSIDOR
Silence, restlessness of the sea, seabirds, wind sweet in the trees, radio, flute. In the glitter of the sea and the shine of fog I find my things, and enjoy long deep northern afternoons.

•

De werktafel: Chambered Nautilus balanced on a glass, *nautilus pompilius linné*, its marmalade and cream tabby markings radial from a center where the spiral begins its flourishing spin, its *ingeschapen* coil sealed off deep in the throat of the outspanning by a hymen of pearl. Its dorsal convexity down the long axis, both front and profile, has the *dop*'s ripe foreswell set and stress of a trim *slipje*. Chosen by Kaatje, bought by Bruno, wrapped in tissue and boxed by Saartje and Hans five times and dithering before they got it right, delivered by ambush, damp kisses, monkey hugs. Good thoughts from good things, said Saartje, is how it works. Art is you look at a beautiful picture and the beauty of it goes inside and spreads around and makes you beautiful. An innocent wink from Bruno. Hans developed the argument into trouble. Papa, he said, says Saartje is beautiful barebottomed but I say she looks like a newt. She's prettier in jumper and jeans.

•

And a spray of golden samphire in a Colman's English Mustard pot, the mature petals a richer yellow than the buds. They grow among the rocks near the sea in buttery, lemony clumps and seams. Three *Arplijk* pebbles, four paperclips, two acorns, and a stray button in a saucer. Postcard with a Red-Throated Loon, a watercolor by Isaac Sprague (1811–1895), a bird dressed in fine modulations of white and grey. A speckled strip runs neatly from the top of its head down the back of its neck to spatter out on the shoulders and fleck away underwing. There is a crimson brushstroke on its bosom. From Sander: Johan de Muynck, chin over handlebars full sprint, eyes down the road, niftier colors, bike and togs, than Sven Nilsson, and a Greek partridge in borage, and a silvery sooty moth, and Hansje pulling off his *voetbalhemd* as high as his shoulders, toes I've never painted better. Wait till you see. That it's my best painting is the thing to say, and I'll praise whatever you've written *hemelhoog. Een kus.*

•

Briefkaart from Paris, Bombois' *Le Forain*. Geliefd Adriaan! We're dossing down with Danes and Finns at a student camp in Vincennes but seeing everything in Paris, Sander saying he needs to see a bunch of things before the final big effort on the show. Blériot's *Antoinette*: a kite by Mondriaan. A hug, and another from Sander. Grietje.

•

Hinault's knee had come to pieces somewhere in the south and Zoetemelk, the papers said, was sure to win. He had come in second for three years previous, and had once pedaled all day with a fever so high the doctors when they got to him wondered how he could be alive. He had shot under the Merlin Plage banner the day before, as I'd seen on TV at the hotel, with his hands clasped victoriously over his head and with a smile that belongs to athletes alone, happy innocent triumph. Winded, bone-tired, gasping, yet he smiled in a glory of well-being. He looks like Vermeer.

•

The Renaissance, Picasso said to Jaime Sabartès, invented the size of noses. Since then, he added, reality has gone to the devil. *Bovendien*, no sculpture has surpassed the primitive. He asked Sabartès if he'd seen the caverns, seen the precision of the lines? The Assyrians had kept something of that purity, that clarity of expression. And Sabartès' dutiful *¿por qué?* To which Picasso's *to think you stop*. And having stopped, to reflect, we lost the faculty to see what's before our eyes.

•

Had renewed the amenity of a Parisian breakfast that summer on the *terras* of the Brasserie Balzac, with *Le Figaro* and the mail from Amsterdam. Keirinckx had written that I must see the Horace Vernet at the Beaux Arts and that he and Margareta might run down for a few days. And there was that *hopeloos geval* of a scribble from Sander, on graph paper. *Achtenswaardig Adriaan!* By doing what you said, memorizing everything, I'm getting through like the bright boy you say I am beneath the squalor and you're right it grows on you that way even English and Latin, treat all information like the multiplication table until it's weightlessly portable and recoverable as if by instinct. I'll bet the cabin is fine on an afternoon like this, yellow leaves on the canals here already, and mist in the trees. I look at things I know you like to look at, paths weeds spadgers flowers in windows treetops doors. Look, there's something to tell you that I don't know I should *yet* but if not now, when? You've met Zuster that one time we went out for sandwiches you remember, trim built girl with long hair down to her butt who you said might be my twin (she says by the way that you only play at being the *fatsoenlijk* man, that she can see the mischief of a willing spirit in your eyes, she's spooky that way). I'm onto moths, splendid creatures, what names they have, The Intermediate Cucullia, and all silvery sooty flecked with mica dotted and zigzagged over and with World War I airplane shapes, even Zuster, about whom much under your hat, likes them, The Nappy Pinion, The Hitched Mimestra, each almost like another but so wonderfully subtly different, The Lost Sallow, The Brown Woodling, not as you and Dokter Tomas know, that poor man with his *bijzonder*

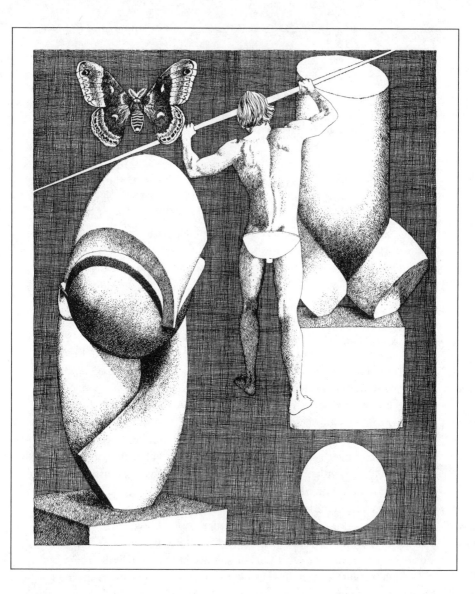

rattle about sex, the first time, but the first time with all our wits about us, in, to speak with awful inaccuracy, cold blood, and is it ever wonderful, The Heterodox Wainscot, The Wanton Pinion, something to do with narrow corduroy trousers bought in England, with the 10 cm zipper, put on barefoot, *keurig nauwsluitend*, The Variable Dart, my big peepee tilts the fly of those corduroys and ridges out across the thigh to the public's universal satisfaction, and mine, even Dokter Tomas would take notice, my continuous tan from the island, and *beetje* French underpants, or perhaps just my wickedly charming self. Anyway, friend Adriaan, there we are. Revolting, isn't it? *Betovering* is her word, that with all her giving it slick and deep to Jan Piet and Klaas she's always from a *kleuter* on, finger wiggly in her panties, been fascinated by *groot broeder* and his exciting ways, imagined natch as being quadruple the nasty reality, and even by *groot broeder* as reformed redeemed turned inside out right way around and renovated by your philosophical handiwork which you say was but that summer and sun and sea and having by main force to exist with a man who reads six books at once and looks up hard English words in a Greek dictionary and made me realize for the first time that I'm a human being with a life all my own to shape for myself or have it shaped for me against my will. I mean to tell you how it started, to deprave you, and even, to deprave you further, wish I were on Snegren Island right now, darting free and brown like my moths, The Wandering Dryobota, The Smudged Sallow, not only for your friendship and talk, but because if you're doing something you absolutely *ontegenzeglijk volstrekt* must quit *ja? neen?* it helps not to be in the same room with it all. I really am studying, the Seychelles coconuts, ginger and cloves, last uninhabited island, spiced air you can smell at sea miles away. And drawing, not only the moths but real pictures, of Zuster and the cat downstairs and the furniture. I'm going to start drawing at the zoo. If I can do the wolf, the handsomest fellow in the whole world, I may throw up everything and be a starving artist, mad about lines and color, thumping Zuster into an early grave (as she says) with unbelievable pleasure morning afternoon and night. *Kop op, kerel!* A ferocious tight hug, Sander. Forwarded from old Duit's Ships Stores and PK on the Point. *God in hemel.*

14 MESSIDOR

Coffee on Sander's rock, in his denim jacket with *stinkdier* armscyes against the chill and his *slip micro*, with explicit musk in the pod, for the fun of it. Terns preening beyond rainbows in sea spray. Waves bobble in a swiveling bounce before they flood against the rocks to shatter and foam.

•

Falanx Samuel Butler, Groep Vliegers Tulpveld, Wervelwind Ned Ludd. Hordes on zebras, Bandes on Shetland ponies. Panisks the one, Vestals the other. The Hordes ride naked except for blue neckerchiefs the chromatic complement of their yellow pennant, the same mushroomcap haircuts for both sexes. The Vestals in white tunics and cloth Mongol boots have long hair embroidered sweatband bound. The series flows from rambunctious to shy, from impatience to placidity, with the attractions distributed thus: forward scouts practiced in kissing, wiggly embraces, grubby foreplay through a half dozen precocious and whiffety orgasms as yet vagrom enough to surge from nape to coccyx in boys, from nipples to clitoris in girls, or chime from scalp to toes and fingers in both. A wingtip of Spartan aversion to gender contrasts, but ardent in allelophily, paired anterotically in precipitately masculine or early feminine couples chaste by fits and starts. A wing of private souls jealous of their independence, ticklish, preoccupied, sexually lively, endogenously. At the center of the chord, varying wildly from day to day, we can place those hordlings whose plasticity shifts them from wing to wingtip to forward scout, so that a sergeant from the Grand Hordes in charge of their mascot attachments will have Nora in the forward scouts on the chart of harmonies for Monday, having seen her joined to Orlando kiss and finger in the quagga fodder, and in the forward wingtip on Tuesday, she and Olga having been observed wrapped around each other in bed, and on Wednesday listed in the forward wing of meditative selflovers passed out with pleasure. Beyond the pivot is the little Bande, two thirds tomboy vestals and one third boys comfortable in their company. The wing commander is a corporal of the Flower and Grammar Police who, when having to consult with her counterpart in the Hordes, never looks below his handsome dusty neck, frequently alluding to decency and civility. She and her Little Bears always precede the Hordes on treks and patrol, taking precedence over all other traffic except the Roitelet's and Reinine's courier. All ensigns must dip at their passing. The wingtip of the Bands are paired into close friends who together make fudge, visit the elderly, compile lists of wildflowers, write poetry, and give their ponies literary names. The rear guard consists of sweethearts who blush to hold hands, stammer, worship their Corporal in the Vestals but dare not speak to her and discuss endlessly what she said to them after she has said it and gone away. They are relieved to be at the farthest possible remove from the Hordes in an encampment or the barracks, and suffer from being just before them on patrol. Their only security is knowing that for a Hordesman to josh or rag the rear guard of the Bandes the punishment is to ride in the Band wingtip for a week.

•

Empedokles feeling kin to the world: I have already been a bush and a bird, a boy and a girl, a mute fish in the sea. And when animals, they became lions with lairs in the mountains, sleeping on the ground, and when trees, laurels. He mentions laurels again: abstain from Apollo's leaves, from laurel.

•

Catalogue for Sander's show to be written, the essay that comes to the two contemporary problems of Fourierist harmonics, back-breeding of the machine to cooperative civility, Eros in rompers. What in the world does Fourier mean by *bee*? Social progress is always in spite of culture, which tolerates change, whether improvement or deterioration, with bad grace.

•

New map of the islands and channels from the Maritime Survey. Flute aslant against it, duck feather paperclipped onto the edge, and the photo of Sander without a stitch standing on the big rock gingerbread brown against a sea as blue as Henri Rousseau would have painted it.

•

Balthus' Passage du Commerce St.-André is an alley that runs from the Place de l'Odéon to the rue St.-André des Arts. His painting looks into the Passage from the rue d'Ancienne Comédie. The dwellings left and right in the painting are now a Watlings pub and a former restaurant undergoing repairs. Balthus' background building (Marat's newspaper office in its day) is just as he has painted it, except that its windows are boarded up. The golden key is still there, and the lettering: 8 LITHOGRAPHIE TYPOGRAPHIE REGISTRES. I remember the alley well from after the war, and may have rubbed elbows with Balthus himself all unknowing. His masterpiece, surely, not only for the tone of Parisian street life but for its touching so much in the French imagination: it is Balzac, Simenon, Maupassant. His figures are Picasso's *saltimbanques* reseen through a Rilkean sensibility. And it *says* nothing, and is as voiceless as all great painting is voiceless. The automobiles parked in the alley, illegally, seemed a desecration, for the site is still very much the painting, uneaten by time.

•

Simenon. Went to the rue Mouffetard, the setting of his *Le Petit Saint*. The market, the shops, the quiet banter of the people. As with Balthus, the artist has caught the full drench of reality. Walked up and down the narrow street twice, looking, taking it in. A house where Verlaine lived. Because Simenon saw such humanity here, such love and genius, I needed somehow to come touch it, with my eyes. I'll never distrust him again, if ever I have. Imagination is a seeing of the real. I savor the street while remembering the Amsterdam evening when I read it, cozy in a room with rain plashing against the windows, a blanket over my knees, imagining a composite, essential Parisian street. Here the mother pushed her barrow. Here lay the cabbages, the red fish, the striped melons of the paintings. For years I have admired Balthus' painting of the Passage du Commerce without realizing that I knew the site of it well, but in another context, from another subset of Parisian memories. I think I may well have been on the rue Mouffetard, years ago: I remember the court, with trees, but it was by night and I was young, and Simenon had not written his novel about it.

•

Graffiti. *Mort à la Chah. Mort à Kominy. La chasse c'est la guerre permise aux tristes cons en temps de la paix.*

•

A walk in the Parc Monceau: Proust could still be filmed here. Joop Zoetemelk was still ahead. Tried discussing this with a bartender, who gave a great French shrug, and said that he could not possibly win. Wrote Sander, to let him know I was in Paris and not on Snegren. And bought Montherlant's *Essais*. He and I share an *oogvermaak*. Epicureans, both, both of different descents from the master. His garden was La Bagatelle, soccer fields, the running track, mine a hermit's island in the North Sea, a lecture room in Amsterdam, my apartment. His love of energy was the duke of the manor's for the hale infantryman. The modern world was a sustained insult to him, except for those who had not become a part of it, the young. Unnourishing fare, one's heart. How he would have liked the Olympics now on TV from Moscow. Poor old man: the pistol to his blind face.

•

English lobster boats, a Swedish freighter. A morning walk after coffee by the fire, a landowner's beating the bounds, Thoreau sifting the familiar to repossess it, Robinson Crusoe patrolling his canebrake paths and desert beaches. In Sander's lenient sweater with its human smell and his ballfondling jeans, *voor de zinnelijkheid, des te erger.* A letter from him, saved back from the batch I brought from the point for after my walk and putting the cabin shipshape. In pencil on a Hermes Herenmodes paper bag: *Boezemvriend Adriaan* but why bosom not chest or *ritssluiting kameraad*? Anyway, a hug and a kiss. You are going to bleat and wring your hands when you see the bill for the big canvases I've been recklessly charging to your account but there we are, if I'm to have museums and Exxon Nederland N.V. executives fighting for my pictures, eh? In one of the Fourier pieces I want you riding a bear in a flock of geese, Hansje on a quagga. How bold dare I be? If I do Grietje and me making zigzig (Gerhard's beautiful photographs to work from, wait till you see, they'll punch you in the *zonnevlecht*), will a big circle moon and plants from Mattioli and posterish wide shouldered, slim-waisted apples and girl-shouldered, big-hipped pears all suspended on a white ground according to the Moldulor be context enough to hold our handsome Sander (eyes scrunched closed with pleasure) 23 cm deep into Grietje arching her back and coming with a yell? She had squeezed off up to a dozen by hand before poor Gerhard arrived and was about to melt down when I took over and chimed and tongued along a couple more before shoving in, so the whole time I was humping her she was throbbing from one goosy orgasm to another, our Grietje's talented that way, *God zij gedankt*, sucking my breath out, in between fits, and squealing when the scrunching touched the quick. Gerhard was stuttering and trembling at the end, grossed out and having second thoughts about skinny boys who jack off to electronic Bach. Grietje handed around hot chocolate which he slopped on his shirt, she in our Laplander sweater that comes to her pretty knees, but I left my pants off, as Gerhard is as you say *Corintisch*, with my thumper's collar back around its neck, to make him spill more chocolate. And you, *helaas!* get a bill for all this. What fun. Will send prints: how long are you on the island shunning us? There's one where I'm in past her bellybutton, her butt lifted by the push, nose crinkled, hair over my eyes, this for a lithograph, as the definition is fine. Max says I must draw and draw: he's going to say *not enough* no matter how much. Says I don't have my own eyes yet. My own hand, yes, though he says that's a quirk of nature. But that I see *naäperwijs*. I'll show him! A bear hug, Sander.

15 MESSIDOR

Time unbounded and limited time, says Epicurus, are equally pleasurable, if we take their measure with a sane mind. This is da Vinci's *an intense life is a long one*. And Wittgenstein's fullness of engagement in which time is of no matter. The elasticity is in the imagination, in attention, not in physical time. The mind must act as a second nature, continuous with but not necessarily

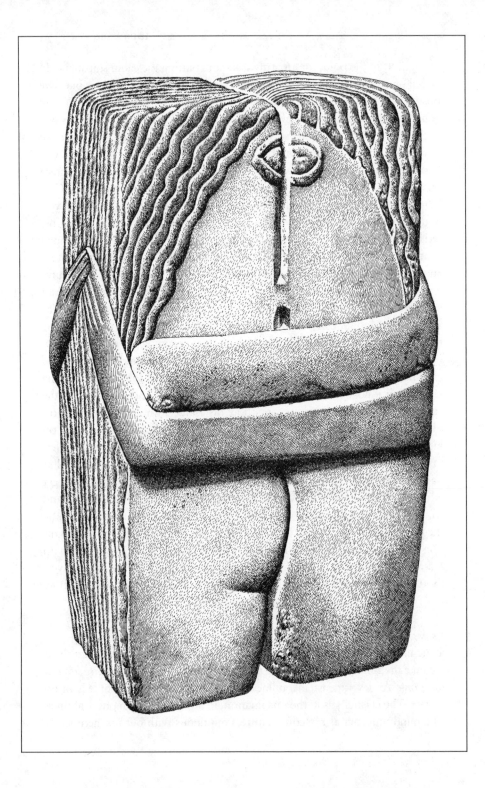

subsequent to the first. Our cultivated nature is our wild nature disciplined and clearer, a transparency achieved in an opacity, keenness in a stupidity, flight in a wingless creature.

•

At the Jardin d'Acclimatation (which Rosa Bonheur helped plan) where I like to see the barnyard animals and cats, there's now a skateboarders' concourse of sweeping and looping inclines, the English word SKATE painted on it in bold blue industrial sign lettering. A boy there taking off his jeans with the greatest insouciance, in the public path, to don short blue pants, which he had in the pocket of his jeans, and knee pads. And further on, poking his finger at the golden Hamburg rooster, a little boy in ratty dirty corduroy britches that just covered his pert behind. He was with his family, but stood, as it were, French-fashion, in his own independence. Simenon would have seen him with one set of eyes, Montherlant with another. I saw him on his quagga, galloping with the Horde.

•

Alexander Floris (which is not, by the way, his name) is a painter who has given no interviews and has made no details of his life available to the press. He is nineteen and Dutch. His nude self-portrait in this show is the only image we have of him, a handsome young man of athletic build, with the trim body of a swimmer. He has painted himself sitting on a gymnasium locker room bench, his shed clothes beside him in a still life of folded jeans, soccer jersey, and modish French underpants, Danish running shoes and white socks in another still life beside his feet.

•

The style in which all the paintings in this show are executed has been described by Max Keirinckx, whose student Floris has been for some two years, as that of a curvilinear Mondriaan who paints figures. We can improve upon that perception by observing that Floris has Mondriaan's precision of space and line but has transposed Mondriaan's Cartesian Jansenism into an Ionian idiom. The style derives from Hokusai and Hiroshige insofar as it restricts itself to black outline filled with flat color. We can recognize as well Keirinckx among the influences, particularly his brilliant experiments in the decade before 1960 with accurate contours and monochromatic areas of color. Keirinckx at this time was himself accommodating certain popular styles (that of Georges Barbier, of the posters of William Nicholson, the pretty archaizing of

Carl Larsson) that kept leading him back, as they have led Alexander Floris, to the Greek vase painters and ultimately to Lascaux and Font de Gaume, where drawing and writing are as yet unseparated, thousands of years before highlights and shadow were allowed into the grammar of imagery. Keirinckx said of his sparely outlined and boldly colored figures that they are silhouettes with more information inside the contours. For Floris every object is first of all a shape in the visual field, and he takes it out with the vigor of the Lascaux painters, for whom a horse or cow or rhinoceros was a word to be spelled correctly and inscribed on the cave wall with the existential obviousness of the word *help* written in snow by stranded survivors of an airplane crash in the Alps.

•

I cannot pretend not to know the painter: I am the Philosopher in a Rietveld Chair, and I posed for the elder in Circassian dress in the Fourier series. Indeed, in the course of encouraging this young painter, I advised him to elude the enticements and snares of publicity. He has agreed, not because my word has any authority, but because his dedication to his work is absolute. Goethe noted that when a man has done something extraordinary, the world enters into a conspiracy to ensure that he doesn't do it again. Epicurus' advice to live unknown is wisdom with more point to it now than then. The telephone, the interviewer, mail from importunate strangers, the collector of acquaintances, invitations into society, moths around the glamor of fame: Sirens, all, indifferent to the shipwrecks they cause. We have seen poets murdered by adulation, writers smothered, actors sent into a spin. Publicity is a blowfly. One of the few details of Shakespeare's blank biography is a note declining a drinking party, pleading that he had a raging toothache. One imagines rather that he spent the evening writing.

•

Culture makes experience possible. Experience does not deposit culture, its symbols, or its tone. Experience follows culture as an orchestra a score. Culture is tacit, unconsciously learned, invisible to the fish in its water. All events are echoes.

•

Mondriaan's Dutch flatness and linearity were once Vermeer's walls, Rembrandt's blank spaces. Sander carries forward Rembrandt's whole figures on an integral ground.

•

For every lack of civilization we pay dearly with boredom, outrage, death.

•

Apple and pear come into history when there are orchards, brick walls, hive houses as in Anatolia, storks nesting, stretching their wings most Netherland-ishly on white mud roofs, houses with mazes of warren rooms as at Phaistos whose apples Sappho sings, barge ports on the brown Indus and yellow Euphrates. People who hung dolls of the twins Castor and Polydeukes in the flowering pear, and Leda in the apple white with blossom.

•

Apple and pear, brother and sister.

•

It was in The Netherlands that Fourier saw the fields of tulips which the Little Hordes were to resemble.

•

Dressing the littles in Magyar finery, to pose for Sander, is like Rembrandt and his trunk of costumes for getting Juffrouw Peperkorrel down the canal onto canvas as Ruth or Naomi. Sander, who calls Fourier a sweet idiot and agrees with Grietje that the Harmony sounds like nothing so much as a troop of retarded Boy Scouts inventing Nationalsozialismus, is nevertheless taken with the vision. A subject matter, he says. After eighty years of bony French women in footbaths and Braque's mandolin and Picasso's guitar and Morandi's kitchen table and Klee's puppet theatre, we need a subject matter. Balthus got through it all and came out into landscapes as beautiful as the fields of Heaven. Picasso ended like Goya, seeing that what we have to stave off the seven sins which are death to the soul is practically nothing: some pages of poetry in Greek and Latin, a round of fiddles playing Bach, a Cézanne and an Henri Rousseau every other century, mint and grass underfoot, the cold sea, the burning sun.

•

Hans on a Quagga. Naked but for Mongol boots, blue neckerchief. Snaffle bit, yellow reins, no saddle, though the quagga is shod. De heer Floris depicts a member of Fourier's Little Horde. The hordes are organized into forward and rear guards, right and left wingtips and wings, with a pivot in the center. This quagga rider would be a forward scout. His nudity bespeaks the season and his virginity. The bandana is an insignia of rank as well as a mop for sweat. The boots are for walking. Quaggas (not yet extinct in Fourier's lifetime) were untameable. Fourier imagined that children in the Harmony could tame them. They would keep, however, a measure of their wildness. Hence the excitement and glory of their belonging to twelve-year-olds. The model is the engineer Bruno Keirinckx's son Hans.

•

Diogenes with Fourteen Dogs. The deployment of so many dogs, each with a distinct character, gait, and attitude, with the philosopher striding among them, staff in hand, seems a conscious following of Hokusai's handling of figures on a white ground in the *Manga.*

16 MESSIDOR
Postcard from Sander: *Hei!* Paris! You once promised. I could come over for a while with the wee bit encouragement from you if you're still speaking to me I mean *Broeder en Zuster* is to *schande roepen over* you were cool enough about it in your letter for which thanks, good man *uw liefhebbende* S.

•

Two Balthuses in the Centre Pompidou: the one with the old hag combing out a naked girl's hair, a fully, rather formally dressed young man sitting beside them. Because of Sander I read them as brother and sister, though Balthus does not hide meanings. And an enormous one of his Japanese woman, his wife I think. I will have to live with it awhile to see it. Clots of middle-aged American tourists looking at everything with hard, suspicious eyes. *Multimedia, Mildred, all of this stuff is multimedia.* And an American man looking at a large Dufy with utter disgust.

•

LILY, Rossini contralto, dove or egret, monarch butterfly, spinning, virginity, Raphael, white, longing, anarchy, girlhood of the Virgin, Joan of Arc.

•

SUNFLOWER, trumpet, lion, wasp, the smithy, moral grandeur, Vincent, yellow, male orgasm after fugal intensity, monarchy, Sparta, Alexander.

•

PRIVET, harpsichord, hen, midge, needlework, patient diligence, Corot, pale green, sentimental solicitude, a good aunt, the early XVIIIth Century, Marianne North.

•

DAISY, a country jig, bee, carpentry, girlish titillation, Denis, golden brown, *l'embrassement de deux jeunes filles*, the management of a dairy, Huizinga's XIVth Century, Chaucer.

•

TULIP, drum, camel, ladybug, glass-blowing, genial arrogance, Rubens, purple, eroticism as gourmandise, zamindary, the Caliphate of the Umayyads, Haroun al-Raschid.

•

ZINNIA, Scott Joplin, Szechuan blue-combed copper-tailed bantam cock, Viceroy butterfly, arc welding, passionate exuberance, Matisse, pepper red, wild Gypsy humping behind the hawthorn in an odor of mint and sweat, feudalism, the Sicilian Vespers, Maria Callas.

•

To Fourier's grave, through Céline territory to get there. *Si la série distribue les harmonies, et les attractions sont proportionelles aux destinées,* some genius of poetic justice must establish the harmonies, or some mathematician find them and show how they generate (like the other Fourier's series), and a more open awareness of attraction and destiny must become a social commonplace. It is a metaphysical intuition that can be traced either to Herakleitos or to the structure of primitive thought as Lévi-Strauss has anatomized it: a symbolic language preferred by children, illiterate societies, and artists, as he has said.

•

PHALLUS IMPUDICUS, Bessie Smith at her raunchiest, billy goat in rut, flea, sculpture, male pride of being, Picasso, olive rose of glans, omnidirectional *zaadgulp*, democracy, the cult of Ta'angaroa, Rabelais, Archilochos, *Deens jeugdherberg*, Marseilles shore-leave.

17 MESSIDOR
Mouthbreathing German tourists with vacant eyes and macaque teeth clattering their goose gabble in front of monuments to Parisians who fell in the

liberation of the city. *The war!* they cackle, *ja!* Have seen a busload of them so gabbling and giggling at the monument to Jean Moulin at Chartres. They sit in restaurants with their legs out to trip the waiters, push their chairs back to take up all the space they think they're entitled to. Nobody else exists for them. Suspicious, stupid, and arrogant, they followed their grimping, mincing Hitler like an hysterical woman who has at last found the occasion and means to throw a tearing fit that will destroy everything, everything there is, every uncomprehended thing that others have made with genius and kept with love. And they did it in the stupidity of assuming that afterwards they could wallow in self-pity for what it cost them, and gorge on chocolates and beer.

•

To Les Belles Lettres, which has all the Budé editions, right around the corner from where Gertrude Stein lived. Some nice work being done on Plutarch. On into the Luxembourg, memory upon memory. Gide sitting on a bench, warming his old bones in winter light. Donkey cart full of toy boats for sailing on the pond. Vistas. Just outside, the deaf-and-dumb school where Itard taught, and where Victor the Wild Boy of Aveyron refused to leave the realm of the animal.

•

Briefkaart from Kaatje: I tell Hansje and Saartje you are staying in the Eiffeltoren, throw parties for all the Parisiennes over 15 and under 35 in the Triomboog, all in black-lace panties (They'll catch a cold, is Hansje's solemn opinion) and eat snails in the Concordplaats. They believe every word of it. Bruno (just home and out of his clothes already) says tell you Zoetemelk can't lose. Wish we were there too. Those beautiful boulevards. Lascivious thoughts from the four of us, which by the littles means toffee and licorice in handfuls though I'm not so certain.

•

Keirinckx sends this delightful lyric, a Shaker hymn from America that an architectural historian at MIT sent him a Xerox of. He wants me to translate it. Says it is Rietveld, de Stijl, and my philosophy all in one.

> Love the inward, new creation,
> Love the glory that it brings;
> Love to lay a good foundation
> In the line of outward things.

Love a life of true devotion,
Love your lead in outward care;
Love to see all hands in motion,
Love to take your equal share.

Love to love what is belovéd,
Love to hate what is abhorr'd;
Love all earnest souls that covet
Lovely love and its reward.

Love repays the lovely lover,
And in lovely ranks above
Lovely love shall live forever,
Loving lovely lovéd love.

18 MESSIDOR

A conversation with some American students outside the Pompidou (they approached me, wanting to know what the great trussed and beamed glass building *was*) leads me to speculate that just as (so Renan charged) Catholicism cretinized French children (one knows what his hyperbole means, our fundamentalist doppers do the same), so it is now the young who cretinize themselves. Manners, none; grace, none; education, none. These were university students: they'd never heard of the Marais, the Commedia dell' Arte, of Racine, of Les Halles as was, of Georges Pompidou. I was foolish enough to sit them down over a drink and attempt a thumbnail sketch of the neighborhood. I showed them the *trompe l'œil* façade and had a devil of a time getting them to understand it. It didn't occur to them to ask who I was, what my nationality might be: I think they thought that all Europe can speak English if it wants to; that is, that we can talk, our own languages being a quaint affectation. They are neither feral, like Itard's Victor, nor culturally alien, like an Eskimo, but nonconversant with their own culture, analogous to slum urchins, except that the ones I was talking to are from well-to-do American families. They make a curious mistake: they assume that what Europe has to show them will be instantly intelligible and meaningful to them. They come at all because their ancestors came, but their ancestors, earnest New Englanders, idealistic Middle Westerners, swotted up their subject before they set out, and arrived knowing a Rembrandt from a Titian, architectural styles, history, places, philosophy, literature. These kids know nothing, and their French is Ningre Tongo.

There were mimes while we talked. The standard blue-jeaned barefoot French boys with May Revolution blind white masks. Torsos bare today, brown as gingerbread, innocent navels neatly punctuating suave mesial dents. The plot, as before, of provocation and face-down: must ask Gerard if he knows where it comes from. Venice, Crete, Sardinia? A leans forward on one leg, stretching the other behind him like a cat that's finished its nap and is planning to prowl. B backs away, a Javanese dancer's steps, feet turned outward. A stalks, B retreats. Then both leap, and the rôles reverse. B stalks, A retreats. *The things these French think up!* says one of the American girls. But what they're doing, I say, is a thousand or so years old. There were mimes here when Hadrian was emperor. *When was that? Roman as in Rome, Italy?* A circles B, nose of mask to nose of mask. Little hops, tentative touching of feet. A's hand spread on B's midriff, slid upward to throat, slid downward to inside jeans. *Hey!* B retreats, dancing indignant, stomping, high-kneed. Stops, dreams with swaying head, repeating A's caress with his own hand, up torso to throat, down torso and inside jeans. *I think this is going to be gross.* A struts around in a circle, straight-legged, with military swing of the arm not holding his mask to his face. B droops, bewildered. He sits cross-legged, leans his forehead to the cobblestones. A strides to him and stands so that when B raises his head it is caught between A's knees. A springs away and does a little dance on his heels. *He's dropping his pants and not a God's thing on underneath!* A stands charmingly naked, his jeans around his ankles. B looks up, stands, approaches, twirling around with every step. When he is mask to mask with A, he unzips his fly, pushes his jeans down to midthigh. One of the American boys looks away. *Jesus,* he says. A and B rock their heads metronomically. Both step back. B drops his jeans all the way, pushes them aside with his foot, and A copies him. They turn their backs to one another and walk in reverse until they meet butt to butt. Each reaches a hand around to the other's tummy. They unmask: a nice touch. They pass their masks over their heads, swapping. As the masks are identical, the gesture is keenly mysterious. *Can you figure this out, Alice? I'm not trying.* A rolls around B, chests and genitals briefly together, until they are again butt to butt. B rolls around A. *Can you explain this?* one of the American girls asked me. What's to explain? I said, and she gave me a hard look. I dearly wanted her to talk about the mimes, but she misunderstood me. A and B swap masks over their heads again. Nice Gaulish darkeyed flatcheeked faces they have, as impassive as their masks. They pivot suddenly and stand front to front, each with a hand on the other's backside. Forehead to forehead, the masks are thereby held on, freeing hands. These they insert between them, against each other's pubic hair. *Cute*, said American Alice. A and B reverse the gestures that brought them close, hands back to the chins of their masks. They pivot, walk backward with locked knees to their jeans, remove their masks, and bow. They entrouser to applause and begin working the crowd for coins tossed into their masks.

19 MESSIDOR

Boezemvriend Adriaan: We have been in the Combarelles cave at Les Eyzies and I know what an artist is. He's the one scratches the elk and horse and cow on the wall. Simple as that, *mijn kameraad kunstenaar*. Some hunt, some cook, some sew clothes, some incise shapes on walls. You draw words, I draw lines, making us kin even more than you finding me under the *jeugdcrimineel*, under the clown, and when we hit Amsterdam you're in for more than puppy frolicking, Grietje says so. The reindeer drinking at the pool, the wildcat marking his territory, the solemn fuzzy rhinoceros (spelling by Grietje who, *klikken van iemand nabij*, is very Modigliani, spelled between a yipe and gasp, with hand by Tiziaan, she thinks he may be spelled, followed by a *woef!*) and the lumbering bear. Anyway, we're dossed down here in an ultramodern blue Danish tent, complete with the Danes who own it and *kameraadlijk* took us in. There's a *Jeugdbeweging Vergadering* and Hippy Jamboree here at Sarlat that's all mixed in with Boy Scouts and a film festival and the odd toothy English tourist and gaping Americans, lots of unwashed Swedes with guitars and brainy French kids talking *Structureelisme*. Our two Danes, Pier my age, and Tom his *maat*, a *verbluffend* 15 with charming big blue eyes and a frisky long *opkrul* of eyelash, so that Grietje says her instincts are fifty-fifty between changing his diapers and seducing him, latched onto us at a brasserie on the square, both brown and goodlooking and under each other's skin, hands all over each other. Pure accident, as these things always are, that we fell in with them: two places at our barrel-head of a table on the *trottoir*. They oh most decidedly gave off what you call an *inspanning* of healthy fresh Danish sexiness, what you say I give off as a good dog gives off dogginess, well the very doggy *beweeglijkheid* of these two got through the solid bone of even my head (I see your smile) though Grietje the Explainer says it was my legs, little *gymbroekje*, and handsome chin with a day's stubble of beard on it that buckled their knees and made them run a temperature. Grietje makes these things up, you understand, wheels whirring in her brain. It was she who after the standard exchange of origins and destinations asked if they were lovers, and then Grietjelijk, admiring, sympathetic, and we the new generation can discuss anything, can't we, she danced into what do they do and how many times a day and what does it feel like. *Let us show you* was what Tom *de jonger* said with a smile like a lighthouse sweeping fullface, and Grietje the goose *gave* me to them, all heart, and Pier said come live with us in our tent and Tom said he would love me up unforgettably well if I wanted him to. This, *liefje* Adriaan, to jelly your mind, as if you weren't perfectly aware of what I'm scheming, *een plattegrond min of meer Fourieristisch*, ha! Anyway, we knocked our drinks back and walked up into a hilly meadow through an orchard (stone path, wildflowers, a tolerant cow) above a Boy Scout camp on one side and the orchard on the other, to their trim ample blue tent all aluminum tubes bent into elbows and nylon ropes and backpacks with forty pockets and snaps and zippers and insignia patches with little green fir trees and orange sunbursts and the Gemini buddies from the horoscope and even one with a circle of Greek saying that where two come together in love God is with them, in between I suppose. Grietje copied this for you. A tent is such a cozy place, like your cabin. So, to get on, here was Grietje babbling about the beauty of boys and golden friendships, *de jonger* Tom dispensed with his jeans, *sapperloot!* and his briefs (elastic frazzled, seam ripping in the pod) and flopped out like 18 cm of suntanned Danish weewee, *hemeltje*. Grietje's Modigliani pose has changed to Klimt, and I'm reading this to her as I write not only for the spelling but to see how to catalogue the doings and still have you speak to us again. In a word, Grietje the stinker gave me to these two pure-hearted Danes raised on buttermilk and granola, and helped them skin me to *adamskostuum*. Pier *de ouder* has a nice body, gymnast's chest, tummy like a plank, and an outsized thumper with the same long backslope to the glans as mine. Grietje says add the knobby bulbing around the eye. Are you still there? *Ach* and *oh me*, but we horsed around and swapped kisses. Grietje shed every stitch and we had a can of worms going, decidedly juicy and unprejudiced. I know, blushes flashing off and on, that this sounds like before you civilized me, but I think it isn't, as Pier is writing a thesis about the Wandervogel kids way back before the wars, for some *theoloog* in Kopenhagen, and Tom aside from being *dol op* his and everybody else's *peester*, is a poet and botanist and is a sweet person. Here they come, back from a dip in the river. More, later. *Liefhebbende*, Sander.

•

The *huiskrekel* chirps over the ripple and thud of the waves. Light weaves time. Mind's boundary's none old Vivante wrote for whom horizon's glare, but our horizon's diketop ruler-straight or inkblue line between sky and sea, sky and tulip field.

•

Ome Adriaan! For apples and pears you said to look. This Picasso which Saartje says she can draw better than is apples and pears on crumpled paper by a French window wouldn't you say, ja? That's a jug and tumbler. I think it's funny. Saartje says it's sad and quiet. Whoopee fuck! Your adoring nephew Hans.

20 MESSIDOR

Max and Margareta in Paris the summer Joop Zoetemelk won the Tour de France. Great fun. There they were, a surprise, on the hotel steps, Max fiercely bearded, behung with cameras and a case for drawing paper, Margareta in what seemed to be a safari dress, walking shoes, a straw hat. Off we went, after Margareta sprang her plans finished and detailed, to Giverny, by train to Vernon, Max a whizz at making French machines spit out tickets. We were lost at Vernon, going off in the wrong direction (a typical country town that could be anywhere, even England). Lunch at a brasserie in back of the town hall, and some questions got us on the country road down some six or seven kilometers of which we got to the house (American tourists held us up, trying to buy tickets with traveler's checks of some enormous denomination, the likes of which the girl at the desk had never seen. The Americans kept saying that they'd learned about this historical garden from a magazine, where they no doubt also saw for the first time, and forgot, the name Monet). All very lovely. The house (resplendently colorful) hung with his Japanese prints. Max and Margareta in an ecstasy. The lily pond (across the road, achieved by an underpass) turns out to be a loop of the little river Epte, along which the poplars, tributary of the Seine, so that all Parisian cooking is done with water from Monet's lily pond. Keirinckx agrees with me that the scenery round-about is even less distinguished than Holland. The studio is as big as a barn. Painted river grass underwater, Max says, which everyone knows can't be done, and the color of air, and glare through the interstices of tangled wistaria. We had a fine leisurely walk back, looking at kitchen gardens and flowers in yards, the spirit of Monet in us. We looked at his grave in back of the church: the family a French rabbit warren. His children by his first wife married the wife's children by her first husband, incest *de facto* if not *de jure*, very sexy, and God knows where the process began in the nursery, everybody's mama having been papa's mistress for years before anybody traipsed to the altar. Hot little hands poking around under flannel nightshirts, impassioned sighs, grunts in changing voices, scandalized nursemaids. Vernon, which we'd first seen during its siesta, was alive when we returned, crocodiles of camp children at the baker's, cars on the streets, citizens gossiping over walls. We had Camparis on a sidewalk, got our breath, had a good talk about Kaatje, Bruno, and the children, whom Margareta obviously adores, and came back by train. Long dinner at the Grand Corona, Place Alma. They want me to go back to Amsterdam with them. I plead that I need more of Paris.

•

The Parc Floral at Vincennes, Margareta's idea. A congenial expedition. Max kept making fun of French pedantry. Even the Tour de France. The Métro an exercise in Ramist logic, he says. But when they abandon logic for inspiration, they soar. Vincent at his most impossible, such as when he tried to draw a grape arbor from inside looking out, never achieved such skeins of wrapped wistaria, tangled willows, perplexed densities of bamboo as Monet.

•

HOLLYHOCK, von Flotow, giraffe, walking stick, flags and bunting, constancy of affection, Hokusai, pink tickled blue, courtly love for the sake of manners, Mandarin hierarchy, the Chou dynasty, Lady Murasaki.

•

DANDELION, *Die Zauberflöte*, goldfinch, lightning bug, chandler, cheerfulness rampant, Georges Seurat, yellow, puppy love, canon law, carmina burana.

•

Saw the Keirinckxen off, Margareta never more lovely, a lesson in seeing old friends against a different background, and when I got back, there on the sidewalk, blue haversack burdened, in scuffy jeans, Sander. Lost for hours! he bellowed. He took a postcard from his shirt pocket before he moved a step: for me from his sister. It was a view of the White Horse of Uffington in Berkshire. On the back she'd written *Braque!* The table by the window, he said, the notebook, everything as neat as a doctor's office. Everything's purest Adriaan! Design, order, sanity! He went about wrecking this admired condition with his gear onto the bed, shirt over a chair, shoes and socks *passim*. Hitchhiked, he said. I've been on the road two days, starved.

•

A joy showing Sander Paris, the Tuileries, the Luxembourg, the Palais Royale, blocks and blocks of the avenues, coffee at the Deux Magots, favorite streets (rue de Seine, Monsieur-le-Prince). We walk and look, look and walk. We have never had so much room, he says, to move about. It is not Amsterdam at all, he says.

•

The center of Proust is when Morel plays the other piece by Vinteuil, the Red Septet, *le rougeoyant septuor*, at the Verdurins, and gets to the enrichment of the magic little phrase of the White Sonata. (Which I associate with a theme in Franck's *Symphony in D Minor* that summons thoroughly Parisian memories of my first time in Paris, the St.-Germain in haze on a November day, the Café de la Mairie du VIe, St.-Sulpice, Sartre and Richard Wright at the Deux Magots, Picasso at the Salon d'Automne, the quais, the grey majestic practical wonder of it all, and, because of Kaatje, a limpidly lyrical phrase in the first King of Prussia Quartet). As Morel develops the phrase in a kind of rapture, his forelock pitches loose and jounces on his forehead. Charlus' ecstasy coincides with the narrator's: a synergy of Epicurus' *I know nothing of the good except the deliciousness of food, sex, music, and the sight of beautiful bodies in graceful motion*. Here the Eurydike in Proust and in Charlus (who is

Proust's tragic destiny) listens to the music her Orpheus plays for Hades and Persephone to free her from irredeemable time. *Elle était plutôt comme une grande déesse du Temps.* At this point he touches the erotic sense to the quick, and gathers every thread of the book around a spindle in one masterful twist.

•

Netjes stout! Sander of a *slip sous-vêtement Hom style nouveau* in a haber-dasher's window, *een blikvanger.* Bought him one, after the saucy, chic, merry-eyed salesgirl had pedantically measured his neck (he looked at me cross-eyed and asked why the silly girl wasn't measuring his hips, to which I replied that she didn't trust herself, or him), a patch of seat continuing in a smitch under-neath to a prow of a pod in front, joined by ischial straps of finger width. White cotton, cornflower blue the cincture. The French eye has a livelier nerve to the crotch. An arm across my shoulders for six blocks. It wasn't until coffee after dinner that I broached the matter he had been itching to have in the open. *Broeder en zuster, wat?* Well yes, he said, yes. She hadn't got along with the folks any better than he had. She's younger. If his wildness, that had landed him in the consternation of the ever-to-be-remembered good Dokter Tomas, had seemed egregious to the disparate parts of his incoherent family—what family? he says—hers was the more abrasive and got her cooped up with an aunt in the Hague. They took to running up phone bills, discovering the in-strument to be a congenial confessional both ways, they who did little more than spit at each other in person. His exemplary recovery from chronic irre-sponsibility and disappearing for weeks with riffraff merited him the Amster-dam apartment that I found for him when I got him enrolled as a student at the university, not without string pulling and special pleas. She too reformed repentantly and convincingly enough for the aunt to consent to her joining Sander in his apartment and attending lectures, the prospect of the two in one cubicle (she was not told about the one bed) being rather convenient and desirable in the aunt's view than otherwise. They could, so to speak, keep an eye on each other. There had been the earlier *paartijd*, out of curiosity on her part, for *kranig stukje* on his, with dash and abandon for most of a week, a day of which moreover he managed, for statistical boasting, a talented girl setting a new record for successive orgasms among her peers, adding three to the count, the forty-first through forty-third of the series (or whatever actual-ity behind Sander's generosity with numbers when reconstructing erotic his-tory), and his own steady girl, *in het algameen gesproken*, his *wisselstroom* friend Piet, and the sister, until fear of becoming the parents, and aunt and uncle, of a very unconventional baby stopped the idyll in its tracks. It was jolly, however, to land eventually in the same bed, the kind of adventure imaginative children might have thought up exploring each other's nature and design, like Eigon Schiele and his sister when they were only a few years into two-digit ages for three days at a country hotel, to be enacted when they were older, freer, and more developed of parts. They were shy at first, even with Sander protesting that he could not sleep in shorts or pyjamas, and with Grietje unable to go to sleep without playing her clitoris for an hour's wiggly pleasure, a habit of years' standing. Has anything *ever* dashed your imagination, Sander? I asked with some point, or failed to drop into your lap? O Lord, no, he said: you, her, all the others. Is unfailing good luck the sign that I'm marked to be squashed by some *folklorisch* goblin who gets boys with healthy active loving hearts? They found that they liked each other's company and preferred it, even, with the practical exception of a lover she ran across again and retook up with, a young mechanic whose only charm, *au fond*, was a member the heft and decidedly the shape of a cucumber weighing a kilo, and on Sander's part several unengaged engaging girls who after a gin or two, some tricky foreplay, and sticky kisses, gave well enough of their virtue and cunning furrows. They told each other of these conveniences, sometimes in clinical detail. They liked dining together at a nearby hash house, economically the great Dutch sandwich and bowl of soup that keep student soul and body together. A slashing rain one afternoon coupled them until dusk. She was in from lectures, soaked. He, toweled and dossy from a like wetting, pondered her grouse that she had to change and get wet again to be laid by the *komkommerlijk* young mechanic who confided in her more than she cared to know of the sweetness of carburetors and the timing of points, and offered a solution which would keep them both dry, warm, and fucked. His words. The rain conspired with a richer torrent, blinding the windows, tearing in a spate off the roof. She was, with perfect timing, peeling off her panties at the moment, and stood there laughing fit to kill in long socks and bra only. He pointed out, good old serious Sander when his heart is in what he's doing, that nobody in the apartment house believed for a minute that they were brother and sister, and thought them naive in offering so moss-covered a wheeze, right down to the old salt of a janitor, who had repeated *sister* several times and remarked that it was sweet wherever you could get it. She laughed the harder, stumbling over taking her socks off. Unhitch my bra, she said, you've uncoordinated me utterly. All very well, *geliefd Adriaan*, but have you ever *kissed* a sister? That's the eery part: I mean the tongue down the throat and painting the inside of her cheeks with your slobber and the ear smooching and nibbling and teats. All the rest is *pas de problème*, that's just girl the world over, and the zigzig is as good as with anybody ever, we're very good at it, championship class and improving, but we're getting to be lovers, if you see what I mean. I knew this when she left a note one afternoon saying she had run across Cucumber who'd pleaded he could come a liter just by looking at her and drooled over her so ruttishly that she'd gone off to a hotel room with him, and put at the bottom of the note *psychologically healthier*. Did I see red! Did I gnaw my vitals, and roll in self-pity and jealousy, renouncing all girls forever as shameless sluts, and threw in renouncing sex as well. Her, or nobody! What saved her from getting biffed in the eye and being thrown out of the apartment to peddle it on the docks was that when she got back, latish, in the full dark of my blackness, she said as soon as she got in, wholly unruffled, that he wasn't nearly as good as she remembered, impressively hung stud as he was and could flush out a cow and smelled of motor oil, and would I hurry and jam her the way she was used to, and don't finick at being second. For her, fourth. So Comrade Adriaan, there it all is. Have I shocked your back teeth loose? Have I undone all the civilizing you magicked into me? Am I a barbarian lunk all over again? All I will say, I said, is that you have a talent for establishing communities of two that exclude the rest of the world. So do you, he said. What if you make a baby? Raise it and fuck it, he said. We're that depraved.

•

His snookily raked new *slip* rode under the huckle and skimped his behind. Makes, he said, my downspout poke forward. I remark that it is a well-fadged fellow now, however obstinate an outlaw when on end and ranting. Which got me a goofy smile and flaunted display, nutbrown, with the plump sleekness of one that has done itself proud as *le grand seigneur*.

•

Drawings, a whole pad of them from the rucksack. The rascal has real talent. Why haven't I seen your work before? I asked in amazement. Never thought about it, he said. Only done it. You think I could ever be good at it? I say yes. Max will want to see these. Max Keirinckx. You just missed him. You *know* him? My oldest friend. He's Bruno's father, though not by Margareta his present wife. Bruno, Sander said. And then in a kind of awe and honest uncertainty: I've heard, well, things about you and Bruno and his wife. Around the university. Several different versions, so they can't all be true. I know nothing of your life, your past, the people you've loved. I'm envious.

•

Drawings of Grietje superbly rendered, some as if by an unripe and hesitant Degas, some as surehanded and mannered as Schiele. Several self-portraits, impossibly good-looking. The best are of mute objects, sneakers and socks, a geranium done in colored pencils, a sweater over a chair, saucepans and lettuce on a table. Something sweetly puzzling about them. I'm constantly amazed at the young being able to do improbable things spontaneously: play guitars, banjos, and recorders by ear, get the hang of a dance step perfectly in a matter of seconds, begin to speak another language in a week. But drawing, no. All children draw, abandoning the talent as they abandon dolls and blocks. They must come back to it as a man exiled in infancy finds his way back to a country he cannot remember. I draw all sorts of ways, he says. Like whatever I see other people doing. I can do Picasso stuff: you just skew things around, like copying somebody's handwriting. Why, I ask again, have you kept this talent unmentioned? Your lines are sure, decisive, economic, expressive. You think I can draw? he asked with genuine surprise. Of course you can draw, you silly dolt. I've always drawn, he said, long as I can remember. I spent my childhood drawing and jacking off, jacking off and drawing. Considering what I drew, the two were the same. Most of it, except for the occasional ship or airplane, had to be destroyed as soon as I'd drawn it. You're bottomless when it comes to disclosures, I said. And each more wonderful than the one before. When am I going to hear it all?

21 MESSIDOR

Like a field of tulips and lilies to see, like a babble of horns and geese to hear, like dogs and horses to smell, like happy puppies and wiggling piglets to hug, like licorice and dusty caramel to taste, the Little Hordes tumble down from their ponies, IX Kabibonokka on detail. The *korporaal*, whose haircut is sugarbowl, torso bare, trig faded jeans with fly fashionably open thirdhand from three elder brothers, linen boots of Mongol cut, proceeds to the barracks of the Tourbillon Georges-Marie Guynemer in what he hopes is a military stride, to report to Sergeant Jean-Christophe, who is fifteen. He gives the salute of the Hordes, grimy hand flat against his dirty forehead. Jean-Christophe returns the salute with two negligent fingers to a bored eyebrow. The porcupines have marched, the badger setts are in order, the stupid chickens have been fed and their eggs gathered by the Young Vestals, the Caledonian boars have had their acorns and garbage, and some mush points garnered along the way. Jean-Christophe, annoyed but conscientious, opens his ledger. Mush points for what? The *korporaal* gives them: they kissed all the sissies in the Bande Oncle

Joseph Fourier. They were policing flowers down in the Quartier Rousseau. They didn't want to be kissed, and in the best interest of the Harmony ought not to have been kissed, but IX Kabibonokka needs the mush points. Kissed how? Affection for thurifer cherubs, regulation which's whatissiz, cheeks, corners of mouth, ears, bellybuckle, dick, with two good squeezing hugs. Six of them, and mine had a snotty nose. Give you ten extra for that, says the sergeant with a sympathetic cluck. That's 610. Then, the report goes on, we invaded Grandpa Florien and climbed all over him and listened to him for half an hour. Give you five hundred, says the sergeant. Better knock off fifty, says the *korporaal*, if you'll give me fifty back for absolute honesty: Jean-Luc fell asleep and Martin got the giggles. No deal, says the sergeant. You're an aspirant, aren't you? Haven't you just turned twelve? What are you opting for in the Striplings? The Spartans, says the *korporaal* with a blush bright as a poppy. And, staring at the toes of his boots, asks if Jean-Christophe likes him enough to have him for a comrade. Eye to eye! Jean-Christophe bellows. All Spartans talk with full eyelock. The question is repeated with an unflinching gaze. I'll think about it, the sergeant says. It'll mean going tritone, as I've started inside with Julie, and I'm about a million points short of champion with the Zebra Marshal, who's determined to hit pentatone major before he's nineteen. So what else are you reporting? Found Madame Orlons' cat for her, carted away the quagga flop from the Avenue Jonathan Williams, where the Nasturtium Spadgers had a parade. Jules and Freckles loved each other in the Jardin Public, and some people came and watched. Any points for that? Give you fifty: that's *composite*, I suppose. Your name's Auguste, isn't it? *Come here*, he says in Porcupine. (They have been speaking in the argot of the hordes and bands. Porcupine is used only by devoted friends and bedmates, but is appropriate for a fifteen-year-old to use to a twelve-year-old who is an aspirant to the Sparticate. It spread from the Porcupine herds, who begin their apprenticeship as Cherubim, and became a favorite language for affectionate assurances and proposals, and is used for tender moments even among twenty-year-olds, who consider it *chic*. Porcupine is always spoken with noses touching, eye to eye. This is Porcupine minor. Porcupine major presses genitals together as well.) *Come here*. And just as they are wucking and snuffling nose to nose and Sergeant Jean-Christophe is parting his fly, in comes the Police. Sergeant! Sergeant! Jean-Christophe stands and salutes Capitaine Lucille of the Flowers and Grammar Patrol, in charge of Bon Ton for the district. She is eleven, wears the white peplon with blue sash of the Angelicat, and sparks flick in her eyes. Sergeant! *Do* you realize that there are ponies in the road eating hollyhocks on one side and roses on the other? What is more, there are two of the dirtiest boys I've ever seen making love in the middle of the road. You there! she screeches at Corporal Auguste. Are you the hetman of these barbarians? *Oui, Mademoiselle la Capitaine,* says Auguste with a snappy salute, the correctness of which is botched by his pizzle still poking out of his fly.

•

Chirico's *Pears* (1918).

•

Kameraad Alexander: *Woef!* We do well, the island and I, and the nattering terns and quarreling kestrels, and thank you for your ruttish scrawl on a filleted shopping bag. *De jongeheer* Cupido has rather made his hammock in the pouch of your *onderbroekje*, hasn't he? Members, *in het algemeen gesproken*, of that pod-dwelling family run loose even here to hassle what they can. While I was having a contemplative walk around the island this morning *de Heer* Eros and his cousin *de Heer* Pothos dropped down, who knows from where, one on each shoulder, with old tales from years ago when my friend Piet and I used to come to the islands in a kayak. No voice has ever shouted among these foggy rocky pine islands that *groot Pan is dood*, and we ran wild and naked, browned by the northern summer sun. Greek these urchins spoke, with a lisp like Alkibiades, and teased me with laughing pagan eyes. One hugged, arms around my neck, legs around my waist, smelling of sage and dry grass. The other, after some puzzlement with the zipper, undid your jeans I was wearing, *liefje* Sander, and with deft tickles bunched my balls tight as an apple. But, and when, and later. I remember a piece of buttery crumbly cake at Sarlat, years ago, and with no Danes or stunned Americans.

•

Ass bray is to cockcrow as an esterházy of kettledrums a haydn of trumpets a sousa of bugles is to quagga whinnock.

•

Coffee by the fire, *schetsboek*, pipe. Out trouserless in Sander's denim shirt with musky essence of Sander underarm and a doggish kindly seasoning of Sander overall.

•

In the crowd swirl around the Beaubourg the boy on the train who was reading Proust. Eyes still bright with attention, still rabbit innocent. White duck tennis shorts, buff jersey with spare white collar, sandals. Blue butt pack like a scut. I'm pretty certain I'd seen him once before, on the Métro, in lively conversation with agemates.

22 MESSIDOR
Silver is sleeping gold. Finch and larch are awake in a world other than ours. How, in the awakened dark of light, do these binaries occupy the same space? They do, they don't. Awareness extends, and over real space, but does not occupy or exhaust the space it fills and traverses. Ten species in one territory inhabit ten different worlds. Ten people in a room are in ten rooms.

•

Pewter and frogspawn green, the sea.

•

Adriaan! The caves, the caves. There's a hotel here in Les Eyzies, as per the front of this card, called the Cro-Magnon Annexe. The food, the food. Actually, I long for a bowl of good Dutch vegetable soup. Sander has gone bonkers over our Danes. I'm not left out, oh no, but the postman's eyes are already out on stems. Sander's sketchbook is, as you'll see, a sight. *Ad interim*, Grietje.

•

What can be learned has already happened, in quanta which, like the frames of a film, are discrete, perhaps independent, but which seem to flow in a continuity and seem to be a series of causes and effects. Thus we imagine reality to be of a piece, whereas every evidence that can be tested shows it to be discontinuous and incomplete.

•

Roger de la Fresnaye gives Guynemer in his portrait of him the heroic frown of Rude's figures on the Arc de Triomphe and large Picassoid eyes of intense concern. In Henry Bordeaux's biography the eyes are mentioned first. His two older sisters and his mother thought them beautiful, and kept his girlish hair long well beyond the age for it. As with Rilke, another *garçonnet en jupes*, he was whisked one decisive day to the barber (who wept). Little Guynemer said, *Now I'm a man*. Anakreon's haircut poem:

> Your bunched curls so crisp
> around your slender neck
> are clipped and lie scattered

in ravaged handfuls, in heaps
on the black ground. Poor hair!
Laid waste by the scissors.
What grief I suffer to see
you close-cropped, like a calf.
And nothing can be done about it,
nothing at all.

Roger-Viollet's photograph shows the same handsome brown French eyes. La Fresnaye's brother built the Nieuport in which he spiraled to his death at Poelcapelle. The crash was into a battle. Before Germans or English troops could find out if Guynemer were alive in his *coucou* (as the brash devils called their planes), the field where he lay was churned by three days of artillery fire and no trace of plane or aviator was ever found. He was almost twenty-three. The official war records credit him with shooting down fifty-three German aircraft (he learned to dance his plane around in a victory jig after he had made a hit). The French, giving him the doubt for the plane he was dueling with when he fell, credit him with fifty-four. He was too underweight for the infantry, and got into the air force by going to Pau as a mechanic, where they called him *the girl*. He and his gunner, younger than he, came into a canteen after a foray, and were seen by a general who was unfamiliar with the squadrons. When told that they were aviators, he boomed, *Mon dieu! this war is being fought by children*. He was tubercular. He wanted to be a mathematician after the war. At the height of his heroism he threw away unanswered all letters except those from schoolboys. He spent his recesses at the *lycée* rollerskating. His first plane was a Blériot.

•

The silk darts into the labyrinth. 1886, Hugo de Vries in the flower market, a basket of wild primroses like no primroses he has ever seen. His mind brims with Darwin, Wallace. By what tediously slow process did this primrose come about? He breeds primroses, goes through gardening books, botanical papers, finds a forgotten paper by a monk, one Brother Gregor Mendel, who charted generations of sweetpeas. The series distributes the harmonies, attractions and destinies standing in exact proportion.

•

On his one-seated Nieuport Guynemer painted his device: *Faire face*. Even before Verdun he wore the Croix of the Légion d'Honneur, and in parade dress at twenty-one, still a sergeant, he sported the yellow ribbon, the red, and the green War Medal with four palms. At Verdun the Germans attacked for the first time in squadrons of eighteen planes together, new types with machine guns firing through the propeller: Albatros, Halberstadt, Ago, Mercedes, Argus, Benz.

23 MESSIDOR

Sartre's *consciousness is not what it is, it is what it is not* follows the Rilkean structure of outward perspective streaming inward, light being a neural event in the mind, the actual world being dark. Sander cries and stomps *No!* Light is not light only in the eye. Light is real. We argue wonderfully, going into leaves, which eat light, and the feel of light on the skin, with its melanin, and rudding response, and uncorridored space hung with fiery stars. And all pitch black, I say, except in the mind. *Ik denk andersom, afschrikwekkend filosoof!*

•

In the unfailing cooperation of accident and design one or the other must be a seamless continuum. If design, then Michelet's vision of harmonic unity is true. If accident, then Fourier's vision of universal yearning of a torn and disintegrated nature for harmonic unity is true. Nature is the extension of seed generating a membrane of cells whose destiny was to be metamorphic, synergetic, inventive, adaptive. Michelet's symbol for this viscous progress was the copulation of Isis and Osiris in the womb, one organism differentiated into male and female. The same blood pulsed through their embranchments of veins as thin and as blue as the phloem of violet petals. Osiris' pink fingertip, gelatinous palp sheathed in transparent skin around transparent bone, found Isis' clitoral tip pelagic under its pellicle as fine as a gnat's wing, as rich a nucular perplexity as the bud of his standing *met*. Their mouths joined, rose-petal tongues twined and rolling. Elf ears. Eyes of gazelle fawns. His finger floats away, her calyx hand guides his peniculus in, and the three-month-long orgasm begins at the meeting of thrust and hunch, a suffusion of light through honey, spreading like music along every course and nest of nerves.

•

Pietro Crescenzi wrote his *Opus Ruralium Commodorum* at Villa d'Olmo in Urbizzano ten miles from Bologna, continuing the work of Columella, Cato, Palladius, Varro centuries before. Rosemary against the moth, borage against depression, convolvulus against constipation, the rose against earache.

•

Ome Adriaan! Alexander and Grietje Floris when they get back from Frankrijk soon are going to draw us, Saartje and me, in a picture poodlenaked together Mama says. They've sent us lots of postcards of prehistoric animals. When can we visit on the island? Your affectionate nephew Hans.

24 MESSIDOR
In The Madonna and Child in the Enclosed Garden with Sint Catharina of Alexandria, Johannes de Doper, Sint Barbara, and Sint Anton Abt (de Meester van Flémalle), Barbara offers a pear to the Christus. A pear balances an apple in the Washington Crivelli Madonna and Child. The pear is a symbol of the Incarnation; the apple, _malum_ (both evil and apple in Latin) is a symbol of the Redemption, the cherry of Heaven.

•

Hoffding followed de Vries into the maze. He talked with his friend Christian Bohr, whose son Niels listened. Everything is a variant of a nonexistent norm. Only the discontinuous individual exists. Individual, nothing, individual, nothing.

•

Adriaan! _Een brandpunt._ What's the opposite of _droomgezicht?_ I mean when you're widest awake, furthest from deepest asleep. At Les Eyzies, across the road from the museum up the cliff there's a little dirt road we walked along, our Danes and us, and there in a grassy meadow was a tree, a youngish pear I think, and while I was looking at it I remembered Redon's delicate lithograph and Leonardo's drawings of plants and quivery trees, and that _Engelsman_ Palmer, and all the Impressionists doing naked light spattered on leaves and grass. But this slender tree all by itself at the edge of this meadow, near the road, was all mine, and spoke to me, you know what I mean. I was stirred up by the flints and bird bones up at the museum (their _spooks_ are fetuses, ja?) and Tom was making a poem right there in his notebook, saying that the word _pity_ must be put near the words _leaf_ and _seed,_ and we were all kissing each other strolling down the hill, to scare some _houten_ Americans (it never fails), and as we got to the road there was a troop of French boys in _driehoekig slipjen_ and brown as _peperkoek_ singing back to their campsite, with yellow and blue pennants on staffs, exciting both Grietje and Tom. And then this slim young tree. Why was it so sweet, so perfect? Tell me. We're headed back. I'm going to paint till I drop. None too soon, as Grietje's giving Pier and Tom ideas about girls, and I'm getting seriously confused by the *allen zonder onderscheid*, jolly as it is. *Spoedig, spoedig*. Sander.

•

And, as ordered from Museum Replicas, a sixth-century BC Athenian athlete's ceramic oil bottle in the shape of a *penis en balsak, de voorhuid* modestly pursed to a tip, scrotal seam in raised definition, the funiculus of a pericarp, the frenal hilum a ridgelet between dimples, the *onderschacht* neatly vascular. Handle to the bottleneck for securing a thong.

•

Four sacred games: Zeus Apollo Palaimon Arkhemoros: Olympian Pythian Isthmanian Nemaian: whose victors wear wild olive coronets apple leaves celery sprays pine branches.

25 MESSIDOR
Bastille Day. Six Phantom Jets over the Arc de Triomphe like the great wind at the end of time, two streaming red trails of smoke, two white, two blue, their vibrant booms going through us into the ground. Some sprightly pomp of a Renaissance march from all the lampposts. Tricolor bunting and flags everywhere. And pouring rain. I had my London Fog and umbrella. We'd put Sander into a Prisunic green plastic poncho, with hood (from which his handsome face looks out soldierly) and zippered kangaroo pouch in front, made in Taiwan. And a fig, from two Dutchmen, for falling water. Giscard d'Estaing came by in a jeep driven by a general. Weapons carriers, tread-mounted eight-inch howitzers, field guns, a hundred tanks each painted with the name of a battle, from Roncevaux to Dien Bien Phu. This was Leclerc's armored division. Les Pyramides. Solferino. Ypres. Agincourt. Marne. Passchendaele. Strasbourg. Quatre Bras. Berlin. Fuck war, said Sander. Infantry, cavalry, a pontoon bridge in sections, field kitchens, the Parisian Fire Department, its twirling lights flashing.

•

Lunch in Chaillot, under an awning, rain splattering at our feet. Mucked about a bit, and decided to give up and go back to our hotel lobby and watch the Tour de France on TV. Raining on them, too. Several cyclists took nasty spills on curves, spinning all over the road. Sander drew cyclists in his pad, and swimmers at the Olympics.

26 MESSIDOR

Tweede jongelingschap. O my. *De herdersgod Pan, zoon van Hermes en een nimf*, stalks in the larches, and his garden cousin Eros mousles here, tigging and throppling his piddler. This racketry from some outback of the will, coming in from the country, like, and welcome, why not. Coffee on the rock, notebook, Sander's gamy denim jacket, shed for the sun's warm kindness, his shared *broekje*, about to be shed.

•

Salsify the root of goatsbeard.

•

Greek *gymnos* does not mean our *naakt*, but *unarmed*. Eros, whose parsnip of a *sathon* jutting over his quince of a scrotum was as presentable as his hyacinth cluster of curls, was naked when he'd laid aside his bow and quiver. There's a poem in the *Anthology* in which he's *gymnos* but carries under one arm a dolphin and under the other a basket of flowers, emblems of sea and land, of *all*.

27 MESSIDOR

The sun! And from Sander: This place swings! This of the end of a long walk on the Left Bank, through markets and narrow streets, sitting awhile in the Luxembourg (*quel beau garçon*, a frank old lady said to me of Sander), strolling along all of the rue de Seine, then along the river. At the Quai du Louvre we went down to the embankment toward the Pont Alexandre IIIe. Not until we were down along the high wall were we aware of so many people out taking the sun after such a long spell of rain. A woman of years, doughy of flesh, very Francis Bacon, was spread in our immediate path, horrendous in a bikini. Next, a man my age had shed his clothes, which lay stacked beside him, and was soaking up the sun in briefs poked up by an obvious erection. He likes the sun, Sander said. Then a boy and girl in their underwear stood against the wall, hip to hip, mouth to mouth. Two more teenagers lay on the cobbles, thirstily kissing, wearing skimpy bathing togs, the boy's being an inadequate container in the circumstances. I thought we Dutch were unrestrained in our parks, Sander said, but we have much to learn from the French. And then a charming curly-haired boy, twelve I would guess, in sweater, jeans, and expensive rainboots of soft leather, Lappish of toe, leaning on a stanchion, watching something with amused interest. He was, as we soon saw, watching two boys about Sander's age. The one lay on the cobblestones of the quai, hands behind

his head. His shirt was off, folded beside him. His jeans were unzipped and open on a rich pubic bush, and his lean torso was thick with hair across his chest and along the midline, whorled around the navel. He was watching his friend with a concerned smile, who was standing braced against the quai wall, his shirt open, dark blue corduroy jeans unsnapped and off his hips and on the fly enough to allow his hand inside, masturbating with a steady deliberation. His eyes were intent on his friend reclined in front of him. They both of them seemed well bred, good-natured boys, kempt, washed, and neat. It was impossible not to stare, especially as they were oblivious to people walking past, camera-wrapped Americans hastening by, others having a good look, the curly-haired boy studying it all with big round grey eyes. Have we, said Sander, seen what I think we've seen? He gave his crotch a hitch and pull. The sun has driven them mad, I said. It has been raining for weeks, with one sunny day in seven. But that's the real knuckle, man, to do it right there with your buddy before you. That's the way I've wanted to live all my life, and nobody's ever let me. Ask the good Dokter Tomas, the brow wiper. That's how I got turned over to you to be civilized. It's all wearing off. At the Pont Alexandre I said, Let's go back. This is like the mimes I've been seeing, but from a hardier playwright. Wait a bit, Sander said. That kid knows how to make it last. Is he going to come down his pants leg?

•

We did not, in the event, go back. We explored further up the river, seeing some girls smooching and holding hands, more sunbathers in scantling briefs, and a boy mother-naked when we came in sight, pulling on a pair of jeans. He was with a bargeman in arrears with shaving who sat on a bench, shuffling his gumboots and batting his knees with his hands, merry as a grig. The boy was laughing, too. I'd have to study for years to understand these people, Sander said, but they seem to enjoy being the French.

•

I remembered and told Sander Julio Cortázar's story about the photograph taken on a Parisian street, of a boy ostensibly approaching a _poule_, a study in the manner of Cartier-Bresson that turned out on being developed to have inexplicable elements in it, or rather elements that could be explained in several ways, such as a man in a car looking over the top of a newspaper, whose attention admits of all sorts of readings.

•

Les Invalides and round about. Vincennes. The bois there, the chateau, streets, markets. We strode through the rain, intrepid explorers. Sander liked everything, asked a million questions, missed nothing. I enjoyed being the cicerone. Here Proust wrote the novel, Colette lived up there. We went into the Gare St.-Lazare, because of Monet. Where he took the train for Giverny. And down nearby, the Lycée Condorcet, where Mallarmé taught English, perhaps taught Proust. On its wall, a terse graffito: *Vivisection crime.* Probably translating, I hate my biology class.

•

To leave the forest just when it is white with mist half the morning and its gold begins to fall, to leave Valvins, these rocks, these trees, these roads, and to take up the school year in Paris in an odor of oilcloth, chalk, and urine, this was the sentence of drudgery year after year, teaching English to rats in stockings and smocks, to giggling bored depraved Walloon geese, to boys. Aubain, Beauchamps, Bloch. *The devil will not come into Cornwall for fear of being put into a pie.* Charron, Delavigne, Drouet. *It would wex a dog to see a pudding creep.* Frontenac, Guérard, Houssaye, Marronier, Proust, Roquetin, Saussure, Weil. *Brag est un bon chien mais Holdfast un meilleur.* Rats' eyes, spitballs, whispers, palmed photographs, erections in their smocks caressed with rolling hands, even when standing to recite. *Parce qu'il est hanté par l'azur!* And from lycée to lycée, Besançon to Paris, by some network, cousin to cousin, the epithet *père*, not quite out of his hearing, always deniable, filthy little beasts. *The Isle of Wight has no lawyers or foxes.* The leaves at Valvins go brown, go gold, the boat is hooded in its tarpaulin for the winter, and wasps worry the windowpanes by day, moths by night, and through the poplars from the walk around the lily pond you can see the hay harvest pitched into ricks by farmers gaitered and hatted like figures in Hokusai. Arrive the rats, by din, by caw, by whoop. One has cracked another with an algebra on the head. An accusation of lice vies with one of sodomy. Grandpa in his plaid shawl is now going to drill us in aspirating the aitch of the English. *Breg is a gid dug bet Oldfest is ze bettair. Le meilleur ou un meilleur?* Delavigne jiggles his foot, holds his crotch like a miser his purse, eyes vapid and fixed, mouth open like a sailor swarming the rigging in a gale. Delavigne! Translate, if you please, *the higher the ape goes, the more he shows his tail.* What page? What line? Never mind what page or line. Were my hand the lilac and yellow at Giverny, April on the Japanese bridge, sheets of light and hollows of shadow, a garden on a river, flowers on a mirror, red and violet burning in the dark of every green. *Plus il montre sa queue.* Bloch's blue discs of eyes tick from Delavigne to Proust, the face of a Poussin shepherd blasted by idiocy. Rat smirks, goose eyes, ferret muzzles. Climb? *Grimper, grimper!* What page, what line? A fart, a red face. *The monkey's tail is stiff and feels so good.* Silence! We are studying the language of a disciplined and well-behaved people, and we should emulate their manners whilst we learn their tongue. Words said by no one, a witching ventriloquy, the Prince of Wales, Jack the Ripper. Delavigne! Quit shaking the whole room with your jouncing foot and put both hands on your desk. And translate. O, but he can still come, by thinking about it, that one! Bloch! Book, essence, faun. The Book. Wittgenstein with his grammar-school children at Puchberg around 1923. Barthes with his spoiled young esthetes, Sartre teaching history in Rochelle.

28 MESSIDOR

Gymnasium. Sweet to get back into old ways, alone. The trees along the canals bushy silver and gold against a bitter blue autumnal sky. Infernal traffic. Gerrit with his *verouderd Ionisch* body, Brabantine blond thatch sheepdog thick and sheepdoggishly blinkering, so that his most characteristic gesture is arching his tall throat to toss it out of his eyes, greeted me. Good workout, swim.

•

Talking Coxeter and Fuller with Bruno, Saartje and Hans getting in from time to time, to butt and squeal, with Kaatje plucking them off against our protests that they were welcome. Max and Margareta over for coffee. He approves of my draft of Sander's catalogue copy, urging me to incite him to even greater boldness. They called, travel weary, around ten, Sander throwing in French and Danish phrases.

29 MESSIDOR

How distinguish between the lurch of the mind into a gritty unevenness that sees everything as uncooperative and this morning's smooth balance, a harvest of Erewhonian luck? After the congenial monotony of coffee and journal, a swim. Refreshed, feeling victorious over traffic, time, and the whole dundering insane botch of the century, rolled up at Sander's, as asked, to find Grietje just back from the baker in sweater, scarf, jeans, and sandals, laying out *café au lait* in the studio, some abominably raucous American record on the gramophone. To shake Sander loose, she explained. Go pull him out of the bed, I've tried twice, and the second time he made a convincing effort to get me back into it, the *seksmaniak*. His head was indeed burrowed under the bolster, the eiderdown was wadded in a crump around his back, with a bare butt and wide divarication of brown legs sprawled therefrom. I tickled the sole of a foot, causing a galvanic contraction and mumped complaint. Grietje kittled his *balsak*, achieving a thrashing spin of Sander entire, bellowing, gruntling, and mussed. A kiss from Grietje on his rigid *peester* and one from me on the nape, corrected by him to one on the corner of the mouth, and he was up and doing. Ach, Adriaan, and aha, he said over coffee, you have no notion what you're in for. I had already seen the big long canvas with a lovely donkey in charcoal, a donkey with a head two sizes too large, jackrabbit ears, and a boy astride. The boy was a frail sketch, quickly superimposed. That's one of the donkeys in the park, Sander explained, the ones kids ride. That's going to be Hans on him. Behind them will be a quagga with Saartje on it. A generous space, and over here on the left I want a Vigeland kind of group, a philosopher with spadgers and chits and striplings. And up here one of my moths.

•

Warm and dry over an able red wine and Gruyère at the Balzac the summer Joop won the Tour, we hypothesized the furtive spectacle we'd seen the day before, which I saw as Balthusian, with a touch of Cocteau, and which stirred Sander's imagination and emulation back in our room. Hypothesis: A (lying down) was a stranger to B (jacking off). This makes A singularly tolerant, accommodating, and, by having shed his shirt and opened his fly, encouraging. Not to be a stranger for long. Sander's hypothesis: A hankers for B, his friend, who will not cooperate further than allowing himself to be adored. The broad daylight scenario is to prevent B from advances. My next hypothesis: A and B are the closest of friends who do everything together that can be done, including seducing each other in public, the danger of which they find spicy. Too novelistic, Sander criticizes, too psychiatric, and counters with: A was taking a sunbath alone with his shirt off. B, passing by, was taken with his body and proceeded to enjoy himself while gazing, a practical sensualist. A notices, is pleased, and at the moment we passed had got as far as undressing little by little. Had we gone back, his jeans might have been shoved down his thighs, the tourists would be bumping into each other, and the curly-haired boy would have his fist in his pocket, planning great things for when he got home. In which case B's hand in his pants was foreplay. Hypothesis: all of this was spinning a web for the curly-haired boy. More sinister interpretations (we'd come up with several) would not fit the amused smile of A or the intent gaze of B.

•

Meanwhile, Sander sighed, my sister and darling is with Cucumber. Asked why he had not brought her to Paris. And both of us freeload off you? Besides, she wanted me to see you. She thinks we do things we don't, though I've told her how I offered you my body the summer of my civilizing and how you eased me down so kindly and expertly that I didn't realize until months afterwards that you didn't actually take it. You're a good man, you know? I said smugly that I knew a thing or two about yeasty boys. For which I got a tongue stuck out at me and a handsome grin. I came to see you, he said, to see Paris, it's wonderful with you, and have you get me, I suppose, out of bed with Zuster Grietje. I said: how can I, possibly? All problems solve themselves. You're happy with her and she seems happy with you. Your account of it all is thoroughly depraving, I assure you. Look. What you're doing is sharing living quarters with a sister. She needs you. She won't always. Nor you her. Time has things to say about these matters. That is, neither you nor she knows what you're really doing. Holding together two parts of a disastrously exploded family? God forbid, he said. The romping in bed is all symbol, I think. Sex is itself a sublimation, not things a sublimation of sex. Warm hearts, a secret understanding, hot pants, and the sweet revenge of breaking a taboo. Not quit? he asked. Do you want to? Good Lord, no! Does she? Not her.

30 MESSIDOR

Sander had called his sister and seemed grandly pleased. We planned to return to Amsterdam as soon as the Tour was over. I felt certain that Max would take Sander on as a pupil when he saw the drawings. We were giddy with the high spirits of making a painter of him, as if by a capricious snap of the fingers. To be an artist! You *think* so, Adriaan? This is crazy! And Grietje. That's crazy. He took his drawing books and pencils along on our walk, a long one around the Marais where we watched a mime, fascinating Sander. We went along the boulevard St.-Denis, and over to the river. The sun broke out in a fine blue sky. Then to the quai down by the Pont Alexandre IIIe, without admitting to each other that we were going there. A clochard sunning himself and nipping from a bottle of wine. A housewifely woman in a monokini, breasts rolling away from each other as in Athenian drawings of *heterai*. Francis Bacon, said Sander. Some almost naked youngsters further along. More like it, said Sander. Sunbathers on barges, the gentry of this part of the river, and making Amsterdammers feel at home. Some wearing *cache-sexes*, so that face down they're stark naked except for a Y of string. Sander, choosing a place, took off his clothes right down to his new *slip si serre et collant*, what there is of it, like pretty much everybody else up and down the quai for a hundred meters, presentable, trim, and brown to the Parisian eye, several of which cast approving and appreciative glances and grins. I hope, he said, your French can get us out of whatever I'm liable to get us into. These Sander pants please me wonderfully. I look good in them, don't I? Let us see that flat hairy tummy you're so vain of. I comply as far as taking off my shirt, the sun feels so good, acting in his fantasy. We sit with our backs against the warm, ancient wall. The Seine glitters, the moored barges rise and rock at the passing of industrial barges midriver. The Left Bank as far as we can see each way is ineffably beautiful. I feel like a straying lover being unfaithful to Amsterdam, or to my island, whose empty loneliness I imagine, afternoon sunlight in white squares on the cabin floor, my books (if things are in any way sentient and Time their god) missing my care of them, my attention. Look, says Sander, scratching the hair the pouch of his *slip* doesn't cover, our friends. The hypotheticals. So they know each other! Now they do, says Sander. I get out my pipe and as I punch in the tobacco I realize that the boy with his hand in his pants of earlier is, I'll swear, one of the mimes outside the Pompidou. Indeed, yes. The other too? No, I don't think. Sander mischievously taps his pouch with two fingers. As if to oblige us, they take station nearby. What luck, says Sander. We must live right. He opens his drawing book. A is wearing a striped soccer jersey and jeans, and confirms my opinion that he and his companion are upper middle class. B wears the same dark blue corduroy trousers and a grey pullover. Their accent is Parisian, the words unintelligible, the conversational tones of old friends. Sander draws. Outline of face, hair. Off come A's sneakers, he's wearing no socks, and his jeans, no underwear, as when he was miming, but with wholly different movements. Well hung, I remark. Sort of, says Sander. A folds his jeans and sits on them, against the wall like us, cupping his hands over his genitals. A passing couple from Idaho, at a guess, stumble in looking back. B takes off his *pull*, shoes, and socks. Sander draws, filling the page with quick, clear annotations of parts of bodies and clothing. B sits beside A, an arm over his shoulder. *Gekakel gekakel,* says Sander. What are they saying? *Hei!* there's the splinter-new nipper with the puky curls and Mongolian boots. Is this a *plaats van samenkomst?* He has on a sailor's middy, French jetting on the tallywhacker, the neckerchief royal blue. He stands with the plummet-line, pert-butted aplomb of a figure by Seurat. He scans the river, the wall, punches his hands into his pockets, and brings his kitten's gaze to rest on our neighbors the two youngsters one of whom is sitting on all his clothes. A mother passing puts her hand over her daughter's eyes, outraged. You see, Sander says, the French don't all hold with whatever in the world we're seeing. Adding, you don't have the beginning of an understanding of my depravity, dear innocent Adriaan. Those kids over there, I'm in love with their *vermetelheid*. They're high-wire walkers, you know? Look at Rabbit Nose. Who was taking off a boot. And the other. And expensive-looking implausibly clean tall socks with blue heels and toes. These he rolled, sailor-fashion, and stoppered a boot with them. The mime from the Pompidou's hands folded in his lap toyed at covert manipulations off and on, causing an American tourist to blinker his wife and knock her harlequin glasses off and to take the name of Jezus in vain. The nipper unknotted his tie, rolled it neatly, and put it in a boot. Off, then, came the middy, studiously folded and laid across both boots. Pants next, leaving him skinnily *gemberkoekje* tan in blue briefs with a white waistband. His absorbed unconcern has not changed. He sits on his trousers, facing us all. He is, says Sander, taking the sun. Mime and buddy become more affectionate. The gendarmerie is going to turn up at any moment, I say, and take us all to the Bastille. Naw, says Sander, not a bit of it. Some Americans in Hawaiian shirts, print cotton dresses, cameras, and sunglasses stroll by just in time to be scandalized by Mime and buddy rolling into an embrace, or tussle of horse-play, or fight. It looked like any of the three, or all of them at once. Whatever it was, it pleased the boy, who opened his mouth and squinched his eyes. After the Americans came a squadron of Germans filling the whole quai across, gabbling. Sander on our side and the boy on his had to draw back their legs to keep from tripping cackling and honking Germans, who were of course not looking where they were going. One of them, indeed, snagged a foot on Mime and buddy, and pitched forward flat most satisfyingly. *Blither blither* went the Germans, chicken-eyed. *Piss off!* shouted Mime, whose anger made him handsomer. *Cons*, said Buddy. *Schweinscheisse!* Sander bellowed, standing. Inevitable, I had to agree afterwards, that Sander would free his considerable *peester* in naked light, from the pod of his *slip*, and stand as if grandly bored, especially by German tourists. Comedy loves the young in the full pitch of their sweet idiocy, and rather than a cold jolt of adrenalin I got instead, *god-dank*, the golden Apuleian fun of it all, and was felled by a laughing fit that felt so good I caved in to it. The Mime cut me a smiling glance, decided that the moment was worth risking French wit on, hooted the Germans away, and joined my laughter. His friend crinkled his eyes, dinted the corners of his mouth in a silvery grin, and we all came together, ridiculously indecent for a public place, including the boy, who got his hair mussed by Mime and a tweak on the nose from Sander. We are, I said, a Dutch philosopher, moi, and a Dutch painter, mon jeune ami. They were, Mime and buddy, students, Parisians, friends. Taking the sun. We had routed the Germans. For a while, said

Mime, rocking the flat of his hand. For him, he added, nodding toward the boy, who was fetching his things and bringing them over to be with us, explaining that he knows one does not ever talk to strangers and that his name is Bernard. Alexandre, Adrien, Georges, Michel.

1 THERMIDOR

The field of cyclists on the wet Champs Elysées, some sixty of them, is wholly silent except for the *whish* of their tires over stone. Their crouch over their handlebars is like a cougar on the pounce. The colors of their maillots, striped, checkered, banded, contrast brightly with the grey of Paris under rain. We watch them double back at the Étoile, return, veer off at the Louvre, race along the Seine, flow onto an overpass, circle the Louvre, enter the Elysées again. They reached Paris yesterday, and have been cycling all day in pelting rain, around and around these last laps. It is not our Dutch champion Joop Zoetemelk who sails with hands clasped over his head in triumph under the Merlin Plage banner at the foot of the Elysées, but his daily time is still less than any other's, and at the finish line the Mayor of Paris helps him pull on the yellow jersey of the winner and kisses him on both cheeks.

2 THERMIDOR

A basket of pears. Blue tablecloth. Freckled Pomona.

•

Mon titre est d'avoir suivi la route opposée à celle de vos charlatans législatifs, comme Platon et Voltaire, Owen et St.-Simon qui veulent changer la nature de l'homme, changer les ressorts que Dieu a placés dans nos âmes pour les diriger. Je suis le premier, le seul qui ait cherché et trouvé l'art d'utiliser ces ressorts, sans y rien changer. Fourier, *La Fausse Industrie.*

•

For Pastoraal VI, four meters by one and a half, Sander needed two children. Asked Bruno if he could pose his, and got, Kaatje shooing them in before her yesterday afternoon, *een echt nimf in de dop en bosgod snuiter, de jongeheer Hans, de liefje Saartje.* They are to be figures on a white ground in the right third of the long canvas, which sat on the big easel already framed in thin black lathing, its other images finished: four silly sheep, very Hokusai of line, black-shanked and with sharp grey-brown triangles for hooves, a suds of milky wool crushed thickest along the ventral swag, clerical of face, their eyes serenely composed upon the simple thought of grass, and, with receding vagueness, the flightier notion of humping one's mother. Sander has placed these citizens in stacked perspective to the left and up. Beneath them, a Sicilian basket of gourds and melons, a moth on a squash. The moth occurs again, a *bastaardsatijnvlinder*, as big as and to the right of the basket. Center, his long back to us, a boy seventeen, *atletisch long en modernaakt* except for the *sportief supporter* the model was wearing (Hieronymus Naaldboom's son Jaap), the waistband belting the small of his back, trim straps curving around the buttocks from the hips and insinuating to a bushy juncture at the perineum with the dip of the cup. Long legs wide apart, a blue javelin grasped upright in his left hand, its slant making a clean diagonal between him and the sheep, basket, moth.

•

Another, O my (Kaatje, thus) of the long paintings with all sorts of things in them, which Adriaan likes so much, *ja*? As Sander knows, *natuurlijk*. She admired Jaap's neck, so straight, like Bruno's at that age, so improbably tall for a neck, and cylindrical, flourishing out into a round of hair that keeps its whorls and spits inside a circle. *Een criticus!* Sander said. Keep on. Not in front of Adriaan. Where are you putting my rascals, in this big painting? There at the right, a brother and sister. A knowing look from Kaatje, as if in on a conspiracy. A brother and sister in ruddy *tankleuren*, nude, glossily but I hope not slickly realistic. Keirinckx's grandchildren! Some grungy iconographer will discover that in the middle of the next century. Kaatje herded them in while they looked around the studio with quick, sly glances, some of which flicked Sander up and down, as if they'd never seen him before, with smiles of doubt and adventure for me. *Ome Adriaan!* Saartje said with sophisticated acknowledgment, and *Hi, ome Adriaan* from Hans with his *elfenglimlach*. Kaatje made them shake hands with Sander, a lesson in manners, and developed them as a theme (talking about children in their presence, a discourse with two audiences), as creatures she loves, as the special beings children are, a breed of animal committed to a human fate. And, with perfect frankness, as admirable children worthy of being shown off, of being seen by the discriminating. Hans, deciding to be superior to the occasion and knowing that as soon as he had been put through his paces in a polite greeting he was free to explore, strutted around with his hands in his pockets, looking at drawings pinned to the walls, inspecting with interest bottles and tubes of color, brushes, easels, photographs. Saartje chose to be mouse timid, clinging to Kaatje, studying the floor. Her *hallo* to Sander had been whispered. You're to be drawn, you demons, Kaatje said briskly, as naked as snakes, so off with your

togs. Both at once? she asked Sander. Together? How, Saartje found the boldness to say, is Heer Floris to be? Saartje dear! Kaatje was beautiful with her
whoop. *Verwonderlijk!* I put in, but Saartje was persistent. Is he taking off his
clothes, too? Kaatje, falling into my arms, said that she had the smartest children in Amsterdam, and with no warning at all they turn into cretins. Call
Heer Floris Sander, wretches. He has studied with Grootpapa and is Adriaan's
friend, and he has been to our house many times, practically a member of the
family, and you know perfectly well who he is, except that suddenly you've
decided to become niddynoddies. Peel, Hansje. Here, Saartje, let me squirm
you out of your sweater so that Sander can see what a sexy and pert *meisje* you
are. Sander, sharpening pencils, whistled prettily. Red sweater off, Saartje held
out a foot for Kaatje to untie her well-scruffed *gymschoenen* and fidget down
the white game socks she was wearing in obvious imitation of Hans. She took
her jeans off herself, and stood there, back arched, comic surmise on her face,
pleading sympathy from me, which I gave her with a wink, suddenly cooperative and in the spirit of the adventure, perhaps because Hans had shucked his
jeans and briefs with casual unconcern, shirt and undershirt, wadding them
into a pile at his feet. Stood there with her thumbs in the waistband of her
scrimped underpants slotted midpudge, which, with a shy flirt of eye, she
slouched down, slid to her ankles, and handed to Kaatje with the air of one
abandoning the wearing of underpants forever.

·

Hans meanwhile tramped about in grubby socks and sneakers only, looking
at drawings. Hansje love, said Kaatje, I don't think Sander wants to draw you
with your weewee between finger and thumb like that, and take off your shoes.
Or do you, Sander? We've seen your erotic drawings. *Woef!* These two barbarians, as I was telling Adriaan last week, have begun playing with themselves, *met vurigheid*, bound to begin sometime, now is as good as any, or I'm
just finding out. Mothers are the last to know anything. Bruno, the beast, said
they're probably retarded to be just now discovering what fun they've been
missing. They may, *gewillig*, and play with each other I daresay, so that's all
right, though they save their racier turns for when the neighbors pop in or the
Mormon missionaries call. You haven't lived until you've seen two of those
really ghostly *mormoons* staring at Hans when he has answered the door
with, as he supposes, at least the minimal decency for a public appearance but
in fact with his little man perky as the spout of the teapot sprung loose from
his underpants. Hans grunted, to acknowledge that Kaatje was telling this
right. And kneeling to unlace a shoe, asked how long all this was going to take,

his voice wonderfully gruff for a boy his age. *Hoe lang duurt het?* What manners, Kaatje said. Hans came for me to pick the knot in his other shoelace. Gave him a kiss on the cheek, which he returned on my chin, squeakily, and grinned. He smelled of licorice and Palmolive *zeep*. Sander picked Saartje up and sat her on his painter's stool, and tucked her ankles inside the second rung down. He commanded Hans to stand beside his sister, please, in whatever pose felt natural. Hans, as I knew he would, clowned his head against her shoulder, his arm around her waist, laughing, and settled into a shins-crossed, arms-crossed stance against her, with a shove and countershove between them before they balanced. Sander drew swiftly. Don't have to freeze, he said. Shift about as you need to, but without moving from where you are. Whereupon Saartje jiggled a finger on her navel, and cupped her hand around a breast not yet there. I could see Sander's block: he was getting line after line as right as Degas, the tender ribby column of Saartje's torso, lyric thighlines, delicious toes, her puddy crotch so plumply cleft before its scrub of silky hair comes along, vulnerable hollows at the collarbones, innocent mouth, nubbly nose, Hans' incredibly straight thighs and rich curve of calf. Kaatje made herself thoroughly comfortable in a chair behind them, facing me. Sander kept up a running commentary as he drew: nifty ears, improbable eyelashes, wrist dimples still. Unselfconscious little buggers, not knowing how beautiful you are. Hansje's fingers strayed to his foreskin, tickled its pucker, slid it from around the glans, wiggled it all, and then decorously pinched it back down, and poked at his chin instead. Careful, said Sander, or I'll kiss you both until you're crazy. Saartje gave Hans a fine look out of the corners of her eyes. It was, Kaatje said, Jenny and Jan Sinaasappel who taught these two. They're a bit older, stunningly beautiful both of them. They, I gather, never quite quit, and were at it when the fast young sporting set here were over one afternoon, not, thank goodness, *voor de schijn*, which would have struck the naughty note and Bruno and I would probably never have heard about it, but, bless their hearts, as a casual pastime. Saartje cast her eyes upward and pursed her lips, getting a laughing glance from Hans. That's what caught their imagination and made their eyes as round as florins, Kaatje went on, obviously enjoying telling us all this. The big Sinaasappels are advanced to a fault, scholarly and into things, Danishly modern and properly psychological. The Sinaasappel littles were watching TV when Saartje and Hans went over, or were rather sitting in the company of the damned thing, which is what kids do, in the *zitkamer*, and Jenny while jabbering about something quite unsexy, I asked, opened Jan's britches, one wants to say rompers, and trotted his little fellow up and down. It was the insouciance that spoke to my nippers' hearts and gave them hot pants. Hans smiled agreement, and gave me a wink. His britches, Saartje said brightly, were already open. He hadn't zipped them up from before we came over. He'd been doing it lots before then, Jenny too. And it isn't little, but big, like Hansje's. Sander whistled a catchy tune, keeping a straight face. Hans caught my eye, glanced down and back, and I nodded assurance. He smiled. Yes dear, said Kaatje, as big as Hansje's, and it was only when Jenny noticed what a sensation she was causing among the junior members of the Keirinckx family that she said, the little teaser, O we're allowed to, aren't you? So they sat there breathless and panting until Jan skeeted a driblet. A sprinkle, Mummy, Saartje corrected. Lots of drops. Hans distinctly blushed, a tender pink under his tan, uncrossed his legs, stretched, and faked a yawn. He resumed his pose at Sander's whispered *please*, and broke into a good-natured smile, man to man. *Maatje*, he said, my dingus is going to stand up *vanzelf* if you keep talking about it. Fine by me, sweetheart, said Kaatje, and Saartje, mischief in her eyes, slid her hand over and patted it, for which she got an elbow in the ribs. *Wat kan dat schelen?* Kaatje went on happily. And when they came home seriously excited, *liefje* Saartje blurted it all out, part scandal, part envy. I'm certain I blushed (you didn't, said Hans), but there was nothing for it but to give a crisp lesson in playing the loving finger in girls and plying the working hand in boys. I *did* call Bruno, as all decisions at command level are joint in our house. He, of course, laughed gloriously. They could hear him on the phone and looked like two worried mice until they heard his *er op los gaan!* and whooshed with relief and fell down unstrung puppets. They both gave an imitation of this, Sander flailing his arms for them to resume their pose. And, Kaatje went on, off to their room they went, skitter scatter, Hans grubbing out his wizzle on the way, and were still there when Bruno came home. Just like him to stride right in and hug them both, naked and doubtless nasty, and kissed them, probably all over. All over, Saartje said with a wild grin. I hope, said Kaatje, all this is getting into the drawing. It's also getting into me, Sander said, starting a third study. God help Grietje when she comes home. Saartje giggled, and Hans, scratching his pubic fuzz, asked why. You see what I mean, said Kaatje, about the smartest children in Amsterdam doing double duty as idiots.

•

Grietje, as it turned out, swirled in when Sander was doing a sixth study, stunning in her brown beret, eyes merry. Hans and Saartje were posed facing each other, his hands on her hips, hers on his shoulders. *Nu ja!* Grietje said, with a kiss for Kaatje, who rose to hug her, and a kiss for me, smack on the mouth, and a warm one for Sander, with a smidgin of tongue in it. These two make you draw, Alexander, they make you draw. *Schoon!* Marie Cassatt! Ingres! *Och*, what beautiful children. She darted a kiss onto Saartje's nape, and ran a hand across Hans' butt before flouncing off to make coffee. I can't stand it if you won't sit on my lap, Saartje sweetheart, pretty please, Grietje beguiled her, laying out cups. Hans assumed his dinky briefs and scruffy socks before joining us. I'm certain, Hansje, that Sander adores your raining cookie crumbs all over his drawings. They're neat, he said. They look like us. You could make my peter bigger, ha! You draw hands and toes real good. Grietje held Saartje, still naked, in a lovely hug.

3 THERMIDOR
The tarpan of Lascaux. Redrawn standing like a Stubbs with groom, as if by Chao Meng-fu or Hiroshige. Its rider, dismounted, a gracefully lean boy with amused eyes and fuddled hair, is patting its willing nose. The meaning of the painting is in the sweetly dumb coquettishness of the tarpan's eyes.

•

Le couple angélique goûte en hypofoyer le bonheur d'être l'objet d'idolâtrie du public, d'être pivot de favoritisme. Ce n'est point une idolâtrie chancelante dangereuse comme chez nous celle de la faveur populaire.

•

Sander asks to go to the island, he and I and Grietje. To work out a structural problem, to let the long paintings go unfiddled with, so that all the changes to be made will be obvious when he returns. This after I had seen Max about the exhibition, and the gallery manager, who was miffed because he hadn't met the artist, and incredulous that apparently he wasn't going to. Turned up at the studio: Sander painting, Grietje working on interior designs for an imaginary house which she says will be given to her by forces and powers she believes in, Kaatje darning, Sarah and Hans posing. At the end of the pose he cupped his hand over her sharebone and kissed her openmouthed, tongue out. *Gunst!* Kaatje remarked, to get a *ha!* from Hans, a *hum!* from Saartje.

4 THERMIDOR
Hansje, being drawn by Sander, tells me about his friend Jan, who is *keurig, knap, goedgezind, vriendelijk, geestig.* He makes geometric figures out of dowels and string that are tight and bouncy and look as if they shouldn't hold together at all. He has been to Sicilië. His sister is always rootling in his pants.

He has books and books of maps. He can say everything in French and English. He's a terrific gymnast. Is it *welvoeglijk* to kiss if it's only on the corner of the mouth? Absolutely, Sander says. It's also *wellustig*. At this Hansje laughed merrily, squidged a chaste kiss upon an eidetic Jan's crimp of a grin, mimed a scruple, and repeated the smooch. You can practice on me, Sander said, but don't dare move just yet. Hans was posing standing with legs in a parted stance, his hands in the pockets of docked white denim jeans, a blue cadet cap all else he was wearing. I can kiss Adriaan, Hans reflected soberly, because he's my uncle, and because I love him, and I can kiss Sander because he said so, and I can kiss Saartje because she's my sister and I love her, and I *have* to kiss Mama and Papa, and I can kiss Jan because he's my friend. I've got to pee.

5 THERMIDOR

That too, Sander said of my remark that the coins and moths in his long canvases are scriptural, the treasure stored up on earth which thieves break into and steal, and the moths that corrupt, Sint Mattheus 6:20. I give it in Greek, *me thesauridzete kai ta loipa*, making Hansje's eyes round and Sander's left hand twirl over his head. One's art, the other's nature. Both are little, both cunningly made. I'm not to explain to the critics, you say. Well, I can't. Money and bugs, Hansje said, relaxing his pose and being shouted back into it by Sander, whose ferociousness puts a smile of innocent patience on his serene face, for me, and a jutted tongue for Sander. Money and bugs, goats and sheeps, boys and girls, fruits and vegetables in a *paaskorf*, all like a big long poster. Your pictures, Sander, are *gek* but neat and bright, and I'm in them, and Saartje and Jan, *ondeugend* and nifty. Tell about working on the baby, as part of my pay. Grietje lies on her back and you stick it in and slide it in and out till you come, *heb ik gelijk? Neen, konijn!* You kiss and sigh and feel and nudge and whisper and laugh. It's love, *wasbeer*, it's all heart. I think I'm blushing, Hansje said. You are, Sander said, it's charming. Let's all take five.

6 THERMIDOR

Gelijktijdigheid. Hansje, delivered by Kaatje, who with a cordial whack on his butt dismissed him as a vexingly cherubic monster, made for the phone as soon as she was gone and had a recklessly frank exchange with Jan. Then, roguish fun in his eyes, he slid his hand inside his trousers, nothing shy, and poked about looking at books and prints, asking the occasional question such as why does Kierkegaard look such a gowk. And wasn't it time we set out for Sander's and Grietje's? What was I doing?

7 THERMIDOR

Expedition with Hansje, rather Erewhonian. Kaatje called (interrupting Sleutelbloem in my office wringing her hands over Kant) and asked if I could take him to Sander's for posing. Also, would I take him by a *winkelzaak in herenmodes* and see if they have a boy's size *onderbroekje naar de laatste mode*, what Hans describes as a *handvol boldriehoek* front and a *dubbelhandvol* of seat. Delighted. We drooled through the stamp dealers first, buying rather more than Kaatje would have allowed, then the haberdasher's, where the clerk was properly scandalized, especially as Hansje was precociously sophisticated with chic chitchat about the scantiness of underpants. We got to Sander's by way of puppies, kittens, and hamsters in a pet-shop window, a display of marzipan at a bakery, the vibrators, dildoes, and magazines in the vitrine of a sex shop (I had to answer questions), a puppet store, and a quick zip down the slide in a park. Sander working on a handsome still life, abstract, geometric, late Corbusier, wonderfully harmonic. A hug for us both. First business was to see if the underpants fit. *Het kan nog net* was Sander's remark, *niet vereist* mine. No blush from Hansje, but much finicking with the set, swiveling of hips, and off to look at himself in a mirror. Sander gave us coffee and milk, a rest for him between the still life and drawing Hans. The room splendidly sunny. Hans sipped his milk, leaving us to talk about the canvas on the easel, padding about in his new *slip*. Neither of us was quite prepared for his coming up to Sander and poking with his index the *ronding* of his jeans *klep*, a prominence which even the most pure-minded must note. You've drawn my peter over and over, he said. Can I see yours? But absolutely, Sander said, unzipping. *In een wip* he flopped over the lowered waistband of his briefs all lucky 25 cm of it. *Gossie!* said Hansje, and whistled. Och, Sander said, but see him up.

8 THERMIDOR

An exemplary *bontwerkerisch* day, Sander said when we arrived at the studio, Hansje and I. A still life's blocked out, we have jogged, fetched groceries, and worked on the baby, like twice, and I see how this *pastoraal* wants to go. That lordly old buck in the zoo with the curled horns, stringy wool down to his ankles, and balls like two Perrier bottles, is to stand here. Hansje *naakt* here. Mattioli's lavender here. Jan in the Sicilian straw hat here, with four sheep. A line or two of Virgilius, perpendicular, an *herleving* typeface. Worked on the baby? Hansje asked, holding up his arms for me to draw off his sweater.

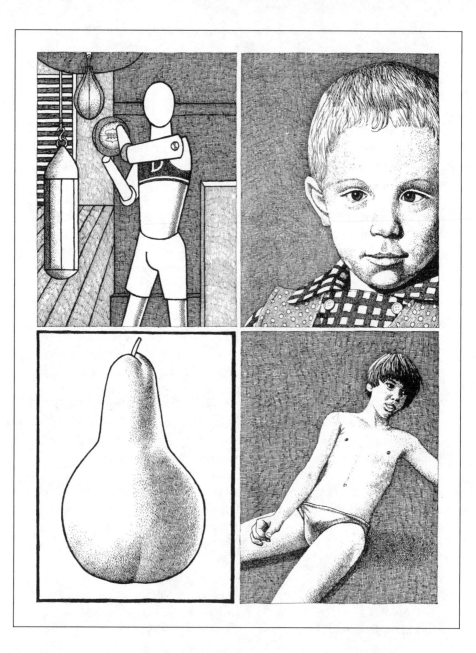

Pairing, said Sander, in the bed, *omhelzing*. You're going in charcoal direct onto the canvas, *liefje*, legs apart, knuckles on hips, chin over left shoulder. Hansje, *leukweg*, in his sly way, delved through all of his pockets until he ran down a toffee while I undid his buttons, zipper, and shoelaces, and stripped him. An amused pursing of lips and tickled eyes, a gape of indignation when Sander combed his hair.

.

Jan. Hans introduced him to me with a surprising formality, and we shook hands. Sander swooped him up and hoisted him onto his shoulders and undid his sneakers' laces, Jan handing down his soccer shirt to Hansje. Leaning daringly back, he pushed his pants down off his hips and in a maneuver worthy of an acrobat, seesaw on Sander's shoulders, got one leg out and then the other, leaving him in a neat blue *slipje* which Sander, heaving him from astraddle to midriff hug, slipped off. *Ziedaar!* If you're going to be *dikke vrienden* with Mijnheer Hans, Jan *mon vieux*, you'll also have to be *intiem* with my esteemed comrade Adriaan here. He and Hans are lifelong friends, from when their relationship was Hans looking gaga at his learned uncle, and waving his arms and legs about, and Ome Adriaan burping Master Hans, changing his diapers and wiping his drool from his Givenchy tie. Besides, I'm going to put *de filosoof* there, on this side of this long canvas, *naakt*, with Hans on one knee, Saartje on the other, and Jan and Jenny too, climbing up an arm, astride his neck, and maybe more kids, heaps of them. Fourier and the Hordes. Teacher and pupils. A scene from Wouter Whitman. *Hoera, ja?*

.

Four masterful sanguine sketches in an hour, Jan on right thigh, Hans on left. So many shins in one area! Sander wailed. Hans across my lap, Jan standing with my arm around him. Things were less than serene from time to time, such as a seizure of giggles quelled by Sander's threat to throw us all out and use other models, and Hans impishly fitching around with his peter, causing Jan's to stand, at which Sander grinned with idiotic good nature.

9 THERMIDOR
Le Nouveau monde amoureux, page 114.
Dialogue entre ZEUXIPPOS, DIOGENES, et DAPHNEUS *sur l'amour des mâsles.*
Should read Zeuxippos, Protogenes, and Daphnaios. Pysias should be Pisias.
PISIAS scène: tu aimeras les enfants jusqu'à ce que le voile [   ] *la*

*face, leur douce haleine et cuisses chérissant [passage haché et presque tout à
fait illisible]*
This is Daphnaios in Plutarch (The Dialogue on Love, *Moralia* IX) quoting
Solon:

> ἔσθ' ἥβης ἐρατᾶσιν ἐπ' ἄνθεσι παιδοφιλήσηι
> μηρῶν ἱμείρων καὶ γλυκεροῦ στόματος.

jusqu'à le voile [d'une barbe couvre] la face: conjecture. *PISIAS s'écrie: O
hercule, bannis le Dieu amour des parcs publics où l'on va à la chasse aux
garçons. Solon a écrit ces vers étant encore jeune et plein de semence, dit
Platon, mais au contraire il écrivit ceux-ci étant déjà sur son âge*

> *Dame Vénus est près mon déduit
> et de Bacchus le breuvage medust*

après qu'il ait retiré sa vie [   ] *comme
d'une tourmente et tempête de l'amour des mâsles et une tranquillité calme du
loyal mariage.*
plein de semence: σπέρματος πολλοῦ μεστός
Solon's couplet:

> ἔργα δὲ Κυπρογενοῦς νῦν μοι φίλα καὶ Διονύσου
> καὶ Μουσέων ἃ τίθησ' ἀνδράσιν εὐφροσύνας.

10 THERMIDOR
The apple, as you can taste, is of the family Rose.

•

Crossing to the island, the sea dirty and tumultuous in an unseasonable fitful-
ness, the wind contrary, fog scudding in, we got drenched to the knackers.
Cabin cold, dark, musty. Lamps lit, a good fire started, Grietje and Sander
into dry shirts, a blanket around them, we had coffee and brandy on the
hearth. Grietje full of herself, having discovered on the train and waiting to
cross in the boat that she could ask questions. To rejoin some of the shattered
pieces of *de Verlichting*, to find structures deeper in the articulateness of things
than we had suspected, to observe with waking rather than sleeping eyes, I
answered her question as to what in the world a philosopher does.

•

To look for evidences of our qualifications for the Harmony.

.

The place itself! Grietje said of the cabin. Lamplight, firelight, books, the worktable, the one bed. And we're not drowned in the North Sea. *Nachtmerrie!* Rain nattering on the windows, wind whomping on the roof. Sander looking like *een engel.* It's all so crazily wonderful! To be here, as I've longed, where Sander got to come when he was *seeing* things, and the cat had his tongue as if he were three again, and when he did talk it was so ghastly that psychiatrists wrote it down in articles on raving teenagers. But listen to the rain, listen to the sea.

.

Supper of tinned ham, cheese, bread, pickles, and chocolate biscuits in front of the fire. Grietje beside herself happy, butting Sander, pummeling him on the shoulders, looking at Sander and me with bolting eyes until he said, he's huggable, try it, as she did, and a sweet armful of girl she is. Middle age, a second adolescence. Sander's not yet wholly civilized, I said to her of his inviting her to feel my tummy through all that hair, it's hard as a Lutheran head, which didn't stop her from doing it. The thing about Adriaan, *zusje lieveling,* is that he's backward shy touchy, not up with the times. Oh, he's way out ahead of the *burgermannetjen* with cubes for noggins, out ahead of psychiatrists and the police, but still very *wat zal de wereld ervan zeggen,* absolutely World War II about all sorts of things. You'll see.

.

Sander's reading of our *kameraadschap* is that in exchange for my *finding* him in the muckmidden he'd dug himself into he has given me Erewhonian citizenship. Your *kindse grijsaard* Fourier, he says, was one of us.

.

Only, says Sander holding his feet and rocking on his bare butt between me and Grietje around the fire, great heroes can sleep together like Adriaan and me. I know the limits of his nature, or enough to behave myself, and despite his tactless remarks about my manners, cold feet, the stiffness and cumbersome size of my dick, he thinks I'm handsome, which is true. So he hugs back when I can't help hugging him, he doesn't think sex is scary or nasty, though his mind wanders. You can be hard as a broom handle with lovingkindness, balls tight as a grapefruit, he'll play along, but just when you're feeling like a stallion half a meter up a mare he'll start talking about Rietveld's eye. *O ja*, says Grietje, Rietveld's eye.

11 THERMIDOR
Grietje fries bananas in the skillet, saying they'll taste of woodsmoke. They do. Sander, having brought estovers and water from the spring, helps himself to a puff of my pipe, hacks, and falls down dead before Grietje, who trills fingers along his mesoventral hair up under his jersey and down into his underpants, bringing him back alive to be fed a slice of banana, kiss her, kiss me, and do the *danse salade* of Isidore *de haasje*, singing what he says is a Frisian catch about fucking all night in a cabbage cart. My brother, says Grietje to the skillet, is an idiot.

•

Sander's resourcefully, mischievously determined *bec et ongle* to impress Grietje with the originality and scope of our friendship. She takes it all in, as so much teasing, and so much big brother's boasting, and foils him by saying that she'd taken it all for granted all along. Out, the three of us, in the early morning, for the splendor of the freshness, Grietje in jeans and Sander's jersey, which she said smells of skunk underarm but of wet sheep otherwise, I in Sander's jeans and cardigan, he in my Finnish sweater, and, to shock Grietje, my briefs, the lug of the pouch making the waistband slight his hips and scant his behind. He took them off me when, dressing for our walk, I had just put them on, causing Grietje to whistle a sigh. So, *onderbroekloos*, I tugged on Sander's jeans, their 10 cm zipper a vexation of scrunching into scrimped quarters. Floc of fog yet in the pines, dull glare on the sea, the air smelling of iodine and resin. Sander, Grietje said sweetly, has goose pimples on his sexy thighs because he must show off, hoping to fluster us this time of morning, what a goof. Well, says Sander, you've got on my soccer shirt when you have a wicked tight sweater you could be wearing, because you're sex dippy and like to whiff your goatish big brother even when he isn't whinnying in your arms. But of course, she said, stepping on his foot and getting flicked on the butt for it. But then you're queer for Adriaan's sweater and underpants because you're trying to magic him into loving you even more than he does. *Grote genade!* He straightens you out when you're so fucked-up you don't know what planet you're on, he makes a human being, sort of, out of you, the neat trick of the century, finds out what God intended you to be, a painter, rents you a studio, buys you canvases and paints and brushes, feeds you, feeds us, encourages you, arranges for a show of your work at the poshest gallery in Amsterdam, writes the catalogue for it, loves you as much as I do, loves us both, so that we cavort in a porno comicbook fantasy that the nuttiest writer wouldn't ask anybody to believe, out of our minds happy, and you, Alexander Brouwer, you want more. Damned right, he said.

.

Apple is to pear as butterfly is to moth.
Bee is kin to apple as wasp is to pear.

12 THERMIDOR

Contiguities chime. Grietje asks about the fifteen volumes of Thoreau's *Journal*, and while telling her about them and as she looked through them and read passages aloud, I saw how I distinguish between books brought to the island and books in Amsterdam. Slocum's voyage, Robinson Crusoe, Amiel, Pausanias, Doughty. Women's curiosity leaps at patterns. She asks about book after book, making her theory grow. She listens with bright eyes when I tell her about the autumn I spent here reading all of Thoreau's journals, underlining, making notes, and about the summer reading Doughty's *Travels in Arabia Deserta* in a deck chair under the big larch, and how, in a way that rarely happens, I *was* Thoreau for an autumn and Doughty for a summer. The here and now became secondary, but more wonderfully interesting because of the imaginary worlds I could go into for so long. Doughty's desert made the sunlight on the cabin's walls and floor have a quality different and richer, and the island became Walden when I was reading Thoreau. I want to feel that, she said. I see what you mean. I see it, I see it. Sander said: When Adriaan writes, he's here, alert to everything, but when he reads *he is somewhere else*. And when he has been reading for hours, he is only interested in putting everything shipshape, and scrubbing and polishing and dusting. After writing he's lickerish and will squeeze you breathless and kiss you in unreasonable places. *Waarom?* asks Grietje. When Sander paints, his balls plump up tight as an apple and you might as well have your knickers off, your butt on a pillow, and your legs spread when he starts washing the brushes. And, says Sander, the better the painting has gone, the sweeter the fuck. Old Matisse, I've heard, ended every posing session on top of the model.

.

Poor Dokter Tomas! Sander said, sighing. At bedtime Grietje said the sleeping bag and pallet were for her, an adventure, like being a *padvindster* again, here by the fire. Us, said Sander, for the bed, zipping down my fly. It was then that

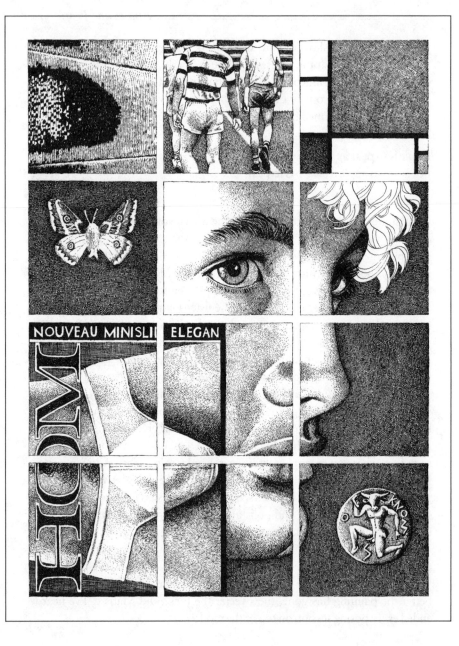

he sighed for good Dokter Tomas. Back and forth, said Grietje. Perhaps we can between us wear it out or at least tame it. Besides, I'm sore from this afternoon. Sander can be rather like a ram his first season in the paddock with the ewes, tongue hanging down to here, ballocks about to pop, humping on the trot, and sprinkling the daisies with the overflow. Sander stripped her and put her into his flannel shirt for a nightgown. Kissed her standing, a hand kneading her sex, the other her butt for an impressively long time. Then he kissed her all down the tummy and between the legs. I tweaked her nose and gave her a chaste kiss on the lips. Sander tucked her in with more kisses, put wood on the fire, and stripped, as I, for bed. Neither of us shaved, Sander said loudly, as if for ships at sea, and it's like two hedgehogs here in bed! This set Grietje to laughing. Quit it! she said. I can't concentrate, and it's so lovely and warm and cozy. A warm hug, a comradely kiss in the vicinity of the ear.

13 THERMIDOR

Fireside. Sander drawing Grietje, telling her more of the summer, as much to acknowledge it as a kind of present of recollection for me as to impart it to her, I think. Tell, I dare you, I said, about the incredible *zaaddoorbrenger* day when you broke all records among reasonably normal adolescents for self-esteem and handwrought orgasms. Sounds awfully like my Sander, Grietje said. *Een niets*, Sander shrugged. I was simply happy. Adriaan, *de drommel*, had turned me loose from all my hangups, had untied all my knots, and I got up that juicy day risen, with my *mannetje* feeling important, all 23 cm from *voorhuid* to *balsak* tight as an orange, proud to the touch, with palpitations and jiggets fluttering around inside. *O lyrische puberteit!* I said, and Grietje remarked that all this sounded strangely familiar. I'm telling this, Sander persisted. I'd been petting the pining fellow and giving him a pull or two while we got the fire and coffee going and it was between sips that I put it to my friend Adriaan here that, to shoo away disliking myself, to advance sexiness in the world, to collaborate with the universe, to oblige a brace of prosperous balls, to chivvy away the mulligrims, to promote benevolence on our island, to perfect my style, I was going to joggle a raving agreeableness and thumping lovingkind-ness into my *peester*, with true pitch and doff, with delicious modulations from *pomposo* to *allegro*, and slog away at it until I passed out or idiocy stayed my friendly hand. You only get a hiked eyebrow out of Adriaan when you say something like that to him. He buttered my roll and otherwise helped me with my one-handed breakfast, reminding me wickedly that it was my morning to wash up. Wash up I did, with a deft left hand, and swept the floor, learning that you don't need two hands for a broom. And then, as innocently as a lamb going *baa*, my friend Adriaan said that we had to wash the windows, which we did together, with Windex and rag, and by the time we were halfway around I had the neb and niddick of the real and essential Sander so slick that they snecked on the draw stroke and slurped on the up. *Om godswil*, Grietje said, *mannenslijm, keurig*. Windows gleaming, the boss couldn't think of anything more for the moment, and I got to sit and concentrate on my *handenarbeid*. And Adriaan, from whom as you know you learn something new every quarter hour on a slow day, brought out his everlasting notebook and the coffee pot and sat across from me, with a philosophical glance ever so often to see how I was doing, scribbling away, heartless as a psychiatrist. What I discovered was that, though I was building up to a ball-jolting spouter, a crazy shyness kept me from coming. So I built up and built up, and the tone of it got agreeabler and agreeabler, and my balls swelled and scrunched. *Looks nice*, Oud Ijsberg across from me would say, or *O jongensachtigheid!* or something equally idiotic. And after a while, in that friendly way that had befuddled me before, because, *dat zweer ik*, I didn't know how friendly the sweet bastard was, he said, *make it last*. Make it last! Gringles along the top of my head, the dry tickles in my mouth, my eyes going goofy, and me beginning to gasp on every pull, and he says make it last. This, Grietje asked, is the famous friendship I've heard so much about? But, oh innocent dumb sister, Sander boomed, tapping her on the knee with his pencil, he *knew* what he was doing, believe me. So I slogged on, sighing. My brain disintegrated, the head of my dick was slubbered over and ringed with froth, every loving whap was slipping smoother and tighter than the one before, and all the kindness for a 100 km around met and danced in Alexander Brouwer's silly *testikels*. The demon Adriaan somehow knew that this funny bashfulness was holding me in, and played me like a game. Invited me to a dip in the sea, which was jolly, and a wander around the island, along which, after a speculative tug or two, I started all over, thriving on resolve. The *filosoof* here, our friend, lectured on the weeds and sticks around us, the trees and bushes. I was sprawled propped against a pine warm with the sun, legs wide, niddling along and sighing, a moronic smile from ear to ear, and it was then that he decided to lecture on the intimate lives of everybody in the encyclopedia. I remember most lecherously some German poet who did it with his sister but felt awful about it and went crazy, and the painter Schiele who when he was 16 fucked his little sister for three days straight the first time in, and Simenon whom Adriaan reads all the time, for years and years he screwed two different women every morning, and two every afternoon, in anticipation of bouncing a bed half the night with Number Five, Victor Hugo, Picasso, Gide who was hale as a plank at seventy and keeping a contented smile on the faces of a half dozen boys a day, and Byron with boys and girls *and* sister, and Leonardo with his Florentine striplings and good old Michelangelo with his older boys, codpieces out to here and with innertube muscles in their arms, and Kierkegaard and Hans Christian Andersen, and Boswell, and horrible Kemel Ataturk who was never happier than with a bedful of nutbrown wolf-eyed eight-year-old boys, and even Max Keirinckx, who fucked all of his models, all ages and flavors, one of them being Bruno's mummy, who didn't want any sort of baby, but Max made her have it, and raised the little tyke himself with the come-and-go forty or so mothers available to him. Adriaan here, along with Max when he noticed, more or less raised him, which is why Bruno is one of the nicest people in Amsterdam, and Kaatje too, who was also one of Adriaan's strays, but about that, about Bruno and Kaatje I mean, you have to piece things together here and there. And through all of this history I jogged and whimpered, especially as a philosopher's *behulpzaam* hand began to smooth the inside of my thighs and graze across a *teelsak* so touchy that I purred and grunted to have it fooled around with. Also, *het was hoog tijd*, came. The first long jet jumped high and splatted from nose to navel. The second spattered on my chest. The third was only a fat spurt that lobbed into my bush and ran down to my balls. More: a spate of glops throbbed out before a last keen kick and squirt ended the romp. For the nonce. I'm not imagining, Grietje said, poking Sander's crotch with her toe, that a salty story about Alexander's *manmoedigheid* ends with one *overstroming*. I want to know what he dares do around, with, and to Adriaan. Coming up, said Sander. A swim, some grub, and some unnecessary prompting from our local skeptic here, and project and measures engaged again, resourcefully, generously, unstinting. There was a flute accompaniment for awhile, much good crazy talk, some hugging, frisking, and a spelling of my jogging fist, unsparingly and with style, from time to time. Well, darling Grietje, Grietje sweet, by late afternoon the island from the rocky end to the sandy tip had been spattered and sprinkled, the cabin and the trees, Adriaan and the bed. I'm taking all of this for the truth, Grietje said, though you probably aren't telling the half. Dusk, and my trusty fellow was sprained, chafed, and wrecked. He was also, as I crowed after supper, feeling sweetly spunky. Adriaan didn't believe me. Even when it stood up as springy as a rib to his grip, and drooled at the nozzle, and jumped when he slid back its sheath. It had to be done tenderly, with slow strokes and a soft hold, taking turns. Our Sander's brain, I said, was a syntectic mush, judgment wholly deteriorated, his happy smile somewhere between daffy and pissed. Don't quit, he kept babbling, even if I lose consciousness or go out of my mind. Which he did: the lout went to sleep. All I remember, Sander said, is that toward the last I was feeling nothing but a delirium of cock, luscious slick, jam rich, and piggishly carnal. I remember coming feverishly and keeping on, and an arm slipped under my head and a hand taking over, my dick only half hard and a gummy slurpy mess but feeling absolutely wonderfully lovely, and then everything melted away. You went to sleep, sighing and grunting, I said, and I kept on for as long as you glubbed and siffled, a good twenty minutes or so. You see? Sander said. Friends! *Hemelse goedheid, ja!* Sander even as a child, Grietje said, had a wild goat's capacity for serial orgasms, scandalizing everybody, and can outcome any lover I've been in bed with. When the *recherche* takes us away in hand-cuffs, I'll plead that, love aside and handsomeness aside, he's simply the best fuck in *de Nederlanden.*

•

Sander talks to free his eye and hand for drawing. Keirinckx, too, likes to draw and talk. Grietje says: this whole story shows what a selfish pig you are. But I'm not, Sander pleads. Am I, Adriaan? Adriaan is *platonisch.* Sort of, in his way.

14 THERMIDOR
Grand loneliness. A walk around the island, copper flakes winking and jig-gling on the sea, the larches red, the pines Tuscan brown. Mosses silvery black, woolly grey. Nebulae of gnats in blurred light. A sense of *duur,* of seamless time, the seasons, the years. Gathered various small agrestal flowers, weeds no doubt, complex tight buttons, for the vase on my desk.

•

Xronos and Eros, our age and youth, were in their proper *paideuma* Time and Love. They are both wavilinear. Love, like time, is a medium, for nothing would be beautiful, no day sweet, or time a gift rather than a burden, without euphoria and benevolence, wavelengths in love's spectrum. Leonardo: the beauty of things lightens our hearts.

•

Out and around the island at the exquisite hour as Sander and Grietje said they needed to bounce on the bed. *Aankweken,* Grietje's word, with wicked laugh. Looked in after a half hour and they were still fucking their brains out. *Bevallig.* A gold of bracken in moss and rock. Saffron thistle. Skeins of mist smoking on the sea. Was watching a bike of gnats when Sander bellowed from the slope. Pulling a sweater over his head, his cock scrumped and shiny wet. Come home, he said, having a pee. Grietje, doing jumping jacks and counting them, hit fifty and said she was going to make us a superior supper. She's always like that, Sander said, after getting laid.

15 THERMIDOR
TAFELBLAD: Dundee Orange Marmalade jar with goldweed, the aryballos, Schillebeeckx's *Jezus*, coffee cup, pipe, pinecone, can of pencils, the mail, Sander's sketchbook (three profiles of Grietje, each a continuous line), bottle of ink, pebbles in a Japanese bowl.

•

GRIETJE, charmed by the aryballos, comes up with a blue ribbon from her kit to serve as a strap, and hangs it around Sander's neck. Not quite, she said, the scarf and slip clasp of a *padvinder*, is it?

•

The colmar, or late burgamot, the winterlong green pear or landry wilding, la virgoule, the poire d'Ambrette, the winter thorn pear, the St. Germain, the St. Augustine, the pound pear, the Spanish bon chrêtien, the wilding of Cassoy, the Lord Martin pear, the winter citron or musk orange, the winter rosselet, the gate pear of Poictou, the Bergamotte Bugi or Easter Burgamot, the Cadillac and pastourelle.

•

Peer, bij, braamstruik. The series of pear growers begins with those who enjoy challenge and variety. To them goes the cultivation of quinces and *sortes bâtardes dures*. The *aileron ascendant* works with hard cooking pears. The ascendant wing: crisp pears. Pivot of the series: juicy luscious golden mellow pears. Descending wing: *poires compactes*. *Aileron*: mealy pears. Rearguard: *nèfles et sortes bâtardes molles*.

•

Avant-garde: boys for whom pears are missiles, Biblical scholars for whom the word *quince* (*enta* in Hebrew) glints with poetry, housewives with the character to make quince jelly.
Aileron ascendant: Cézanne, practical grocers, hill people who like things with substance and durability.
Aile ascendante: adolescents learning the taste of the world, girls who pride

themselves on having different eating habits than their brothers or younger sisters.

Pivot: Dunoyer de Segonzac. Gide. Matisse. Patient voluptuaries, for even these pears must be wrapped in paper and put away awhile to ripen to their mellowest. Bees and wasps, for whom the fallen ripe pear, slightly fermented, macular with nectary brandy-flavored sprits and bruises. Keats, Rubens, Poussin.

Aile descendante: Vintners, distillers of *alcools*, Spinoza, people who admire nature's organization more than its prodigality.

Aileron descendant: millers, Protestants, those who have accepted spiritual deprivation and made a virtue of it, sentimentalists.

Arrière-poste: spoiled brats, gourmands, procrastinators.

•

Oxen under the yellow perpendicular of noon, hares in the blackberry bramble, bees in the quince. A trembling silence. August a young man browned by the sun, straw-hatted, loosely mantled, barefoot, under his arm a basket of pears, plums, and apples. Grietje in a long blue towel, drying herself after a dip in the afternoon sea, eyes muscadine purple silvery with laughter, breasts tight and pointed. The little musk pear, or supreme. The Chio, or bastard musk pear. The Hasting, or green chiffel. Sander brown-straked with blue shadows from the larch, wet hair drying wild. I play a Corelli sarabande on the flute. The red muscadell, the little muscat, the jargonelle. A blue sky! Grietje says, I thought the sun would never make it. The god Pan with his pipes. She spread her towel in the sun and lay naked. The Windsor pear, the orange musk, the great blanket and long-stalked blanket. Why, says Sander ruffling my hair and knuckling the back of my neck with a wet fist, is Mijnheer Pan overdressed for the last fine day of the year? The musk robin, the musk drone, the green orange. Autumn a Braque Ceres with wicker panniers of gourds and wheat. Sander on all fours straddles Grietje, up to mischief. She tickles him mercilessly in the armpits, he collapses onto her, she traps his neck between her shins and drums on his behind. The cassolette, the Magdalene, the great onion pear. They wiggle and wrestle, slippery wet, until Sander allows himself to be bested. The August muscat, the rose pear, the summer bon chrêtien, or good choaky. Sander with a fish flop frees himself, and stalks on all fours to where I sit crosslegged, music book on the moss before me, a gigue of Bach. He butts me in the midriff, pushes me backward, unzips, unseats, and drags off my trousers. *Wat leuk!* says Grietje. Snatch off everything. Between being so furry and having such *een aantrekkelijk lichaamsbouw*, Adriaan makes you look like such a gawk, Sander brother. Peel him *spiernaakt*. Which he does. The salviati, the rosewater pear, the russelet. Let's do something untellably silly, Grietje says.

•

The great mouthwater pear, summer bergamot, the red butter pear, the autumn bergamot, the dean's pear, the long green or autumn month water pear, the white and grey Monsieur John, the flowered muscat, the vine pear, the rousseline, the knave's pear, the green sugar pear, the marquis's pear, the burnt cat or virgin of Xantonee, Le Besidery, the flat butter pear, the dauphin, the dry martin, the villain of Anjou or tulip pear or great orange, the amadot, the little lard pear.

16 THERMIDOR

Morning coffee on the high rock, the air warm and sweet. Grietje wearing Sander's *studentenpet* cockily, my blue shirt unbuttoned, and floreted French underpants, said out of the blue that she knew who she was, had never properly known before. That's awful, said Sander, kissing her nose. Are you going to tell us who? Of course not, she said. One thing you are, said Sander, is a girl dressed just like that on the far right of the long canvas that has Adriaan and the littles on the far left, and in the middle goes old Fourier on a quagga. In floppy Mongolian trousers, with Chinese boots, a Gypsy shirt, a rakish freebooter's felt hat with a lilac scarf around it that hangs down his back to the quagga's rump. The first canvas they're to see is Hansje stitchless holding an apple in one hand, a pear in the other. Then Saartje with her armload of autumn flowers. Then the ten long *pastoraals* with their people and animals and moths and pumpkins. Then the portraits and still lifes alternating. And at the end the big one: Adriaan with the littles sitting and climbing all over him, Fourier in the center, Grietje in flowery little pants, open blue shirt, and my student cap, on the right, weight on left foot to get a slant of hip and *contraposto* shoulder, right arm gesturing, or about to gesture. Meaning what? O, said Sander, everything. Everything good.

Erewhonian Apple, New Harmony Pear

I7 THERMIDOR

He trumpets through cupped hands, the boy standing hipdeep in the Seine at Asnières in Seurat's painting, a water god sounding a conch, a French child imitating the foghorn of a *paquebot*, a Wind from the corner of a map bellying the sails of a galleon with Favonian trades.

Arion calling to his dolphin, young Triton rallying nymphs. His bell hat, the color of a tangerine, matches his bathing drawers, bought by his mother at the Bon Marché or Samaritaine, *la mode* being the vernacular common to the middle class, their identity and coherence.

An admirer of the hat can have one just like it, must have one just like it. To frolic in the river on a Sunday afternoon, he has shed a cotton nautical blouse, tight gabardine culottes, a *sous-vêtement combinaison tricot de corps en co-ton*, socks, hightop button shoes.

1884, this painting, the same year as Thomas Eakins' *Swimming Hole*. Four years before Pater Hopkins wrote his poem about a summer bevy of bellbright boys with dare and with downdolphinry in earthworld airworld waterworld thorough hurled all by turn and turn about.

1884 is also the year *Huckleberry Finn* was published, with its river idyll of Neger Jaap and Huck on their raft. Why this moment a century ago of sudden *pastoraal* found in reality, not a quotation from the neoclassical? And Coubertin and Henri Rousseau, the rebirth of games.

Geestelijke gezondheid is de conditie die in fysiek, intellectueel en emotioneel opzicht een optimale ontwikkeling van het individu toelaat, volgens de Wereldgezondheidsorganisatie, opgesteld in 1948, voor zover deze verenigbaar is met die van andere individuen.

Woke to find Sander in my Finnish reindeer and Lapps cringlecrangle sweater and briefs, making a fire. I slept in the camping bedroll, sound as a block of teak, so's they could have the bed, where they fell asleep after a charitably curtailed sighing, humping, and grunting.

Grietje, peeping from under the covers, blew me a good-morning kiss, and pointing to the snooked-out crop of Sander's *onderbroekje*, said: *woof!* He only wants to pipi, said Sander, making a face. Here, he said, throwing her my raincoat, come along and you can pee with us.

Come, Adriaan. So we three went onto the porch in fog and drizzle, Grietje squatting under her tenting of the coat, Sander and I shoulder to shoulder, crisscrossing our streams. You two! Grietje said. *Indrukwekkend*, Adriaan. Dare you, said Sander to us both, stripping.

We threw clothes through the door and ran to the sea, the shock of it exhilarating. It bites! Grietje cried, and Sander showed off by swimming out and doing porpoise dives. Back inside, blue around the gills, we toweled down before the fire, tingling and fresh, happy.

> From every one of the four regions
> of human majesty
> there is an outside spread without
> and an outside spread within
>
> beyond the outline of identity
> both ways
> an orbed void of doubt
> despair hunger thirst and sorrow

Here the twelve sons of Albion (that is, humanity) join in dark assembly, jealous of Jerusalem's children (the imaginative, those who have kept what Fourier calls *the flame*), become wheels turning upon one another into nonentity, murdering their souls, building a dead city.

The outside spread without is the world, the outside spread within is the perceived (Rilke's taking in of essence, as a bee gathers nectar, to be made into the honey of memory). The outline of identity is Wittgenstein's eye, field of vision on one side, vision itself within.

Blake's grief is for things seen flat and empty, without their charge of spirit. Jerusalem is the imaginative frame in which things exist in an harmonic wholeness. A Shaker chair must be worthy of an angel's visit. A Rietveld table is a philosophical statement in a discourse.

Lovely body, Grietje's, her sex virginly sparse of hair, her legs and butt coltish and trim. Sander dried her roughly and affectionately, buffing and kissing. And combed her hair, whistling, having wrapped her in a blanket before the fire, himself as naked as the day he was born.

He assumed the Finnish sweater for breakfast, thoughtfully giving me his ratty cardigan. So this is it, Grietje said, where wild boys are civilized. You even taught Sander manners. I said I only put him to work. We finished building this cabin together, the two of us alone.

We brought every plank, nail, brick, dish, and pot from the mainland. The windows and doors were readymade. The chimney is our masterpiece. It was all so much fate, that whole summer. Tomas, Sander's favorite doctor, told me that he had a completely disoriented boy on his hands.

A boy who, he felt, needed normality in great heaps and doses, and I said I could use a strong back here on the island. I convinced Dokter Tomas that I'd had experience in the feeding and care of other people's children, and he handed over to me one Alexander Brouwer.

Who was one of the most mixed up people I'd ever seen. I was *scared*, Sander said, fussing about pouring coffee, setting plates, tossing us rolls, poking up the fire. Scared, gone to earth, afraid to be alone. The Finnish sweater left him *homerisch* naked from hipbone to toe.

This is my brother? Grietje asked, charmingly lost in Sander's jersey and jeans. You've made a street dog into a cottage cat. If he had on britches he'd pass for civilized. O no! said Sander, making rabbit teeth at her, the style here on the island is according to Fourier.

The idiot philosopher Karel Marie Frans Fourier, in whose design for the redeemed world you dress to please your friends. Grace and beauty tickle Adriaan's particular eye. In our summer we spent whole days bare assed. What, said Grietje, do you two *do*? Something wildly lovely.

O but nothing, said Sander, or almost nothing. I was crushed when I got it into my bone head that Adriaan doesn't give a hoot whether I'm the handsome *knaap* I am or a weaselfaced drip with mouse meat. It's my soul he loves, God help us, not my blue eyes or big long hangdown.

I protest that Sander had just contradicted himself. Sander's soul, Grietje said, if he has one, does tend to nip back and forth between his big blue eyes and horse peter. It has a weakness for the latter. Not horse, said Sander, donkey. Or quagga maybe, Fourier's steeds.

Once sun and work had healed his bruised spirit, Sander was desperate for affection. The body is an animal and at his age it was a puppy. Still is, she said. Don't explain it, Sander said. It was lovely and sexy and friendly and wonderful and like nothing ever before.

You don't know this charmer, Grietje. Imagine you're a donkey with a donkey's simple hankering to have its head knuckled, its ears scritched, its tummy stroked, its butt patted. I don't think I'm up to hearing the details, Grietje said, except that I absolutely must.

Spare me nothing. Oh, bear hugs, Sander said, and nuzzlings and pawing and squeezing. All I know is that I needed it and had no notion what we were doing, no words for it. But O how I hugged back! That was the sweet nuttiness of it, as it still is, ragdoll and teddy bear.

A big rough sprawling shameless romp, and the delight that made me blubber and laugh together was that I could accept it as just that, even though my scheming mind was as rich in lechery as a rutting girl on her back being fucked blind, with a whole football team waiting its turn.

I'd come in from nipping around the island. Adriaan was writing his things there at the table. I sauntered in and while unlacing my sneakers, which was all I was wearing, I offered him my body, brassy as a hustler. He smiled. The bastard smiled. Didn't even look at my dick.

I really honest to God don't think he knew what I was talking about. *Ongelooflijk!* The smartest, most understanding friend I'd ever had, and there he was revealed for what he was, an idiot. I mean, he'd patted me on the behind when I got the carpentry straight, hadn't he?

And squeezed me around the waist to say goodnight, and fluffed my hair, and swapped sexy adventures while we worked or lay in the sun, and he was perfectly understanding when after weeks and weeks I couldn't stand chastity any longer and jacked off half of a night.

This, deliriously good, at the other end of the island, not noticing that it was raining frogs and herring. How was I to know that I could have done it right here by the fire, as I did afterwards, or that he would spell my hand in one of my longplaying endless orgies?

So in that first roll and hug I was snakenaked and my generator rigid as a lead pipe, but my *kameraad* here was in *borstrok* and jeans, which, considering my helpless evidence of affection, seemed unfair. I'm waiting, said Grietje, for Adriaan's version of all this bragging.

After the first wallow, Sander went on, rolling like bear cubs squeezing the breath out of each other, butting like calves, winded and laughing, I wriggled his shirt off, and with him helping, got him out of everything, hairy as a bath mat. *Het was reuze!*

We went back at it, silly as halfwits, and my black heart thumped doubletime when there was evidence, as against my leg, of my friend's humanity, a decidedly stiff, unphilosophical, sporting and proud humanity it is, too, making me saucier, fresher, and much happier.

If I was going to disgrace myself I had already done it. May I tell it all, Adriaan? Grietje offers to wring his neck if he doesn't. But all I'm telling, Sander said with open hands and big honest eyes, is that we learned how to have fine long friendly fits of affection.

No questions asked, no rules to break. Making us friends forever. He's a great philosopher, Max Keirinckx says so, I'm going to be a great painter, famous as far away as Belgium, collected by bald Americans and jetset Japs. He is Adriaan, I am Sander. Beautiful.

Beautiful, Grietje said, but I'm disappointed. Sander seems to have met someone he can't deprave beyond the utmost ingenuity in what can be done with tickled flesh. O *that*! Sander said, looking improbably innocent. Chums are chums, and some are chummier than others.

Third grapple of that sweet day, after a swim and lazy time in the sun and another roll under the pines, we got more reciprocal and wigwag in the bed, more inquisitive, liberal, broadminded. So that in one ferocious hug the sliddering was slicked by a volunteer liter of slosh.

Out of a philosopher, in, I'll swear, punchy spurts that would have splatted on the walls had they not been stopped by the chest and tummy of a happy Sander. We squished and slid like oiled wrestlers. I came, too, in glops. Something in a Danish magazine, Grietje said.

Didn't slow us in the least, Sander said, as that wasn't what we were hugging for. Why, said Grietje, must we try to figure out why we're hugging anybody, like a brat all brains and no manners? Fuck why, and also by whose leave and with whose blessing. Love is love.

18 THERMIDOR
Apple brother, sister pear. Apple Virgil, Theokritos pear. Erewhon, apple. New Harmony, pear. Helen is to Castor and Pollux as apple is to pear. Painting is apple, music is pear. Apple is the letter, pear the spirit of the law. Bee and wasp, moth and butterfly, dog and wolf.

Analysons les ressorts de leurs vertus: ils sont au nombre de quatre, tous ré-prouvés par la morale; ces sont les goûts de saleté, d'orgueil, d'impudence et d'insubordination. C'est en s'adonnant à ces prétendus vices, que les petites hordes s'élevent à la pratique de toutes les vertus.

And move in the Tartar, or Curvilinear Mode, wheeling their quaggas with yells and hoots, their mustards and reds, jangle of harness and ripple of flags tangling in with the storm of their drums and whistles. Their dogs and cheetahs wheel with them, bounding, circling, leaping.

There is a happy squinch of smile peculiar to the Hordes, a lift of small shoulders and dip of coppery cornsilk hair, ruckle of nose, a display of snippety teeth, nip of dimples, and jiggle of eye. They josh, flirt, and steal impudent fingers into their britches.

They make tactless comments on each other's fug of pungent quagga, damp dog, prodigal sperm, and garlicky armpits. Maartens, says Frits to the world, shouting above the racket, has quagga come in his hair, from jacking it off all the time, getting two liters the spurt.

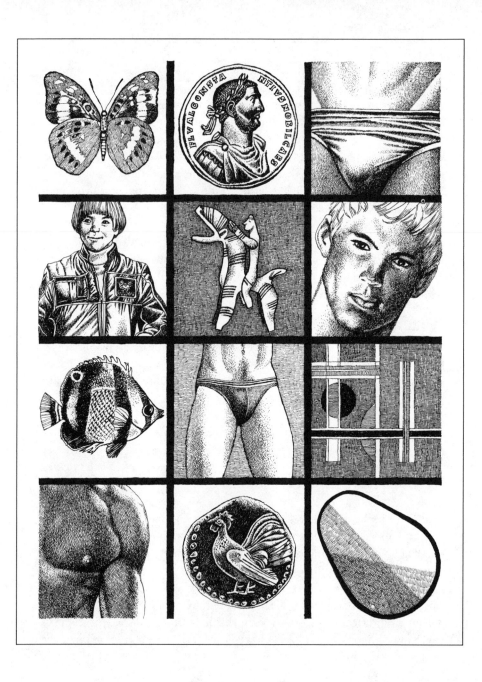

Neen, says happy Maartens, it's all mine from an hour of steady work and help from Hendrikx, Nollet, Gerrit, and Kees, who know how high I shoot, up and over into my hair, thick and creamy, none of your *peutertroep* whey, and they can't keep their hands or eyes off it.

Whoosh! *Gunst! Hemeltje! Leve sekse!* Splat! With an aftersplash from chin to bellybuckle, one more from bellybuckle to hand, and some leftover plops that run down the stalk around my balls. Zibber flop! somebody hoots. Quagga pee, another. Band piffle, yet another.

19 THERMIDOR
Slender Saartje honeybrown slipping two fingers down into her drablet of red-and-white-checked underpants in Sander's studio, being drawn so, Kaatje and I chaperoning, is an image that has worked in me, in my most guarded spirit, a quick sweetness drenching the imagination.

What's beautiful about it? Hans challenged. *De bejaarden* call anything beautiful, and it's only skinny Saartje fiddling with her *speelgoed*. I mean you have to know where it is to find it. I know exactly where it is, Saartje said, and gave him a saucy look before closing her eyes.

Sander's studio, as summoned. Fourier in his parson's hat, and Anakreon aromatic with dill and hyacinth came in with me. Pencils ready, drawing table untilted to flat, studio tidied, Sander confessed to being dithery, wholly unlike him, a glitch *nu en dan* in his pulse.

Said he would be relieved when Kaatje turned up with the little fuckers. I asked why I was there. For morale, for courage, for reasons he'd forgotten, like Kaatje wanted me there. Placidly matter of fact *an de telefoon* with her. She said the idea was Hans' and Saartje's.

It would be better, wouldn't it, to take them up on it, than dashing their eagerness? he had said, mentioning complexes. *Wat drommel!* What *is* a complex, anyway? Of course I want to draw them *erotisch*. Bruno, Kaatje said, was perfectly willing, and wished us great fun.

For *een ondeugend steendruck serie*, the second of which they owned, leggy teenagers sprawled around and on each other. The first, pedantically sexy, was of Sander and Grietje, drawn from Gerhard's photographs, I'd shown Bruno and Kaatje, Sander's best lithographs to date.

It was the second suite that inspired Hans and Saartje to volunteer to pose, taking up the hint of Sander's which Kaatje had dodged. Not at all, she said, I wanted to put it to Bruno first. A bit breathless, Kaatje, and the lovelier for it, grinning wickedly, after the stairs.

Saartje up to her impish eyes in raincoat collar, a beret cockily on the back of her head, Hans with hair jutting all around from under his cadet cap, fists socketed in jeans pockets, pigeon-toed, underlip tucked behind buckteeth, eyebrows up where presumption overtakes surmise.

Kaatje was for pushing them in, and leaving. Oh no, Sander said, I need you. I need Adriaan. There's coffee, just made. I don't really know children. Grietje didn't know whether to be here or not, so she left. I'll say or do something awful in the first five minutes.

He explained the transfer paper, how the printing was to be done from a polished stone, how he was to draw with colored pencils for some details, and with the lithograph crayon, how it would all be brought together for the finished plate. Kaatje fetched the coffee for us.

I've explained to the monsters, she said, that this is not a film, that it's all illusion, but they argue that they must do the real thing. So they began practicing, they called it, a good hour ago, squealing and grunting. Hansje tends to moo when his jacking off gets mellow.

Well, said Sander, let's hear it, gathering Hans and Saartje in a swoop and piling them on the bench across from us, and with his arms on their knees asked them, *tussen de mensen onderling*, what they wanted him to draw them doing. *Juist wat, he?* I can draw anything.

You drew us bare butt, Hans said wide-eyed, and put us hugging, sort of, in that big picture, and we looked at the *fijn* drawings Papa showed us you did of *tieners* all *opgewondenheid* and *allerliefst*, and, well, you could draw us too, didn't *Maatje* call you up, like?

This is when Saartje shed her jeans, and, bouncing on her toes, slipped two fingers inside her tiny red-and-white-checked underpants. Whee! said Sander, nipping to the drawing board. Fourth pair of undies, Kaatje said, tried on before the mirror. Hans and I voted for these.

Hans watched the drawing awhile, impressed with how fast and accurately Sander worked, stripped his jersey over his head and was soon in briefs only, of curt fit, *Amerikaans Grieks Y klep*, a rich blue with white trim. Woof! Sander said, you're next, in those, peter out.

I thought, Hans said, you were going to draw us real good doing real good things real good. In a bit, said Sander, fish your peter out through your fly. Let it hang down, half hard, like that. Saartje, sweetheart, take those dainty scanties off, eh? Keep your hand playing.

For just under two hours Sander drew real good things real good. Hansje, Saartje explained astraddle Hans' thighs, jacking him, is going to be *onuitputtelijk*, though he has to let a while go by before he can come again, five minutes maybe. I understand, said Sander.

The two sprawled in a kiss, Hansje's fingers gentle and expert with Saartje. Hans jacking with Saartje lying across his tummy. Can they, Sander asked, whose jeans were warped out by an erection, pose as if fucking? Kaatje, who'd been good at chatter all along, said no.

Why not? Hans asked. Please, said Saartje. I had been in a kind of euphoric shock from the beginning, reality in and out of focus, partly with an arm around Kaatje, partly watching the drawing, the quick long lines that went busy at spread toes, an open mouth, hair swirl.

Sander kept up a patter of appreciative grunts, whistles of astonishment, and commentary. He criticized both their techniques. *Goeie genade! Poef! Wat trilling en klopping!* O come on, Kaatje! he boomed, coming around the drawing table to squeeze Saartje in a lifting hug.

Lord knows what he whispered into her ear before he set her gently on the floor, quickly made a roll of Hans' jeans, and tucked it under her behind. He then lifted Hans in as crushing a hug, and turning him prone lowered him onto Saartje, who opened her legs, raised her knees.

Up onto your elbows, Hansje boy, Sander said, but bend down and kiss. That's right. Press your hips right down against. Saartje, raise your heels higher. Tilt your hips up. If this were for real, Hans couldn't shove in good. Can I, said Hans, put it in just while Sander's drawing?

No, *liefje*, Kaatje said evenly, though she was pretending to have gone limp in her chair. Sander was drawing with great concentration. Don't move, he said, even if you begin to ache all over, just don't move. I don't ache, Saartje said brightly. Me neither, said Hansje.

20 THERMIDOR

What eye among the rungs and hordes
of angelkind would turn and find
my long call through the storm of time?
And if one took me in his arms
I would be nothing in that light.
Sweet of beauty gathering in
is fear's beginning: we love it
because our longing stands uncrushed
in the strength of its harmony.
An angel is a fearful thing.
I keep my loud call in my throat
and stop the deep dark of my grief.
Is there any to turn to then?
Neither angel nor brother, no,
and all the animals are wise
to our bewildered stumbling
in the dark of our signs and myths.
What do we have? That hillslope tree,
our walk in the afternoon,
our customary faithful
things remaining year after year.
And the night, there's always the night
with its wind from across the stars
which we can close our eyes and drink.
She's always there, the night, kind witch,
always, if your heart can love her.
Is she kinder then to couples?
They are hidden from each other.
Have you not learned that secret yet?
Unclasp your empty arms and throw
that nothing into breathless space
to quicken a bird's pitch and dip
if your riddance traverse its flight.

Aprils needed you down the years,
the stars waited till you found them,
forgotten days have sought you out.
As you passed an open shutter
a fiddle under ravishment
was surrendering to delight.
Such was our animal faith.
Was your response in proportion?
Were you not worried with waiting,
thinking it prelude, ruining it
with expectations and designs?
Wanting rather someone to love?
What room had you for a lover
with so many overnight thoughts
arriving and leaving in droves?
Yearn, calling to sight those lovers
whose desire filled all their being,
whose power to feel strengthens us,
whom we would almost choose to be,
whose longing was denied ripeness.
Hymn their praise justly you cannot.
The Hero persists. The background
for his splendor was promise
that he would be seen there again.
Lovers, however, are returned
to nature, exiles home at last,
for good, so exquisite a force
released but once to lovers' eyes.
Have you taken in the meaning
of Gaspana Stampa enough
to understand that you must long
like her, for a love that, lost, lasts?
Should not our oldest pains have borne
their harvest by this time? When will
we begin to last in our love
vibrant without our beloved,
be as an arrow to the string,
which breathless in its singing jump
is more than arrow, string, or bow?

To stand still is to be nowhere.
Voices. Listen, heart, like a saint
raised into the air by voices,
still kneeling, voices lifting him,
so native to his ears the words.
We cannot stand to hear God speak.
Our ears can bear the aftersound,
the enriched silence full of Him.
A hush, as from those who died young.
Have churches in Rome and Naples
not told you all about themselves?
Inscriptions have made you read them.
Remember the lettered stone in
Santa Maria Formosa.
What do they want of me? Must I
then take the wronged look from my eyes
that obstructs their pure onwardness?

It will feel strange not to be here,
to leave our familiar world,
to leave the roses, their meaning,
things in which we'd placed so much hope,
strange no longer to be cared for
by the solicitude we'd known,
to abandon our given name
like an old toy. It will be strange
never again to feel a wish,
see all arduous knots drop loose.
All will seem random when we die,
hunting hard and gathering up
until we find some lasting sign.
The living draw their lines too sharp.
Angels, we hear, sometimes don't know
the living from the dead. The wind
across eternity confounds
both realms and chimes in the voices
of each.
        The early slain, what more
have they to do with us after

a while? They have been weaned from things
earthly as from their mother's breast.
But we need them, we for whom grief
is the spring of our best efforts,
we need the great secret to live.
Without the dead would we exist?
Is it an empty myth that once
in lamenting Linos with cries
which were the seed of all music,
weeping for a godlike young man,
we first filled death's anguished hollow
with the ringing sounds that help us,
that we must hear to understand?

21 THERMIDOR

A transparency, Rilke's angel. How distant Tobias' time when one of the brightest came to the door, dressed for a journey. And the most perilous blinding archmessenger will stride from beyond the stars and our hearts will beat their last under the drop of his closing wings.

Jan in little white pants, looking in at the cabin door, for Hansje, his body slender and brown, like that of an archaic dusty Eros, like that of Tobias' angel a little disguised, the shoulders of a bird with folded wings, hair gilded and windblown, said I must change my life.

22 THERMIDOR

Weather golden and holding, splendid for so *impudique* a pastoral. Reached the island over a sweet blue sea, Hans and Jan in their vermilion lifejackets as bright as pennies from the mint. They held hands, swapped gleeful glances, tossing hair from their eyes like foals.

Knowing winks from Sander. The island flecked green and yellow in fine summer light. They went exploring while Sander and I squared away the cabin. A working visit, said Sander, his drawing pad out, pencils ready. Writing to write, drawings to draw, the boys to pose.

Two naked impudent lovely boys, on the double! Sander hollered toward the beach. Hans came and stuck out his tongue for the fun of it, with a *you can't catch me* tilt to his shoulders. Sander had him in one spring and brought him back over his shoulder. Jan followed, eyes green, dubious.

I've done this lots, Hans explained, Saartje and I. Stripped, he rolled his fists and pranced in place, as graceful a channeling of fidgets and shyness as one is likely to see. Come on, *vriendje*, he said, *poedelnaakt* like me. Jan knelt and undid his shoes, dawdling.

Tugged off his pullover in handfuls. Turned away from us to shinny out of slender jeans. Across implausibly strait hips, neatly kiltered briefs. *Idioot!* Hansje whooped, we've done this before, in the studio, and why be *schuw* undressing when we're going to be drawn bare-butt?

Mine, he said of the briefs Jan was edging down. We wear each other's *voor de grap*. Natch, said Sander, and kiss and slidder half hours of jumping bliss into one another's peters and feel importantly sinful. Trimly finished, Jan's body, a blush drenching its tan to the shoulders.

Well hung for his age, he has the famished Spartan look of well-nourished flesh that would like to prosper into muscle and volume but must deny itself and stretch to keep up with lengthening bones. An encouraging smile to say that he has survived the heroic blush.

His penis, as with Hansje's, seems a gratuitous carnality in contrast to the calm innocence of his animal gaze. Arms around each other's shoulders, said Sander, if you please. *Vervloekt! Uit de tijd van Koningin Victoria!* I can see the *vijgblad!* Come on, hug for real.

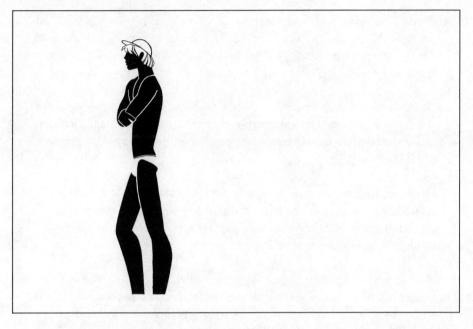

Look, gooses, join the times, *ja?* My paintings are alive, sexy, modern. Go away, go run wild around the island. Forget you're bare-assed. Jack off, tumble, wrestle, hug and kiss, anything to keep from looking like department-store dummies and Italian valentines.

When I was a shrimp your age I jumped on everything that moved and fucked everything that would have me. I jacked knots and welts on my dick, kept a crick in my wrist and cramps in my balls, jellied my brains. Hansje grinned at this from ear to rosy ear, eyes teasing.

Jan veritably gulped, curled his toes, and looked to Hans as if to ask if these godsent people were as delightfully crazy as they sounded. With shy sidewise glances, to make certain we were watching, they curled fingers around each other's penises, drew together, and kissed.

What light, what clarity of moment and talk. Sander tells me how much Grietje longs to have a child. The *Volkskrant* review of drawings pleases him more than he will admit. He savors the huggermugger of ducking all interviews, all appearances, of remaining invisible.

He wants to do scenes from Fourier, the little bands and hordes on ponies and quaggas. Queries things I wrote in the catalogue to the painting show. Archaic eyesight. Innocence of irony and despair. All I'm doing, Adriaan, is what I know how to do. I don't know what it means.

Grietje is beautiful, so I paint her. Moths are beautiful, bicycles are sexy. Do you really think people are going to buy these things and I can make a living at it? I would be the luckiest bastard in the whole world, and the goofily happiest, *ja nu! Dat geloof ik!*

From time to time, voices as the wind plays tricks with sounds over the white ground of the sea wash, the hush of the afternoon. A yipe, spates of uncadenced chatter, windborne gibberish, laughter, long silences with only my and Sander's voices vibrant against the ocean.

Against the lurch and tumble of the waves. After the good part of an hour, Sander bellowed for the boys, striding off in the direction of their babble and scurry. I strolled behind, my mind rich with apprehension and curiosity. Already? Hans was saying, diddle daddle drat.

Are you cool enough, Sander said, to pretend I'm not here drawing? They were, sweet nippers, lying on red larchfall in citrony mellow light head to foot, holding each other's erections, and each, when I rolled up, staring with vague eyes at the sky. Hello, scamps, nobody's here.

That's not Sander sprinting from the cabin with drawing pad and pencils. You're beautiful. Feels beautiful, too, Hans said to the sky. Feels great, Jan said, taking up his stroke. Sander drew, sitting crosslegged before his pad. I sat beside him, watching, mouse quiet.

For a while they kept to fiddling and coddling, and then, accepting us as company, put their hearts and some style into it. Sander drew with wonderful skill, study after study, changing his angle of vision. Jan skeeted first, an opalescent sprinkle that stippled his brown tummy.

He sighed and whinnied. Nice, Sander commented, and you're making my balls snuggle together. Jan raised himself onto his arms to get a better purchase on Hans, who shot a creditable squirt. They compared *ejacula*, Jan attributing his superior amount to assiduous practice.

Sander asked for, and got, poses: the two sitting, arms around each other's waists, Jan's head affectionately on Hansje's shoulder. Standing cock to cock, hands on each other's butts. Facing, on hands and knees, looking into each other's eyes. Jacking each other, sitting.

A triumphant drawing, in colored pencils, of Jan standing, his long hair in disarray. Hans sat and watched Sander draw, his arm around his shoulder. When Hans posed alone, in a wide-legged stance and pulling his peter in a lazy rhythm, Jan came and sat beside me, leaning for a hug.

You're very broadminded, do you know? he said in an honest, chummy way, nuzzling into my hug. He was as warm as bedclothes and his hair smelled of hay and clean dog. Sander's a beautiful person, don't you think so? he asked. He makes me blush. That's only natural, I say.

Sander thanked them courteously for posing, and they went off, arms around each other, not to be heard or seen until they turned up while Sander and I were making supper and having a Campari on the porch. Leaf trash in their hair and stuck to their bodies, knees smutched.

Hansje's right cheek was daubed with woodsearth, and Jan's back was criss-crossed with pine needles. Smears of forest muck on their legs and chests. Their eyes gleamed. Two happier, nastier boys I've never seen. Ah! said Sander, passion. Cold beef sandwiches, cheese, pickles.

Cold blond beer from the spring. Neither boy had had a whole glass of beer before. They ate like wolves. With coffee Sander hefted Jan onto his lap and methodically picked leaf trash off him. Hans went to help and got hauled up and scrunched in beside Jan. You two! said Sander.

You two are wildly in love with each other, he said, tweaking their dicks, a lovely thing to be, and you're as filthy as sewer rats, fine by me, and Adriaan couldn't care less, except that you're to sleep, if that's the word, in our bedroll, which will look like a badger sett.

So off for a bath in the sea before it's too cold and too dark. Besides, you're giving me a hard on, and it's not me you're in love with. I made a fire the meanwhile. Sander came back later with a leggy boy on each hip, a subject the Greek sculptors missed, or the world lost.

23 THERMIDOR

Friendly conversation with Jan, who had strayed back to the cabin from an outing. Hansje's and Sander's shouts and hoots sounded like a zoo down the way. Jan wambling to show he'd had enough of chinning limbs, sit ups, push ups, sprints around the island, all Sander's idea.

Honeybrown in underpants of negligible modesty hanked down at the waist, held on more by the poke of his genitals than the low relief of his behind. Asked him how he got so richly tan. On a camping trip with his parents and sister, in Sicily. Wore nothing for weeks, he said.

Onverschillig, after breakfast, he and Hans had stood just beyond the porch, not five meters away, and brushed lips, as if nectaring, while pushing down each other's briefs, brushing balls with fingertips, meddling with foreskins, making my stomach flutter and a seep of saliva.

Thumped Sander on the shoulder, who clucked his tongue and whistled. *O them!* They're under each other's skin something wonderful. Nothing for it but to put up with their *poppenkast*, though they're making my balls run a fever. Whereupon, defiantly, they kissed, tongue and all.

And now Jan wore a great seriousness in his green eyes. *Zaadsmet* on the pouch of his briefs. Heer Hovendaal, he said, Hansje's mother when we were leaving said to Heer Floris, to Sander I mean, that Hans and I were to be allowed to do anything. You and Sander are very liberal.

Hans and I think that you are wonderfully nice, even with your making a little fun of us, that's one of your ways of showing affection, isn't it, but what I want to ask is do you think Mevrouw Keirinckx meant that Hansje and I can make love? You are, I said, aren't you?

You're as loving, dear Jan, as frolicsome puppies licking and chewing on each other. He winced. I mean, he said, swallowing awkwardly, making love. Not just playing around. I remembered Sander's despair, once, of adult understanding, and answered with an insouciant shrug.

I've known Hans' mother, I said, since she was a teenager, and his father too. They are, as you say of me and Sander, wonderfully liberal and contemporary. But your own parents? Oh that's *in orde*, he said. They showed me and Jenny how to masturbate when we were *kleuters*.

I have at home, he said, the book *De Seksueele Bevrijding van Kinderen*, which they've seen in my desk, because I heard them talking about it, and they haven't thrown it away, as they once did some other things, and it has pictures in it of boys Hansje's and my age making love.

Does Hans want to? O yes. *Akkoord*, I said, with a tweak for his dick through his briefs to show that I understood. We then talked about Sicily, Sander's drawing, what kind of book I'm writing, his interest in history, the planets. Hans and Sander turned up shining with sweat.

24 THERMIDOR

The boys washing socks, underpants, jerseys under Sander's demanding supervision. A swim. In radiant late afternoon sun on the porch of the cabin, coffee for me and Sander. In jeans, Sander, with the fly left unzipped, characteristically, his signature, the boys naked.

They, who had been blatantly smooching and daring mischievous salacities since our talk, calling it *twaalfjaaroud bevrijding*, soon colloquialized to Badger Liberation, were mucking about with their dicks in front of us, full of themselves, unblushing and eager-eyed.

Hans sat in a canvas folding chair sipping a jelly glass of beer, picking his nose. Jan sat crosslegged between his knees, jacking Hansje's dick in a bike-pedaling rhythm, occasionally grazing the inside of his thighs with the flat of his cheek. Friendship! said Sander.

Nothing like it. Absolutely, said Hansje, and is it ever good. If only, said Sander reaching for his drawing pad, Dokter Tomas could be here now. Who, said Jan making his pulls up taller and his downstrokes deeper, is this Dokter Tomas? Hans, drumming his heels, asked who cared.

The boffin, said Sander, who when I went berserk as a teenager, gave me to Adriaan to help build the cabin here, and to get me back into the mainstream of Dutch middleclass normality, like being here now at an orgy in a Greek gymnasium drawing amorous spadgers jacking off.

Jan added his other hand, caressing Hansje's balls, which had drawn up tight as a quince. And then, making me and Sander trade stares, Jan, squiggle-eyed as he leaned and cupped the head of Hansje's dick in his mouth, shoved onto it cross-eyed, forcing it in with sliding nods.

Een derde, drie vierde, het geheel in elf opsicht. Hans, boggled and blushing, was utterly, seriously silent, staring at what was happening. Nose mashed against Hansje's pubic down, drawing back with a slick slow drag to the acorn, Jan slogged through a brave cadence before he kecked.

Eyes watered, gasping, he scambled up, jiggeting his foreskin, for Hansje's turn. Who, holding Jan by the butt, ran his kiss on full glut, gagged, tried again less impetuously, made a go of it for three slippery thrusts, stood beaming to crush Jan in a hug, and went back to it.

You little buggers! Sander bellowed. I can't stand it. We're going for a walk, Adriaan and I, out of temptation's way. He mussed their hair, kissed them both, mouth, navel, and dick, and strode off. Make it good, I added, and followed Sander to the other end of the island.

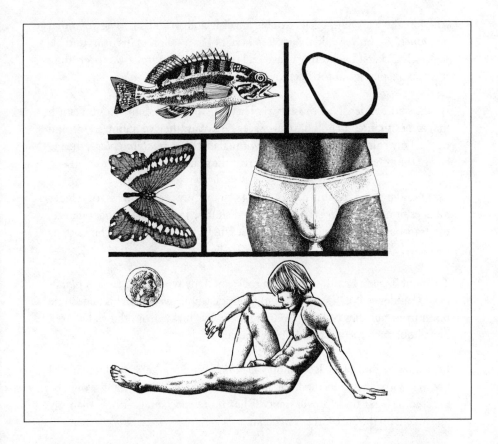

He walked with barefoot Choctaw tread through the larches and pines, silent for a long while. Kaatje and Bruno won't mind? I said I didn't think so. Jan was a best friend, a bright, just, affectionate boy. Affectionate! Sander shouted. He could seduce a Calvinist archbishop.

He's back there loving sweet Hansje into an orgasm that will start with a supersonic tickle in his grubby pink toes, zing up his pretty brown legs, wiggle through his spine, dance in his heart, slosh out the top of his head, and ripple and buzz out to his fingertips.

That's, of course, only the buildup. Then it will scrunch in to hum around in his balls and trill and jump in his trim little dick. He flexed his knees and hauled his out of his open fly, and walked on with it flopping. Watch, he said, this one come all by itself.

And Jan, the scalawag, a della Robbia angel, a lamb, a Poussin *jonge Johannes de Doper*, as you've said, and look at him, hot as a sailor. O his heart and his seasick knackers! Lucky little charmer. I remarked that Sander was overrating their sexual play as far too Beethovenesque.

Nyah, said Sander. Not those two. They've studied carefully more Danish magazines than you and I have ever seen. Anyway, they've unhinged me and trashed my calm. We came to our favorite flat rock, *the talking place*, the tag end of the afternoon lying silver out across the sea.

I sat, Sander stood, poking things, a moss clump, my foot, with his toe. Under a fidget of fingers his cock distended and snubbed up. A silly Sander glance, the transparency of which I met with a laugh. I'm being awful, he said, as awful as I've always been, always will be.

The jumbling sea heard, the solemn rocks, and my wondering ears. A *platte-grond* Sander calls it, a scheme for my consideration, evolved in his handsome brain from hunches of his and Grietje's, always lucky, from things I've told him about the *stapelgek* philosopher Fourier.

Item, that he and I buy Roseknop's *De Stijl* house on the Spiegelgracht and live in it with Grietje. Its top floor, half the roof of which is skylight, would be his studio. Next floor down, mine. It has more space and airiness than my apartment on the Suze Groeneweglaan.

Extensive bookshelves. He and Grietje will have the first floor. Every painting, every drawing he sells will go into paying for his part of the house until it is all wonderfully ours. The place is in the hands of some national trust, which wants somebody to buy it and live in it.

Item, that he and Grietje want children, lots of children, and have already dispensed with precautions. They are not afraid that it will be a sweet and lovable *idioot*, as it will be nephew or niece as well as son or daughter, but genetics are genetics. Bound to be beautiful.

Item, it would improve the little bastard's chances by half if I put myself in the way, alongside, as it were, Sander, of being its father. I am Hansje's real father, am I not? I don't know, don't need to know. He has Kaatje's beauty, but no telling resemblance to me or Bruno.

Item, that Grietje with female bloodymindedness says this will also get us into each other's pants. She says you're shy. There's a *vrouwenbeweging* trollop she had been to bed with, for the fun of it, just a silly frump of a tomboyish girl who comes for hours.

Groot God! They can squeeze out orgasms all of an afternoon and part of a night, having convulsions the whole time. Anyway, we'll be close in her. Not in *goedgezindheit*, and we know you're not shockable or *preuts* or *puriteins*. You don't want to believe that I love you.

The three of us would make books and paintings and children as fine as Hans and Saartje. All of our days will be charmed and sexy. We won't let anybody in. Never answer the doorbell. The rest of the world can go gibber as it will, shut out, in rage. Just us inside.

Except for Bruno and Kaatje, and Max and Margareta, and Grietje's *wildzang* with the outsized talented clit, and Hans and Jan, we'll make them a corner somewhere for as long as they're liberated badgers, before they wise up to girls, and your spooky professor friends, natch.

O yes, my models. But nobody else. It will be an island, like this, but in Amsterdam. What did I think? What did I think! First, that it's a knot of unsolvable problems, each reinforcing the other, and like all knots has stability. Adriaan, he said, there are tears in your eyes.

25 THERMIDOR
Samenstelling. Table on porch, big camp coffee pot, archaic Japanese blue vase, the gift of Minoru Hara, with buttony yellow summer meadow flowers, sharp green of fragrance, coffee mugs, solid Dutch plates with crumbs of rolls, marmalade and kipper wreck. My pipe.

Two pairs of briefs, Jan's and Hansje's, one white with blue band, pucked and dimpled along the elastic, the other a pale Greek blue with white band. Wet towels over the backs of chairs, Sander's docked jeans. Summer morning sun through pines. Flat green, the sea.

On the bed, well beyond credence and probably beyond human capacity, Sander remarks, our champions of mutual esteem intently and devotedly at it. Back from a dip, he looked in, slapped his forehead, and came onto the porch with one thumb in his mouth, the other jabbed over his shoulder.

I looked. Tousled mops of heads held deep between brown, narrow, shifting thighs, a working of sharp shoulder blades, traveling of hands from pert butts along ribby flanks to virginal napes, a voluptuary of restless caresses, hips hunched in slow and exact pulsings.

They were thus *negen en zestig* on the bed when we got back last evening from the flat rock, causing Sander to spin on his heel and raddle his hair. We made supper, noisily, to which they were a while in coming, hand in hand, with shiny wet dicks and chins, brazenly.

Sander marched them by the ears to the sea, hoisting them on the way to smatch a kiss onto a midriff, a navel, a thigh. They splashed and washed each other. I followed with a towel, as there was a nip in the air. Began to see what talents Sander has for being a father.

We dressed Hans in my Finnish sweater: it came to his knees and his head was half swallowed by the high neck. Jan asked to have Sander's jersey, which fitted him like socks on a rooster. Neither seemed the least flustered or unbalanced by their homemade orgy. *Integendeel.*

They wore their excitement openly and happily. Is, said Sander with a mouth full of corned beef, Badger Liberation all that your salty hearts expected? Jan, at whose age with such a question I would have been at a loss, welcomed the question. I'm hooked for good, he said.   .

Me too, added Hans. Slyboots looks at each other as they answered. *Amor meliores facet.* So they laid the fire, washed up after supper, brought coffee, looking very Little Hordes in the outsized sweater and jersey. Love makes their eyes brilliant and alert. And soft.

Zaad, Jan offers, tastes like celery. Like soda, Hans said, sort of. We wanted you to see us all wiggly and drooling, but you went away. I got Jan to yipping and mooing a lot, and then we did it together on the bed, both at once, you know, and it got better and better.

Sander put his head in his hands. We're going to do it all night, Jan said. Is it all right to kiss? O God, Sander moaned. Hans was puzzled by Sander. Jan saw through him. Kissing, I said, is what you're doing. I suppose it is, at that, Jan said. Sander's going crazy.

Why? asked Hans. Because, said Sander, never mind why. Because, I said, he's younger than both of you and feels left out. He's like an eight-year-old who wants to play with the big boys. But, said Hans, Sander's peter is 25 cm long, *gossie mijne*! And it's girls he fucks.

I fuck everything, Sander said, though I've never had an eye for goslings, not before today. I didn't know you were such sexpots. Sander's pulling your leg, I said, he wouldn't remain interested over an hour in something as wet behind the ears and pure of heart as a boy.

When we're older, Jan asked, we'll have more *zaad*, won't we? Scads, said Sander, glad to have the subject changed. He heaved Hans onto his lap, hugged him, and said, you come more the more you come. And this fellow will get longer the more you love each other into fits.

Look it, said Jan, that's mine. They went early to their *slaapzak*, to discover that the one with his head deep inside tended to smother. Sander suggested they have a good hug and go to sleep, heads side by side, both breathing. No way! they said together. Sex is too good.

I suggested the bed until Sander and I turned in. Afterwards they could be in front of the fire in tall socks and sweaters for as long as passion raged. This they did, so that when we went to bed it was warm and redolent of boy. We talked quietly a long while before sleep.

Sander calmly assuaged his concupiscence while we talked about the plan to buy and live in the Roseknop house. When I woke deep in the night, the boys by the fire seemed to be some eight-limbed insectoid creature in a spasm of contractions, part caterpillar, part cricket.

They were snuffling and sighing. I got up, livened the fire with wood, said hello, and looked at the time: half past three. Jan detached and gave me a ruckled grin that hitched into a rictus of felt pleasure, eyes closing, and slid back onto Hansje. I pulled up his slipped sock.

Tugged down Hans' sweater that had ridden up his back. Patted each's behind, twitted Jan's ear, and was going back to bed, cock rising, when a whispered *Ome Adriaan* brought me back. Could they have, Hans said, cocoa or something? Where was it? He would get it and make it.

Stay there, I signaled. I swung the kettle over the fire, fetched instant cocoa, mugs, and spoons, and a bottle of Perrier and cognac as well. They disconnected and, swapping a kiss, sat watching me open bottles. Their eyes were glad and tired, hair tangled and matted.

Gave them each a mug of Perrier into which I tipped a smidgin of cognac, which would either put them to sleep or urge them on to more piggery. Brandy for strength, I said. Cocoa for a treat. To Badger Liberation, I toasted. Best uncle in the whole world, Hansje said.

The Badgers' best friend, said Jan. And nobody I know would ever believe I'm on an island way out in the sea making love with Hansje and sitting by a fire in the middle of the night drinking brandy and cocoa. It's not real, it isn't happening. But it is, said Hans.

A hint of dawn in the cabin when I woke again. The fire had died down. I could just make the little bastards out. They were asleep, heads still between thighs, still hugging, breathing softly. Goose pimples on an arm showed me how cold they were, and curled toes and pink ears.

I scooped Hansje up, who said something inarticulate in his sleep, and kissed the empty air. I put him in our bed, next to Sander, and fetched Jan, who woke briefly but was too sleepy to care what anyone was doing with him. I slid him in beside Hans, and got in with them.

Sander woke, turned, and muttered that he seemed to be in bed with several more people than he'd thought. These buggers fell asleep by the fire, I whispered. Don't wake them, they'll start all over here between us. Keep them warm. Aren't they lovely, Sander said.

Quagga

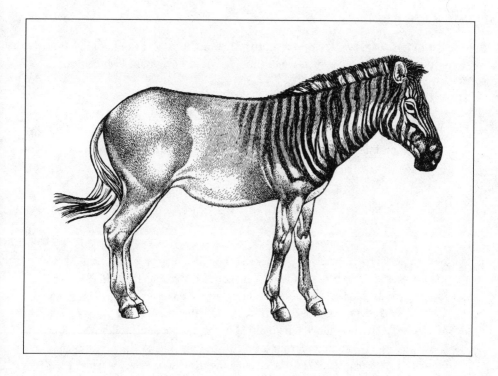

1 FRUCTIDOR
A basket of summer fruit.

                    Amos, He said, what do you see?

And I said, a basket of summer fruit.

Then *de Heer* said to me, the end is come upon my people.

I will not again pass by them this way anymore.

   •

It sits rich and fragrant on altars and sills, this harvest hamper of mellow apples and speckled pears, red pomegranates, fat blue figs, clumps of olives and clusters of grapes on a bedding of emmer and spelt, the round white moon of Elul promising the rains of Tishri. Here, green and yellow in wicker, was earth's plenty for table and manger and granary, bounty and blessing which nevertheless the wind spoke of to Amos the shepherd and dresser of sycamores midway the 208 furlongs from Hevron to Yerushlim as the sign of the end of all.

•

Sycamore: *shiqmah* (Ficus sycomorus). Fig mulberry leaf hook. Shepherd's hook, the hook with which we cannot draw out Leviathan. Fish leaf hook.

    There shall no signe be given,
but the signe of the Prophet Ionas.
                    And *de Heer* stood upon a wall
with a plumbline in his hand.

•

Hook leaf fish.

•

No skateboards, no bicycles, Jan ticked off on his fingers the fun of the island for Sweetbrier, who was on the next bus after Hans' and Jan's, having been lost all over the Netherlands. No TV, though there's a radio that gets England, France, the Federal Republic, and the DDR, sometimes Spain. Only half of Sweetbrier's face was shaved: he realized in the middle of his toilet what time it was and barely caught the train from Amsterdam. His clothes don't match, one shoe is different, and there's a lens missing from his spectacles. This he has in his pocket, using it as a monocle to read with, which predicament, along with the eerily asymmetrical one-sided shave, the odd shoe, and his obviously very capable, good-natured intelligence, gives Hansje fits.

•

Good lord! Sweetbrier cried after Sander had stuffed himself in and given his hand, you're the painter? Alexander Floris. Sander did his I Am A Handsome Idiot act, speaking a Dutch so demotic that Hans slid his tongue across his upper lip and cut a glance at Jan out of the tails of his eyes. Sweetbrier had taken the wrong bus several times over. Only the kind guidance of a tulip farmer with a firm grasp of country busses got him to the Point at all. Accent Midlands, which Jan is picking up already. Hans too, though his English is that of a Chinese waiter.

•

An island, is it, out there in that mist? Piet took us out in his motorlaunch.

•

In dressed stone and tilled field Amos found God and man working together, creating together, for *de Heer* will accept none but the common effort, wherein there is justice and the bond of hand with hand, heart with heart. And in the work between them of man and God shall the plowman overtake the reaper, and the treader of grapes find himself hard upon the heels of the sower of the grape seed, and the hills melt under the weight of the harvest, and work shall be the rites, not a sign.

•

And there it all is: the meaning of still life, the sign to return us to the rites. A sermon in gourds. The sanctuary was in the winnowing flail all along, in the winejar, in parched millet kneaded into mashed dates.

To answer in somewise Denys Sweetbrier's question, which was, with wide open laughing English eyes, why in Sam Hill I'm concerned, if only as a philosophical exercise, to redesign Fourier's preposterously impossible utopia just when this awful century seems about to repeat its hellish world wars with an exchange of atomic missiles in total futility and consummate madness?

•

When there was a Sweetbrier to ask the question, by our congenial fire. Over for the antinuke march in Amsterdam, he asked if we could get together, go over his paper on Fourier's architecture, and have some jolly talks, what? Jan it was, looking more like a quattrocento *Florentijns* Johannes de Doper than ever, not Hansje about whose English we all know, who managed, first crack out of the box, Mijnheer Zveetbrier, I am delightful to meet you! Who replied (Britishly crinkled), Absolutely right, don't you know. *Delighted* is the word for me. He wasn't at the Point when Sander and I rowed over, only Hans and

Jan, whose selfmade invitation was prior to Sweetbrier's.

Sander amused by all this, and his smiling sigh, followed by a lickerish whistle, meant that I would be sorry. The whistle was for Grietje. He could see, said Sander, this Brierpatch van Oxford rumpled and vague, demanding tea *om het uur*. And with the Greater Amsterdam Vandaalvereniging in residence to boot, *jandorie*! They will take him apart, the boys, a matter of honor for them, and throw the remains to the gulls. He'd stay and watch, and help both me and them, except that Grietje would have his ears, and the big canvas was calling him home. So to the Point, Sander rowing, his mane awash in the wind, for stores, the mail, and Hans and Jan, who attacked as we climbed from the boat, walking up Sander until each bestrode a shoulder, and for Sweetbrier nowhere in sight. *Zo?* asked Sander from under Hansje's student *muts* topped by Jan's cricket cap, you're surprised? The English get lost in their own houses. Or these two have assured him that he was in Sweden and sent him off again on the Paterswolde bus. *Jawel!* Jan agreed, *de hond van de Baskerwillen* glupped him, right over there. *Ik denk van niet*, said Hansje with a calm seriousness. It was *een fliegende schotel* skimmed down and juddered along the dock, *gepiep gepiep* and *bimbam*, with lights that hissed and blinked. Jan hissed and blinked, Sander hissed and blinked. It hovered and put down steps. A round kabouter with silver eyes waddled out, rolling his tail. *Bak bek bik bok buk*, he said. And your *Engelsman*, Ome Adriaan, had had it. In he went. Off they whizzed. I rather think Jan and I were the only ones to see. Truly, said Sander, cupping his hand over Hans' crotch and kissing him recklessly smack on the mouth. The same for Jan.

•

It was when Hans had monkeyed up Sander's back and toppled him into the piled haversacks, and Jan had sprung from the front and was trying to squeeze Sander and Hans into the one comprehensive hug, and Sander, pinioned fore and aft and hollering that he was being kissed to death, was nimbly unzippering all three of their flies, unbuckling belts and unsnapping buttons, grubbing inside, that Sweetbrier, shaved on one side of his face only, asked me if I were Adriaan van Hovendaal.

•

The only mercy to descry in the death of Coubertin's two-year-old son in 1898 is that, had he lived, he would have been twenty in 1916, and death would have found him, as it did all of Coubertin's nephews, whom he loved, at Verdun or Dompierre. There walked unseen in his funeral procession Albert l'Ours in a yellow bowtie and waistcoat of Scotch plaid, Pierre Lapin in a scarlet coat and jockey cap, Madame Poupette-à-l'Épingle in her best apron and bonnet, Madame Hortense l'Éléphant, Monsieur Noisy Noisette, Madame Sophie Canetang with parasol and reticule, Thomas Tigre, who had come from Malaya in a balloon, Madame La Vache in a calico dress, la Famille Flopsaut with bouquets of dandelions, Georges l'Hippopotame, who came by train from Sénégal, Milord Chanticleer and Lady Pertelote, Herbert le Hérisson, and all the sheep and chickens and goats from the Jardin d'Acclimatation. They were conducted thither by Orfée himself, who did not mind, in among his herds and flocks, from time to time, a human child. And they all went to Heaven on the Caen Express, the locomotive's bell and whistle playing calliope marches from the Cirque Médrano all the way.

•

Jan, with splendid manners, disengaged himself first from the seething wiggle, and fastening his jeans with one hand held out the other. *I'm delightful to meet you, Mijnheer Zveetbrier.* Unfazed Sander, penis out and all, shirt wrenched around his ribs, rose with Hans still grappled around him. Hi! he said with a silly smile. Hans, realizing at last that we had company, managed through some thrill of genius the Quakerly *I am the better for seeing thee, friend.* The Greater Amsterdam Erewhonian Society, I introduce us as. A collusive sparkle in Sweetbrier's eyes, and mock scandal at Sander's putting Hans' clothes in order while he himself was indecent and dangling. The hordes, I said. Yes yes! said Sweetbrier, quite! But in public? O, they know us around here, I said, indicating three fishermen taking the sun in front of the store, complacently smoking their pipes and watching the most interesting sight they would see all week.

2 FRUCTIDOR

Sweetbrier will do as a guest. Affable chap. Knows boats, so he wasn't a clunk (Jan's approving observation) coming over. Teaches at a boys' school in Oxford, which is not all the advantage it might be (his candid remark) in getting the hang of Hans and Jan. He admired their dispatch in stripping and remaking the bed with army corners, shucking and recasing pillow, fussing blankets flat and even of side, salutes inviting inspection, no wrinkles and no fuzz. Mijnheer Zveetbrier's. We're *slaapzak*, us together in this one, Adriaan in that one beside us.

•

Supper on the hearth by a good fire. I've never felt so unreal, says Sweetbrier. He calls the cabin marvelously cozy, shipshape, *Dutch*. Everything done right, Hans explains as if to a Patagonian, racks up grace, like money in the bank. Do it wrong, or come up with a tacky excuse for getting out of it, and Ome Adriaan will remember in the stamp market. Actually, you can get away with anything out here on the island except being a *biggetje*.

•

Jantje's dignity in every movement is the same as Hansje's animal grace: extremes that have met. Jan sits, Hans flops. Jan walks like a Red Indian, Hans clomps, skips, saunters. Jan puts his foot up to tie his laces, Hans leans over his shoe, kneeling. Jan gazes, Hans stares. Jan grins boredom, Hans yawns. And yet they're constantly imitating one another.

•

Conversation by the fire. Fourier's series of harmonic attractions, a charming make-believe parallel to his uncle (as he would have you believe) Joseph Fourier's mathematical series (Jan cocking his head in sharp interest), are a conscious structure exactly like the furtively harmonic and unconscious structures found by Lévi-Strauss in primitive cultures. Society as poetry rather than the newspaper prose of history. Practically all that's tacit in civilization is concerned discourse in the primitive. Most twentieth-century art has longed to submerge significance inside structures, forgetting the otherness of art. When style becomes habit we become children. Jan asked to have this explained, with a nice turn of English probably not idiomatic: How is it that you mean? That, says Sweetbrier, our heritage is uncritically accepted. A child does not question that a chair is. It belongs to him in the same order as sun, trees, oxygen. The Japanese once faced the existence of chairs, *Christian beds* as the Chinese say, something they did not have but which the Chinese had adopted, and which, they knew, Europeans sat in. They considered, they rejected. The Erewhonians, Jan said softly, rejected machines.

•

Kaatje, of Hans and Jan as Free Badgers: something new. Sounds exciting. Bruno likes Jan. They talk math together. She finds the prospect of our renovating and living in the Roseknop house more interesting by way of gossip, and urges me to take Sander up on his offer.

•

Fourier's architecture begins in the country house of the landed gentry, to be lived in and played in by the Harmonian phalanstery. That's the beauty of his imagination. Shepherds, having folded the sheep, bathed and spiced themselves, come into the *grand salon*, curls oiled, leggings and smock exchanged for alpaca jacket, with decorations, and Turkish trousers. Here they mingle and chat with blacksmith, mathematician, turnip farmer, and historian. They sit on silk divans to read the evening paper. Fourier has moved the neighborhood brasserie into a Parc Monceau drawing room, exactly as Henri Rousseau would have done if he had painted a Citizen's Ideal World.

.

The phalanstery is a whole village in a building as big as the Louvre: Corbusier's inspiration for his Marseilles apartment house. A Shaker Louvre full of practical things like looms, printing presses, kitchens, pantries, libraries, artists' studios, sacks of wool, conversation rooms, lecture halls, ballrooms, concert chambers, cozy rooms for lovers.

.

Sweetbrier agrees, wrily, that no phalanstery anything like Fourier's is possible without an Erewhonian revolution, canceling machines. To return movement to walking, horseback riding, and the true dance. To return music to the instrument and occasion. To return the casual to the deliberate, the planned, the expected. To return reading to daylight and the lamp. To return love to passion as it arises. To return work to communal duty, to the sense of usefulness. To have the beginning and end of everything kept in sight and in the discourse of the whole phalanstery. To take happiness from money and restore it to the harmony of work and its reward, ambition and its achievement. To put mind and hand in concert. To reorganize society after its disastrous dispersal by train, automobile, airplane.

.

Butler's insight was that the machine enslaved us, changing all work to drudgery. All work became pandering to the reproduction of the machines.

.

To return the body to its beauty, the mind to tranquillity.

.

Impossibly idealistic! Sweetbrier cries. But you're right, you know.

3 FRUCTIDOR

The three hundred thousand who carried their banners in Amsterdam to protest *de bom* set out in an Ohio that never was.

If, I say to Sweetbrier, we need to define our studies in a phrase, the phrase must be: to locate in the geography of the imagination, and go back to, the Ohio of Fourier's vision.

These protesters against megadeath set out from the phalansteries of the Susquehanna, from Mennonite communities, from the round barns and angelic symmetry of the Shakers, from the Schwarzwald of the Wandervögel, from the Olympic flags of Athens in 1896, from Danish classrooms in which the ideas of Holberg, Grundtvig, and the brothers Brandes were heard.

And you were in the march, too? Sweetbrier said. O I say, how jolly. It was so worth coming over for.

•

O *ja!* said Jan. I was on the shoulders of a man I more or less climbed onto without really asking, in the Jeugd en Jongere Groepje of the COC, which my folks weren't raving happy about. I rather bullyragged them about it afterwards. They, and my sister Jenny, were with the Ethical Society. Oof! Which did have, I'll admit, scarier *doodshoofd* masks than ours. But I saw the Free Badger folk and nipped over. They were just behind the Voor het Kind people. Hansje got to ride on Max Keirinckx's shoulders, his granddaddy, and Saartje was on Grietje's. Yes, Hans said, but we were in with a Lutheran Sunday School from Brabant, bunch of hicks singing Jesus music, and a wimpy Neighborhood Association. Wild, I'll tell you! Grootpapa Max called the *Rus* Head Rabbit and the *Amerikaans* Head Rabbit senile old farts. *Who*, Sweetbrier said, I was with I couldn't say, I assure you, but we were hundreds strong, and we had a *papier-mâché* nuke missile with the President Reagan's pompadoured face on it, don't you know, and another with Brezhnev on it, with those eyebrows, don't you know, and those sliding-away corners of the mouth.

•

For the Renaissance to complete its dream of antiquity it had to recover the athlete who as symbol and presence is the opposite of the chivalric horseman plated with armor, trussed in silk and taffeta, shuttled between honor and shame, more skilled in manners than in fighting. From the grocer's son Gambetta, the republic, and from his twelve-year-old admirer Coubertin, the soccer fields and swimming pools and bicycle races without which we cannot imagine modern Europe. Both their revolutions were so successful as to be seen inevitable.

Both revolutions were against guile, stupidity, superciliousness, arrogant privilege. The French for all their republican passion are still suspicious of democracy, but no one can remember a world without football, bicycles, or swimming. That is, without the age's *daimon*.

·

The zebra has the figure and grace of the horse, joined to the swiftness of the stag. He is about seven feet long, from the point of the muzzle to the origin of the tail, and about four feet high. The color of his skin is beautiful and uniform, consisting of alternate parallel rings of black and white disposed in a most regular manner. He is generally less than the horse and larger than the ass. The zebra is found nowhere but in the eastern and southern provinces of Africa, from Ethiopia to the Cape of Good Hope, and from the Cape of Good Hope to the Congo. The Dutch have been at great pains to tame and use them for domestic purposes, but with little success. He is hard-mouthed and kicks when any person attempts to touch or come near him. He is restless and obstinate as a mule: but perhaps the wild horse is as untractable as the zebra. For it is probable, if he were early accustomed to obedience and a domestic life, he would become as docile as the horse.

·

The Olympics are reborn in Rousseau's *Les Joueurs de Ball*. It was his sense that games are played, as at Elis, in a clearing in the wood, that the players are friends, that they are playing for the fun of the game, not to be a spectacle for the entertainment of an idle crowd. He knows that the game is a dance, and creates what also might be a ballet by Stravinsky or Satie. Huizinga and Montherlant were meditating on sports much later: *Homo Ludens*, 1938. *Les Olympiques*, 1924, with a new edition augmented and with a new introduction in 1938. Nice rhyme and synchronicity.

·

How now (Sweetbrier with one of those English sideways looks, a kind of wise gawp, to Jan being walked in circles as a wheelbarrow by Hans) can you say you *think* you've been to Oxford? Goodness gracious! You remember Sicily and Paris and Florence. You would remember the curved High Street, gardens, walls, colleges. A big park with ducks and cricket players, said Jan.

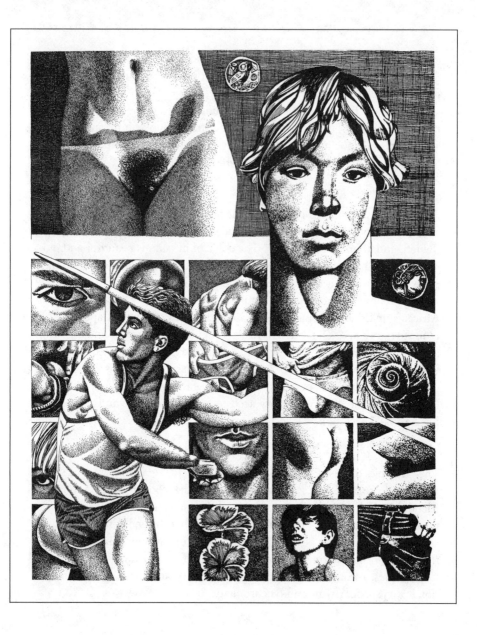

Bateaux pushed by poles on a river. I add a memory of an evening hearing Paul Wittgenstein play the piano at Balliol. Ludwig's brother. He'd lost his right arm on the Russian Front early in the Great War. This evening was in 1949, a concert at Balliol. I never met the great philosopher, and I've often wondered if he were present that evening. Very likely he was, Sweetbrier said.

With one arm he played the piano? Hans asked. Far better than most pianists with two. Sweetbrier corroborates, with a whoop of laughter, my memory of the coffee. It was made by undergraduates who were my hosts by putting coarsely ground coffee in a flower vase of tepid water. *Gossie*, said Hansje. So throughout Wittgenstein's concert I kept finding grains of coffee between my teeth and under my tongue. All very Oxford, said Sweetbrier with delight. And whether Wittgenstein was actually there, you can take the probability in all its rich potential and believe that he was. There may be, don't you know, ways of finding out. It would be a jolly bit of detective work.

Why would it matter? asked Hans. I can see why, said Jan.

•

Moisei Ginsburg's and Mikhail Barshch's plan for a linear city submitted in 1929 to the Green Town Competition of the Soviet Planning Commission, to be built in 15,000 *hectaren* of forest, was inspired, they said, by the hypothetical sociology of Comrade M. A. Okhitovich, who in turn was inspired by the French utopian economist Charles Gide, Fourier's disciple who spoke his eulogy at the Cimitière Montmartre in 1837, October the twelfth, and laid a heap of roses on the coffin. Ginsburg and Barshch in fact took their plan from the American Edgar Chambless, who published his plan for a linear city in 1910, a continuous house with a subway train in its endless basement and a highway and arcades on its roof. Outside every door was the forest, or prairie, or garden, or orchards, or fields of grain. He likened it to city skyscrapers laid on their sides, made continuous. Here civilization could not puddle, stagnate, or congest, as it was strung out room by room along an axis, a molecule of humanity, a syntax that could articulate every human expression. China! says Sweetbrier, moving into the Wall and setting up house! Chambless' plea was for all cities, towns, and farms to be dismantled and built into his continuum, to prevent their deterioration into slums or alienated byways, before the corrosion of estrangement set in.

•

The cry of the horse is known by the name of neighing, that of the ass by braying, which is a long, disagreeable noise, consisting of alternate discords from sharp to grave and from grave to sharp. He seldom cries but when pressed with hunger or love. The voice of the female is clearer and more piercing than that of the male.

•

Harold Schimmel writes from his guard post overlooking *de Jordaan* that a fox brings her two cubs there and teaches them to steal. They are frisky, bright, impudent *jongen* with none of their mother's craftiness. The bored soldiers, glad of something to watch, pretend they don't see them. One cub secures a bit of bread and looks to his mother for approval. The other gets a green banana and is full of doubt that he has the right thing. Yes yes, Mama says. Stealing is stealing, and off they whip into the desert, where Harold can see them through his binoculars, on blond rocks like those in a Renaissance Sint Hieronymus, Bellini or Leendert van Vinci. The little fox is taught to kill the green banana by shaking it in his teeth.

•

Jan whistles *There Was an Old Man with a Blue-Eyed Daughter* and Hans does a *klompschoen dans* in my gumboots, fingers snapping, hair flopping, grinning like an imp. I add a flute accompaniment, with fancy sweetenings and trills, and Sweetbrier, clapping the beat, joins in.

•

You're writing this *down*? asks Sweetbrier. Essences, I say. Annals of the Harmony in its cradle days. I'm convinced that some wrenching catastrophe is about to happen. He suggests that the four of us draw up a list of details of civilization which can function as modules for the Harmony, for our diversion on a rainy day, for the good of humanity.

The Rietveld Schröder-Schräderhuis in Utrecht, 1925. Étienne-Louis Boullée's Hôtel Alexandre in Paris, 1763. The one is the father, the other the mother, of all modern architecture that's fit to live in. The city of Amsterdam with automobiles banned. Our island longhouse. Adolf Vigeland's sculpture complex in Oslo, as an epitome of Scandinavian idealism. Seurat's *Grande Jatte* and *Bathers at Asnières* and all his drawings, formal beauty in the service of French wit. All of Piet Mondriaan, all of George Herriman.

        Monet's house and garden at Giverny. Carl Larssen's house at Sundborn. The Jardin d'Acclimatation in the Bois. All the houses on the Singel. Bicycle. Fountain pen, typewriter, printing press. Jeans, *slipje*, Adidas, soccer shirt, down jacket, wool scarf, the skateboard.

        Bachelor uncles to supplement parents and brothers and sisters. More cooperative sisters. Wagner's Scupperdine Preserves. The custom of Oxford visitors to The Netherlands. James Keiller's Dundee Orange Marmalade. Pelikan India Ink. Ice cream. Toffee. Whiffet isonomy.

        The Olympic games restored to Coubertin's rules and regulations. Raoul Dufy's woodcuts for Apollinaire's *Cortège d'Orfée*. Centre Pompidou. Windsor and Newton watercolors and gouache. All the photographs of Imogen Cunningham. Chess and checkers. Chocolate and gingerbread.

        What in the world, asks Sweetbrier, is whiffet isonomy? Free Badgerdom! says Hans. Equal rights, says Jan, for children. O I say! says Sweetbrier.

4 FRUCTIDOR
Fourier could imitate the voices of all the animals.

    •

A zebra, Jan says, is a black horse with white stripes. And the only zebra that's a zebra is a horse. *Dol op de zebra*, says Hansje. That is, Jan persists with a twirl of fingers around his hair and indignant eyebrows, there are, or were, four species of *Equus* which Adam named zebra. They are, or were, Grevy's Zebra, with ears like *Michielje de muis* and very thin stripes, the Mountain Zebra, stripes German Expressionist, as if by Emil Nolde, Burchell's Zebra, stripes Late Picasso, and the Quagga, with stripes on its shoulders and neck only. Quaggas were exterminated by German hunters before 1900, so that Hitler's mother could have nice quaggahide gloves to wear to the zoo. But in this list, dear friends, there is a mistake. The Mountain Zebra, says the *Amerikaans zooloog* Stephen Jay Gould, is a horse. A black horse with white stripes. And it is the only one in the batch with the family name. Grevy's Zebra is *Equus grevyi*, the quagga is *Equus quagga*, Burchell's Zebra is *Equus burchelli*, but that horse in a zebra suit, he's *Equus zebra*.

    •

Sweetbrier wonders if the quagga can be backbred, as with the tarpan? And wouldn't Fourier's Harmony be in effect a backbreeding of mankind, back at least to Lewis Mumford's neolithic communities?

•

Rousseau's football players are wearing not the white duck *caleçons* and wool jerseys of English fashion but *maillots de bain* such as Albert Bloch and Robert de Saint-Loup wore at Cabourg to the delight of Palamède de Charlus, and Tadzio on the Lido to the despair of Aschenbach. Moreover, they are playing in a bowling alley in the Bois. Rousseau may have known that Coubertin had been given a soccer field, that it had trees in it which the authorities refused to have cut down, no matter how often Coubertin pleaded that soccer fields are treeless.

•

Jarry: bicycling, rowing.
Degas: Sparta, the ballet, horses.
Delaunay: football.
Fourier knew only the transition from medieval play to an incipient sense of modern sport, but felt the lack, noting the pallor of city children and the rubicund faces of country children, and thus designed work itself into an elaborate, playful *agon*.

•

The ass is as humble, patient, and tranquil as the horse is bold, ardent, and impetuous. He submits with firmness, perhaps with magnanimity, to strokes and chastisements. He is temperate both as to the quantity and quality of his food. He contents himself with the rigid and disagreeable herbage which the horse and other animals leave to him and disdain to eat. He is more delicate with regard to his drink, never using water unless it be perfectly pure. He looks upon the world with innocence and courage. As his master does not take the trouble of combing him, he often rolls himself on the turf among thistles and ferns. When very young, the ass is a gay, sprightly, nimble, and gentle animal. But he soon loses these qualities, probably by the bad usage he meets with at our hands. He becomes lazy, untractable, and stubborn. When under the influence of love he becomes perfectly furious. Although the ass be generally ill-used, he discovers a great attachment to his master. He smells him at a distance, and searches the places and roads he frequents. He easily distinguishes his master from the rest of mankind. The ass has a very fine eye, an excellent scent, and a good ear. When overloaded, he hangs his head and sinks his ears. When too much teased or tormented, he opens his mouth and retracts his teeth in disgust. This expression of disagreement gives him an air of ridicule and derision. If you cover his eyes, he will not move another step. Whatever the pace he is going at, if you push him, he instantly stops.

•

Mice, Hans and Jan in their *slaapzak*, squeaking in spite of themselves, chirruping and rustling. The promise to be *omzichtig* whiffles above the dull suff of the night tide, getting busier once there was a regular grump and wheeze from Sweetbrier in the bed at the room's other end. My drift into sleep was jolted by Hans crawling into my bedroll on elbows and knees, a badger butting into its sett, wiggling around until the capsheaf of his hair snuzzled under my chin. Ome Adriaan. Yes, Munchkin. Where's your wristwatch? Because it glows in the dark and we're timing. A hug all ribs and shoulderblades, a tickle for his damp *teelsak*, a charge of *snoezig snuiter*, and help with creeping out, watch in fist, back to Jantje who, whispering thanks, pulled on his nape.

•

My *hemeltje!* when we were undressing for bed, despite Sweetbrier's dithering about, was for Hans' *onderslipje* on its way to laddering into lace, scruffy, and jaundiced. A common property, as I knew, worn time about. Sweetbrier out on a call of nature, the rapscallions dived for each other, hugged, rubbed noses and chins, ran heels up the back of legs, clutched crotches, burbled and whoofed. Mice rubbing whiskers. Well, said Jan, jiffling out of his jeans, we can all go have a pee, too, *ja*? A great white sea owl in the larch back of the landing. A wet wind from crosscurrents brings all sorts of creatures to the island, once an otter, once a brace of storks who looked at us with aristocratic *hauteur*. Hans, said Jan with a swipe of tongue across his upper lip, is the big-eyed nipper who runs this place, *ha ha*. Yick, but if you want to be spoiled rotten what you need is a bachelor uncle. *Jaloers*, counters Hans, and ungrateful pig. Whereupon they circle each other like tomcats. I am given, to hold, Hans' jeans raining a pocketknife and coins, and the scruffy briefs, Jantje's next, they say. Their skinny legs flick in and out of the dim late light and swallowing shadows, flouncing gleam of hair, silvery ankles, curled toes, sweet yipes and grunts. Where are you? Sweetbrier calls through the dusk. Up, monkeys. Fried apple pie! cries Jantje flicking trash from his legs. Dutch vegetable soup! shouts Hans. All the photographs of André Kertesz, I add, getting a kiss on the chin from Hans, and a kiss from Jan on the cheek. *Fromage Gruyère!* shouts Sweetbrier.

•

It is precisely, says Sweetbrier, those rhythms that have become dissonant we want to study. They had an harmonic origin. They changed. We changed. We are quite often mistaken about origins.

•

A long evening's talk by the fire, synod of quaggas and zebras. We cut out paper masks with lenticular eyelets and round mouths for Hans and Jan to do a mime such as they've seen in Vondelpark. Hans' mask rucks his hair into a shewel, and in a twink, with my sweater down to his knees, arms lost in the sleeves, he is a chimpanzee shoggling about. How a mask changes the rest of the body! Jan, barefoot in jeans and soccer shirt, loses his charm, his body becomes a stranger's, his gestures unfamiliar. He walks woodenly on his heels, a robot, Hans doing a limber monkey dance around him, gibbering. While they cavort, a mummery of robot and chimp, Sweetbrier asks about Hans' prayers. While, last night, Jan stood patiently and barebottomed, Hans knelt, fingers to lowered chin, and thanked *de Heer* for our health and wellbeing, for Jan's love, and Ome Adriaan's, and Mama's and Papa's and Saartje's, before rabbiting into the *slaapzak*. His mother Kaatje, I explain, raised a Catholic, feels that Hans and Saartje should know a moral code at its source, and have, as she says, religious passions of some sort, a real meaning to Easter and Christmas, if only to be easy with religious people and ideas. So they attend a Calvinist Sunday School.

•

Fourier's rooms were a Mexican jungle by Rousseau the Douanier, potted plants with paths among them negotiated by cats. The Harmony was to display in its windows the flowers peculiar to each day's symbolism. His notes for this are obscure and a little insane, but the general idea is clear.

•

The Harmony, says Sweetbrier, must feature Yorkshire pudding served with cold beef and mustard, beer to drink, or he won't belong to it. Apple pie, says Hans, with lots of juice and sugary crumbly brown crust. Jan and I vote for vegetable dumpling soup, lots of carrots, as the Harmonian staple.

•

Fourier was terrified of frogs, caterpillars, spiders. Against spaghetti he had an aversion, calling it rancid library paste. English cooking he couldn't abide, and was persnickety about bread. His favorite dish was potatoes baked in their skins, buttered, with onions.

5 FRUCTIDOR

Stately, to Sousa, behind the floppy silken strides of a brace of afghans flanking the Corporal Major of the Angelicat, eight, who bore their colors and whose quagga sported the yellow crupper, surcingle, and bridle of the Burgundy Hives, the Little Hordes rode out prancing. Tornado Squadron IX, Suzette Bright Eyes Tibble Wing, pranced out from the Phalanx Hortense Cézanne like a slope of thistles and wild carrot to see, silvery trumpets and stormy drums, sopranino commands. Glory to the Harmony! With impish swank (it was the Feast of Coubertin, 5 Frimaire, white puffs steaming from their quaggas' nostrils) they galloped to meet the Dandelion Band from the spadger barracks, on ponies, their captain a girl, their mascots Dalmatians. The toggery of the Band was what they called Greek: last year their orator Skeeter Boussy swallowed a wad of his medicinecabinet cottonball beard in the middle of his ode and had to be pounded on the back by a Vestal, whose oakleaf garland fell off and to pieces.

The Grammar and Manners Police fined the lot for giggling. Thus the Horde in its Magyar finery of silver-buttoned vests and scarves and boots and gaucho breeches, its long banners and decorations for valor in love and courtesy, stared at them with superior eyes.

•

We're, said Hans, Kangoeroekind I and Kangoeroekind II, and the sleeping bag is Mevrouw Kangoeroe. Jan thought better, as one could see from his eyes, of remarking on this. Ome Adriaan is Washer Rat from the woods behind the red windmill on the Point, who smokes appleginger roadtar tobacco in a rosebrier pipe, takes The *Tulip Grower's Weekly & Dutch Reformed Lutheran Bugle*, and reads Aristotle.

What am I? asks Sweetbrier. An English badger! says Jan. They visit sett to sett. You have come to visit Adriaan in his *weekendhuis*. Now, says Hans the honest, that you've shaved both sides of your face we don't find you silly at all. English, please, dear Hansje. Say it in English. Jan helps with whispers. *Nu*, now, have you, hast thou, cut the beard of you, *een* half face, aren't he now, are not *schrik*. Jan turned once on his heel

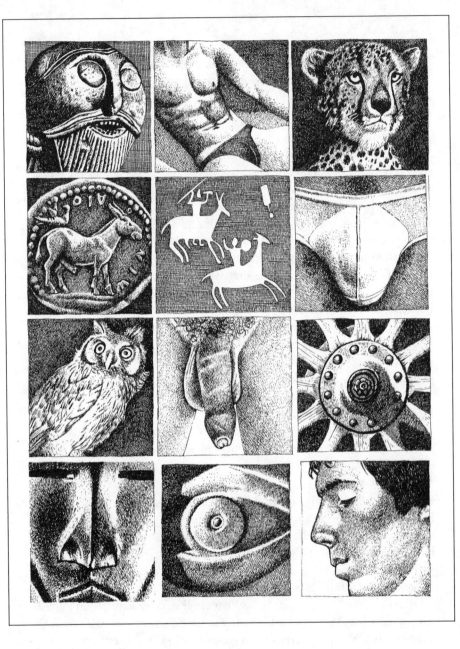

and fell upon Hans with a hug. He offers, complete with Midlands accent, all sides of your face you have shaved now and do not look peculiar. That's it, says Hans. What I said, *ja.*

Whereupon Sweetbrier, losing his make-do monocle, tripping on the way, squeezed Hans' shoulders and called him a brave fellow. Foreign languages require more courage than bearding lions in their dens. Hans gave him a kiss on the corner of the mouth. Ha! said Jan, repeating the salute, which Sweetbrier took with the slightest of flinches. O dear! he said, I feel I'm blushing rather dreadfully. You are! said Jan. It is a nice blush.

•

Of Jan's saying that the sea's doing Sibelius' *Fourth*, sloshing *largo*, dull and dark, Sweetbrier says, do these tykes always talk like this? I explain the game. Poetry in the Harmony will be a system of analogies and correspondences noted by children and gifted adults. It is an ongoing research project among the cultural and natural inventories. In Amsterdam we have a bulletin board on which the Keirinckx, Hovendaal, Floris, and Sinaasappel households tack conceits, haiku, similes. In the Harmony these will be displayed on posters. Hansje without looking up from coloring his sneakers with Magic Marker recites what's currently up. Vermeer is Rembrandt with the lights turned on. Bad, says Jan, very bad. Algebra is a detective story about arithmetic. The fox is the cat of dogs. A bee is a Dutch wasp. A wasp is a Japanese bee. Korfball is football for giraffes. An apple is a Protestant pear. To get a poplar, starch a willow. If Robinson Crusoe had met Tuesday, Balzac would have had to finish the book. Seurat is the Poulenc of painters, Poulenc the Seurat of composers.

•

De vlinder en de wesp, or as Sweetbrier shows us, with much guffawing at Jantje's Babrius out of Greek by way of an English crib, *the butterfly and the wops. Ja ja,* Jan agrees, *Broeder Wops de wesp.* Uncle Remus!
Butterfly seed a wops. Hans, not following, cries for help.
O me O my! moan the butterfly, didn't I used to be a member of Congress could orate like thunder and lightning? Jantje knuckled his hair, turned in his tracks, and came up with *Didn't I in the Ridderzaal talk like a silver waterfall?* Hans stared at him in unbelieving admiration.

Good show, said Sweetbrier to a smug Jantje, but too clever, my dear fellow, too clever by half, and it's not Uncle Remus. *A colonel of the regiment with my monument downtown, a man who when he went out, the street raised its hat.*

               Resigned comic disgust from Hans, chin on fist, out of it altogether. I did it into *klomp* Dutch for him, and got a *golly am I dumb* squinch and a grateful *kusshandje.* Jan thumbed his nose at him.

                               Now would you look at me, Sweetbrier went on, *a bug! But you, Wops, was a mule. Don't matter what we* was, Wops come back with, *it's what we* is.

                          Explain it! Explain it! Hansje wailed, beating Jan on the shoulders with his fists. Sweetbrier had found another, reading with the lens unseated from his broken spectacles.

    Crow lit on sheep's back. Sheep walked on, giving Crow a ride.

                                        Jan translated directly into Hansje's ear, his arms around his neck. *Hateful old bird! Sheep got up the gumption to say. Was I a dog and you lit on my back, I'd snap you into a bunch of feathers and cat's meat. To which Crow says: If I didn't know who to pick on, Sheep Old Boy, would I have celebrated my birthday of one hundred years old?*

•

Hans and Jan splashing highkneed from the sea, where Sweetbrier and I had been keeping an eye on them. They have been very good about their *konijnge-tand bevrijding,* containing it in the bedroll at night. We have all worn *zwem-bad slipjen* on the beach, out of deference to Sweetbrier, God knows why, some Dutch sense of British propriety, and I might have known that Jan's courageous zeal to be unconventional and revolutionary would move toward its moment. I say! said Sweetbrier, were we supposed to see that? Which was Jan pulling down Hans' swimslip and kissing his tummy. And Hans pulling down Jans' swimslip and kissing first his navel and then his smattering of pubic hair. Naked, they whacked water from their *slipjen,* making glittering arcs, and snapped them at each other until Jan, his shoulder stung, cried quits. I think, I said, we were supposed to see. They're rather full of themselves. Are they now? It was Hans, when they came and flopped beside us, who said, and in English, sex be wonderful.

•

Melnikov's Green City comes from Jules Verne, who was raised on a river island and had the bargeman's sense of an isolation enviably private but which could nevertheless observe its surroundings. And Melnikov's childhood was spent in a forest outside Moscow, a deep green silence of a childhood.

·

In the dissonances and divergent energies disrupting the harmonic dance of the phalanx Fourier finds his sociology, the debate between the ill-fitting shoe and the foot that must wear it. Go barefoot, get a better shoe, abide the discomfort. Sweetbrier opposes the human, which he defines as reciprocated good will, to money, or the systematic exploitation of desire. The great difference of the Harmony will be a substitution of faith in good will for the Capitalist assumption that all exchanges are of something for money. Once people walked in the gardens at Giverny, and around the lily pond, because they were friends of Monet. Now they walk in those gardens by paying a bank, ultimately, for the privilege. In the Harmony, we will walk in those gardens when through good will and love we've earned the welcome to walk in those gardens. That is, Sweetbrier sees Harmonian space in a primitive way. Everywhere is sanctum, being there is a rite. What kind of rite? Social courtesy bred from justice and a poetic configuration of the world.

·

Chinstrap penguin, Jantje hoots at Hans, and reindeer together! South Georgia, says Hans as cool as you please.

Buffon's gazelle

and the moustac monkey!

Cameroun.

Galago, potto, and colobe d'Oustallet!

Republic Centrafrikaans.

Terriers, thistles, grouse!

Schotland.

·

Kleuters en kinderen in a wading pool on the roof garden of Corbusier's Unité in Marseilles naked and skinny except for some in sagging *cache-sexes*, though there's one boy with a mist of early pubic hair, easy thicklashed eyes, brown as a brick, his spout straight out. Wholly *fourieriste*, Corbusier's Unité, Sweetbrier says. The mode is urban rather than rural. The shops inside, on indoor streets, took awhile to catch on, French businessmen being wary and unimaginative, but they're working quite well now.

·

Time dissolved? O yes, says Sweetbrier, we've done that, too. That's why I wanted to talk with you. This bloody hateful century. It has made us all mean, vulgar, discontinuous. Nothing can be expected from anything except that some scoundrel will find a way to suck money from it.

•

Jan, his long maizesilk hair batched out around the high collar of his sweater, talks happily with Sweetbrier about his friendship with Hans. It is very beautiful, he says, and not at all sneaky. He tells of two older boys at his school, popular and good-looking both of them, who are in love with each other. One of them has a girlfriend, and sleeps with her a lots, and sleeps with his friend, too, when he can. It was a talk with these two that emboldened Jan. They showed him how, Hans put in.

6 FRUCTIDOR

Rilkean angels, complex essences in a wind of light, fibrous with articulate memories, accidental events enriched into significance, a cherished smile, a long afternoon, a concupiscent dream, disappointments salvaged by courage, are the quiring that Fourier saw as a destiny of attractions. They are harmonies of essences. They are kin to us. They are messengers in that the composite knows how to appropriate the random, knows what to do with lost time, with the found moment, with a memory of apples on an autumn afternoon, of pears eaten at a kitchen table, longing in our eyes.

•

Rosa Bonheur's sister Juliette married Hippolyte Peyrol, their stepmother's son by her first marriage.

•

Amsterdam by evening, Sweetbrier seen off, Jan and Hans delivered to Bruno and Kaatje. Jan, *tout nu*, gave Sweetbrier a hug while he was in his pyjamas our last morning on the island, and Hans kissed him on the nose. Called Sander and Grietje, who asked me over. An enormous painting well underway. I tell them, so as to think no more about it, that I'll see if we can buy the house. O but we know we can! they say together. We've checked it all out. *Zo.*

•

Titian's blond Turin on the brown Po turned into the dream cities of *i metafisici* before Nietzsche's eyes. Through the geometric autumnal light of the arcades, citron and blue, he paced in his student overcoat, his every step reported by agents to King Umberto and the Pope. *Carmen* every night, ice cream and coffee while reading the *Journal des Débats* long melancholy afternoons. Here Teuton nostalgia for the classical fused with the new century only a decade away. Absence and presence pass through each other here like treble through bass. The agon is between Bizet and Wagner, between the Italian guitar and German horn. *The sidewalks,* he wrote dear Peter Gast, *are serious, and the patrician architecture of such a dignity that no silly suburbs have dared face them with bourgeois impudence. And yet this philosophical city is gaily all yellow and reddish brown.* And when Nietzsche strolls into a café and takes a chair at a table, someone says, *eccolo!* that man is a German officer, a professor with a degree. Give him the *Journal des Débats* to read. His thought is lectured on in Danimarca by Georg Brandes. People stop each other on the streets of New York to discuss his books. The yellowhaired youth of Norway and Sweden have thrown their Bibles away and parade through town with locked arms, shouting *Nietzsche! Nietzsche! Nietzsche!*

•

France is my watchlight,
England is my tree,
Spain is my city wall,
My sword is Italy.

Ireland's my strong arm,
Germany my word,
Ohio is my heart's love,
And prophecy my Lord.

Build me a high house,
Angels at the eaves.
Grow me an apple tree
With a thousand silver leaves.

Grow me a pear tree,
A daughter of the sun.
Put yellow pears upon it
And bless them every one.

•

When we clasp our hands, the Shaker ordinances specify, our right thumbs and fingers should be above our left, as uniformity is comely.

•

Angel sitting in a Shaker chair. Bovid eyes, bonnet with long ribbons tied under chin, dulcimer with bow, red apron rich in pockets over blue dress, feathers as neat on the wings as scales on a fish. *Be certain*, it says, *of the light*.

7 FRUCTIDOR

Letter out of the blue from one Godfried Strodekker, chairman of the Nederlands Student en Arbeiterverbond voor Pedofilie. Admires my work on Fourier, the essays on sensuality, and my critique in general of industrial capitalist society. Hopes I may be in sympathy with what his group feels they have an ethical and moral responsibility to carry out as a social reform. Indeed, an imperative. That children are deprived of erotic affection and a fully sensual life is an injustice too long imposed by puritanical prejudices, ignorance, and the narrowness of bourgeois propriety. Kindred organizations in Denmark, Germany, and Sweden have made fair progress and have aroused great curiosity and interest as well as, needless to say, violent opposition largely hysterical. Invites me to a steering committee coffee on Wednesday next, to meet the leaders of the group, all of whom would feel greatly honored by my attending. Why do I imagine a balding scoutmaster with halitosis and eyes too wide open?

•

Pinecone, drachma, snailshell. My Rietveld table, my Spartan bed, my books and notebooks, clothes. Moving into Florishuis, as Grietje has named it already, will be simplicity itself. Not quite three trips of a wheelbarrow through Amsterdam streets, but close enough. Aside from paintings and the easel, Sander can carry all his possessions in one armload. Grietje, two suitcases.

•

Kaatje, of Hansje's friend Jan Sinaasappel. He is impossibly *heerlijk*. He seems to know everything about animals and botany, postage stamps, the solar system, and *God weet wat*. He sits and discusses continental drift with Bruno, who says that for two cents he would steal him from the Sinaasappelen. Kaatje protests that she would die rather than snoop in Hansje's or Saartje's room, but when things are left in full view, they're there, *ja*? Well, suddenly there are *fisiek* and *erotisch* magazines in several languages, with photographs and drawings of a very advanced kind. They're Jan's, else Hansje has snitched them from newsstands, which she rules out. But she has met Hilda and Gregorius Sinaasappel and all is as clear as daylight. Gregorius, a good sort if chuckleheaded, is some kind of museum curator, philologist, and scholar, and Hilda is a warmly messy tweedy toothy woman into charities, flowers, ecology, sociology, and what not. She said right off that her Jan and my Hansje seem to have bonded in a charming friendship. She and Gregorius had allowed Jan and Jenny to explore each other's sexuality rather early on. Jan was now going through a phase of erotic imaginativeness which she and Gregorius were allowing to develop as it would. At home things were little short of incestuous, and she gathered that Jan and Hansje were cultivating a nicely sensual intimacy. She said all of this with lots of overlapping teeth and flashing intellectual glasses. So Kaatje feels the challenge to be equally liberal.

•

The animal that persists so stubbornly in portraits and family groups, genre scenes and townscapes as an accent or punctuation, descends from Jerome's lion, itself a continuation of Orpheus with animals. Orion and his dog would be a beginning, or any animal bonded loyally to a human master. The interesting thing is that thereafter the portraitist feels the structural need to include a casual animal: it is part of the syntax. The animal is always low in the picture space, an iota subscript, usually minding its own business. Jerome's lion sleeps. This symbol of tame domesticity, as taken for granted as the artist's signature or traditional props (classical column, drapery, a glimpse of landscape) sometimes enters the painter's alertness, as in Velazquez's *Las Meninas*, where the dog is being prodded by a playful child. Picasso, in his variations, kept putting his dachshund Lump in place of the royal hound. What does it mean when the animal isn't there?

•

The figures in Seurat's *Bathers, Asnières* might be characters in a Maupassant novel. The *Grande Jatte*, Proust.

8 FRUCTIDOR
Modern karakter en openhartigheid. With Bruno and Hans in the park, a splendid afternoon, rows of sunbathers, an arterial flow of tourists, the benches occupied by nurses, regulars from the neighborhood gossiping, and those types you only see in parks who seem to range from well-appointed business-

men looking over the top of newspapers to frayed old parties having a social hour alone in the public cordiality of civic leisure. Dame Partlet and her boon-sister sandbagged in on their bench by outsized purses and Bijenkorf sacks just ahead of us were busily ignoring the teenagers not three meters away naked, enlaced, and kissing as if they never meant to quit. That's fun, Hans remarked. You don't know the half of it, Bruno said. *Some* of it, Hans said.

•

Darwin's Notebook N. As forms change, so must idea of beauty. Surely we have taste naturally: all has not been acquired by education. Pleasure in the beautiful, distinct from sexual beauty, is acquired taste.

•

Quoi de plus moral que les hollandais, dans leurs pays? The question is Fourier's (v.iv), probably without a smile.

•

We agree to a community of shared work to ensure that work which only each of us can do will be done in peace. We will all be each other's servants, as needed. The important thing, says Grietje, is that we love each other. She and Sander love each other in defiance of custom, law, and biology. Because, she says, Sander is retarded in all the social graces, and is moreover about ten years old. His painting is a miraculous reversion to childhood, just when he was about to grow up. Saved in time! And with it, the passion for drawing. Perhaps, she reconsiders, not a reversion at all, but being fixed in midchildhood. A triumphant return to where he was before he got lost trying to grow up. He will never massacre innocent people or starve the hardworking. He will simply paint pictures and raise idiot sons and daughters. We'll fuck ourselves into idiocy, so's to be like the children. We will love Adriaan however he wants to be loved. He won't tell us, Sander says. He likes me, he likes you. He likes Kaatje and Bruno. He made Hansje on Kaatje, and Bruno hugs him as lovingly as I do. But he and Bruno can talk, O how they talk, geometry and philosophy. Me, I don't have any way to express how I like people except with my body. Sex, says Grietje, is everything, or it is nothing.

•

Of the Schröder-Schräderhuis Grietje says there are no sides to the sides of things. In Florishuis the mad Theosophical designs of Malevich and the red squares and blue slats and white boxes quit tumbling about, as they do in a

Kandinsky. In the art books a De Stijl room smells of fresh paint, sawn wood, and glue, but our rooms must smell of coffee, washed boys, Adriaan's pipe, toast, linseed oil, turps, and potato soup.

•

Gossie mijne! said Hansje at the door, peeping around, his hair tussled into a jumble. It's Ome Adriaan, he said for someone behind him to hear. *Gode zij dank*, came Saartje's voice. And Jan's *Ha die Adriaan!* Hansje in full view wore a recklessly assumed pair of underpants with Sinaasappel J Kastje 27 stencilled along the waistband and an inconvenient salience inside. Hoisted him and smooched his navel, getting a rib-squeezing hug of legs around my thorax. I'll go away, I said, hiding my face in his midriff, I won't even look, if I've trod on a scandalous romp. But Bruno did invite me over, and I'm not early. Whereupon a stitchless Saartje climbed my right elbow, lightly as a monkey, and holding onto my and Hansje's necks, straddled my shoulder. *Ho!* whooped Jan, climbing the other side. They squealed, I groaned. With a confident wiggle Jan got astride my left shoulder and kissed Saartje crisply. By turning my head in the crush I could kiss three tummies, as I did, getting a *hei!* from Jan, *oof!* from Hans, and *fijn!* from Saartje. Again! said Hans. *O ja!* said Saartje, we all like it. Unbespadgered—they all jumped down backwards on the chanted count of three—I sprawled crumpled on the couch. They sat leaning against each other on the floor at my feet. Jan had pulled on short but unzipped pants. We were experimenting, he said brightly. Mijnheer Keirinckx told Hansje that his technique in jacking off is greeny, too quick, and altogether incompetent. He said, Hansje chimed in with a matey grin, that I do it like an urchin whipping off in an alley. He says I ought to take my time, get it feeling good, and keep it feeling good for as long as I can before skeeting. Girls, Saartje said, can go on and on. Jan stuck out his tongue at her. This generation! I sighed, for their amusement. They like to be reminded of their privileged modernity.

•

Ongelofelijk, said Bruno, but this afternoon I saw a *tiener* and his girl doing it in the park, all their clothes enlisted as a cushion for her behind. Several of their pals were telling a policeman not to have an evil mind, and not to suppress *joie de vivre* with tiresome statutes written by *Calvinistischen* in the days of Rembrandt. Jan had a *why not?* look on his face, Saartje and Hans grins that they meant to be knowing. Adriaan and I, Bruno said, remember when it was the last word in daring to be bare-assed on the beach. Hansje had something to say about this, but swallowed it. Jan, who had listened with concerned eyes when Bruno told about the lovers in the park, was not to be deterred. How long, he asked, is long? His dubious upper lip arched over chisely teeth. You're going to say it depends. Ask for information and you always get *it depends* for an answer. Saartje called him impolite and a grump. I complained that I wasn't being given a chance to answer. So how long? Hansje asked. Sander Floris, I said (and Bruno looked relieved), for whom you've modeled, was an adolescent when I took him under my wing. Still is, said Bruno. He'd had a disturbed childhood and was in and out of considerable trouble before he discovered that he was an artist of great talent. In getting turned around right, he backtracked, so to speak, through a misspent adolescence, and lived it over again, his mind a veritable sun of alpha waves. I gave statistics for Sander's stamina. Jan whistled. Bruno looked smug. Hans said, *O wow.*

•

Fourier's chaste children were an invention of his age, a moral injunction of middle-class propriety. In medieval schools you could have seen little boys with rumpround taffy hair hiking up their smocks between grammar and noontide oatcakes, as it may be, to jiggle their stipes stiff and springy, the tips of their tongues like rose petals between their teeth. The best moralists said that such fleshly play was inevitable in children descended from Adam, and was not to be considered any more serious than giggling at Mass or vagueness in one's grasp of the catechism. And you would have seen older, quadrivial youngsters with codpieces untied vying with each other in spattering the stable walls. The great doctor Gabrielus Fallopius accounted it useful, moreover, in lengthening the member and preparing it for its mature use in propagating the species.

•

Fourier's harmony is designed to cause dissonances, or divergent energies, which is the subject of its constant watchfulness. Human nature is at all times both civilized and uncivilized. To keep it from feeding on the weakness of others, of using others' despair as an advantage, there must be a common justice easily available. But first there must be the sense that we can agree what common justice is.

•

Mimi personati in the park, a girl in jeans and red shirt with a large United States flag wrapped around her, as toga or cape, a boy barefoot in jeans and

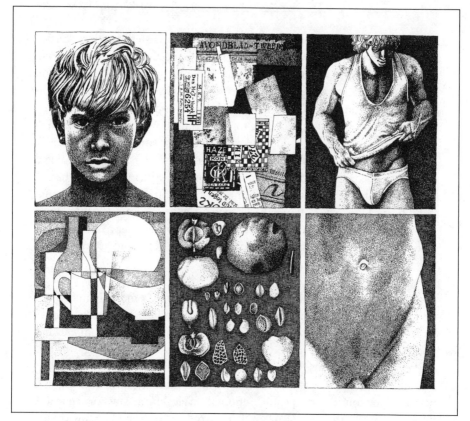

unbuttoned tattersall vest over a naked torso, and another boy hooded and
cloaked in a large tricolor of the Netherlands. All wore masks in the style of
Art Deco shopwindow mannikins, blank of eye and inanely serene of mouth.
The girl did the Standbeeld van Vrijheid that became, with a snap of her
fingers and handclaps in jazz rhythm from the boys, a seductive dance. Jan
interpreted: imperialism giving the glad eye to the sheepwitted European _bur-
gerklasse_. The boy in the tattersall vest with histrionic boasts of his masculin-
ity, did a forward roll, and waltzed with American Flag. Dutch Flag took a
fetal position. _Onzinnig!_ was the stout remark of a doublechinned woman,
who then skewered Jan in his scantling _slipje_ with a stare of _schandaal_, and
looked daggers at me. Got one! Jan whispered, squeezing my hand. That the
game, _burgerschrik_? He butted my arm for reply.

•

We staked a territory in the shoal of sunbathers. Hansje shimmied out of his
jeans, Jan unslung his _poche_ with a downslide of thumbs. _Zo._ The voice used
for crowded open places is like no other. It finds the ears it wants. Ome Adriaan is _schuw_, Hansje teases, and is not about to go natural here as he does
on his island.

•

Tsunami VI, Grand Hordes of the Vincent Willem van Goghfalanx, przhev-
alski mounted, _een vloedgolf van zaad_ their motto. The hetman is eighteen,
beamshouldered, hair a hummock of brassy silk sprucely swirled and trimly
edged. He wears mulberry linen Chinese cavalry boots, a blue vest rich in
badges and insignia patches open to the navel, white briefs scorched nutbrown
in the pod. His merit badges are a golden scallop for fucking daily since fifteen, a brace of acorns for Spartan Friendships with agemates, chrysanthe-
mum with leaf cluster for friendships both celadonian and erotic with elders,
crossed Cupid's bow and arrow for friendship with minors, silver crotchet for
his piano sonata in B Flat, bronze ladle for a potato and leek soup made for
the Sodality of Poets and Geographers on Founder's Day, panpipe in walnut
for his _Frisian Eclogues_, Olympic medals for swimming, the javelin, running,
and the pole vault, enamel palette for second prize in landscape painting, red
sunburst for charm in conversation, phallus erectus with ejaculum jettant for
a Midsummers Day when he offered as an exercise in Composite Harmonics
a display of squash and beans at the early market after waking and kissing all
sixty striplings of the Little Bands and Hordes attached to his comitatus,
mouth, bellybutton, and genitals, captaining his soccer team in a match after

reveille, sitting with the Council at its weekly session, playing the clarinet in an afternoon concert, chairing the Philosophy Club, preparing a dinner for friends, and six exploits of gallantry, the first with Belinda of his whirlwind before the soccer match, classical tumble with full foreplay, throbbing deep orgasm, and silly talk afterwards, kisses, hugs, and gossip, the second with Carolus before the Council meeting, a dusty and wiggly *soixante-neuf* under a laurel bush in the Parc Floral, the third with Daisy, who was fond of blonde teenaged girls with athletic interests but who had a weakness for strapping young men like our captain from time to time, a frolic in a bed frilled with lace and chintz, the foreplay longer and more elaborate than the coupling, eighteen orgasms by finger and tongue but one only while being tupped, the fourth with Erasmus, a corporal with carroty hair, a spray of freckles across his face, capacious thorax, terse waist, a top-heavy dick, and rowdy smile, after the concert at the barracks of the Sparticate redolent of armpit, sperm, and socks, swimming pool and wrestling floor, the fifth with Clémentine after the Philosophy Club, a *jouvencelle* with beautiful eyes and high breasts, an accomplished sensualist whose style in bed was a topic for long quaggarides, one lover praising her nimble rhythms, another her versatility, another her wit and generosity, the sixth and last, a valiant harmonian *coup de maître* with a faunlet named Rutger, longflanked, big-eared and ten, who had declared his fancy through Corporal Erasmus, who got the consent of the Directorate of Good Taste, which issued its indulgence after considering that Rutger had seduced his every agemate, both Band and Horde, outjacked every challenger in duration and repetition, and was inordinately pretty, a pairing in barracks, with onlookers invited by Rutger.

9 FRUCTIDOR

We agree to an isonomy of continuous visual field for the second floor, and *oningehouden en onbeperkt* tactility and affection. Grietje writes this in crayon on a postersize card, different color for each word. There are indeed no doors to shut between the two bedroom spaces at each end of the long center room. Shall we have Bruno remove these two partial walls? Not everybody's us, Sander says. We've promised the Liberated Badgers a cozy corner that's always theirs. Ask them, Grietje says. Unrestricted is unrestricted, say I. The cabin has no divisions of space: we have inhabited that territory. We will have five levels: roof garden and sundeck, Sander's studio, our bedroom in its unboundaried three parts, Adriaan's studio and library, and the kitchen below.

•

Imagination chilled by apprehension, apprehension relaxed by imagination.

•

Admire the angle of his fly, says Sander of a nubbinnosed sprout of a Swede in *De Volkskrant* hugging his sweetly dippy sister and their croodling *peuter* on the occasion of their marriage by a liberal and practical judge, and the glimpse of zipper at the prod. We're not, says Grietje, moving to Sweden. So they sunbathe naked and marry brother and sister. They're also buttermilk-fed lunks and bores and alcoholics and walk around bumping into things, chronically depressed. What's worse, they sing folksongs.

10 FRUCTIDOR

To Strodekker's house in Uilenbos. I had fixed him in my mind as a Weimar intellectual in his mid thirties, abundant dark brown hair brushed straight back, an enthusiast and crank under the eye of the ss for deportation. Check shirt, grey sweater, narrow blue slacks, good shoes, eyes too wide open. He was, instead, a younger man, early thirties, sunbrowned olive umber, eyelashes sooty black and seemingly inked by Modigliani around large aniline blue eyes. Coal-black hair in a boyish cut. The face of an Etruscan god of adolescence, or Balkan military hero whose death devastates a whole population and gives rise to a hundred-stanza ballad. Eyes *are* too wide open, but in idealistic good humor rather than fanaticism. Shook my hand with both of his at the door. In a room with many glass doors looking out onto a garden enclosed by a high brick wall he introduced me first of all to his sons Nils 13 and Tobias 11, charmers both. Nils sunripened at beaches, in cocky short blue pants, rugger shirt, his father's black hair saucily run wild and ruffled, eyes amiable, witty, and gentle. Tobias in snug kneelength nautical pants, white middy, full head of amber-brown hair, waggish smile, chipper dimples. They shook hands, both, nothing shy. Dokter Roelof Groenvink, psychiatrist at the Gemeentekliniek for disturbed children. Warm handshake, effusive greeting. Olaf, about eighteen, autochthonously Danish, blond hair in eyes, full-lipped, flat-cheeked, in jeans and pullover with an Art Deco decal, the Gemini twins encircled by the words *Paedofil Frihedskaemper*, a wzw button on the slope of a hummocked pectoral. Spoke to me in English, saying it was an honor to meet me. Gymnast? I asked, feeling free in such company to shape in the air the contours of his narrow hips and wide shoulders. O *ja*, he said, and weights and swimming. A young printer named Joris Oudveld with black close-cropped curls like a sheep growing back nicely after being shorn, stockier but with as wrought a physique as Olaf, the grace of a soccer wing in his walk. Elsa Boonwijn, smartly feminine, good legs, Athena's nose, fingernails trimmed round and short. Welcome, she said with a laugh, to the most revolutionary group in all the Netherlands. A bearded photographer with an eagle's nose, thirtyish, English cap on the back of his head, leather jacket, grundgy jeans, Ulric Kuller by name, German, from Düsseldorf.

•

Strodekker a history and geography master at the Conrad Busken Huet-school, *bijzondere*. Coffee handed around, pleasantries exchanged in so congenial a room, Master Tobias, with compliant if ironic good nature, stood with shuffling patience while his father stripped him mothernaked, brown as a gingersnap, his *suikerpot knippen* topping his elvish slenderness in the lively flesh as that of the museum copy of a Pommier Chaillot boy in a corner of the room, the Despiau adolescent in another. They had, Strodekker said, been photographing Tobias in the garden with Olaf and Nils, and that we ought to keep him around *au naturel* to be, as it were, our presiding daimon. Blinking in acknowledgment of his daimon's status, whatever the fuck, his scrooged shoulders said, that might be, Tobias palmed two cookies and an orange slice, and went to sit astride Olaf's thigh and to arch his back against Olaf's hand kneading his back.

•

Strodekker, nodding to Nils that yes, he could be excused to go out, outlined their goals, distinguishing factional disagreements with similar organizations. What freedoms, and to what extent, were morally due the young and the very young. He himself had taken up the movement, he and Dokter Groenvink, because of the infuriatingly repressive restraints imposed on children forbidden any sensuality whatsoever. Pamphlets, lectures, films, study groups with parents and teachers. Psychological studies, theories, arguments. Great strides, of course, since the war, and astounding progress since the last century, especially in the Netherlands and Scandinavia, but still everything yet to do. In Germany there's a squabble between those who go no further than an early acceptance of our sexual nature and the radicals who want to include children in the full spectrum of sexuality, ardently, passionately, and, as they say with German wit, below the belt. A grin from Tobias. La Boonwijn spoke of sensitivity, of the love of which children are so capable, of honesty, of beautiful friendships between boys, and between girls, of smooth rather than traumatic transitions from childhood to adolescence, as in Polynesia. Groenvink spoke of security, reciprocity, sophistication, communication, moral awareness, giving and taking, erotic sophistication. Olaf, rather ostentatiously caressing Tobias, who was making a joke of caressing back, explained the vast leap ahead of the Danes, clubhouses, outings, camping, magazines, a newspaper, articles in the regular press, manuals, posters, buttons. Films to show to interested groups. He parked Tobias in Oudveld's lap and, limping cautiously to make fun of the prominent ridge across his groin, fetched me a portfolio of brochures, clippings, posters, some cranky, some done with taste, all bold. Oudveld, addressing me as professor, and stammering, said that he was the radical of the lot, as well as the proletarian, and further felt that any present, always excepting Tobias the Red here, whose peter he squeezed, and that regardless of the humanity of it all, the struggle of the oppressed against bigotry, the nasty superstitions of the bourgeoisie in their arrogant ignorance and stupid propriety, we must gross out the meanminded prigs with the basic fact that kids are, *goddank*, sexy. He stammered dreadfully, and blushed, and looked pleadingly for understanding. His hand forgot Tobias, who guided it back. Professor van Hovendaal, he plunged on, is probably thinking of the *Anthology* of the Greeks, and Else of *het Ideaal*, and Roelof of *mens sana in corpore sano*, and Godfried of nobly affectionate boys and girls, but for the kids it's whether they're in a moral concentration camp or free to love and be loved. Right ho, said Tobias, in English. More talk, more theorizing. The most I hope I agreed to is to address their group on Fourier's blueprints for childhood in the New Harmony. Warm gratitude, and prompted by Olaf, a kiss on the corner of the mouth from Master Tobias, whom I picked up and kissed on the navel, for good measure. Joris Oudveld left with me, anxious to talk.

•

A cap, like Lenin's, the tread of a pard. He wanted me to know, Joris Oudveld, that he believes in truth, social justice, and beauty. He said *schoonheid* with a stutter, and after a quick questioning look. He has, he wanted me to know, an extensive paperback library, works out in a gym, plays on the company soccer team, and is an admirer of the finer sensibilities. Is trying to teach himself to appreciate classical music, has a room of his own, is treasurer of his workers' solidarity. Loves nature, in which he takes meditative and appreciative walks when he can. Did I know that was Lenin's ideal for the worker? To appreciate nature, like a poet. Longs to be able to speak correctly. Would I help him, some? He doesn't waste his time, not him. Others, lacking idealism, might squander their leisure time mindlessly, not him. Thought Bertolucci's *1900* the best film ever made, and had I seen the Danish film *Du Er Ikke Alene*? The rich make him furious, ill, out of all patience. Exploit is all they can do. He loved going to Strodekker's, the most cultivated and civilized home he'd ever been in. His whole life had changed, and this recently, since he'd joined the Cause, a truly revolutionary group, didn't I think? The barricades of liberty! He'll be nineteen his next birthday. This was only his second time at Strodekker's. Hoped he hadn't overstepped himself in his remarks or in squeezing Tobias' wizzle, the little sexpot. Olaf he'd met only today. He'll be showing films. Would I come see them?

11 FRUCTIDOR

A naked man on a naked horse is a very fine spectacle. I had no idea how well the two animals suited each other. As the peons were galloping about they reminded me of the Elgin marbles. Darwin's notebooks, Argentina 1833.

•

Sander, the agent of chaos, is suddenly a fanatic in ordering both time and space. He and Grietje draw plans of every room. His studio is to be like Klee's, like Mondriaan's, like Corbusier's. Back to the Shakers! Gerrit Rietveld! Our time is to be in segments we can control: meals at regular times, exercise, walks, conversations. Only work and love are to be without form, to be initiated and prolonged by inspiration.

•

Kaatje, dear soul, it is not that the past can't be changed. It will not cease changing. How I have sat in the island's meadow this summer, watching dancing gnats, butterflies with winking wings, and, thrilled to the quick, two thumbsized black-eyed fieldmice fucking, high summer holding its finest light and sturdiest green, and parted your thighs again, and put my animal soul deep into you to find my human soul again. Your eyes know what's in my inwardness, and no one else knows. That is our lovely secret.

•

Space, its flow in a house. Its territorial character, a metaphor of freedom, security, privacy. Windows are for the French to look out of, for the Dutch to look in, for Italians to talk through. Sander howls that he grew up in houses with doors closed, too many walls. He wants to see in all directions.

•

Don't you love me? he says. Now that I have Grietje to love, like to idiotic foolish happiness, I know that I love you, too. I'm not afraid of that. I've loved you, I think, from the time you couldn't be bothered to think of me as raised wrong, a headache to good old Dokter Tomas, a disgrace to my parents. Nothing to do with me, you said cheerfully. You wanted boards sawn and sawn straight, and treated, O God, with creosote. It was days before you parted with so much as a grump of approval. What a bastard, I told myself, but a bastard who knows what he wants, and one who doesn't meddle into my fucked-up past. You showed me how to drive a nail and to chisel and to sink a screw and bore true with the brace and bit. You muttered in strange languages, Greek I think, and swore in German and English. I'd never met anybody like you at all. You hurt my feelings. But in making me respect a straight line, a nail placed just right, things squared away, neat, you put me back together. We built a cabin that summer, and we built one Sander.

·

Sander to make us a copy of Gerald Murphy's *Wasp and Pear* (1929) for the living-room wall. Ozenfant in the spirit of De Stijl, and wonderfully by an Irish-American painting in France.

·

Grietje for all her rhetoric of liberation and Bohemian airs has a *huisvrouw*'s animosity toward motes and microbes. She says that although I undoubtedly plucked Sander from the gutter and found the gold beneath the grime, I deserve a statue in the park for making him hang up his clothes, put the towel on the rack, and change his underwear before it looks like a *Honderdjarenoorlog* fieldkitchen dishcloth.

·

The greatest achievement of civilization may be detaching the individual from culture to function as a contemplative and creative force. Civilization ought to ensure freedom, and culture security. To be there when wanted, to be ground and a nourishment, but not a hindrance, as both have proved to be. This balance is the most difficult, most delicate of cultural structures. By such detachments we got Darwin, Balzac, Beethoven. Many interesting private people. People who do not exploit, who are not parasites.

·

Any architect reading Fourier, as Sweetbrier observes, sees that he anticipated all our concerns, or what should be our concerns: space as congenial as a grove of trees, the right space for work. Nothing like the department store, hotel, gymnasium, or apartment house had evolved by his time. The private room had to wait for chimney, fireplace, and stove to proliferate from the center of the house, and for glass panes to windows. Fourier would approve of the military encampment, the tent city, becoming the youth hostel of today. He would have liked the bicycle and would have put the bands and hordes on

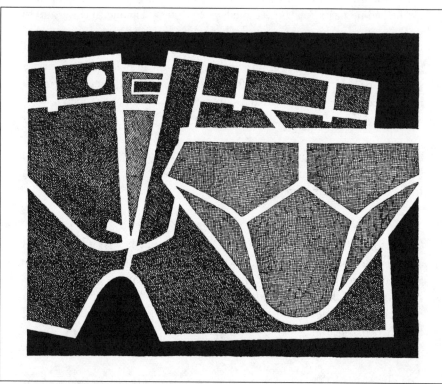

them. But the industrial revolution, which in a sense his phalansteries would have prevented, was the end of his hopes. It was humanity moving into a new serfdom to the machine and to the monotony of treadmill regularity that he was calling to in his books, without knowing what he was warning them away from. He was inviting us back onto the land, bringing the city with us in small neighborhoods, to a future of eccentric, local, imaginative city-farms incapable of warfare and intent on being rich in the necessities, opulently luxurious in the passions, in the arts, in civilization, just when mankind was being drawn into the slums of cities and the hell of factories. The machine, which thrives best on war, claimed them as its vassals. Ned Ludd had been right. Butler had been right.

•

The machine cannot produce without overproducing. It gluts its market. To force this excess onto the market, Capitalism began eating itself, like a hyena its own bowels when it is wounded. If the investors in a business think there's a market for quaggahide, they kill every living quagga. Because (and here is where Fourier began to think) it is not gloves from quaggahide that interest the industrialist, but money. Capitalism recognizes two values only: money, and what can be sold for money.

12 FRUCTIDOR
Yellow pear, red apple. Tante Magda wrapped green pears in twists of newspaper and put them in the bottom drawer of her wardrobe until they were mellow. We ate them on autumn evenings.

•

The apple is a kind of solid rose.

•

Screening of Olaf's propaganda films at Strodekker's. *Hemeltje.* Joris called in the afternoon, asked if I planned to go, and suggested that he drop by after work. Perhaps we could grab a bite of dinner and go out together.
                                                                    He turned up in the Lenin cap, black fisherman's sweater, work trousers, for all of which he apologized (this Radical Socialist), holding up a shopping bag of what he said were his evening duds. *Jandorie!* he sang of Sander's painting of Hansje wearing only a bandana around his neck. *Mijn petekind*, I said. *Boffer!* As he admired other paintings, books, furniture, I explained the boxes of things, and that I was moving to a whole house which I'd bought, where I'm to live with the painter of Hans' portrait, and his sister.
                                                                    Strodekker, he said, I thought was cultivated, but *this*! All these books. He admitted to vast curiosity about where I lived, how I lived, chattering and stuttering about everything he saw, darting from one thing to another, running his fingers down the backs of books, reading titles aloud. The more he talked and paced, the more he stuttered. I suggested a drink to calm him down. Doesn't touch the stuff, but would join me in a sip. Can't figure you out at all, he said with a big grin. Nor I you, I said with I hope as affable a grin. You came to our committee coffee, he said, the most radical group in Holland, and didn't bat an eyelash. Talk about cool!
                                                                    He began a running self-critique of the kind the selfmade bore you

with, but piquant enough. That the NSAP had shuffled his life and reorganized the parts. He felt new, fresh, clear-headed. He was different from his fellow workers at the printshop, not only in lusting for his own gender, but in being a reader and a thinker. He was an optimist. He was well on the way to understanding the finer things. He'd seen an ad in the magazine *Zuigen*, had written, had been invited to meet Strodekker and his group. *Goddank!* he said, slapping both thighs. You must realize, he said, looking at me so earnestly that his head turned sideways, the silly wonder of talking for the first time with an educated man about *brooddronkenheid*, a hankering to hug gossoons, about social justice, boyish charm, biological imperatives, and even the laidback lift of a throbbing good hourlong wank. Strodekker was over Joris' head in lots of things, but what counted was the man's plain honesty, his easy friendliness, ja?

Soup and sandwiches here, a happy idea that pleased Joris immensely. He jumped at the offer of a shower before changing for the films. It is common among the shy to plunge into overconfidence when they've overcome reticence, and Joris, toweling, asked me to check out, as he said, his build, which is splendid, and to note, as I already had, that he was hung by Mother Nature when she had cock on her mind. He's filled out a bit, Joris said, dangling it out of plumb, because he knows we're going to see towheaded cubs with freckles.

His dress clothes were not all that different form his work clothes: soft clean faded snug jeans, plaid cotton shirt, the fisherman's sweater, the cap. Smile even friendlier.

•

The films. Olaf made a stumbling talk about the Cause in Denmark, picking himself out of syntactical wrecks with stunning blushes. Strodekker straightened a phrase or two. First film, *Hvalpetid*, voice-over in Danish, began with a close-up of a *nimflijk* girl, thirteenish, a secret in her eyes and lips puckered to tease us with it. I thought of acting lessons and aspiring directors. Then a boy in fuller close-up, snubnose, serious longlashed eyes, lips parted in amused amenability. Camerawork adroitly modern in abrupt transitions and an elliptical grammar of images. Boy and girl in school togs, books overshoulder in satchels, skipping along a path in a park. They stop, look into each other's eyes, laugh, kiss. Kiss on sunroom wicker chaise longue, well-appointed middle-class household. Kiss on swimmingpool edge, girl topless, breasts in their springtime, her *slipje* a white triangle held on by a string. The boy's as cursory. Accelerated sequence of the two undressing fast, fingers scurrying, shirt and blouse tossed aside, shoelaces undone in a flurry of flickers. This intercut with slow motion: as if the afternoon light in which they undressed were as dense as water, a sock drawn off with a dreamy sluggishness, panties languidly hauled down. Close-up of lips nearing to kiss in lyric delay. Exploded by a frantic speeding up in which every stitch is snatched off and they collapse entwined into a bouncing jumble of chintz pillows. Followed by the two playing tennis, bicycling, holding hands in a museum interspersed with shots of his hand on the crotch of her panties, the two reclined nose to nose, his finger quiddling her clitoris, two fingers exploring inside. Her face in the gasp of an orgasm, his eyes closing in pleasure and flying open in delight. The girl snuggled naked in the arms of an older sister (says voice-over), learning things and liking what she hears. The boy and girl suiting up in pyjamas for bed. Then a medley of images, every other one of the boy's or girl's face smiling happily, the others of suntanned fingers opening wet labia, a cherubic mouth sliding onto his penis, her back arching into a climax induced by fingers, her behind bucking. The first shot of them at it was so intimate that the eye had to resolve the bulb of flesh in and out of focus, and the shuttling stalk, into fucking seen from a hand's length away. Next was from the top of their heads, a saucy little butt thumping beyond tumultuary hair. Ended with their walking complacently along the hallway of a very modern house, bejeaned and sweatered, holding hands. *Zichzelf verklaren*, and a film that hived an agreeable cordiality into me, for all its sentimental didacticism. Glossy magazine sex, Joris commented. Capitalist myth.

•

Second film, West German, *Wenn Sie Wollen*. Fine color tones, silvery highlights. Summer house, lots of glass and natural wood. Pines, a lake, July or August. People at a trellis table, a family eating out of doors. Two boys, a little sister. Cut to boys, fourteen and twelve, in a canoe. Older wears an orange cap with bill, low-waisted slim short pants that come to just above his knees. Younger, blue-and-white-striped sports shirt and slight yellow *slipje*. Shots of soccer fields, Boy Scout tent encampments, school gymnasium, scads of naked boys running along a beach: voice-over keeps saying *comrades*, as in all these takes our two exchange winks, beaming glances, shoulder hugs, knowing looks. A bedroom at the summer house, the two dressing after a swim, no evasion by the camera of the *veertienjaaroud*'s sparsely bushed, or the *twaalfjaaroud*'s hairless nakedness. A nimbly-paced sequence of the two hiking through romantic meadows, wrestling on a river beach, bicycling, riding horses naked. The images then begin to find the *wellustig* with a telling eye, camera moving down from older boy's fetching grin to the fly of his trousers. In an idyllic view of the older reading a book while scrunched down in a chair boy-fashion, camera noses around to close in on the poke of an erection under compliant cloth. A run of full-screen details in abrupt succession, repeated in different order: longing eyes, a tan nipple, laughing eyes, a boyish penis, succinct briefs plump of pod, flat abdomen with tight navel, adolescent penis with eyelet and disc of glans wet in the foreskin's ellipse of aperture, a jeans zipper drawn down and parted by spry fingers, younger boy's nose wrinkling like a rabbit's, back of boy's head with long perfect cylinder of neck rising from naked shoulders to a sunny involution of muddled hair, an impudent, lean behind, the dimpled corner of a mouth kissed in friendly salute. Exposition of theme thus developed, film bounds the two upstairs and into a meticulously modern bedroom congenial with northern light. Earnest-eyed, radiant with sincerity, they rub affectionate cheeks while undressing, nudge their cocks together, flop on the bed, and jack each other with practiced skill. They kiss, awkwardly, as if trying to locate something in each other's mouths. Camera wanders from kiss to rigid cocks to flexing toes to stylish Danish clock on dresser, which advances twenty minutes in a sweep. Camera looks at things in room: shirts, jeans, briefs, and socks on the floor, an Olympic poster of a male swimmer full length, the magazine *Emanzipation* on a desktop, cover depicting two very healthy boys nose to nose and cock to cock, their arms over each other's shoulders, eyes keen with exalted aspiration. Back to boys on bed, rocking their hips and shuffling their heels. They sit up, swivel around, and address each other's crotches in a sprawl of long legs and too many elbows. Close-up of lips sinking onto a cock. Much agitated flopping and arching of backs, fingers closing around a scrotum, heads bobbing between thighs. Final shot is of the boys, dressed and looking smugly pleased, with the family on the lawn around the summery outdoor table (grapes in baskets, bottles of wine, books, a frosted pitcher). Pecked kisses all around, Mama, Papa, *und kleine Schwester*, and for each other. Fierce idealism in everybody's eyes.

•

Naderhand, Strodekker making notes in a minutebook with a silver pencil, having the air of a man in his element, the dedicated secretary of a committee with a cause. What did I think? What I thought was *gunst*! Which got me a tolerant, friendly smile. The fucking little rascals, *in de fleur van zijner jaren* (such phrases, said Strodekker's look, will get you nowhere at all), Joris said, unsnapping his jeans to resettle his underpants which, he happily explained, had squirmed awry. Olaf said the films were topnotch, from the cinematic point of view. Joris brought up social realism. Strodekker felt that their effectiveness was in educating sensitivities, beguiling away ingrained fears, but not, dear Lord, overnight.

•

Some clips from an *erotisk instruktionsfilm* which Olaf is working on, these sequences of his *Spartansker Yngling* troop, of which he is scoutmaster. *Mig*, he said of the sturdily upreared whopper that appeared on the screen, its slathered glossy glans and vascular stalk almost instantly sloshed in a mesh-work of guttering *zaad*, webbing the fingers of the attending hand. *Wel alle-machting*! Joris said in honest awe, that's you, yours? *Personlig*, said Olaf. And in English, jolly good, what? Look at this dazzler: a Ganymedish tow-head, around thirteen, who runs his briefs down long tan legs (Bandaid on one knee) with the grace of a deer bending to nibble, shakes his hair back into place with a smile for the camera, tugs on his penis with a doorhandle grasp of the foreskin, and, sitting with spread thighs, gives himself over to the hand of an older boy who's half-dressed in student cap, open troop shirt with Gem-ini shoulderpatch, and tall white socks. Continued, camera changing angles, until three milky driblets seeped out, appropriated by a tonguetip. A mere tad of a spadger with big brown eyes and *raagbol* hair, is the younger brother, Olaf explained, of the fast kid there with the *opstopper* nose (fast kid wallow-ing on a cot with two others, a tumble of puppies). Thoroughly and preco-ciously trained at home by Big Brother, he's one of the yeastiest of the gang, never quite running down.

•

Olaf whistled the *Padvinder* marching hymn he wants to use on the sound-track, along with some passages from Sibelius.

13 FRUCTIDOR

Florishuis, as we name it, is structurally sound. Our brooms and the new vacuum cleaner uncover a beautiful interior that wants paint and spackling and scrubbing only to make it the exact plainness of space and surface we want. Lights and water activated, roof inspected. We've set up a camp in the studio, top floor, as HQ from which to work. Pallets to sleep on, a hotplate for coffee.

•

In this new house my mind balances in an unexpected serenity, as if I had fallen into step with the pace of time. Place has become peace itself. One side of the brain treats space temporally, the other time spatially. In the moment of balance, place achieves a harmony with time, and their two mysteries of infi-nite extension, omnidirectional for space, a forward direction only for time, become one mystery, for all the directions of space move in the direction of time: upward, downward, out along the radii from all points. *Ubi* coordinates with *quando* if the larch has reddened and geese stream overhead, *quando* with *ubi* if our train slows.

•

An adventure, says Kaatje. Trust you, Adriaan, to make this happen. Sander and Grietje enjoy the illusion that they thought it up and talked you into it. But they did. *Caca*, she replies.

•

Culture, says Lévi-Strauss, is not merely juxtaposed to life nor superimposed upon it, but in one way serves as a substitute for life, and in another, uses it and transforms it, to bring about the synthesis of a new order.

•

François Marie Charles Fourier, born at Besançon 7 April 1772, the second birthday of the English philosophical poet William Wordsworth. *A six heures du matin*. Eighteen years later he would change the spelling of the family name from Fourrier to Fourier, perhaps to claim kin with Jean Pierre Fourier de Mataincourt, who in 1597 founded the School Sisters of Our Lady. A cloth and spice merchant, his father. Three sisters, no brothers. Mother a Muguet, illiterate but devout. Little Charles a serious and scholarly child, with a sensual streak in his gravity. He was passionately fond of sweets, and when he was seven wrote an ode on the delight of eating, read as a funeral oration for a pastry cook. He also loved flowers, geography, and music, so that his room in childhood, as for all of his life, was full of potted plants and maps. Quite early he saw that businessmen and bankers are unprincipled scoundrels, crooks, and jackals.

•

The series distributes the harmonies. The attractions are proportionate to our destinies. Character is fate.

•

Studied classics at the Collège de Besançon, after which he was placed in a commercial firm at Lyon. Business took him to Paris, where he admired the arcades of the Palais Royale and appropriated them in his imagination for the family houses as large as villages which he called the Phalanx of the Harmony. Business took him to Rouen, where he was disgusted by the mud and traffic, to Marseilles, where he saw a shipload of rice dumped into the sea to keep prices high, to Bordeaux, to Strasbourg, and to The Netherlands, where in the polychrome tulip fields he had a vision of children dressed in the colors of the barbarians riding in hordes and bands on quaggas from phalanx to phalanx in a New Harmony.

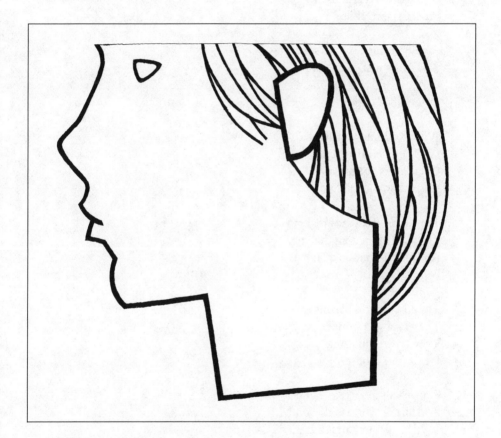

The gospel is advancing
And freedom is commencing
With leaping and with dancing
We'll hail the Jubilee.

The fire is increasing,
The flame is never ceasing.
I feel I am releasing,
And now I will be free.

Now in the strength of union
Subdue the great Apollyon.
Believers in communion
Proclaim the Jubilee.

And while the trump is sounding
And Antichrist confounding
Our love and zeal abounding
Determined to be free.

With freedom I'm delighted,
I will not feel affrighted
Come let us be united
And sound the Jubilee.

The bands of sin are breaking,
The devil's kingdom shaking,
And his foundation quaking
Because we will be free.

The gospel fire is blazing.
The world will wonder, gazing.
They say it is amazing.
Is this your Jubilee?

But we will shout like thunder
And fill the World with wonder.
We'll break our bands asunder
And then we will be free.

•

In 1793 Fourier inherited eighty thousand *livres*, which he converted into merchandise: cotton, rice, sugar, and coffee. The troops of the Convention besieged Lyon, trying to subdue the extremist wing of the Gironde. Fourier's cotton bales were requisitioned by the city for the defenses, his rice, sugar, and coffee to feed the populace trapped in the walls. So says Pellarin. Hémardin-quer says that Fourier's fortune was lost in a shipwreck in 1799. Like Henri Rousseau, Fourier distributed various versions of his biography. In any case, his trials under the Terror at Lyons left him with a lifelong hatred of violence and of revolution. The wars of The Harmony would be of kindnesses outdo-ing kindnesses. The besieging armies of the Phalanxes will arrive singing to horns and drums, laden with carts of flowers and pastries. Spermando, stand-ing in the stirrups of his quagga, shouts at the gate that the Grand Horde Jaufre Rudel with all its stormwings and whirlwind attachments has come to love the Phalanx Jules Supervielle into idiocies of ecstasy.

•

To breed meanness out of human nature.

•

Escaping from Lyon to Besançon, Fourier joined the Eighth Regiment of Cav-alry Scouts, under the command of a Colonel Brincourt, who had married a cousin of Fourier's. Most of the cavalrymen were young, idealistic, and full of a sense of glory. From them he saw how the entire economy of France, and of the world, could be taken from the greed of merchants and the vicious manip-ulation of the stock market and put into the care of children on ponies.

•

The word *cell* in biology comes from Robert Hooke whose microscope showed him that nature in fine was a honeycomb.

•

Back in Lyon Fourier fell in with progressive minds and Corinthian morals. He began to write for the newspapers. On 25 Frimaire XII he wrote that Russia would try to take over the world. The police came to his boarding house (girls being hidden in closets) to arrest him for spying and trading in international intelligence. His friend Ballanche vouched for him at the Gen-darmerie. The police in The Harmony would be little girls and sissies on Shet-land ponies.

•

On 4 Nivôse XII Fourier published his Kafkaesque *Letter to a High Judge*, outlining the vision of a New Harmony and offering to the First Consul Napoleon the title Emperor of the Earth and to all a permanent frenzy of happiness.

•

Desire, insofar as it has reference to the mind, is the very essence of the mind. But the essence of mind consists of knowledge which involves knowledge of God, and without which it cannot exist or be conceived. A man will love the good which he desires for himself and loves, with greater constancy, if he sees that others love it also.

•

Citoyen Grand Juge:

Great good news, if you will allow me a page to extract a universal harmony from a matter that will seem to you trivial. I understand that certain persons have brought my political comments to your attention, on their own and through the police. It is on the advice of the Commissioner that I write you this letter. I have frequently written the Directoire and the Foreign Office, giving them the benefit of my observations. They have always replied courteously, and with gratitude. I am sure that you will receive my criticism in the same spirit, and appreciate its essence if not its style. That my ideas run counter to common opinion is all the more reason for you to pay careful attention to them. The situation is crucial. In a continental war, such as I feel is about to happen, Germany will split in half, and the triumvirate of which I spoke earlier will become a reality. At first it will look like a duumvirate, for Germany, caught between France and Russia, will have to serve one or the other. If Germany chooses Russia, France is indeed in danger of defeat. But this I have already said, and what I write you about now is not the child's play of power politics as manipulated by various idiots and buffoons, that is to say, politicians and those whose butts they lick, the bankers, but the matter of Universal Social Harmony and the Imminent Downfall of All Societies, Civilized as well as the Barbarian and Primitive. I am the Inventor of the Mathematical Calculus of the Destinies. The celebrated English Savant Lord Isaac Newton had this calculus within his reach without knowing it. It was he, great genius, who discovered the laws of attraction among masses in the material world. I have discovered the laws of passional attraction. No one else has ever even dreamed of such a law. I am the first, O Citizen High Judge. Passional attraction is the matrix in which God has cast all the characteristics of nature, the ordering by divine plan of all action between human beings. As long as we fail to reckon the laws of attraction by analysis and synthesis, our minds step from darkness to darkness, and we have no clue as to the structure of the world we inhabit, the order destined by nature for society, nor the function of the passions in our lives. My theory of the destinies divides into three parts. First, Creation. Which is the shape God has given to matter, everything from the galaxies and the invisible stars to the most exquisite designs in the animals, vegetables, and minerals. I will disclose the plan by which God has distributed passions, abilities, forms, colors, tastes to all the diversity of creation. Second, the societies of man past and future. Third, Immortality, or the destiny of the soul through world after world. You comprehend, Citizen Judge, that a whole exposition of this extensive theory would be too great for me to complete. I have therefore worked out, as yet, only the most necessary calculations, that of the societies of industrial nations. I have drawn the mechanism of a Harmony in finest detail, from its administration at the top down to the home. This Harmony is diametrically the opposite of everything we know in our civilization. I will turn these plans over to the savants, retaining for myself only the eternal honor of the discovery of them. These laws should have been discovered twenty-three hundred years ago. It is due to the pride of metaphysicians, the blindness of moral philosophers, and the stupidity of political scientists that mankind had not, until I came along, discovered the plan and work of God. They should have seen that God's design for society is implicit, as it is with the stars and the animals, in the natural attractions immutably built into our being. A synthesis of these attractions reveals the code of a new Harmony which will last around sixty thousand years. I would place it longer, except that the cooling of the globe will curtail our sense of pleasure considerably. And pleasure is the pivot of the Harmony.

14 FRUCTIDOR

Who could they be, these acrobats?
Wanderers, lives briefer than ours,
wrenched by a will since their childhood,
and, can you tell me, for whose sake?
A will that twists them, tosses them,
hurls them, rocks them, spins them upward,
catches them in uncoiling leaps.
As if from a silkier air,
denser than ours, they somersault
onto their worn old padded mat
trod thin, laid down as if to dress
some wound inflicted by the sky.

All but not there, the letter D
of *Dasein*. Presence, being there.

•

Picasso's pensive figures are still as dogs are still, between movements. Seurat's bathers at Asnières are still with the sense of being where they are on a summer afternoon. They watch, play reveries through their imaginations, feel sun wind and water. They are French, acute, alive. Picasso's figures in blue and rose come down through time from Rome, from mimes in the Forum, from melancholy village squares in Roman Spain.

•

And O around this middle place
A ghost rose blossoms and closes.
Around this pestle or pistil,
snared in its own dust or pollen,
seeded by its own fruit, boredom,
the smile for show, the tedium
of surface without inwardness.
The defeated lifter of weights,
who, grown old, only beats the drum,
whose skin would fit two men his size,
the other dead, perhaps, buried
already. This is the widow.
That young man seems to be the son
of a neck and a nun, so fine
a joining he is of muscle
and virginity.
        Suffering
just beginning has long delays
with a kind of playtime in them
before it grips for good.
          O you
that drop like green fruit from the tree
a hundred times a day, a tree
that knows spring, summer, and autumn
in one whirl, the tumblers' tree.

•

Paulus Zetmeel the Platonist by to see where I've moved, a pleasant enough conversationalist and exponent of beauty hypersensitively grasped. Sander positively growled at the poor soul: I made soothing excuses for him. We'd been lugging boxes of books, outsized canvases, and furniture for hours. Grietje's girlfriend turned up, more hindrance than help, and the two had gone to bed, I wasn't certain where. Sluts, said Sander. I was ready to sit for a while, even with Paulus for company. He kept admiring everything, disordered and unpacked and cockahoop as everything was. He approved of what he called the splendid arrangement, the young painter, his sister, was she, to keep house for us, such a modern and sensible *ménage*, such a scope for the creative life. What so openly and beautifully you have to *give* them, Adriaan. For all your notorious reclusiveness, you are, I've always insisted, to people who think you standoffish, on the furtive generosity of your concerns. Whereupon, Paulus dithering on, Sander singing sea chanties somewhere above while painting a wall, I having a comforting pipe, up the stairs galloped Jan and Hansje tearing at their zippers. They were well inside the door when, taking in Paulus, they skidded to a halt, one bumping the other from behind, and stood popeyed, pulling their britches back up. Try the floor above, I said, where Sander's doing walls. That's him singing. My nephew, I said to his interrogative stare, and his friend Gregorius and Hilda Sinaasappel's son Jan. *Bof!* we could hear Sander bellow, grab those brushes. You can suck your thumbs.

•

Often, pausing, a tender look
begins in your eyes, toward her,
your mother, who's seldom tender,
a sweet look that wanders instead
all over your supple body,
lost in its ripples.
        A handclap
signals the dive, before your heart
can feel a throb, there's the tickle
in your heels before the bound
that can start real tears in your eyes
and, unexpectedly, that smile.

Find it, Angel, that healing leaf
and turn a jar to keep it in.
Shelve it with delights yet to come.
Let its flowery label read
Subrisio saltatoris.

15 FRUCTIDOR

Open slatwork flooring for the roof garden, or sundeck. Sander has painted the chimney blue and the ship's vent yellow. Bricks and coping of the parapet scrubbed. Shipshape, boxneat. And private.

•

White walls for Sander's studio, one corner of which is an area with chairs and coffee table. The three of us painting my room (Italian Stone, say the buckets), I tell about going to Strodekker's, and about Joris and Olaf. Bring them around, says Sander, I want to meet them. I don't care about their arguments and justifications, Grietje says. It's what people are that matters. The only thing that matters. The mind is a washout. Only the soul counts. Only feeling.

•

Books accurately aligned on my new wealth of bookshelves, floor to ceiling, around two walls and part of the third. Rietveld table in place. Paintings. My spartan bed with its Shaker quilt. Cot for Hans and Jan at the far end.

•

Sander, wordless, also britchesless, came and stood until I saw why. Grietje wonderfully gentle and bright about it all. I really can't go away, Sander said in a voice I'd never heard. Nobody wants you to, Grietje said. So he sat on the floor, his elbows on the bed. Get in there, Nipper! he cheered.

•

Godfried Strodekker. The fire beneath his affable and cultivated mask is one of banked coals, deeply stocked. Coffee with him today. Judge all men by the coffee they make: Strodekker gives you a winey black thick sweet espresso, a cup Diderot and Chamfort would have admired. Coffee, not wine, goes with the *bonnet rouge*. It comes to Paris with the guillotine, with Marat and Fourier. It is in the series with tobacco and honey, with chairs and tables (the French, both aristocrats and peasants, drink wine standing), with good talk among friends. Coffee adds, wine divides. Strodekker did not know about Alan Turing, that tender genius, who had fallen in love with a little boy some weeks before he salted an apple with arsenic and impulsively refused a problem which, unlike the mathematical, cryptological, cybernetic ones his unique genius could solve, he could not live with. I trust the compassion in Strodekker's eyes.

•

In Holland Fourier saw the fields of tulips which the Little Hordes were to resemble.

•

Strodekker distrusts sentiment, the invisible tradition of courtly love, and feints and sublimation of all sorts. A matter of camouflage, very complex, he says of all the delusions and fantasies, the erotic daydreams and neurotic searches for one's own lost childhood, idealistic velleities, every manner of archetypal identification of the child with purity and innocence which the movement must analyze as a study group. He has read widely, thought carefully, but admits with candor that his own emotions blur all but his most lucid ideas. Liberalism itself is its own worst enemy.

•

Strodekker, a conscientious notetaker, was writing *Montherlant, Plutarch, Herbert List*, when from upstairs sauntered Master Tobias in all his amber-brown slenderness and robin's-egg blue *slipje*, hair raggedy and eyes lazy from a nap, smooth armpits displayed in his yawning stretch. Hallo, he said, you're the *filosoof* was here once before, when Olaf came from Denmark. He gave Strodekker a kiss and came and shook hands with me, grinning at his politeness. He strode out again, returning in a bit with a cup of coffee and a spanking new skateboard for my inspection and approval. *Gunst!* they're costly, Strodekker said, and I was able to name the price of Hansje's, and even to talk ballbearings and kneepads. Hansje? Strodekker asked with amused interest, but Tobias made the question easier to answer with a gruff *Who is this Hansje?*

16 FRUCTIDOR
Een schittering! Een glans! De Schudders marching to God! Lineaments by Mondriaan, Fuller, Rietveldt: our house unclutters area by area. Grietje has the kitchen functional. Beds are still hard to get at over heaps of impedimenta, except for the narrow daybed for Hansje and Jan, with a plaid blanket for cover, a plain russet rug alongside, and a brazen poster from the Jeugd en Jongerencentrum of a large photograph in glossy color of two boys undressing (a nubble of *onderbroekje* pouch pokes from the unzipped fly of one) with the vertical caption between them: *Alle dagen!*

•

Adnotatio libidinosa: Olaf vel masturbator vel paiderastos mentulas mutuo sugens quinquiensve septiens per diem ejaculatur. Ipse dixit sponte. Appetans manet. Copiose fundet relatione amanter Marci, abunde pocillum coffeae replere, gloriose et ridens impudenter.

•

RB Fuller: From here on we have learned that it is success for all or for none, for it is experimentally proven by physics that unity is plural and at minimum two—the complementary but mirror-imaged proton and neutron. You and I are inherently different and complementary.

•

A *kladschrift* of a letter from Tobias and Nils to Olaf, to help me understand, as Strodekker says. Kameraad Olafje! Come visit Amsterdam and us as soon as you can the color pictures you took of us all stripped down O wow *flinkgebouwd en broodmager* in english good built body and lean how could you stand us we would love to be wolfcubs in your pack are we soft headed for you who do not have you said a favorite in your pack but love them all but we hope you do and love him Papa says hallo and love you made a big hit with Joris do come back *kameraadschappelijk* Welp Toby en Welp Nils.

•

It eventually received punctuation and was signed with the outlines of their virile members made with a magic marker, traces of which are still on them, nontoxic it is to be hoped. Olaf and Joris are the best outlook for the movement, being young, attractive, dedicated, idealistic. Olaf a commercial artist and designer, of sorts, working in advertising on commissions, but most seriously interested in making films. His afternoons and weekends go to the *kønsligfrihed* clubhouse, study groups, showing films.

•

Postcard from Olaf (two Danish boys naked in a rowboat): Hallo Nils! Hallo Toby! When your handsome papa invites me is when I'll visit again. Drink your buttermilk and try to behave. Hopeless, I know, but then you don't know how lucky you are. A hundred kisses, fifty each. Big Olaf.

•

Joris when he was a schoolboy of fifteen living with his Tante Mathilde and Ome Hendrick wrote a very plain letter to the Nederlandse Vereniging van

Homofielen Cultuur en Ontspannings Centrum on the Frederiksplein, hoping for great things. He had a cache of magazines, some stolen, some bought, to supplement his even more graphic fantasies, and in several of them he had found the center's address and offer of ministrations. He got back a note with an appointment at the Jeugd en Jongerencentrum Ruimte for the following Tuesday. Oof! he says with jiggling eyes and fine smile, you can't know what it meant, that card! Nice people, and they were gentle with me. After a prissy and superior secretarial type who asked some arch questions and read from some statutes, and blithered about moral responsibilities, choices in a free society, and ideals, which withered Joris' hopes and peter together, he was put in a room to wait, together as he remembers with a pitifully scared man biting his nails, until a university student named Martijn turned up grinning affably (tight jeans, cadet cap, wool pullover with high collar) and asking for the _melkbaard_ communist. Decent and even likable chap, Martijn, well-off, middle-class, a keen enthusiast. They had but the one thing in common, but after a walk, all their conversation _overhoop_, they went to Martijn's room.

•

Briefkaart from Joris, Tuke's _August Blue_: Do you know, Kameraad Adriaan, that Coubertin wanted _jochen_ in _de olympische spelen_, and as naked as newts? _In de open lucht_ he called it, about the time of these English scamps, _ja? Uw liefhebbende!_ J.

•

Een ander, a Georges Minne _knaap: —Alors, dit-il, je saurai nager—toi, tu sais—et nous irons loin dans la mer. Puis, nous resterons longtemps allongés sur le sable, au soleil. —Oui, dit Alexandre d'une voix étrange. Et nous échangerons nos maillots. Snoezig, hej!_ J.

•

Voor Joris: _Der Männerbadeanzug war schon um 1900 aus Baumwolltrikot, meist blau und weiss oder rot und weiss quergestrieft; ausserdem trug man damals die knappe kleine Badehose in Dreiecksform aus rotem Kattun, die Vorläuferin der heutigen kleinen Wooltrikothose._ Ruth Klein, _Lexikon der Mode._

•

Briefkaart, Eugène Janssons _Badtavla_, 1908: Ten naked Swedish boys in their teens and twenties against a background of boys and sailors in uniform at a swimming club. *O jee!* Adriaan, *lieve hemel!* Who is this Janssons and where can I see more of his work? Were the Swedes as dull as *bordenwasser* in 1908? What happened? *Makkerlijk*, Joris.

17 FRUCTIDOR

There came in from the garden at Strodekker's a boy the left of whose handsome eyes is a minim out of line, slightly inward, intent on some fixed concern while its twin follows the affairs of the world with an interested open gaze. Fifteen. Face northernly *dolicocefaal*, yet the cordovan brown of his longish hair and the ruddy evenness of his tan argue a Spanish grandmother who cooked everything with garlic and olives. White denim short pants, a light blue pullover, an easy smile, bare feet. Erasmus, said Godfried, meet the philosopher Adriaan van Hovendaal. Erasmus Verlangerspruit. Surely not, I said before I'd thought. Well, said Godfried with an expansive swing of his arm, try Prinsprong or even Peereboompje. Strodekker, when we get the adoption through. Ha! said Erasmus, the adoption. Nils has described you, he said shaking my hand. He said you are an old man of forty or so, well-preserved in your decrepitude, talk like a book, look at everything, missing nothing, are kind and polite, and sport British *pulletjes*. The little bugger, Godfried said. Tobias saw more of you. He said simply that you're brainy and wear brown ties with blue shirts. All of this took Erasmus as a wonderful joke, over which he batted his eyes and limberly dealt with an itch inside his left thigh with his right toes, and with zest, no tilt of poise. Godfried pinched thumb and forefinger in a short downward drop of a gesture toward Erasmus, who obeyed, unzipped his pants, plucked off his pullover, and stood naked, lips pursed in an irony of understanding and comic compliance. The proportions, Godfried said, putting a hand to his brow, the harmony. Big cock, too, said Erasmus. And Godfried thinks the cast in my eye is sexy. Then, straddling Godfried, chair and all, in a lyric leap, legs wide, like a gymnast on the parallel bars, diving over his head into a somersault, out of which he uncoiled with a bounding spring, Erasmus came and sat at my feet, his chin on my knee, pleased with himself and with the moment. What, he said, do you do? Write books and essays. What about? How things mean: words, statements, art, history, manners, philosophy. Godfried teaches history and geography. He's a good teacher, too. You're his student? *O ja!* I get bad grades, because Godfried expects twice as much from me, and doesn't want the class to hate me as the teacher's pet. It's awful. He's going to adopt me, if the judge, who's a woman, can get away with it. She thinks she can. My folks are split, the old man going off to the USA with his secretary, and my mummy has gone bats on Theosophy

and is holed up in their lamasery, in touch with forces emanating from a
second moon that's always aligned straight behind *the* moon. Only initiates
know it's there. Anyway, I'm sane. I like books and music and swimming and
hiking and camping and sex, lots of it. How Godfried knew this, I'll never
figure out. Saw it in your magic eye, said Godfried. It's not as if, Erasmus *liefje*,
you don't sit in class hugging your crotch with your hand, or grubble in your
swimsuit at the pool, or wear jeans that fit like the skin on a sausage. Erasmus
has this *zwemslipje* that weighs half a handkerchief and is sheer, despite being
Norway blue, except a white smitch of liner in the pouch. As soon as he's out
of the pool he shoves it down, jostles his balls, and tugs at his peter. Then he
strides around a lot with everything hanging out and bouncing prettily. Well,
said Erasmus, a jigget in his off eye, here I am.

18 FRUCTIDOR

Cockleburs, sticktights, and puppies that follow you home. Ten lengths of the
pool at the gym, Gerrit with his coffee making conversation along the side,
conquests of girls driven mad by his technique and longwinded loving. The
secret, he said, is to turn them on good, slide it in and let it soak awhile up to
the hilt while kissing and sucking teats. Then (with a sip of coffee for punctuation) you start off real slow, nudging along while holding it in deep. Tone is
what it's all about. Once you've got it tuned to a fine tone, you can start in
with long strokes getting faster. Petronian all this, the baths and the hale atten-
dant drinking his essence of roasted and ground tropical bean, talking skill in
affection to a philosopher vain of his body crawling through crystal water, but
all transposed into antiseptic Dutch practicality. When, dear Gerrit, I said on
the way to the sauna, are you going to settle down with one good girl? Who
knows? he said. My problem is that when I'm with one and fucking her eye-
balls back into her head, I'm thinking of how I can get it better with another.
Een vlinder.

•

Drenched, soothed, the crick fading from my neck, tensions melting away,
alone in the sauna except for a clerkly soul with a hangover. We exchanged a
word about the weather and another about the miraculous powers of clouds
of vapor. He was sighing and feeling his eyelids and I was sinking into a luxury
of wellbeing, planning the day, when Gerrit slipped in two boys, not under
eleven nor over thirteen, saying with a snap that if they gave us any trouble
he'd snatch them out and sail them into the canal. They'd paid, it was a free
country, and he could heave a *snotaap* with one hand through the door. The

taller, a *z'on jong broekje* with curly brown hair, *snoezig* and slender but firm as a plank, gave me a bright smile as he stretched and sat with a whistled sigh across from me, having given a cursory, dismissing glance to the clerkly soul. The other, coppery blond, pretty as a boyish girl, plopped beside him and laid his head on his shoulder, limp with fatigue. Up all night, Curly Hair boasted, by way of explanation, *gammel en gezogen*. The clerkly soul gaped his pale face with alarm, time already to summon Gerrit. I spiked his jitters by remaining calm, raising interested eyebrows. Their penises, well developed for their age, had the pulled and bruised look of having been lovingly jacked with enthusiasm and regularity. Their argot was affected but down pat. All fucking night, Curly Hair said. Copper Blond admired him out of the top of his eyes. Was I up all night? I explained that this was my gym where I kept in shape. Neat shape, said Curly Hair, the kind of kid who smiles everytime he speaks. I deprecated the compliment with clicked eyes and a squinched grin. You're hung heavy, golden smile. I'll say, added Copper Blond. The clerkly soul, trying for a scandalized face, managed to look constipated instead. This is great, smiled Curly Hair. I've only been to a sauna twice before, and Michiel here never. I only lasted all night, cause I knew we could afford a sauna to soak out feeling shitty. I said, returning Curly Hair's smile, that I wouldn't dare ask what has kept two schoolboys out of bed all night. Out of bed, said Copper Blond, my ass. Curly Hair looked at me satirically with wide-open eyes, showing broad buckteeth under a rucked upper lip. Well, he said with full awareness that I was pulling his leg, Michiel and I, we're friends, my name's Wolfgang, we met these kids wearing their *vay zet vay* buttons and smoking a joint on the Prinsengracht and they liked our looks and we liked theirs. They took us to a place with nobody home. Clerkly Soul swallowed his cud. I turned my palms up and tried to look knowing and appreciative. Talk about horny, Michiel said, squeezing his dick idly, so that the glans slipped free. You like boys? Wolfgang asked with his shining smile, not that either of us could do a fucking thing right now. I'll handle this, I had to say to Clerkly Soul, who was gathering himself to call Gerrit. To Wolfgang I rocked a hand and got from him a wink and a nod. He also unsheathed his glans, meaning God knows what. *Wanneer zij willen*, I said to show that I knew the button. Michiel sat up at my pedantry: everybody knew that. Clerkly Soul was confused. I explained, to his consternation. You can get *zwemslipjen*, Michiel helped, with little *vay zet vay* circles just here to the side, and patches for jackets. You see 'em on sneakers and chains you wear around your neck. The kid last night named Klaas, he's fifteen, he had his on the side of his cap, Tomas on his sweater, Pier on a beltloop front of his jeans. Details, blandly imparted in the swelter of the steam, got through to Clerkly Soul, and he left, not without a word from me to tell Gerrit that all was serene, and details were getting through to me, *geleerde* as I'd thought of the erotic, not certain whether I was playing Diogenes at The Silver Hound or Montherlant on the *plaine de Bagatelle*. Wolfgang stood after Clerkly Soul departed, gave his peter a few gingerly pulls, and reported that it felt OK if sore and sprained, and lay along the bench on his back. Healthy ribcage, knobby knees. Michiel imitated him on the bench above, tummy down. I imitated Michiel, across from them, and we talked.

•

Outside, in the bustle of the street, they looked even younger. We'd all come giddily alive in the cold showers. There was the information of our clothes for the three of us to learn from: I was not wholly surprised to see them wiggle into illfitting skimpy briefs grey with indifferent laundering and pissburnt, into socks worn too long, cheap snug trousers, doubleknit pullovers with sprung elbows. No WZW badges anywhere. Of my tweed jacket and jeans their shrewd eyes made much. They asked if I were a businessman, what kind of car I drove, if I had been to Germany. I invited them to have breakfast with me, and they proved to be starved, mannerless, wildly appreciative. It was like dining with barbarians for whom generosity and kindness came naturally but to whom a code of manners was alien. They wolfed and glupped, ate with their mouths open, talked while they chewed. I was a *what*? A philosopher. An hilarious word, which they thereafter said without warning.

19 FRUCTIDOR
Grietje and her friend Bunny to do the kitchen. Curtains, pots, pans, spices, and making all that will gleam gleam. Clitoria, Sander calls her. So we, with Hans and Jan in tow, head for the island by train, bus, and boat.

•

Women who love women it was that gave Fourier the impetus to write the *Nouveau monde amoureux*. Grietje calls it supplementary sensuality. With, she says, a good gossip and lots of deeply satisfying meowing. Girls can get into each other with an ease and warmth men know nothing about. Their role as diaper changers and wipers of butts makes them intimate in a practical as well as a sweetly carnal way with the body. They can have forty orgasms in a row, whereas a man after one or two is a dead duck. Another meaning to continuous and discontinuous in the contrast between male and female. Sander explains it all on the train to Hans and Jan, in rather more clinical detail than Hans is comfortable with, though Jan chooses to be sophisticated, and a bit bored. Then they slide their eyes into looks at each other and get the giggles. Sander calls them brats.

•

The boys *sprokkeling*, Sander and I savor, without saying a word, the cabin's healing sense of refuge. He gives me a tight, long hug. Buffer, says Hans coming in with an armload of firewood, friendship everywhere.

•

Woke, richly rested, to a squeeze of my shoulder by Sander, who brought mugs of good coffee to the bed, faunishly upreared, clad in my Finnish sweater. Rubbed noses for a greeting. I've pissed, he said, but he's still stiff as a grenadier. Nifty. I like my body, I can say to you, *vriendje* Adriaan, but what I like best, after Jongeheer Jaap here with his plump long noddle and stout shaft and brace of goose eggs in his shotbag, is the dense strut of the top of my nose, and the runnel line from the scoop at the bottom of my neck that goes right down to my bellybutton, and my knuckly knees, and my toes, I'm wild about my toes. *Groot God!* I said, and got a thousand-guilder smile. It's those little buggers, he said, so mad for each other. He swiveled off the bed and crept over to the bedroll full of boys, only their hair showing in two collided whorls. He poked them with his toe, mussed their hair with his heel, and knelt and stuck his arm in between them up to the shoulder. Are you two stuck together in there? We're only two badgers, Hans said. *Sakkerloot!* Jan said of Sander's *pompslinger* morning erection so proudly curved up in a jaunty slant. Sander hauled him out by the armpits and brought him, a long naked boy with hair in his eyes, and dropped him beside me on the bed, turning down the blanket with his foot. He returned for Hansje and plopped him beside Jan. He offered each a sip of his coffee, which they took. Good, said Hansje, and got kissed by Sander on the dimple by his mouth. Good morning, badgers, said I, and was kissed by Hansje on the chin and by Jan on the cheek. Sander kissed Jan on the back of his neck, with a loud smack, and trotted off for more coffee. Jan kissed Hans on the lips, and was kissed so. Heigh ho, sang Sander. You two little buggers can drink from the same mug. I put in heaps of that nonmilk gunk and loads of sugar. Move over. Two of the little horde, one of the grand, and a philosopher in his prime. Hans and Jan looked charmingly dissipated, as no doubt they were, whereas Sander looked ready to win the Olympics. His erection held. This is neat! Hans said, with an arm around Jan's waist, and around Sander's, butting both on the shoulder, and a butt in my direction that didn't reach. Is this breakfast? It's coffee before breakfast, Sander said. For friendship. Whereupon he leaned and kissed Hansje's peter, Jan's, and, flipping back the blanket, mine. Pleased mightily with himself, he sat tall and grinned a doltish smile, gathering Hans and Jan into a lopsided hug. Hans, confused, crawled over and gave me a sound squeeze around the neck, and received my kiss on ears and nose with animal grace. Jan, breathing Arcadian air, pulled Hans off me and climbed across to copycat his embrace, straddling my chest. Hugged and kissed, he shifted to my knees, dabbed a kiss into my crotch, turned to Sander and swanked a reckless smack dab on his glans. For Hans, he put rather more nudge into his kiss. *Wel allemachtig!* Hans said half aloud. Fine doings, said Sander, but me, I'm hungry. *In de looppas*, badgers! Up and out. First Badger, fetch in more firewood. Second Badger, down to the spring for two buckets of water. They skittered off. Damn, said Sander, whose musky denim shirt I put on. I went down to the sea for a stroll and quiet moment to myself.

21 FRUCTIDOR
To explain is to evade.

•

Crossing the Vondel, what do I see but *een kastanjebruin krullende raagbol* atop one Wolfgang sitting cross-shinned under a laurel studying a supply line of ants. Black crescents under fingernails, nape dingy. Two meters away I can see that his fly is open, a pink tip of peter poking out, foreskin drawn back. I halted, his eyes went to my shoes. If, I said in a jolly voice, I were looking for a minnow, I wonder if I haven't just found one? Refulgent smile, rosy blush. *De filosoof!* And where's Michiel? I asked. A redder blush. Cancel the question, I said. What about some lunch? Your fly's gaped and your *mannetje*'s looking out upon the world. He smiled the brighter. I know, I said, a *broodjeswinkel* a hop and skip away where a philosopher and a spadger can glup the lunch of the century. He was not comfortable with my taking his hand to cross the street, but got the hang of it, with a delightful squeeze, and we held hands the rest of the way. For the utter mischief of it I compared Aristippos and Antisthenes while we ate, both to keep myself from asking questions and to have talk going. Happy smiles his only response. He tucked away two large beef, cheese, and onion sandwiches, a glass of Pilsener, and pineapple pancake. Coffee he conspued, but helped himself to a puff of my pipe, going crosseyed. Any engagements? I said with acted archness through a blue puff from the retrieved pipe. *Wat zal 't zijn?* he shrugged. Tag along with me for a bit? *Buff,* he said. Hand in hand, we made for a _warenhuis_. Bought him, to his smiling wonderment, two niftily striped soccer jerseys, a pair of real American jeans, three pairs of cotton briefs, sturdy socks, and a pair of sneakers. He made all the choices. He was in a kind of trance when I handed all this over in a shopping bag for him to carry. Outside, he said, butting my arm, I don't care what I have to do for this, it'll be good. First of all, we have a stroll to where I live, _in orde?_ This, with interruptions to look in the sack, another pull of my pipe, and some disagreements about waiting for a light to cross at the zebras, went well. I rang the doorbell, for the fun of it. Grietje came to the door. What is it? she said, pointing to Wolfgang, whom I picked up, shopping bag and all. A nipper, I said, who is going to live with us, if he likes us. Sander can use an apprentice. You can practice on him, like running a bath straightway and putting him into these spiffy new _pulletjes_, and taking him to a dentist very soon. Those curls! Grietje said. I set him down inside, closed the door, and showed him that anytime he wanted to he could walk out of it. I want, he said, to put on my new clothes.

The Vestments of the Band

DE HUISKREKEL

Adriaan, Adriaan! Sander says, Wolfgang on his shoulders. Where did you steal this fellow? You can't have him back. He's mine. Grietje sprang him on me awhile ago, scared as a mouse in a corner, and the cat's got his tongue. We're still sniffing each other, that's fine, but I can tell he likes me. Grietje says you and her washed him in the tub and stuck him into all these new clothes. He's the little brother I never had. He's the nipper, for now. Is he German? I love the little fucker.

UITSTEKEND

One of the bands or hordes, I say. Technically, I suppose, he's plying his trade, the world's oldest, though I think we can give him a stabler job as brush cleaner, errand boy, adopted mascot, early nipper, friend, model, and house cricket. We can put his bed on your floor, a rack of those modish trays in a stack beside it for his togs, soccer ball, ice skates, and such. Bedtable, with lamp. A bookcase. I can't read, says Wolfgang.

NIPPEROLOGY

When Grietje undressed him for the bath, to see, as she said, how a boy works, I said just like Sander. Surely not, she said, pulling down his briefs. You're beautiful, young man. I plied the shampoo, Grietje the washrag. He acted for a while as if we were boiling him in oil, but relaxed after a while, and even laughed. After we'd dried him, and Grietje was getting his arms into his shirt, he asked if both of us were going to suck his dink. Neither, I said, we're going to eat hot buttered muffins with jam, and drink big glasses of milk, some of us tea, and get to know each other.

GRIJS

Sander painting, muttering *grey grey such a color*, Payne's Grey (who was Mijnheer Payne?) with its flavoring of purple hidden in with its blue, the color of English sweaters and Dutch clouds before rain, of some of the granites and seabirds. There are more good greys than good blues. The friend of brown, of white, of black.

HELEN IN PEARWOOD

Philologus, said the horse. Nietzsche, having his afternoon walk in Turin (dashing student cap, officer's overcoat, Viennese yellow-and-black-check suit, English underwear), stopped. *Yes, O horse?* Of time, said the horse, we can say that its structure is like that of the restless sea in its great bed. Without continents to dam its tides, the sea would slide around the earth as smoothly as brandy rolled in a goblet, its bulge toward the moon, fatter at the equator than at the poles, because of the spin. Time would be like that, except that we are its continents, and we experience it as one wave on the back of another rather than, as with God, one hyaline mass. *Ganz recht!* said Nietzsche.

RED FLAG AND BUST OF LENIN

Windows onto warehouses and canal for commercial barges in front, onto alleys and brick rowhouses in back, Joris' long room surprised me with its clean organization of space, its totems (Soviet Baroque plaster bust of Lenin against a large red flag, hammer and sickle and crossed wheatears making a diagonal with Lenin's noble gaze), plain secondhand furniture, scraplumber bookcases, kitchentable desk, barbells, exercise board, neat military bed. *Pan* and *Kouros* on coffeetable. DSAP posters. To the left of the red flag a tall framed photograph of an *inblijde* and *posthaliskos* thirteen-year-old wearing a wristwatch and student cap, cornflower blue of eye and blond. On the other side of the flag a bulletin board collaged over with clippings of soccer players, swimmers, skateboarders, naked boys on beaches, handsome young faces, penises, backsides, underwear and bathing suit ads.

PLUTARCH

The concept of infinity eludes both understanding and language, even our sense of the sacred, but into all relations it brings a play of chance and accident (*týche kai automátos*).

SLAAPMAAT

Coffee, bread, butter, and jam up to Sander and Grietje, for the fun of it. Wolfgang, *oho!* asleep between them, in *gilet*, skinny arm across Sander's throat, a leg over his thigh. It's when this *langpootmug* climbed in with us, said Sander reaching for the coffee, that's most interesting. We were working on the Blue-Eyed Nipper some more, beautifully, and here was a brown-eyed one, with curls, wanting, as he said, to see how it was done. Thought storks brought them in a nappy, safety pin and all. Good coffee. Sander, I said, you're making this up. No, no: climbed right in and felt around, gawking. Grietje's mind at the time was melted down, she couldn't have cared less that a boy all legs and scrunchy curls was in bed with us. Good morning, O my, said Grietje with a sleepy and doubting look at Wolfgang. Yep, said Sander, still here. Elbows sharp as the corner of a table in the dark, lots of ribs, knees, and hipbones. Nice peter. If you slide the sleeve on it back and forth over the mushroom, it skeets watery goo in your eye and its owner tends to smile all disgusting dimples and milkteeth. Coffee, said Grietje, coffee. You're hearing the unvarnished truth. Sander said he was practicing in case our Blue-Eyed Nipper arrives equipped with the instruments of male arrogance and female oppression. Whom, said Sander pressing Wolfgang's *eikel* between forefinger and thumb, we will have to jack off, all of us, time about, until he's coordinated enough to do it himself. Whereupon Wolfgang woke, and without transition from deep sleep to wide awake, sat up grinning like an elf. Jam, he said. Butter, too. To Grietje and Sander, touching each with a fist, he said, you fucked.

WASHSTAND WITH TOWEL
Canary yellow, white jug and basin, blue towel. Oval mirror on wall above, plain unpainted walnut frame. Grietje's idea: a bit of the early century to relieve, as she says, some of the look of a barracks for reformed Calvinists.

ONTBIJT
Grietje in her fetching kimono (and nothing else), Sander in white bib overalls (and nothing else), I in corduroy jeans and pullover, Wolfgang in the nightshirt Grietje bought him at Buffy's Kindermode, a light cotton short-sleeved shift, midshin length. It has an archaic air, vaguely biblical. Truly, says Sander, he must be drawn in it. Doesn't impede access to Meester Rozeknop, our *zoete-lief* here. No TV, says Wolfgang. Some of us, I say pointedly, can read the newspaper. Glup your kipper, Sander says, there's heaps to be done today, but in the science of nipperology we're going to see what to expect from the blue-eyed one, if male, by jiggeting the brown-eyed one off, off and on, on and off, happily, all day, a grand idea, wouldn't you say? My dink? says Wolfje. Grietje and I look at the ceiling, each other, Sander. Whose drunken smile couldn't

have been jollier. Absolutely, says Sander, in between other things, like a reading lesson from Adriaan, and helping me on the painting, and going shopping with Grietje. Wolfgang eats with a will, his eyes think and give Sander silly looks. We're very serious people, Sander says with a mouthful of kipper and toast, I'm a great painter, and people all over the world read Adriaan's books, but we like lots of play in our seriousness. Whereupon Wolfgang hiked his biblical nightshirt up around his ribs, as if to ascertain that he has a dink, as he calls it, and to have Sander's agreement that this particular is the one meant. It was, moreover, erect in a tight shallow upward curve, the hairless scrotum neatly seamed with a funiculus more vegetable than fleshly. That's the spirit, says Sander.

IK BEN

Being, the precious something in such extensive nothingness, is a system sturdily balanced in nonbeing, for the nonce, but with metabolic wear, such as the going away of the pterodactyls and the explosion of stars a hundred times larger than our sun. Metaphysical light is too brilliantly cold, even for those with eyes to see it. It is twin to dark. To know everything would be to know nothing again. Opposites meet, the circle closes. Nothing is charming but the road there. The mystery is that there are no mysteries, only ignorance and limits, our home. There is the moment, and the moment to remember the moment, or place and perspective. All else is waiting.

SNAILS

Everybody, says Hans, should see snails in love. They kiss with their feelers, and roll and dip their heads. A sweet tickle, I'll bet, and the little heart *ging van rikketik*. He has come so far, so slow, to meet Mevrouw Slak, with his house on his back, his stomach for his foot, and it feels so good to jiggle his nose against hers.

THISTLE

It is wrong to think that time rings like a bell. Nature makes a thistle, or a child, with a patience no clock is fine enough to follow, and with a harmony in time of enzymes, proteins, cunning acids and capable alkalis, bonds of oxygen and hydrogen, of iron and nitrogen, on schedules that correlate the stars and the seas. It makes the kingly thistle's seven heron's-shin stalks bear bright mauve hispid discs as pannage for bees. Circled by artichoke leaves, these thistle blossoms of delayed purple (as Jan Parkinson says in his *Paradisus Terrestris*) seem to flourish in parking lots, untended yards, desperate soil in seams between a desert of asphalt and concrete, with majestic disdain for the tackiness of their surroundings. Wolfgang is such a thistle, oblivious of his nobility. We have put him in a garden. His stamina that throve on the main chance and hunger and meanness, will it go nerveless, soft of fiber, dull? Gardens of thistles: Fourier's aching heart's longing. All this in so many words over coffee with Grietje. Jan and Hans are garden stock, our *wolfswelp* a weed. Me, I like thistles.

SILVER FANFARE WITH NIGHTINGALES

Rights of conscience in these days
All deserve our silent praise.
Here we see what God has done
By his servant Washington.

Who with wisdom was a dove
By an angel through a cloud
And that gave him wisdom's plan
To secure the rights of man.

THE RIPPLING WOBBLE OF SHEPHERD MOONS

There are shepherd moons, Jan says with a flutter of hands around his head, inside Saturn's rings that cause the bands of ice rubble through which they pass to swing and twist. The orbits of the solar system are the rings of the sun. Hansje makes a hash of his hair and spins on his heel.

BRAIN

Thinking is, as Valéry said, a by-product of sleep, though sleep is thought, as witness dreams, which go on all the time, at every moment of consciousness. This is the mind scanning its data. What we call a dream is this process seen with all the receptors off, but not off duty. Dreaming is more logically at the center, midbore, of the mind than *under*. It is inmost.

PHALANX NFS GRUNDTVIG EN PARADE

Color guard on three quaggas, a Séraphine from the Tiger Lily Band bearing in the center the flag of the phalanx, a triad of daisies on a yellow field, a scout from the North Wind Wing of the Fridtjof Nansen Horde bearing the Danish flag of protoharmonian times, a Jouvencelle of the Band Mère Ann Lee bearing the flag of the League, dove volant over a wheatsheaf.

THE DRUMS
Behind them, on foot, forty drummers of the Grand Hordes playing Lully's *March of the Turenne Regiment.*

ROITELET
Alone on a zebra. Mongol dress: lilac shirt, kumquat britches, T'ang blue boots, Tabasco neckerchief.

NOURRISSONS
In goat carts and in the arms of Chérubins and Chérubines, some asleep, some crying, some astonished out of their minds.

POUPONS
On Alsatians, some in Peruvian dress, some in Chinese, some in Greek. Each has a Séraphin to prevent spills and to command the Alsatians.

LUTINS
In dog carts drawn by Saint Bernards with shoulder reins. A Gymnasien shepherd precedes them seated backwards on a yak, to keep them more or less in the same direction.

BAMBINS ET BAMBINES
Thrinters on tricycles, both sexes wearing bloomers and skirts, Norwegian student caps, and such merit badges as they have so far accumulated: shoulder rosettes for friendships, manners, rhythm band, coloring, singing, flower arranging, and ring dances.

CHÉRUBINS ET CHÉRUBINES
Divided into Hordes and Bands, both on Shetland ponies, the Hordes (two-thirds boys who prefer the companionship of boys, one-third tomboys) in drab Hun cavalry jackets and legginged trousers, with yellow waist sashes, the Bands (two-thirds girls and one-third boys who prefer the companionship of girls) in Saint-Simoniste smocks and ruffled pants. Many sport the violet ribbon for dyadic bonding, and wear the steel ring thereof, some the decoration for ambition (red ribbon, copper ring). The Band leads, the Horde rides behind.

SÉRAPHINS ET SÉRAPHINES
Bands on zebras, Hordes on quaggas. Like a field of tulips in March wind. Argot Porcupine Minor.

HORDES ET BANDES

Company after company to a trill of drums, the Grundtvig Harmonian Silver Cornet Marching Band, and the commands of sergeants each in the key of their quagga's whinny, Lycéens et Lycéenes, Gymnasiens et Gymnasiennes, Jouvenceaux et Jouvencelles, Adolescents et Adolescentes, Formés et Formées, divided into Hordes and Bands, further divided into Vestales et Vestels, sashed in white, and Damoiselles et Damoiseaux in dyads, triads, and quartets of lovers wearing blue sashes.

DAPPLES IN PAIRS

On horses, the Grand Hordes and Bands of Athlétiques et Athlétiques, Virils et Viriles, Rafinés et Rafinées, respectively nude, dressed as Janissaries, and as nobles in the court dress of Louis XIV.

THE ACHIEVED

Preceded by a Band of Grammarians and Flower Police on bicycles in weaving formations, singing The Harmonian Hymn *a capella*, squadrons of Temperés et Temperées on Morgan horses, Prudents et Prudentes on Tennessee Walking horses, Révérends et Révérendes, Vénérables et Vénérables in carriages with guests and friends.

VICTORIAS AND LANDAUS

Patriarches et Patriarches. They are led by a color guard of the Little Bands bearing flags of all the orders and decorations of the Patriarchate: banners for prize custards and gravies, marches and waltzes, symphonies and string quartets, poetry and prose, histories and biographies, buildings and gardens, theology and philosophy, painting and printing, the lilac jack of friendship joined into circular iron, the azure jack of love divided into elliptical tin, the dandelion jack of paternal and maternal love subtracted into parabolic lead, the red jack of ambition multiplied into hyperbolic copper, the indigo jack of intrigue progressed into spiral silver, the green jack of alternating passions balanced in squared platinum, the orange jack of composite attractions calculated into logarithmic gold, and, borne by a spadger on a quagga front and center before the first rank of the Patriarchate, wearing on his frayed and bemucked vest the crocus of a Spartan Imp, the sugarcane tassel of a Cookie Master, the rosette of an Early Damoisel, the compasses of a Pioneer Geographer, and the sheephook of a Goblin Shepherd, the white jack of unity strengthened into cycloid mercury.

OHIO

Antéar carmacel volpur alvic orante finedis oblumen ravile ostramador molaine salamas tourmac talamalente affedice iperbouc altermadule udor.

ROSE COMB BLACK SUMATRAN BANTAM

Kokkos! Kokkoi! Kokkydzo!

BEETHOVEN

Grietje and Wolfgang in a ring of art books on the rug. He is happy, baffled, cooperative, lost. He's in a new shirt and looks grand. They'd been shopping, the two of them. A yellow shirt, latest French mode. Yellow socks. Yellow underpants of fetching neatness and brevity, as I'm shown, with white trim. A russet wool sweater. *O ja!* says Grietje, for fashion plate and stunning dazzler, look no further than our Wolfje here. The salesgirl at Buffy's on Prikkestraat was all adither. And now we're learning paintings and drawings and sculpture. Wolfgang! Who painted this? He tucks his lips at the corners, ruins his hair, looking hard. Beethoven, he says.

WE SHALL ALL HAVE TAILS
Like Pan, like satyrs, like quagga colts. The tails of northern Europeans will hang in a jug-handle curve to the calves, with a blond tip like a watercolor brush, and will switch friskily. Oriental tails will be hairless, African tails will have a hyacinthine tuft.

RIVER AND SKY
Here the antiwhales will preach, here the odor roosters tread.

AMOS
Can two walk together, except they be agreed?

ZWEM
Thirty thousand atomic bombs. That, says Joris, is what the VSA has stockpiled, and poised to fly in their silos. Actually, the number is 29,200, but they are right now making 19,000 more. It is insane. This in the locker room at the gym, and without transition, he says, how *medegevoeland* can you be, Friend Adriaan? Try me, I say. One of those days, he says, when because I, the radical rationalist enemy of superstition and sentimentality, am wearing briefs that once belonged to a fellow name of Jaap. Which, off and slung between his thumbs for me to see, were dappled all the yellows from cream to lemon, and smelled of soaked straw. First glop on them was Jaap's, he says, they're his, were his, and night after night I've added my own. The mind of a monkey, *ja*?

WARDEN PYE
English warden, or garden, pears cooked with sugar, mace, nutmeg, saffron, prunes, ginger, and raisins, covered with a lattice crust rubbed with eggwhite and butter, is one of the first desserts to be served at Florishuis. The pear was brought to England by the Romans. Sander said that it was the best thing he's ever eaten, or ever expects to eat. Which, said Grietje, was what he'd said about the chocolate cake last evening, and the Chinese compote the evening before, and the apple flan the evening before that. You're beautiful, replied Sander.

ROSALES
Three families. The Rosaceae, comprising four subfamilies: seventeen genera of Spiraeoideae, thirty-four genera in two thousand species of Rosoideae, fourteen genera in six hundred species (Malus and Pyrus among them) of Maloideae, three genera in a hundred species of Prunoideae (Prunus and Amygda-

lus among them: apricot, cherry, almond). The Neuradaceae: three genera in ten species. The Chrysobalanaceae: twelve genera in three hundred species.

AFTERNOON IN THE PARK

Onverschilligheid. Jantje's grey gym shorts, of such *inkorting* as to leave his lean brown legs bare from crotch to toe, are of a *dubbelgebreide stof* that gives and clings with equal deference to cleft, plane, and clump. His soccer jersey, striped mustard, white, and slate, he pulled over his head, fluffing his hair. Undermost, *een minimaal schuilseksezak, Hermes stijl micro*, which he proposed to wear in the park. *Precies!* he said to Hansje's doubting squinch. *Iets van de nieuwe tijd, ja?* My *waarachtig zeg!* got tolerant pity from Hans, whose formal response was to simplify his outfit to docked jeans and nothing else, to be shed once we were in the park. The anthropology of all this is taxing and encodes structuralist wonderments. Called Kaatje to report that a patrol of one philosopher and two all but naked urchins were off to sunbathe in Vondel Park for reasons apparent to the urchins but not to the philosopher, quite possibly inspired by the *bosgod* Pan. By, said Kaatje, the TV and newspaper pictures of *tieners* in the raw. It's the *manie* nowadays. The police have given up. If you get a good offer to sell or rent the monsters, I get half. It's foreplay, if you want to know, in *jongetje's* Choctaw. There'll be a *wervelstorm* in the bed here afterwards. *Voorlijk!*

BORDEAUX

Great whales stand in the sea and preach.

ONSTUIMIG

Wolfgang serenely applying paint beside Sander, cooperation itself. But Grietje tells me that Wolfje was impudent after breakfast and that she spanked him for it good and hard. He wept rather more bitterly than the tragedy warranted, causing Sander to pucker up, all heartbroken, and weep hot tears, a greater spate of them when Grietje offered to slap him if he tried to comfort Wolfje. Good God! she shouted, is this what men are! Tears skeeting in all directions because she had to whack an insolent butt? Fortunately Wolfgang, little devil, thought it hilarious that Sander was crying because he was crying, whereupon Sander spanked him, got bit, and got called a cocksucker. At this point Grietje left to discuss all this with Kaatje, expressing grave doubts about the charms of children. They agreed that they'd seen nothing like the worst of it: that if I'd been there, I would have wept to see Sander weeping. Bruno was consulted. He suggested, helpfully, that we'd brought it all on ourselves by taking in a gutter rat. This put Grietje on the defensive, damning all men as aliens, pigs, and bullies. When I got home, Grietje was still hot under the collar but relieved to find Sander and Wolfje happily at work on a painting, Sander on the lines, Wolfgang on the fill. Men, said Grietje.

GIGUE

Grietje, in from jogging cycling paths before breakfast, full of herself: O God the kinks in my shoulders and legs! Bragging by complaining. Coffee made, and she'd picked up rolls at the bakery. These panties, she said, showing me, ride my clit as I run, and between the exhilaration of lungs full of oxygen and the outrageous fun of a playing panty crotch I was as close to coming as you can get without hand or man. Whee, I'm slick! Did an extra kilometer to see if I could come running. Built up and built up, better and better, but no popped cork. Adriaan, your mouth is hanging open. Plucked her gym shorts down, and the cooperative panties, and sat, sweet creature, in the kitchen chair across from me, my newspaper and coffee, and with knees wide and eyes closed, gasping, clitoris nipped between two trembling fingers, she came. Oof! Sweet and sharp as a chime of bells, she said with a pleased, silly grin. Woke horny, sweetened matters with some zippy foreplay (Wolfje asleep on top of Sander, like a lionness on a limb in Kenya), suited up, had a splendid run, and a neat one-ring orgasm, all before breakfast. Bundled her into a hug around the hips before she put herself together, a petting kiss on the warm clump, a tongued one on the tummy, smooch for the navel. Whoopee love! she sang as she sprinted upstairs, returning with Wolfgang over her shoulder. Yawning Sander followed, fighting his way into a sweater, cock and a lobe of scrotum drooping free from his briefs. These Grietje poked back in, tidied the fit, and went to work on Wolfje's curls with a comb while he swigged orange juice. Clever elves to know such knots. Kiss Adriaan. Wolfgang recited the rote of kissing: kiss everybody first thing in the morning, when they go out and come in, and at bedtime. Lot of kissing, do you ask me. He was in his Old Testament nightgown. The robe of Amos, Sander said, as Adriaan reads us about, except that Amos probably didn't have sperm on his. Who's Amos? Wolfje asked, giving me my kiss, orange-flavored, on the corner of the mouth. Grietje's full lips, Sander's on his ear. Sander, a long swallow of coffee down, lifted the scriptural shift and paid back the kiss on Wolfje's lizardy penis. The Harmony! What, said Grietje handing around rolls buttered and bejammed, if the case-worker who noses out stray boys raids us someday, and Hans and Jan are in their ancient Greek position with legs at both ends, and Adriaan and I are making the Nipper, and Saartje and Jensje are rippling orgasms through each other and cooing like doves, and Sander is licking Wolfje all over and showing him how to jack off longer and oftener, never mind the bare-tailed population in the paintings all over the house? We'll plead, said Sander, an accomplished talent for love and affection, and say that when any of us looks at any other of us, we start coming then and there, crotches overheat, cocks leap up stiff and bounce, and it doesn't do us the least good to fuck each other crazy, because we're so simple-minded that we see all over again how lovely we are, Grietje's long trim legs with the brown crimpled crump of hair curving down and under, my handsome self and manly dick, Adriaan's noble eyes, furry chest, and freehanded love, Wolfje's curls and snipsnub nose, and we're back at it. Would that make it clear? Placid smile from Wolfgang glossy with gooseberry jam. And then, said Grietje, the longnosed social snoop may arrive when Adriaan's piled around with books in his private pipesmoke weather, writing, and Wolfgang's lettering *Africaland* in South America on his big world map, and I'm reading Proust with Kaatje, and Hans and Jan have their zippers up and are talking ballbearings and skateboards, and Sander's painting a still life with pumpkins and figs. You never know.

GAMME
Avant garde. Embryo, *Homo ignorans*.
Aileron ascendant. Baby, *Homo infans*.
Aile ascendante. Child, *Homo imaginator*.
Pivot. Adolescent, *Homo pubens*.
Aile descendante. Youth, *Homo juventus*.
Aileron descendant. Middle age, *Homo faber*.
Arrière garde. Old age, *Homo senex*.

A WALK WITH JORIS
He pads, pigeon-toed, his wide shoulders seesawing counter to the rocking of his narrow hips. Thumbs hooked into jeans pockets. Always looks at my eyes to talk, but listens with head down. He might be taken for *een straatschender*, especially in his Lenin cap, but this mistake corrects itself in his cropped glossy curls, the fineness of his nose, the apologetic sweetness of his eyes.

WHEATMEAL BISCUIT, BORDEAUX, AND GOUDA
Well, says Hans, I'll probably be an engineer like Papa, and reclaim more of the North Sea bottom and call it The Netherlands. I will be a Radical Socialist like Joris, and reform all the laws, and fight for the good old rights of man, so we can all be free and happy. I could be a philosopher like Ome Adriaan if I

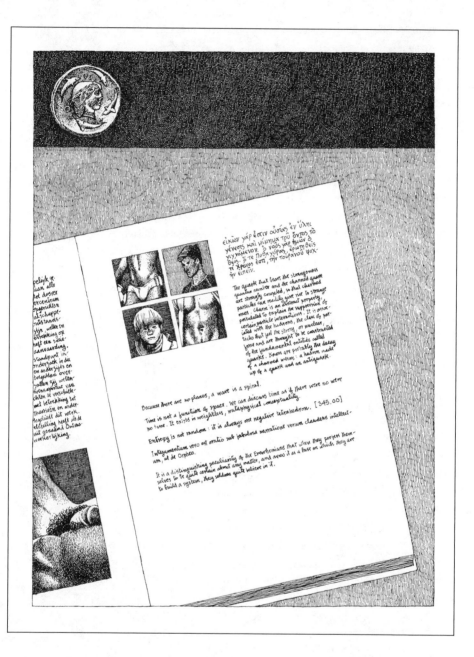

learn how to spell, or a painter like Grootpapa and Sander. That would be neat. Jan and I might be explorers together if he becomes an anthropologist and not a mathematician wearing a stocking cap like Einstein. We'd be like Humboldt and Bonpland. I'm going to marry Jenny, and he Saartje, if we still like them when we grow up, and live in a house together. Jenny wants to be a judge, can you imagine, but Saartje thinks she might like to be an architect. But if the Americans and Russians blow us up with their crazy bombs, we won't be anything but dead. America is all automobiles and gangsters, and all their kids want to do is zonk out on dope and listen to pukey music. Russia is all concentration camps and factory workers. Bunch of dumb clods, both of them. Americans all look as if they owned grocery stores.

FULLER'S *SYNERGETICS* 1056.15
Human awareness first apprehends, then sometimes goes on to comprehend. No guarantees.

LA FOUGUE DE SALETÉ
O I'll buy them, Kaatje said. There's no *not* buying them. The good of being a mother is that nothing fazes you, nothing can. *Een gekeperd katoen broekje voor een jongen van 12 jaar, 4 cm ritssluiting, wit*, O God. They come with an elasticized nylon belt. No need to call Hilda: she'll think it charming. My official line is that it's nasty. That's predictable parental backwardness, of course. Thus Kaatje on the phone. White denim short pants for Hans and Jan to wear without briefs and never to be washed. To sport stains of piss and sperm boldly and frankly. Jan it was, the enemy of hypocrisy, who asked me if I thought they could get away with it. Really messy, Hans elaborated, come all over inside and out. We'll wear them here and at home, and on the island if it's just us. Beautifully grubby, spitterspatter you won't believe. Makes you wish you'd never met us, doesn't it? Where your peter pokes the pantsleg out will be the gunkiest and ripest.

A BASKET OF PEARS
Red feckles brown on pale yellow, once green.

WOUTERS
Rik Wouters' pears scattered on a table. Musées Royaux des Beaux Arts, Brux-elles. One of the most brilliant colorists of his time, Wouters died in the Great

War (1916) after only four years of work in the style freed by Ensor, integrated by Cézanne, brightened by Van Gogh, and launched by the Fauves.

BLUE VASE OF CHRYSANTHEMUMS

Bruno by to collect Hans and Jan. Why *badger*? he asked, pulling on Hans' briefs for him, with a smooch on his navel, hauling on his jersey, combing his hair with his fingers. Why not cubs, puppies, colts? It seemed right, said Jan drying his dick on his undershirt. He leaned over Hans having his shoes tied to give Bruno a kiss on the corner of the mouth. Regulations, he said. Bruno squeezed him into a hug, which Jan passed on to me, and which Bruno redelivered in person. Come have a drink, and supper, can you? Cleared with Sander and Grietje downstairs, working on the nipper with Wolfje huddled against them, each with an arm around him. His invention, and not as impossible as I thought it would be. His bony shoulders fit under Grietje's arm around him, his head against her breast, his hips under her spread thigh. I lock him in with my left arm, my right around Grietje. Scrunches his eyes with the pleasure of being included, but looks worried when Grietje groans. Fine, says Sander, you want Wolfje with you, or does Wolfje want to go to the flicks with us? The flicks. So we drop Jan off at his home.

GAMME

Avant garde. Camphor (Raspail, koala bears, mothballs)
Aileron ascendant. Musk (billy goats, skunks)
Aile ascendante. Floral (pear, apple)
Pivot. Mint (beebalm, peppermint, all four-sided stems)
Aile descendante. Ether
Aileron descendant. Pungent (pepper, the savory)
Arrière garde. Putrid (faeces, *E. coli*, carrion)

SEURAT

Hans in his yellow straw hat, blue shadow across his eyes.

RIETVELDTAFEL

Because we have more lumber than we need, Hans and I cut the pieces for another Rietveld worktable, paint the slats blue, yellow, and red, and take all the makings tied to the tabletop of thin strong plywood over to Joris', and in fifteen minutes assemble it before his astonished eyes, complete with a white oilcloth thumbtacked underneath drumhead tight over the surface. There, I say, when someone asks about De Stijl, show them this table, and say that you have it because a philosopher and his nephew were making a batch of them for Florishuis, and thought it fun to give their friend Joris one. We aim, said Hans gazing at copies of *Pan* and *Kouros*, to please.

KUS

In the sunroom beyond us, Hans and Jenny wrapped around each other on the wicker lounge. Apparently, Kaatje said, giving me coffee, they don't need to breathe. They've been like that for an hour. Tongues in each other's mouths, hands in each other's jeans. Makes Jan pine away. He and Saartje smooch, but don't like each other that way. They'd rather talk books and films.

FREE BADGER OUTING AND RAMBLE

Jan's report for the Bulletin Board. Joris the corporal, Hans & Jan the troops. Errands first: two bladders of Payne's Grey, one of vermilion, four of raw Sienna, ginger and lemon drops for Jenny and Saartje, pipe cleaners for Ome A (Joris' prize idea). Swim at the Jeugdgroepje COC, everybody nice and naked, but we had to wear a Parental Permission Supervised tag around our necks (orange plastic bit with blue printing, on a short stainless steel chain) which Joris called our leashes though he's the one needs a leash (you said absolute truth in unvarnished words). He blushed to his shoulders when we all stripped and his whooper rose and nodded, *sakkerloot*! The boffer *lijf-wacht* (seatless orange pouch for a *slipje*, stencilled COC, *fijn fysiek*, patted us all on the behind, Joris too) is named Karel and is a student at the university and did his jaw ever drop down and his eyebrows shoot up when Hansje said brightly he's Ome A's *neef*. Ome A will get us for this, but we discovered that Joris blushes like a tomato if you kiss him, also his hangdown bounces, and I think we may have overdone this maybe to see if it ever quit working but it never did. Kiss, blush, jump. Made friends with Joop and Jaap, good swimmers. Hot chocolate afterwards at the canteen, the Family Sinaasappel doing the handsome thing with half my allowance. Joris says that getting kissed by people eating glazed doughnuts should be written out of *De Eengezindheid*. Why then does it make his eyes shine? To his place afterwards where, as per orders, we called home and got Bruno on the air, to say that we were there and to see when we had to be home. Joris got invited to supper by the Keirinckxen. New *Pan*, with Danes big and little. Horsed around, talked sexy, did our best to drive Joris out of his mind, and were generally impossible. J. Sinaasappel.

EXPEDITION

Picked up J & H. Sander's paint, pastilles for sisters. Signed us in at COC where we swam and had refreshments. To my room for conversation and looking at books and pictures. J & H beautifully behaved the whole time. No complaints. Joris.

BADGERS ON THE LOOSE

Report as required by snoopy family. Submitted by Hans K. We were taken by big Joris our friend and keeper for the afternoon and bought things as Jan says in his version at the art store and candy shop and tobacco shop and we went to the swimming pool for Free Badgers at the club Joris belongs to and made two good friends who collect stamps and went to summer camp in Denmark and the lifeguard who knows who Ome Adriaan is, fancy that, and we teased Joris something awful. The pool has too much chlorine in it. Joris has pictures and books in his room all to himself and let us see *Pan* from Denemarken (golly). Then we came home and brought Joris with us as the folks invited him to supper where he was shy as he wasn't with us. Hans.

KRIETIEK

Never do things to make people feel bad. Joris can handle your teasing, which seems to have been within the bounds of friendship. *Pan* is *in orde*, the *Noorweegs* edition is even more *wellustig*. Glazed doughnut kisses with chocolate backlash are what the Harmony is all about. The *gamme* should be from licorice to raspberries rolled in sugar. The university student who's the lifeguard will probably ask to buy you two for $f100$ down and $f50$ a week for a thousand years, at 20% interest, but I imagine Joris would outbid him.

ANTWOORD

Yes and nobody was impolite enough to complain of kissing a wirebrush no matter how good Joris shaved.

KRIETIEK

Sounds puky but who cares? Note well, long-legged Hamsters, and brood on Adriaan's words about other people's feelings. Kaatje.

SCOUT

Joris has the gift of friendship, and in the scale of things, *de weegschaal*, is a forward scout in the chord of the passions. If genius is the courage of talent, and if friendship is a talent, a natural inclination and affinity, he will prosper.

GIRLS

Komaan! Sander pleads, joshing Wolfgang, not until the *kopje* of your *onder-broek*'s fat as an oatfed figpecker will you see what a looker Saartje is. At this Saartje, posing for Sander, kecked and held her forehead. Wolfje fipped his thumb at her. *Peuter!*

GRIETJE

Thought you didn't like girls, Shrimp, Sander says of Wolfje in Grietje's lap, in fine late afternoon sun by the window, the two looking at a picture book with animals and the alphabet in it, Wolfje's arm around Grietje's neck, his head snuggled against hers. Grietje's not a girl, said a vexed Wolfje, Grietje's Grietje.

THE BLUE-EYED NIPPER

With, says Sander to the ripping downslide of his zipper tab, a neat slot with clit at the top, which I shall kiss as soon as she has howled hello to the world, or cunning little spout and clever little balls, which I shall also kiss. What's going to be little about his pisser, Grietje asked, if he takes after either of his daddies? We'll have twins, says Sander, if we have the best luck in all Amster-dam, *knaap en meisje*, and they will go at it as soon as Spermandillo can climb on top of Clitorella. Rock their own cradle. Was anything ever so much fun! Here's Grietje between us, and half of the nipper is somewhere under all that hair around Adriaan's testicles, or here in mine, and the other half's up here in Grietje, aching to fuse and grow, and squeeze out, a sweet little blue-eyed fucker. Two little blue-eyed fuckers.

FOURIER SERIES

It was in the attempt to write a mathematical formula for the vibration of a violin's string that d'Alembert, Euler, and Bernoulli asked if the extension of an arbitrary function of x be possible. A series of sines being both periodic and odd, an arbitrary function of a single variable must have these two properties to be developed in an infinite series of sines of multiples of the variable. f is what x does when acted upon by an arbitrary force: what course a trajectory takes in the grip of gravity when a space rocket blasts off from Cape Kennedy, with what frequency does a violin string quiver under the bow's friction, how heat radiates. Our Fourier wanted a science of the heart's *chaleur*, its warmth of affection, its repulsion. He saw that attraction is cunningly complex, and that happiness depends on the vibrancy of a feeling, on depth of tone and range of variations.

APPLE GLANS, ROSE VULVA

Ashen violet, says Grietje, to give a name to the color of Wolfje's *eikel*, snuz-
zling it between two fingers, having nipped it out of its foreskin's snurp. Wolfgang, snugly britchesless in her lap, suffers Grietje to study his penis. Feels
good, Wolfje says. I'm glad, says Grietje. Some people, says Sander. Shall I
keep this up? Grietje asks. O yes! says Wolfje.

ONTMOETING

Sander painting, Grietje darting about with pots and pans, screws and nails, I
unpacking books and hanging prints and maps, the doorbell buzzed: Jan in
cutoff jeans and tall socks, red billcap and an undershirt so deep of neck and
scye that more of his trunk was naked front and flank than clothed. He wandered about, watching, saying in his grown-up voice how spiffily everything
was shaping up. Wolfgang, painting alongside Sander, stole glances at him,
and at Jan's *Hullo Wolfgangje*, snapped his fingers and mimed a smile. Only
area in place is the Free Badger cot on my floor, with its Danish rag rug,
Navajo blanket, *schuimblusser* pillow, Shaker canebottom chair (for clothes),
and the three-leaved folding screen acquired for Sander's models, rarely used,
relegated to the Free Badger territory but denounced as prudish and counter-
revolutionary by the Badgers, and by Sander. In *this* house! *In ieder geval*, Jan,
watching me clean glazings and reframe a Klee *Angel*, conspued the dressing
screen, unjeaned and debriefed, desneakered and unsocksed with what level
ease, *grote genade*, and cool unconcern for boring convention, leaving on the
airy undershirt for some abstruse erotic motive, whiffling a flutter of fingers
over a dapperly lifting cock and tight balls. Hansje's somewhere on the way
over? I ask. His fly ricked out by a jumping hard on? An indulgent grin and
stuck-out tongue for my joshing. The phone, Grietje answering, and then
Grietje herself looking at Jan through fingers crossed over her eyes: Hansje
has been levied by Pastor Duckfoot or Turnipseed to work on posters at the
rectory. O Lord, and Jan's heart, so to speak, is all set. The rectory! Jan cried,
those Jesus hooters and Godhoppers have my Hans? For how long? All afternoon, I'm afraid, Kaatje said on the phone. Help us paint walls, pitch in upstairs, help Adriaan shoo microbes off all his things there. Jan sat on the cot,
disgusted. Hold on, I said, and nipped up to Sander and Wolfgang. Explained
the situation tersely. Oof! said Sander. Send the scamp up. We'll put him to
work.

ADFABILITAS POST COITUS

Dubonnets *rouges* with twist of lemon peel, deep late afternoon, only the
crumpled whirl of bedsheets evidence of our spirited tumble. Two helpings

from each papa, said Grietje, sipping and smiling with closed eyes, of nipper makings. A wink for me. I'm glad we're not doing it in cold blood. We can get a girl who paints, a girl philosopher, a boy who loves his sister. Have both of you been swigging rocketbooster fuel? I'm still coming in little blips and tickles. It was, said Sander, the two rascals up there. I thought I'd slammed goal on all the facts of life, but no. Dear sweet cool brainy Jan came up to drown his disappointment in work. He dwelt on the exact nature of his disappointment in such gutter Dutch that Master Wolfgang grew a lightheaded grin all dimples and squeezing eyelashes. Something else, these *kleuters* with permanent erections and steadfast willingness. Traded smiles, those two, and Wolfje shed his overalls in two flicks for the galluses, a push down, and a kick, but Jantje was quicker still and had skinned back his lean peter with the chubby noddle while Wolfje was scrounging his out of his diapers. Poked the heads of them together, the buggers, and rolled them around each other. And hands slid to shoulders and hands slid under balls and hands felt butts. So I made an armload of the two of them, lugged them over to the cot, and left them hugging each other with arms and legs into rather a tight knot. Eros, I said, with his famous inspiration. Passed around, said Grietje. Fucked silly.

CASTOR AND POLLUX IN TORINO
De Chirico moved from dreams of Italian plazas at four o'clock in the afternoon with train trestles which are also aqueducts with impost arches to a butterscotch neoclassicism generated by the motif of Castor and Pollux, and painted as if by a blind Raphael. They were there all along, *questi eroici fratelli, questi gemelli*, invisible among the metaphysical pineapples and shattered Niobes, invisible as stars in daylight. Nietzsche put them there, seeing them athletic and blank of eye beside the black-blinkered smoking carriage and dray horses who spoke to him from time to time, of time, of the eternal return, of character and fate. I know you, Horse, Nietzsche said. You are the floss-silk-maned stallion of Alkman's dawn dance for girls dressed as doves. I have heard of your rolling eye in Anakreon, the hollow thunder of your hooves in Sophokles, the noble pace of your gait in Homeros. And, replied the horse, Kastor and Polydeukes, tall and square-shouldered as gods, have walked with me in Spartan pastures.

SPACE
Joris immensely happy to come with me to the island for the weekend. Says he has too few outings, that Lenin liked outings, that in a people's republic the outing would be a ritual. He made on over the boat, the crossing, the cabin,

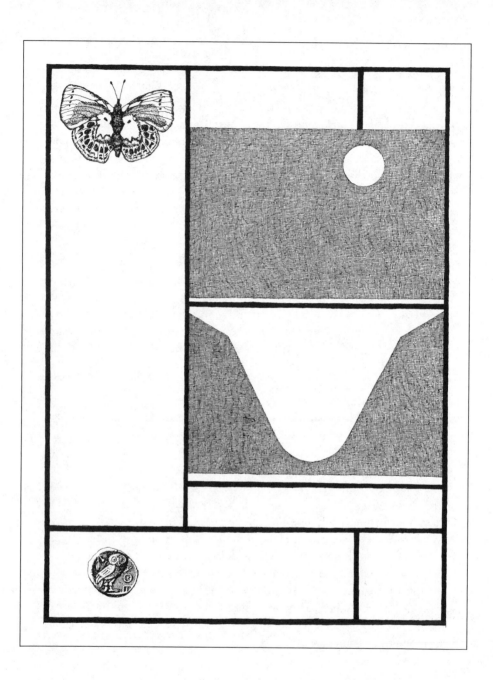

the perfect isolation. A philosopher's place, like Lenin's quiet place in the Moscow woods, and how easily he could have missed ever seeing one! Particularly taken by the open fire, vistas of trees and sea out the windows. Would I, later on, read him poetry, or some pages of a philosophy book? Asked me to teach him table manners. He has felt lost at Godfried's, having to learn by looking. Would I help him with grammar in Dutch and in English? Good talk by the fire. Bedtime, a choice of sleeping bag or bed. This confused him. Share the bed! Whyever not? What was the problem? It's a chilly night. We snuggle under good wool army blankets, and sleep. The bed's narrow, I admitted, but Sander and I manage to be comfortable in it, and we've made do, several times, with Hans and Jan between us. Seems he'd never slept with anyone. That is, not to sleep. Considering his leanings, he'd thought I wouldn't want to share a bed with him. *Godsnaam!* We'll be the snugger and the easier. *Wel zo!* he said, grinning and blinking, thumbs hitched in the pockets of his narrow jeans with the *uitspringend* crotch, I'm as clean as a whistle, no crud between the toes, no microbe cultures anywhere, all surfaces and crannies neurotically policed. Us Dutch! He undressed with studied grace, folding socks across parallel sneakers, jeans packed square, shirt rolled, Lenin cap and wristwatch, down to a hard-fitting undershirt and sexy blue briefs. Wry inspection of my flannel pyjamas and a question in his eyes as he peeled down his briefs, pouched his cheeks in doubt, and tugged them back to a neat fit again.

POLIS KAI EROS

A dark uneasy sea outside: weather is always part of a conversation. By our kind fire we work on Joris' brochure for the NSAP. In any consideration of erotic isonomy, Erewhon appears. Joris admits that the spadgers and striplings in *Spartansker Yngling* open before us in their lean leggy comeliness toasted by August light are the very ones his revolution is to free from the thralldom of capitalist repression. Physique he does not doubt is character. Fourier imagined the phalanx to be a genetic pool, like a people, Chinese or Zulu or Mongol, so that beauty would be in the local idiom. Joris' theory is that ugly people are unloved, unhappy people. We must, he says, free society from its fear of itself. We must free the troll from his iron burrow, the politician from his lies, the economic system from its dependence on war. They say to Eros, these trolls, you may not, you cannot, you must not.

FELICITER

Genoeglijk kan de voorhuid gemakkelijk over de eikel worden teruggeschoven.

A LETTER FROM SWEETBRIER

My dear Quaggamaster! Fondest remembrances to Hans and Jan. Have you read Serres? The genepool is, among other things, a reservoir of differences. Big feet, little feet, big ears, little ears, all the anatomical distinctions catalogued only in *ars erotica*, Hokusai's *Kinoye no komatsou*, and the Dutch Erewhonians: encoded in genes, concentrated or diffused in the gene pool. Difference is potential energy. If we are to believe the second law of thermodynamics, differences in temperature, in electrical charge, in gravitational force are what get dissipated in closed systems. Without differences, everything becomes homogenous mush. Entropy is not chaos but uniformity. Reverberant bounce must be the Harmony's dance, difference caroming off difference, energy jostling energy. Mathematically, information measures improbability. If one of eight equally probable events happens, it carries more information than an event that's one of two equally probable states. Diversity, you see, informs. And improbability turns out to be another way of talking about difference, which in turn means information, like energy, which is yet another way of talking about difference. Meaning moves by contrast. In Serre's essay on Lucretius, he distinguishes between science inspired by Venus (that of Lucretius, and let us add, Fourier) and science inspired by Mars (that of everybody else, to hear him tell it). The science of Mars is obsessed with laws of regularity. Regularity, of course, turns out to be repetition. Thus Serres thinks science is dedicated to abolishing novelty and change. His science of Venus starts with the *clinamen* of the atomists (the swerve atoms make when they fall), which he identifies as the minimal angle to laminar flow that can initiate a turbulence. Turbulence is Aphrodite's work, Leonardo's sinuosities, Pound's sea-swirl. *Turbantibus æquora ventis*: pockets of turbulence scattered in air or water, breaking the parallelism of repetitive waves. This is a physics of vortices, of sweetness and smiling voluptuousness, the sea-swept movement of intertwined lovers (one force plunging like waves in tidal wrinkle, the other spiraling like spinning water). *Suave ventis vexari voluptas*. Lovers, winds, trees, grasses move in the voluptuous roll of the high seas, the turn of the galaxies. Desire is linear, its achievement a convolution. Poincaré's protoform of the earth was pear-shaped, evolving toward apple. The Bands and Hordes swarm. Their passional movement is curvilinear. Eros is design mastering accident. Our point of view, of course. From an angel's, it's like what you say about accident and design. Aphrodite's wild chance, and Ares is symmetry.

HORDES

1881, the year Franz Hellen was born, swarms of the red admiral (*Vanessa atalanta*) encrimsoned Russia.

RAMS' HORNS ARE CURLED

All this sociology and psychology, Godfried says, even with Frits Bernard, all these case histories and cobbled together Greek and Latin medical words, none of these can get anywhere near Eros. Our alienation of the animals is like our alienation of children from the characteristic events of human fate. Both are a gratuitous cruelty, the result of timidity and fear, of smallness. We've disguised ignorance as science. Human nature does not change, only humanity. Greek love of children may have been a survival of a common Neolithic sentiment, or it may have been an invention, unlikely, to link the Theban Phalanx into a fence of shields.

THE CAUSE

Olaf's article for *Spejderpatrulje* a candy box of idealism and Erewhonian logic, Godfried consulting Erasmus while adding Nietzschean tinges, Erasmus vastly pleased to be consulted, his canted eye acquiring a tickle. Knuckles to chin, he agrees and questions, jumping up to dash at Tobias playing spaceship at the windows, who has remarked a dozen times, if only we would look, *you can see every star.*

NAZOMER VAN SINT MAARTEN

Islandbound, we're to brown Wolfje in the last summer sun. Jan in his buttcheating nasty pants carrotyellow at the shove of his pecker's neb in an oval stain, tugs on jersey, socks, and sneakers. He asks the time, says he must nip home and see if he and Jenny can go to the island with us, *wat leuk.* A ferocious hug for Hansje still poodlenaked, handshake for me, and kiss, *een smaakje van eikel.* And strode off on slender brown legs with horsy knees, out to the parade ground milling with zebras and quaggas to mount his Strookstreep and prance with the Ned Ludd Spokkelmaandwind. *Eskadron!* Erewhonian pioneers on patrol! We shall ride along eating strawberries, bred upon Terra by the silver planet Mercurius. We shall ride along singing in Porcupine.

GIVERNY

Fourier's *attraction* is the dialect of the logos which every individual imagination finds most articulate. Whitman's grass was such a dialect of the logos, Einstein's light, Homer's fire and wheat, Monet's lilypond, rivers, and fields of haystacks. Monet's eye kept to the processes of water and light, from watertable to clouds. The haystacks stand in fields reclaimed from the old European marshlands, the draining of which was the basis of culture. The lilypond is a remnant of the marsh restored by Monet. The Japanese footbridge across it spans where he has diverted the Epte to pool in his garden before it flows into the Seine at Vernon, detained for study. Symbol, or focus of attraction, is pivot, generating a series of affinities in a territorial parameter of the functions of the series. The phalanx of attention correlates accident with design.

COFFEE, SCHETSBOEK, PIPE

De Volkskrant and Wolfje's bright citron underpants with wolfcub pawprint where he left them by Strabo to niddle his dink, *sic ait*, until every slide was jam. Grietje, reading Columella in her nest of cushions, had lent a hand, Wolfje patient with her good intentions until Sander, sorting out ideas with me about Seurat's *Asnières*, noticed his fastidious pout, hooked him across to us with a long reach of foot, laid him on his lap, and took over his advancement into sweet idiocy as absentmindedly as Grietje but with a resourcefulness more to Wolfje's liking. *Nu ja*, Grietje said, they're the same age. What, Adriaan, is your notebook with all the neat writing and *collages* for? His work it is, said Wolfje. He told me. My work is to help Sander, to learn to read, and to be the house cricket. Also, when the Blue-Eyed Nipper comes, to talk to it and wash it and kiss its bellybutton to make it laugh.

BODIES AND PLEASURES

The focus of resistance to sexuality as a deployment of negations ought not to be sexual desire but bodies and pleasures with comprehensive desires in a harmony of attractions synergetic of integrity. Subtitles, please, says Grietje. To assign all knowledge to Homer, Strabo writes, is zeal beyond its limit: as if one hung apples and pears (*mela kai ongknas*) on an Attic garland of flowers and leaves. Sander! she howls, translate the subtitles. It means, says Sander, that if you're nibbling peanuts while reading Proust and playing with yourself, you should also grab Wolfgang and kiss him if he's near. Isn't that right, Adriaan? Better, I say, a Belgian hare in the cabbages at Angelus. Pears of Anjou, apples of Brittany, a wooden bowl, lace curtains at the rectory windows. Hollyhocks. A family of hedgehogs. That's what I said, says Sander. Adriaan speaks Adriaan. I speak Sander. Wolfje speaks chocolate from ear to ear, getting the paint on flat, even, and within my lines. He speaks hugged by everybody, peterproud in his spiffy togs. Ideas come from tall trees along a country canal, from cabbage gardens as along the Epte, from swimming, walking, watching the sea from a window of the island cabin, from a sky thick with mares' tails.

PROSPECT

On canvases four meters square Sander sets out to paint us all in Hokusai curvilinear Mondriaan, as Harmonians, to make, he says, brush in teeth, hands in backpockets of his jeans, with a shuffle of feet, the future a little less impossible. Hans and Jan ask to be painted with their arms around each other's shoulders, dressed in the cavalry outfits of the Little Hordes. Beside Hans, sitting, a fennec. Beside Jan, a silver wolf. Very Pisanello, he specifies. Grietje on a quagga, Wolfgang on a pony. Studies for the big *Island*, these portraits. Sander's *Grande Jatte*.

SLAAPMAAT

Phone rang midevening, all of us in the studio, Sander and Wolfgang painting, Sander revising the lines of a quagga, Wolfgang whiting out the ground around a zebra, Grietje and I reading. Hilda Sinaasappel. Jan rather imaginatively and very seriously wants to come over and spend the night with Wolfgang. He put it to us so frightfully honestly. What did I think? Fine by us, I said. Is this something Wolfgang and Jan planned? No no, said La Sinaasappel, I rather suppose Jan thought it up, brooded on it, and sprang it on us. Whistled impoliticly. Why do you whistle? she asked. Just being stodgy, I said. Hans and Jan had spent the large part of the afternoon with their moppy heads stived between each other's thighs in assuaging and arousing, arousing and assuaging, natural urgencies with abandon and affection. Just who, Hilda Sinaasappel asked, is this young Wolfgang? A stray boy I took in from the streets, adopted freehandedly by Grietje and Sander. At the moment he's applying flat color to one of Sander's *Hordes on Patrol* canvases, apt as any Dutchman with a brush. Jan came on the line, asking to speak to Wolfje. Whose telephone style turns out to be all *huh?* and *I guess so* and *come on over* and *yeah, I could want to*. Hilda back on: Gregorius will drive Jan over. Wolfgang, hand in pocket feeling himself, returned bowlegged and tiptoed to the painting. Sander, mouth hanging open, looked him over gawking, shook his head. So Grietje and I went downstairs to say hello to Gregorius and take in Jan who, pyjamas and toothbrush in hand, kissed his father goodnight and greeted us with a handsome good-natured smile. Something new, Grietje said just before they arrived. O God, I give Wolfgang his bath, he seems to like it, and tuck him in, though he has yet to stay in, coming to sleep in whoever's bed he can invade. Do I tuck them both in? Where, in the Badger Sett in your room or in Wolfje's bed in ours? Sander will put them in bed with us, for the fun of it.

THE STAR MILL

At Time Zero where the equinoctial hinges of the sky were Gemini and Sagit-
tarius with the Milky Way arched between them, both signs made of two
bodies, like the Fish and the Virgin with her wheat ear at the two other corners,
the road was open for gods and men to come and go into each others' realms,
wisdom seeking the ears of the perplexed, loving arms coming upon beauty,
odd dancing with even, and will again, when the wheel of time has rounded
its turn.

WHITE LIGHT

Asémanthropos the Electron Man has clicked on the lights of his eyes. Too
bright. The wall cracks, the air smokes, shadows go red, charts scorch, time
melts. He dims down the scale: sunlight on polished steel, anti-aircraft search
lights, firetruck headlamps, Hegel's brain after a bait of phosphorus, Roman
candles, sixty-watt bulb, nightlight.

MORNING LIGHT

Sander in, bawdily curious, bringing me coffee, a cunning hilarity to his stare
at both boys in my bed, asleep not quite so much in each other's arms as in
each other's legs. Cozy, said Sander. Very, I said. Do they stink? Anything that
looks that much like two della Robbia choirboys collapsed in bliss must have
something to make them human. Human! First, when I finally got to sleep,
here was Wolfje helping himself to my bed. And after some conversation I
won't shock you with, he scampered out and came back with Jan. Between
them they have sixteen elbows, thirty-two knees, at least four heads, and
enough damp penises to wreck Comrade Joris' composure for a week. All this
around 2:30. If, said Sander, you don't tell me that conversation I'll pour this
coffee over all of you. Well, translated from the demotic, they had sustained,
by mutual excitement, a hyper-sensitive euphoria in the neural ganglia of their
weewees for some unconscionable time, expressing their pleasure therein with
whimpers, yelps, and whispered salacities long on expressiveness if short on
polish, then they had swiveled and swapped spermatozoa, this reciprocal affection and piggish rootling being replayed five times, if I could have heard
correctly, after which their central nervous and cardiovascular systems shut
down intercommunications for the night, and Comrade Wolfgang began to
nod off, but had the energy to nip over to me and curl himself into my hairy
bosom. I asked him, kindly enough, if something had gone wrong that he had
left Jan. Left Jan? They had, he said, done all they could do. Yes, but Jan came
to spend the night with you, and you've left him. He'll be hurt. Do you think

so? I know so. His heart will be broken. Silence from Wolfje. Then he went away and came back with Jan. And here we are. I think it's rather much that both the little buggers have erections. You too, said Sander. Bladder, I said. They have erections because they're both sloshing about in wet dreams about spaceship commanders, soccer teams, Saartje and Jenny, and probably you. Naw, said Sander, I'm big brother to Wolfgang and grownfolks to Jan.

GAMME
Avant garde. Selfless friendship (Damon & Pythias, Hans & Jan)
Aileron ascendant. Friend through admiration, attraction, delight.
Aile ascendante. Friend through common views, hobbies.
Pivot. Love (Jonathan and David, finding oneself in another)
Aile descendante. A friend abided.
Aileron descendant. A friend for company.
Arrière garde. Selfish, with ulterior motives.

FLORISHUIS
The Shaker Submarine, Grietje calls it. Shipshape, whistle clean, as sharp as Dutch Calvinist Platonism can make it. Sander grins. But it is a house of houses: Adriaan has scads more room than in his old apartment. He has us in his hair all the time. We have a flow of space top to bottom, side to side, for visual generosity and agrophilia. We redefine privacy.

PARTITA
Przewalski gingko Sander grass
Tarpan hornbeam Grietje Val Dordogne
Jack Russel sweetgum Wolfgang parkwalk
Brown bear beech Bruno forest
Dikdik mimosa Saartje savanna
Shetland pony laurel Hansje tulipfield
Springbok olive Kaatje meadow

FUGUE
Reason, but people are irrational. Honesty, but people are hypocrites. Decency, but people are mean, jealous, and spiteful. Candor, but people are cowards and liars. Irony, but people are stupid. Stoic forthrightness, but people are lazy, careless, and selfish. Satire, but people are humorless and their minds without dimensions. Example, but people are witless. Admonition, but people are sheep. What then, O Diogenes?

EYE

Sander's eye, focused on sturdy sensual beauty, never veers from the immediate. He has no distorting mannerisms or ideal of form. You can't improve on Grietje or Wolfgang, he says. It's hard enough to get them just as they are.

TAFELGESPREK

Correct enough for our house, Grietje ruled of Wolfgang and Jan coming to breakfast barebottomed but undershirted. Always wanted to, Jan grinned. Hansje does at his home, and Saartje. Wolfje said we could, it's great. *Voorhuidsadem*, said Sander of a goodmorning kiss from Wolfgang, tushed by Grietje. A loving twit, said Sander. Our house cricket has magicked us all into spoiling him silly, and now Jantje can't keep his eyes off him. Sander! Grietje pleaded. Quit teasing the whiffets, Jan's blushing, and Wolfje is about to bolt.

JAN

Sex, says Jan at lunch, is *prachtig* and, trying out the word, beautiful. You're beautiful, Sander says. Silence and thought. What does that mean, Sander, I'm beautiful? Jan covers the question with an awesome bite of sandwich, *I'm beautiful* coming through much bread, sardine, and cheese. Well, says Sander, you have all that long light hair and sexy blue eyes and a body that's on its way to being tall and trim. You smile a lot. But beautiful? says Jan. Sure, says Sander. Not as beautiful as I am, because you're still a squirt. Don't you think Hans is beautiful? More thought, more silence, more sandwich. Hans looks left and right, liking the fun. Wolfgang studies Hans to see if he can see the beauty. I love him, Jan says, that makes him beautiful. Do you think Hansje's beautiful? *O ja!* Sander says, drives me crazy.

LINE

Sander, like Bruno in his day, only wanted a context, and a fellow conspirator. Man at his most animal is not animal at all, but radically human, wishing to dissolve boundaries precisely where the animal needs to create them.

TYXH

Everything happens by chance (the wild) and by law simultaneously and integrally. Water is wild, contained by the contours of things and obedient to natural law (gravity, the chaotic nature of its own liquidity, evaporation, freezing, wind). That is, chaos and order are everywhere, their purposes opposite yet cooperative. Spirit is as wild as water, seeking its own equilibrium, as water its own level. The planets are trying to move along a wild line, held in by the sun.

XPONOC

For weeks there has been no time, or undivided time, all the hours elided, *legato*, none with a number, so that after abandoning the habit of supposing the day to be *around four o'clock* there is a fine feeling of uninterrupted time. Time becomes an ocean, air streaming above an empty field, primeval and generous.

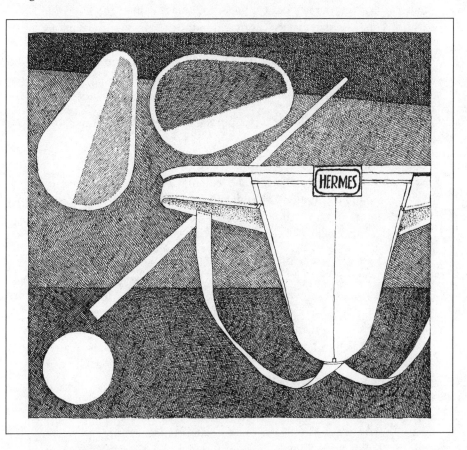

ORCHARD

Apple and pear can be eaten at the tree, like cherry, peach, and fig, and Plato in his *Laws* says that hospitality should allow the wayfarer to eat, but not carry away, pear or apple in the orchard, and that children may do the same, except that they may be driven away but not hurt. Plato distinguishes between an adult fancying an apple and boys and girls who have no doubt in their minds that they can eat a whole tree of ripe cherries or half a grove of yellow pears.

JAMAICAN SUGAR
The Harmonian Compote. Fruit heaped over with a pound of refined Jamaican sugar. Apple slices shredded coconut grapes figs orange pulp, all under a hillock of sugar. Six of these a day for children. As they achieve the damoiselat, the Compote Pause in work or play becomes affectionate coupling. Willy and Sally, peuters, have a recess from setting out strawberry slips when the compote cart arrives, donkey drawn, under the supervision of the Little Bands, who must be kissed in thanks. Gerrit and Marjorie, damoisel and damoiselle, have a five-minute entanglement, tongues in each other's mouths, hands in each other's britches. *Yick!* say the peuters, when you could be glupping a compote.

ANIMUS INGRATUS
In this century we have lived off the spiritual cultures of former times, having none of our own.

EQUUS
Sander bellowing supplications to the sculptor of the horse in Niaux, to Hiroshige, to Stubbs. Painting a splendid przewalski such as we saw at the Jardin des Plantes, a mare with a daughter, and Pan Przewalski had a meter of *peester* out and dangling.

THE AUTUMN OF THE WEST
Reading Lévy-Bruhl's *Carnets* iii/iv (1938) alongside Montherlant's for the same months, both on walks around the Bois and at La Bagatelle, the one rethinking his life's work on the primitive mind (taking prelogicality from it, finding that it's all a matter of attention, the mind being what it knows, not how it reasons), the other (the last Hellenistic sensibility in Europe) observing at random, with irony, with haughty disapproval, with precision. Germany in an hysteria of illusion and obscene idiocy. Huizinga walking with his hands behind his back, head lowered, along Dutch biking paths. The vigor of Lévy-Bruhl's thought about the magic of religions and man's allegiance to the imaginary, the acumen of Montherlant's dark contrast of generosity and vulgarity: Europe continuing to think before the most violent barbarian attack of them all. And I a little boy, knowing nothing.

O JA!
Apple pear.
Apple apple.
Pear pear.
Pear apple.

THE ORDERS

Hero Major: scientist, agronomist, mathematician, philosopher.
Hero Minor: artist, poet, composer, architect.
Saint Major: gastronomist.
Saint Minor: lover.

FIELD

Attraction's an invisible field of force defined by the pattern of the things attracted. Poles of Monarch butterfly's migration like iron filings in a magnetic field. Fields in time, fields in space. Curvilinear (Crete, Jugendstil) gives way to rectilinear (Hellas, Bauhaus, De Stijl). Until identity by character absorbs again identity by sexuality we will suffer our present shallow sense of being, where psychology, looking at nothing, thinks it sees everything.

HERO

Regard. Jan home with Joris after a swim, Hansje told me bravely and only half-confused, but furious with himself for his confusion and needing somebody to talk to. They'd teased Joris, as usual, making him blush, and Jan said (the smart alec) he was going home with Joris. This to Hansje in Joris' hearing, who, swallowing a frog, said that he wasn't. Yes, said Jan. Joris said he was on his honor not to touch Jan or Hans, except for a friendly hug or irresistible kiss. *Ook zo?* He, said the cunning Jantje, wasn't. Nor bug-eyed Hansje. Foraging, said Jan. Hans can come along next time. So Hans turned up at Florishuis, looking as if he might cry. He didn't want me to think he was snitching on Jan. And after a while here were Joris and Jan improbably innocent and looking for Hans. Oh no, Comrade Hans, Joris said, reading his face, all Comrade Jan here and I did was have a good, an awfully good talk about friendship and about his love for you and yours for him. True, said Jan, every word. When, said Joris, do they pin the medal on me?

HOURS

Fabian says that communication is, ultimately, about creating shared time. Hans' days are long, mine short. Sander's days are longer than either. Genius knows rhythms. He does not stop work to talk, and likes to talk while he paints. He has begun work before he gets up, saying things like *What I'm going to do today is put yellow and blue and grey together like Vermeer.* Wolfgang mixes, Sander comments.

COMITATUS

Godfried and his brood. Greek hygiene and Scandinavian candor. Dutch pragmatism, also. Everything must be modern, progressive. And narrow-mindedness is not modern.

JAN SIX, WITH GLOVE

A crocodile of *peuters* crossed the zebra to the *gracht*. Dimples skipped, Freckles hopped. *Hummeltje Tummeltje! Winterkoninkje!* Their teacher wore a cape with a big paper daisy pinned to its collar. Cruise missiles, Joris said, will blast them all into phosphorescent ash. Sniff, he added, they smell of mint, soap, and waffles, *ja?*

ISLAND

On my second cup of coffee, savoring the grey rawness of the morning, when I heard a launch. Sam from the point, hallooing that he brought me friends big and little: Joris full of the triumph of his surprise, which was Hans and Jan, all of them in slicks and souwesters, the combined brightness of their three smiles outshining Sam's headlamp. You don't believe what you see, do you? Joris shouted from the boat, handing over Hansje, then Jan, then a rucksack and a hamper of provisions. Through stinging swiveling drizzle to the cabin, the boys jumping as if on springs, Joris with his arm around my shoulder. No hassle at all with Jan's folks, even when Kaatje said pretty bluntly over the phone that I'm a DSAP organizer in spite of being improbably young, a handsome devil, and not to be trusted two steps with Hans and Jan. How exciting for them! she said, so help me. I could hear her. And Kaatje, I can see how you like her so much, gave this double-take at the phone. She then grilled me pretty closely. I was so honest with her I blushed till my ears rang. Bruno rolled in, and we went through it all again. *Gunst!* is he cool. If, he said, Adriaan thinks the rascals would like going to the island with Joris here, fine. They'll worry the piss out of you. So here we are. I can't believe it.

AZURE TIN ELLIPSE

True, I'd written Joris saying it would be nice to see him for the weekend, and added, more to throw out a congenial idea than to be wholly serious, that it would be jolly if Jan and Hans could come along. I did not really think that he would show Kaatje the letter and tell her Lord knows what, and actually arrive here with two boys with whom he has probably already fallen in love. *In love!* Joris howled pounding me on the shoulder, *asjeblief! Look* at Jan, *look* at Hans. I've eaten the rascals all the way here with my eyes until my balls have set like concrete, my heart is jelly, my poor heart. *Lieve hemel!* Hans at all this bent double laughing and Jan staggered stiff-legged around him cross-eyed and with his tongue stuck out. A whinny from Joris, and: Don't think, Kameraad Adriaan, that I won't come right here, right now, just by being here, in my pants, all down both legs, running out over my shoes, squishing through the teeth of my zipper, splashing up over my belt buckle. Jan's eyes were radiant, Hans lay on his back and kicked, I pulled Joris' Lenin cap over his eyes, and commanded a firewood detail to get with it before the dark closed in.

SPIRAL SILVER

They were treading about, Hessians on patrol shoulder to shoulder, heads down, when I hallooed *Ducks! a word from your captain.* They saluted. What is all this? I asked sweetly. Hansje looked out of the top of his eyes, studying the weather. Jan ran his tongue over his lips. Are you miffed? he asked. Did we goof coming out with Joris? What, I asked, do you know about Joris? He prints books, Jan said, and is a Radical Socialist, he's *your* friend, his cap is like Klaas Lenin's, he belongs to the NSAP, and likes boys our age. O God, are we teasing him and making him miserable?

FIRESIDE

A sizzle of graupel mixed with fine rain made our fire with pea soup on the pothook the more friendly, exciting Joris to shine, voice and eyes and smile, with the compatibility of it all. He made the cheese and sardine sandwiches, poured the beer, set places on the hearth, patted whatever boy's behind came within reach, and kept the fire steady as if he'd lived in the country all his life. It was Hans first who, as we came in with estovers, gave Joris a kiss on the corner of his mouth, and got one in return. That, nipper, he said a bit stunned, makes me happy, do you know? What it's for, said Hans, it's our way. Ome Adriaan helped us decide it. Kissing on the mouth is for girls, on the cheek is not for real, but for friends the corner of the mouth is right, and has a good tickle to it. Also, said Joris, makes my knees turn to water. See, said Jan rather ahead of things and with a mouthful of cheese, sardines, and bread, we're not going to be horrible, Adriaan says we mustn't, unzipping with one hand (sandwich in the other) and some trouble wriggling his penis around the pouch of his briefs so that it poked out of his jeans fly unhooded and pink. And, with a kiss for Joris that left breadcrumbs on the corner of his mouth and unbelieving surprise in his gaze, you can fiddle around with it, like after supper, if you want to. Adriaan says he won't barf or go tharn: he's some kind of Pythagorean Calvinist, *oh ja*! This with *spleetogig* mischief lost on Joris who put his head against the floor, holding his crotch with both hands, whimpering. Hansje, crosslegged beside me, parked his sandwich on my thigh, scrambled to his knees, and tried opening his fly like Jan, jamming his zipper halfway, needing me to get it unstuck. Between us we got his penis out, but when he sat it slid back in. Jan's stayed out, two fingers clamped behind the glans jiffling a shake off and on. Joris with a shivering hug gathered him closer beside him and they ate thigh to thigh. While I laid out gingerbread and coffee Hans with determined fussing almost got his penis to stay on the jut out of his fly. I solved the problem by taking off his jeans and briefs altogether while he stood munching gingerbread and grunting approval that some grown-ups knew how to treat a boy. If, said Joris spilling coffee, closing his eyes, I get to take off Jantje's jeans and nappies like that, will you give me a decent burial at sea? O wow! Jan yipped, scurrying up, hands over head to be undressed. I nod to Joris: *fijn*. A critical amusement on Jan's face as Joris peeled him of his clothes, ironic misery and whoofs of pleasure on Joris'. Hansje slid backward onto my lap, butting my chin with the top of his head. Pulling off socks Joris risked a caress on Jan's bare butt, making his cock dance its head. Naked, Jan straddled Joris' legs and gazed at him eye to eye. Joris hugged him awkwardly, with confusion, and gave me an *Oh God what do I do now?* look. They rubbed noses, and Hansje said, I'm next up there, and Joris won't think we're prigs or that Jan and I think it's icky you like boys. We like it that you like us. We like you because you like Jan and me to love each other. Jan, ankles locked behind Joris' neck, leaned back in his lap and said with head upsidedown: Hansje's mama's not worrying a whit about us because she says she knows Adriaan and she knows Hansje better than Hansje, and that nobody as good-looking as Joris would hurt a midge. To Moeder over the phone she said that. Is Joris good-looking, Adriaan? What Hansje's and Jantje's lucky mothers do not know about good-looking Joris, Joris said with a whistled sigh and wide smile, is that Joris comes, as he just has, half a liter, in his pants, when he has Jantje bare-bottomed on his lap.

VERHAAL: HANS

O me O my. Well, Joris and Jantje and me, we came by train happy and excited all three of us, then by bus and boat to spend the weekend with Ome Adriaan on the island. Joris told us about printing and socialism, which Jan says is for Balkans, and the English soccer teams and all sorts of things. He's a good talker, like Jan. As this report is real sexy I won't leave out that Jan had a volunteer erection on the train that made his fly stick up and he sat so everybody could see it, and Joris closed his eyes in prayer. Ome A was kind of surprised to see us. After supper, or sort of in the middle of supper, Jan and I took off our britches, or rather Joris with Ome A's OK took off Jan's with the result that Joris shot off in his jeans, which was really true love and a great feeling, but Ome A said some of his funny things.

VERHAAL: JAN
What Adriaan said was two Arcadian panisks and a satyr with circadian erections. Joris for all his big talk is a gentle person afraid of doing something wrong. Not that any of us had much of an idea what came next. It was sexy to see Joris get out of his jeans, damp in the crotch, and his soaked and gummy briefs. Wet penis. Talk about big. So Hansje and I made love, and when we started Joris said to bury him in the Red Flag and to sing _De Internationale_ for his funeral.

VERHAAL: HANS
So Joris was sitting Japanese and Ome A said it was _in goede orde_ for Joris to be silly with Jan's peter again, and Jan showed what and how and lay on his back with his legs forked out on Joris' knees. So Ome A whispered how we could match them but backburner slow so I could take Jan's place and drive Joris happy mad, and the space was right so that when I got spread-legged and in the sporting hands of Ome A I could pillow my head on Jan's shoulder, and Jan his on mine. Easy for kissing and for killing Joris, who whimpered a lot, and Ome A whistled Telemann, Jan identified it, in and out of kisses and begging Joris to take his good sweet time.

VERHAAL: JAN
Add that Joris while these ardent pleasures were being administered tried to sell us Lenin, of whom Joris says I'm disrespectful, and he and Adriaan agreed that the NSAP has two purposes: to give all young folk the right to be Hans and Jan (and Saartje and Jenny, I put in), and to blend Greek love in with all friendship and thus smooth away the abrasive edges of its difference in the context of middle-class propriety.

VERHAAL: HANS
Whoopee.

VERHAAL: JAN
When I was about to come, Joris broke our rule that he could play in our game but not us in his, and broke it again when we changed places, with Hans.

Adriaan was ominously silent about this turn of events, though he pointedly handed us shirts and socks after we'd both kissed Joris on the corners of the mouth and got hugged wonderfully, and said he was a good person and our friend. We also kissed Adriaan, who hugged us as hard as Joris. Hans, naturally, had to ask him if being loved by Joris was right, and he said No. Wash the dishes and pans.

KRITIEK: ADRIAAN
Because it's unfair to Joris, who can only want to play for keeps, whereas you two, enjoying a permissiveness that's at best experimental and, shall we say, experiential, are simply playing.

KRITIEK: BRUNO
So? Zipper down, zipper up. Jan is making fine progress with Bach on the harpsichord and plays a mean game of checkers. Hans shows signs of someday learning to spell. Hilda says that she had not expected that Jan and Jenny would prove quite such a joy. She's inviting Joris to supper, and will make him blush purple.

KRITIEK: JORIS
ICBMs with nuclear warheads in silos all over the VSA and Rusland.

PASTEUR
The universe is dissymmetrical. I am inclined to think that life, insofar as we can know anything about it, must be a function of the universe's dissymmetry and all that follows from it. The universe is dissymmetrical: if the solar system could be seen in a mirror, its orbits and local motions and motions as a unity could not be superposed as an image upon reality, as a left hand can be superposed on a right. I can even foresee that all living species are primordially, in their structure, in their external forms, functions of this cosmic dissymmetry.

GERTRUDE STEIN
Human nature is not interesting. The human mind is interesting and the universe.

COPENHAGEN
Opening Olaf's door at the rigorously modern apartment complex the station taxi took me to was a long-headed fourteen-year-old blond with dark blue eyes, tall for his age, in an American Army shirt, unbuttoned, Gemini shoulder-

patch, a wolfcub pawprint in a yellow circle on the zipper ply of his jeans, rotten sneakers, and dirty white socks. You're the man from Amsterdam, he said. At least I hope you are. I skipped school to be here when you came. Olaf will be back. He was, he said, practicing holding action foreplay while waiting for me to turn up, and (checking a Rollex oyster on his left wrist) had been at it for an hour and fifty-two minutes. I made signs of being impressed. He took my briefcase and overnight bag to a table piled with books, magazines, and a scruffy blue rucksack I took to be his, as well as a pair of briefs. I asked his name. Pier. He zipped down his jeans, took them off, dried his glans and foreskin on the briefs, and pulled them and his jeans back on. No need to stop because I'm here, I said. Save it for later, he said. He was in a film of Olaf's, and Olaf wants runny splats and loopy strings of sperm for a take later in the afternoon. Age? Almost fifteen. Incredible blue eyes. Silence. Asked him to tell me about himself. Tell what? What, for instance, interested him. At school, at home, in general, how long he'd been with Olaf's *fribørn* group. Or anything at all. Three years, two years, something like that. Time flies. Films, photography. Reads a lot. Acting, maybe.

DISTEL'S DRENG

Olaf's wolfden. *Overnydansk* long box of glass and brick with decisively proportioned corbufibonacci modulations, narrow intensely reticulated verticals dividing Shakerly rectangles of urban brick from *Bauhauslijk* squares of glass. High wall all around. Flagstone courtyard, bicycles, skateboards, boxwood in concrete cylinders. Lifesized neoclassical Art Deco bronze boy on stone cube base, incipiently adolescent, anatomically ideal, head leaning pensively forward, hips canted, one hand holding a soccer ball against a thigh, the other knuckles down on a hip, penis punctiliously modeled and precociously advanced, scrotum chastely small. Toes worthy of Bourdelle, butt of Maillol, face of Despiau. Sander would approve. The work of a young Belgian named Distel. Olympia by way of Erewhon.

WOLFDEN COMMON ROOM

Large sunny room, ultracontemporary chairs, tables, bookshelves, sexy posters bold of sentiment (*Wen sie wollen! Weg mit dem Scheisssystem! Auf zur sexuellen Revolution! Konsfrihed for altid! Pik eller kusse alle dage!*). With designs variously styled from the photograph to the abstract, all smartly graphic, all explicit.

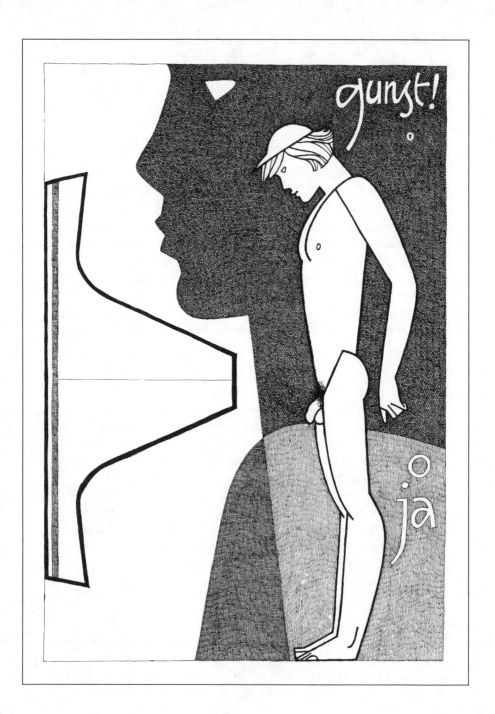

THE WOLFDEN BULLETIN BOARD

Clubgebouw aanplakbord, een Fourierlijk verwondering. Emil: after tumbling Tues: Tom. Thorvald: grounded come over to the house it's OK: Ejnar. Sven + Tom 1600 all of next week. *Frivillig* needed for *paedo arbejder 26 muskelstaerk smuk 17 cm. Frivillig* needed *nydreng* Adam Fleming 14 Thurs or Fri 1700. An abandoned scantling *slipje*, blue, was thumbtacked, spread frontward, across a poster (handsome young man in denim workclothes with an arm around the shoulders of a handsome grey-eyed blond boy in short pants) for the Düsseldorf Deutschen Studien- und Arbeitsgemeinschaft Pädophile e.V. (*Für sexuelle Selbstbestimmung von Kindheit an*). A forlorn long white sock hung from a thumbtack at the bottom of the board. A pair of grubby shoelaces shared a drawing pin with a film brochure and schedules (*Masturbation: sa meget man lyster, forlaengelse og hyppighed.* The Red Planet: BBC Science Film. *Ungt Menneske og Lille Dreng. Hygiejne og Kneppen.*)

KONTORET

JCH Ellehammer skimming over sawgrass dunes in his ornithopter kite hangs behind Olaf's table, a speckle-grained enlargement of a photograph made 12 September 1906. It is flanked on one side by a poster derived from a woodcut herbal (black winter cherries), and on the other by a poster in the same series, of double anemones. Superbly modern swivel chair. Oxblood carpet. Benches, chairs, shelves of art books.

SKRUB AF!

Introduced by Olaf to two teenagers with remote and untrusting eyes. They'd just arrived themselves, had satchels of schoolbooks, and had greeted Olaf with kisses more military than affectionate, me with nods. There was the gaze of the wolf in their eyes, an animal alertness. Olaf said why I was a visitor: to learn. But how dare you, said their eyes, come snooping around here, whoever you are. Writer and philosopher, my ass. What they said was nothing. Olaf stamped his foot at them, furious. *Skrub af!* the two of you! Go love yourselves crosseyed. Come back when you think you have some manners. A stammer from one, apologies from the other. Six demerits apiece, Olaf said. You, Peter, that makes ten for you in one week: remember what you said to Diderich when he was only paying you a compliment. And pull Jens and Edvard apart and tell Jens to come down here. *He's* been known to have some manners.

BILLY

You could go quietly insane talking to my Billy, Olaf said, but he's off for the afternoon seeing *Stjerne krigen* with some pals. Rare for him to be out of sight.

He's adhesive. Our mascot, I pass him off as. But for prelogical thought and a total innocence of cause and effect he has few peers among those who can come and go as they like.

JENS

Fiks, eleven. Saucy-eyed, harumscarum hair, trim, smiling compliantly, expediently wearing an unavailing brief with a wet spot on the pod. Long torso, long legs: going to be tall. Dimples, chubby upper lip, baby's flat nose. *Hallo!* he said brightly, nothing shy, giving me both hands to shake. Introduced as a pal and fellow *ungdomsfrihedskaemper*, to be called Adriaan. And your *trusser* are on inside out, *bonkammerat. Ak ja!* he laughed, slipped them off, whipped them right side out with a snap, and resumed them. *Held i orden, nu, perfekt!* He watched me with cocked head and wide eyes as Olaf said who I was, why I was there. He tended to answer my questions with *perhaps* and *I forget* and *I don't know*, and everything became awkward and the pulling of eye teeth, not helped by entanglements between Dutch and Danish, and my and Olaf's English. Apprehensive glances from Olaf, who was helping wonderfully, but getting nowhere. *O pokker tage det!* he blew up, heaved a hugging Jens over his shoulder, whoofed kisses into his hair, and wiggled a tickling hand into his briefs. All this is too *uelsket* for this *hedensk slurkpik*, the cat has his tongue. The pool, the pool's the place. Jens is a fish when he isn't everybody's *lille skat*, and a crack scholar when he doesn't do his algebra with his hand in his fly. Upstairs to undress, and you can see the barracks.

THE BEDS

Barracks upstairs: a Spartan double row of precisely made iron cots, army surplus. Well-lit by four skylights and high square *nydansk* windows. The two *ulveblik* were clamped onto each other head to crotch as tight as breeding frogs.

ULVEBLIK

Three others: two *halvvoksne*, just arrived, were undressing and bragging how horny they were, and a straw blond in a thin-bretelled white undershirt. This was Edvard, Jens' bonded mate. I was introduced to him as the friend from Amsterdam who wants to learn how we do things. Call him Adriaan. Olaf, stripping (a gymnast's body, nothing naked about his nudity) expatiated on Edvard, fifteen. Marvelously talented at drawing, the guitar, photography, woodcraft, canoeing, and civilizing stinkers from the fast skateboard set, like Jens. Jens, Olaf said to Edvard with a voice suddenly loud, turns out to be as useless a spokesman for the *sag* as *rend mig i røven*, so we're having a dip. Adriaan can learn wonders from Edvard. Adriaan! *Barmhjertige Gud!* but you've kept in shape, *kammerat!* You're blushing! *Yndig!* I was given an unabashed inspection by the *halvvoksne*, now holding each other by the hips. The clinched *ulveblik* held, full-throated, to their unhistoried hour of Arcady beyond time and statute.

THE POOL

The four of us down to the swimming pool, Edvard abiding, Jens patient (the young's greatest defense of their inwardness is to wait all occasions out), Olaf confidently doing his best, I feeling very much the tame fox in a henhouse, character giving way to instinct. We swam, tossed a tired ball, had a splashing fight, a ducking chase, all within any Lutheran burgher's notion of men and boys at play except for the quick kisses in passing, sudden halts at the poolside for puppyish fits of affection. Edvard, no matter what else was happening, had a practiced way of plunging toward Jens, sinking just short of him, and surfacing to kiss him full on the mouth. Olaf kissed everybody, including me. The boys were wary of the *hollaender* until Olaf caught me in an impulsive hug that sank us both in a boiling swarm of green bubbles. We porpoised up, I returned his salute, and we capsized again. Edvard and Jens crawled over and hugged Olaf together in a tumult of splashing. I got them next, half drowning. We swam in circles with them around our necks, Edvard Olaf's Arion, Jens mine. Winded, acquainted, we dried in the level sun with towels Edvard fetched. I went up to the barracks for my pipe, tobacco, and matches. There were three braces of boys on cots. The *ulveblik*, holding tight, moving only at the hips, were still at it.

JOHANNES

Tall boy, sixteen, longish hair the brown of walnut stain, as coarse-grained as weathered wood, large thin-nostrilled nose with high bridge. Hornrimmed specs. Works out in the gym thrice a week, bonded to one Ejnar, also sixteen, with whom he couples (*dobbelsug*, the argot) daily, usually twice, with swim and second foreplay between, more on weekends and holidays. Jacks off nightly, *aldeles bestemt*, for (I must have blinked) the fun of it. The only *ulveunge* who has heard of me, to Olaf's delight. Eager to be interviewed. Very much the young intellectual. Has good English. Conducts the pack's study group, is the clubhouse librarian. Shook hands and said he was honored to meet me. A three-note whistle from Olaf got me a smiling kiss on the corner of the mouth. That's better, said Olaf, and Johannes said he wasn't sure. Our manners, said Olaf, are our manners. We kiss. Poolside, this interview, in fine green light. Olaf asked with his eyes if he should leave: I signaled *stay*. So peel down, he ordered Johannes, this is for the *frihedsbevaegelse*. Skinny boy, big feet and hands, good rusty umber suntan, chest muscles worked to finished anatomical definition. The fore distension of his briefs (I'd thought the strain on his jeans fly was the push of an erection) seemed an excess of design in a body so lean, tail flat, and shallow-fleshed. Of his oversized penis horsily ponderous, fat of girth at root and head, Olaf boasted that it was the prize thumper of the troop. Johannes, a pink tinge in the brown of his flat cheeks, shifted his pinched grin to a guffaw. I love it, he said, but it's cumbersome and embarrassing. Discussed penile awareness intelligently and wittily, causing Olaf to give me a smug smile: his boys are smart. It's not bigger than Olaf's whopper, inviting me to compare the two (Olaf stark naked except for his whistle on a string around his neck), but he has the physique to go with it. Erect, it's really gross: and showed me. Began keeping it in shape at age nine, tutored by a cockhappy brother (thirteen). Parents magnanimously broadminded, both sons being obedient, bright, talented, affectionate, assiduous in school. Family has traveled considerably. Johannes reads French, German, English, Italian, and is learning Spanish. His brother boldly brought home a girl at fifteen and fucked her for five days, coming out of the bedroom only to fetch food for the two of them, Johannes banished to the living room couch, the parents uneasy but determined not to be prudes. On the fifth day Ulrik emerged from his harem tanglehaired and glassy of eye, saying that he had come forty-seven times, the girl several hundred, but now she was too *modbydelig* sore to *kneppen* more, and was having hysterics. Inspected (Ulrik's penis livid as a bruise and puffy, the girl's vagina raw and swollen shut), washed (Mummy helping graciously), properly fed, and put into pyjamas, they slept in a fresh bed around the clock, Johannes tiptoeing in from time to time to look at them with awe. Girl went away for a week, replaced the meanwhile by another: much glee in Johannes telling us all this, a dubious slide of eyes from Olaf, who was enjoying it. First girl returned, joined the other (Mummy did allow herself the observation one breakfast that two girls at once might plausibly deplete one's stamina) and has been there, off and on, ever since. She's a sweet kid, devoted to Ulrik, who's *pisseforvirret* crazy about her. Johannes, turned thirteen, organized his emotions: he was giddily and happily excited by fellow males, their bodies, their charm, their smell, their grace. Claiming the license given his brother's loving heart, he proudly announced at dinner one evening to the family and two of Ulrik's *serail* that he was *homoseksuel*. Mummy turned white, Papa red. But Ulrik whooped *juhu bravo! brave Johannes! honest Jo-*

hannes! and they sat up most of the night talking about it. His first tumble, mind like a kite in March wind, was with Ulrik, who, a week after Johannes' family news, inquired if little brother had seduced or been seduced by any-body interesting, and (again at table, making parents turn colors) fraternally offered himself, to get things started and for practice. Prince of brothers, Ulrik. Heirs, both, of the lineal inclination to good measure, they had between them 46 cm of penis to work with, and Ulrik, putting in double time as banty rooster and *gammel graeker* bedmate, became disgustingly vain of the universality of his affections, demanding raw oysters, vitamins, fewer tactless remarks from the old folks, and lots of sleep. Can't touch the sweet bastard now: the *ulveun-ger* get booted out if they bring in alien germs. Olaf hauls us all to the doctor quite enough as it is. Johannes joined the wolfden at fourteen, out of his mind anxious that he wouldn't get in. A patch of ancient Greece, a logical progres-sion of Scandinavian liberality, a frontier: his answer to the question variously replied to by others as crazy fun and why should we have to wait? The men's longhouse, girls excluded, stodgy middleclass prurient taboos subverted. Jo-hannes has the earnest passion of the young revolutionary: in really repressive countries like *Forenede Stater*, he lectures us as if we didn't know (and Olaf pretends he doesn't), the punishment for killing a boy with an automobile, even if the driver is limber drunk, is six months in jail, whereas the punishment for loving a boy is thirty years hard labor. *Sindssyg!* His theory is that capital-ism won't work if people don't hate and distrust each other, and hate them-selves, and savage each other. *Kristus!* They're out there, sadists, breaking their children's arms with beating on them, and telling them that they're de-praved idiots for jacking off. After he'd worked himself through an oration, I remembered, and told about, the case of an American child, an orphan adopted by straitlaced puritans, who was caught masturbating in the barn. A local doctor was of the opinion that he was a moral degenerate for whom no hope was to be entertained, and he was confined in an insane asylum for the next thirty years. This is true, Adriaan? Olaf asked, tears brimming in his eyes.

NEJ TAK

Johannes' Ejnar turned up, a Standard Danish Boy, short and compact. Some quick words in the argot of the troop, a huddle with Olaf, Ejnar undressing as he talked. Ask him, Olaf said. And Johannes with unsuspected shyness, ex-plaining that on very rare occasions they were allowed to make it with out-siders, put his and Ejnar's bodies at my disposal. Hugged them both (Johan-nes' shoulders warm, Ejnar's cold), thanked them kindly, and pleaded other arrangements. Olaf gave me a very odd look.

POOLSIDE TALK

By not differentiating between the sensuality of the whole body, Olaf says, and that of sex, common opinion has on the one hand damned all sensuality in damning sex, taking affection, loyalty, and comradeship along with it, and on the other burdened sex with representing the full range of sensuality. Sexual attraction is, I should think, far too effervescent a reason to marry, and yet the divorce courts show that an awful lot of people suppose it to be. Better to enjoy a game of checkers together. Human affinities come from any direction. My *slubberter* here are after affection one way or another, and are also heroically generous in giving it. Their puppy longing to hug and lie close is as God intended. They are silly, selfish, conceited, cheating little buggers as well, but most soon learn to leave their unlovable nastinesses at the door. We have a tearing fight from time to time, and the occasional emotional crisis, which we all deal with as best we can. I've jettisoned all psychology, terrible guff written by cold fish anyway, and learn from Billy. Who can't sleep unless he's got a monkey hold on me all night, arms around my chest, legs around my waist, hair in my mouth, peter tickling my navel. In the morning I put a sweater on over the two of us, and make breakfast so.

ISAAC NEWTON PHILOSOPHE

Attention is attraction, surveillance, or critical inspection. Civilization discourages all three as immoral, as leading to more efficiency in industry and government spending than bankers are happy with, and as embarrassing. The Harmony will come into being through attraction, grow through surveillance, and make a habit and delight of critical acumen. The people will be the mind rather than the bowels of their community.

PLACE

Grietje, solicitous for and respectful of Sander's privacy, and of mine, worries that Wolfgang doesn't have any, especially after his mysterious running away, that he may not even know what it is. We build him a table, with bookcase. On his own carpet, defining a territory. He likes the table because Sander has one, and Grietje. The model's screen rejected by Hans and Jan for the Free Badger area he has appropriated. Something, he says, to look around.

PROVINCIA GALLIA

In early Atlantic Hazel Time, apple was analogue of grape in northern forests. Apple the only tree to keep its name after the imposition of Roman horticulture.

INGENIUM

The French readiness to dismiss, like the German suspicion of everything on God's earth, is an annoying habit which prejudice calls national and psychology an attitude taught children generation after generation. One is haughty, the other pathological. Both are meannesses caught by children, a true contagion. It was Fourier's idea that children are their own best teachers. Chronic suspicion is unlovable. Children will soon correct it in an individual. Haughtiness is easily brought low by a democracy in rompers. Nor will children idolize each other with fixations that have invaded and corroded the adult mind. They are, all unknowing, followers of Holberg's observation that to be a Christian (or Harmonian) you must first be a human being, or you will never be a Christian (or Harmonian). There is, as Fourier set out to discover, a human nature which never wholly dissolves in culture, which is candidly naked in children, and reappears often in the old, who are weary of custom and impatient with pretense. Harmonian manners will all be transparent, human nature showing through.

PATROL

Gallop of quaggas beyond the pear orchard. A girl's voice above the silver call of a horn. _Patrouille! Voorwaarts!_

FILM

Digt, idyllisk, hyrdedight, den slags ting, says Olaf of his short films, studies in invention. One is a hundred stills, each held three seconds before the next clicks into place, like a series of color slides shown at a steady rhythmic pace. Details of a cornflowerblue-eyed nickelblond Danish boy, midteens, _en kondi,_ all close-ups, beginning with the two beautiful eyes with white feathertip lashes: brown nape with frisk of woodshavings curls across the top: eyelet of navel tucked flat, trapezoidal knee as lean and compact as a fist: hiplevel profile of innocent rump and supple penis limber over pudgy balls: sandy toes, wisps of hair on the knuckles. Palest pink glans crimpled across the boll: ruddier glans plumped smooth as a plum: gingery pubic thicket by waistband of briefs flapped down: chest with copper nipples: penis erect as a bowsprit: and every fifth image the eyes.

DRISTIG

Olaf's _Selvportraet_ is entirely of his penis jauntily hanging limp, stiff as a rib, jacked rich-veined and slathery, swallowed to the root, tongued, kissed, coming in snappy globs, fingered lovingly, runny with pearly rivulets of sperm, knotty and sagging its head, knurled with rootlets of risen veins, bulging in briefs, standing out a jeans fly, peeing, butting another glans to glans, hummocked in tight pants, lugging out the cup of a *skridtbind*, lying curved over a thigh in morning light.

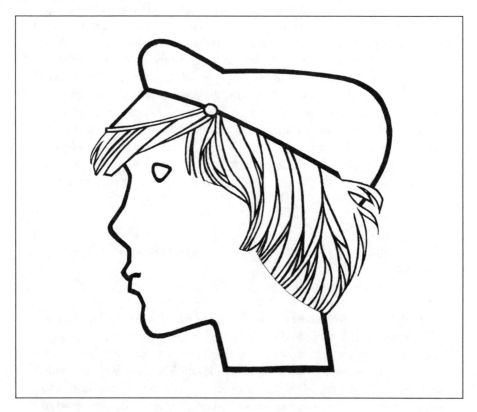

OLAF'S EROTIKSTUDIE FILM *Billy*

Billy the golden tadpole frogs around with a school of naked darting *ulveunger* swimming, ducking, dolphining in a pellucid dazzle of water bobbing green and blue. Heaved out glossy and blinking in an armpit heft and licked on the spout by Olaf, he stomps a devil dance, eyes jiggling with glee, gets picked up and hugged by two boys trotting to the pool, passing from one to the other and back to Olaf for a laughing stare nose to nose and lift onto his shoulders, tummy against Olaf's face, legs hooked around so that his heels are in Olaf's hands. Flops backward and hangs upsidedown. Twists up again, looking dizzy. Olaf flutters his penis with his tongue, sinks a tight sucking kiss around it, waggles his chin on its stiff shaft. Shift to Billy asleep, coppery leafshadow-spattered light on bed, gilet rucked up underarm, flat, grooved concavity from sternum to pubic boss very Modigliani. Camera tracks arm from heron hike of bony shoulders to elbow slightly bent to oblique wrist to fingers bunched around scrotum, tip of foreskin puckered. Tracks sienna gold-brown legs from cleft of buttocks to blunt knees to trim ankles to stubby toes.

UNGDOMSFRIHED

Poolside. Olaf nipped away, returning in sweater, jeans, socks, and with a box of lemon drops. Edvard, shawled in a towel, his chin on Olaf's thigh and his arm around Jens' waist, asked me what it was I wanted to know. I saw the nudge of Olaf's foot that got the question asked. *Jo*, Olaf agreed. Kammerat Adriaan has come all the way from wicked Amsterdam to innocent Denmark to talk with liberated loving boys in their own clubhouse, and Peter and Tobias, *skridtvild* those two, treated him like an evangelist, and Jens, given his chance to shine as a *frihedskaemper*, was about as conversational as a two-day-old calf. Olaf fed Edvard a lemon drop, who turned and gave it to Jens, tongue to tongue, and asked for another like a nestling, with open mouth. Olaf obliged, and repeated the nudge. *Rigtig!* Edvard said, scriggling his nose, thwacking his knee with a flat slap, sliding one foot over the other. I can tell you, he said, how scared I was, and shy, and ready to bolt. It's one thing to write a *brevkort* to the *postboks adresse* in the *ungdomsfrihed brochure* when you've got a hard on, and something else to turn up at an office with a woman in it and your face's red and your ears on fire. *Modbydelig, satans osse!* I'd sent the postcard with super schemes in my hot little heart, and filled out the form that came back, dick in hand, sneaking a year onto my age, 10 cm to my height. Zap! A postcard back in two days with an appointment and interview on it, something I can tell you to wonder about and wonder about and feel great jacking off about. I was OK right up to the time itself, turning up in clean underwear, clean socks, and the only foreskin in town that had been washed twenty times in one morning. One happy boy! It was when I got to the building, just like any other building, that I began to ask myself how crazy I was, what in the world I was going to say, and just what it was I thought I was doing. I'd checked out every letdown by the time I pushed the doorbell of the office: it was all a hoax, there were cops on the other side, the truant squad, sex muggers. And inside, a woman! That did it. I was blushing like a crossing signal, my palms were sweating, and general paralysis set in from head to toes. She knew my name, I didn't. She did get me to understand that there was a chair I was to sit in until they came with the handcuffs. It was a while before I took in the photo on the wall of a kid without a stitch on and some friendly booklets and folders on a table and began to come out of shock. Even so, I jumped like a goosed nanny when a door opened and a man laid a big hallo on me. His office was an OK sunshiny room with a desk and couch and book-cases and filing cabinets. And another boy there, Emil. We seemed, the man said, to match up, but that we'd have to see. This Emil looked as scared as I was. The man was doing his best to make us easy, but he asked questions about things I didn't even know words for. Emil, who scared me worse than the man, was sitting there hunched in his chair saying that he'd jacked off since he was *en lille spinkel fyr*. He had a tale about all kinds of crushes on school-mates and lifeguards and teachers, and a tale about almost getting somewhere with a friend several times. *Alligevel*, this character gave us a pep talk, sort of fruity but to the point, about friendship and loyalty. But what, Jens asked, did you do? I like Emil. He's great. What did you do, *hva'*?

HALLO
Peter and Tobias the wolf-eyed came down for a swim, which they executed with cleanly slotting jackknife dives, swift crawls side by side four lengths of the pool, hiking out effortlessly at our end, panting, gleaming, appropriating Edvard's towel for drying each other. Seeing the lemon drops, they went over and stood with open mouth, each getting one, undeserving, as Olaf remarked, of lemon drops. *Hvorfor?* they asked together. You have the manners of Ger-mans, Olaf said. Puzzled, concerned, they distributed kisses smartly dabbed on the corners of all our mouths.

ONENESS
The awareness of harmony, of oneness, the only noncontradictory reality, is reflected in the mind as the first law of reason, the principle of noncontradic-tion, and in the psyche as contentment. We have become blind to the hard truth that reality, because symbolic, is a function of dreams.

THE STARS ARE STILL THERE IN THE DAYTIME
Quia non est nobis conluctatio adversus carnem et sanguinem: sed adversus principes et potestates, adversus mundi rectores tenebrarum harum, contra spiritalia nequitiae in cælestibus.
Blossom lives on in the apple.

EARTHSPIN
Rutger wakes, Corporal Holter having licked his face. Hi, Holter! *Hrgkao wroof wroof.* Ark ark! Holter replies, pure wolf, silver with agate eyes, tail

down to indicate that he is on duty. He growls *do*, and *do* Rutger whistles back. If he is not up in a minute flat, Holter will pull the covers off and laugh. Rutger snuggles down for half a minute, one eye open. Then, Holter giving him a hopeful look, he rolls out. Holter prods his foreskin. Cold nose! *Hrgkao!* Off with Titus to the pool, past dogs and cats at breakfast. Then, wolves supervising, he makes Titus' bed, Titus his. They rub their hands, cheeks, and scrota with beebalm, sage, or lemon geranium.

LES NYMPHEAS
Essences on the ground bass of a mind at peace with itself, through the rhythm of monotony, the generosity of work.

Monet at Giverny. Lévy-Bruhl in the Bois.

SILVER WOLF EYES
Pulled on jeans to the flat hollows underhip, saddling the *wortel* of scrotum and *schacht* out over the crotch seam of his spread fly, standing with knees hasped straight, bare feet parallel 30 centimeters apart, animal cunning in the nipped corners of his mouth and flat grey eyes. I fix his stare and best him. He blinks first, gapes a smile all big white teeth and wolf's tongue. No English, no French, no German. My Danish between pratfall and stage fright, gets only a puzzled grin. *Fotograf?* he asks. *Nej. Elskovskval? Penis? Nej, nej. Underbukser?* We both laugh, *nej! Et lille øjeblik*, he says, off his mark, almost pitching on his head hobbled by his open jeans, teetered on his toes, tucked in, zipped up, and sped away like Merkur in both heels and beauty.

LES ATTRACTIONS SONT PROPORTIONELLES
An aggregate of entities or systems is said to be polythetic if each individual possesses a large but unspecified number of the attributes of the aggregate, if each attribute is possessed by large numbers of these individuals, and no single attribute is both sufficient or necessary to the whole.

FIELD NOTES. DUTCH ANTHROPOLOGIST
Thirteen-year-old translator with hair like an English sheepdog, scuzzy gympants with Gemini patch, fetched back by Wolf Eyes by the wrist. English functional if basic. Dutch anthropologist writing a book about us here. How come? For people to read. What for? So they'll be the less idiots. OK. You want Blinky's britches off, too? I don't want anybody's britches off. Olaf said when we talked to you he'd smash our butts if we didn't hang free or if we didn't sport the best manners we could find.

JAKOB

Blond. Almost fifteen. Has seen a *flyvende tallerken*, believes in them, and would welcome a ride in one. Thinks an ET crew would find him neat. Younger sister, older sister. Father works for some chemical firm and has an *elskerinde*, or *veninde*, whatever. Mother dotty, wimpy, and a Christian Scientist. Big sister picks on him, is ashamed of him, calls him fag. Little sister a friend, likes to hold his penis, and watch him toss off. Makes good grades in school, does gymnastics and swimming, belongs to a hiking club. It was, in fact, a hiking friend who got him into the wolfden. Father knows, doesn't care, but doesn't like hearing about it. Mother thinks it's Boy Scouts. Olaf, did I know, is an Eagle Scout? And is an artist and shoots movies, proudly added. Olaf is very *sjaelfuld, jo*? *Spartansk*, beautiful, and just. An idiot, *naturlig*, about little Billy, but that was sweet. Jakob bonded to Niels, sixteen, the hiking friend.

UNGE HR. BILLY

Returned, babbling of starships and robots, he was scooped up by the two he'd been to the movies with and brought to Olaf's lap. There, one said, you don't get to scalp us. Billy, Jakob said, is Olaf's cock with arms and legs.

OLAF

Apartment Scandinavian Erewhonian. Gropius chairs, rugs designed by Laplanders and Navajos, reproductions of a Dufy *Regatta*, a spirited Richard Mortensen abstract, a Kupka of 1913, a Jansenist Ozenfant, a firmly simple Max Bill, a melodic Helion. On a row of Shakerly pegs hung a *Deensblauw* backpack splendid with zippers, straps, and pockets, an Olympic *zwemslipje* with its slight strip of filmy lining outward, a denim jacket with *Ungdomsfrihedsfront* shoulder patch, a satchel of cameras and photographic gear, two English caps, one a child's. *Hov!* he said, are you learning anything, even *hulter til bulter*? It's all rather much, I remark. Right, he said. A monkey house of *gamle græsk* Boy Scouts. Whatever the ethics and sociology of it, the reality must be as Scheller says in the Düsseldorf Manifesto, in the *besondere Fähigkeit zur Einfühlung in die kindliche Psyche*, what *they* want. In the frame of the *Idealismus*. Which, of course, is as Danish as buttermilk, and very like. We find moral clarity exciting and invigorating. Northern Spartans.

BATH

Billy bathed and dried pink, Olaf took off his undershirt and dressed him in it. The philosopher and I have business to talk over, he whispered in Billy's ear. Just a little? Spoiled, said Olaf, rotten. Nevertheless, he jacked Billy for some five minutes in his lap before kissing him pretty much all over and sending him off to bed. A kiss for me, *for Olaf's friend*, and a hug. Olaf, sliding a smile across every phrase, said that if I wanted to know only clear and true things, *kun lige akkurat*, he could speak plainly. He is not *gaga* about the little buggers in his charge. The pioneer committee of the Students and Workers Coalition asked him to organize and captain the clubhouse. They knew that he kept a boy, a stray who had taken up with him and toward whom he had been both big brother and lover, as the kid expected it. At the same time he was in and out of bed with a girlfriend whom he shared with another fellow. He'd listened to the *ideelle motiver* in havering assent, quiddits and quillets nattering at both his conscience and measure of *bonsens*, however vellicative and advanced it all was, however *revolutionaer*. It was as if, just when he was getting well into layout and design, coming by as many commissions as he could handle, settling in with a round of friends, his life, the part of it, anyway, between *navle og forhud*, was doubled back to puberty and before, to a *fantasiverden*.

SPADGERS

Veelsoortig, he says, searching my eyes for understanding. Your Fourier built a utopia in his imagination, yes? *Min tro*, but in Düsseldorf the Indiansk group there gave me an *umyndig* little squirt closer to ten than eleven, as full of *livsglaede* as a lamb bouncing in clover. Yours, their *kaptajn* said, to show you, hefting him onto my lap. Frisky, cocky imp of a heathen with smart blue eyes, rabbity teeth, and a skint knee patched with *haefteplaster* and painted with *jod*, he chattered a wholly incomprehensible German at me, which, translated, made even me blush. Following instructions from the *kaptajn* and a helpful teenager with uncertain English, I parted this sweet brat from his *spejderbukser* and *trusser* while he blinked and beamed and wriggled helpfully. And then he was all over me like a monkey. His *pastinak pik og figen pung* were charming, if you will, but not *sexet*, not then. His *yndighed* was all over, integral can I say? So here I am with all these fanatic Germans, slobbering in spirit if not in fact, clicking out abstract nouns. *Unge hr.* Eros, whom I felt up and petted as I would a puppy, got my hand where he wanted it, on his *erektion*, which, as we got on with the policy talk and exchange of ideas I was there for, I cockered and jacked and fondled. *Idealismus* they talked, like your Oudveld and Strodekker in Amsterdam, law they talked, psychology, sociology, enlightenment, Gestalt theory, group dynamics. There was one Teutonic wonder of a teenager who was britchesless when I arrived, who must have spent the whole summer naked to be so brown, and who, continuing an awesomely prolonged pleasuring of his peter, denounced *Normalität, Familie*,

Schule, Maloche und Heterosexualität. Also war, prostitution, capitalism, fascism, hypocrisy, the police, colonialism, and other things as he thought of them. He was recommending friendship, collective economics, free love for all ages and combination of sexes, when my *Unge hr.* Eros abandoned my affections for his, and the two locked onto each other in as breathless and slogging a prodding of uvulas as ever wriggled about in the middle of a conversation. Everybody seemed pleased in a German sort of way, and I began to see something fetching in the scamp, so that when the spontaneous orgy was over and he came back to my lap licking *saed* from his lips I began negotiations for a wildly lovely frolic with him before I showed my films, and another after, and spent the night with him. He was good. And then, out of the blue, dropped Billy. About him he was, he had to admit, indeed *gaga*.

TABLE MANNERS

Joris (fisherman's sweater, jeans) and Wolfgang (new winebowl haircut, knee-length poplin pants, tall socks, red jersey with narrow white collar) at our dinner table, hands in lap. Full setting by Grietje. Joris frozen, daring not look at Wolfje. Wolfje trying not to laugh. I call *pâté*. Fork on outside left. Bread is always broken by hand, not sliced with a knife. Wine glass at right. Cut bite size of *pâté* with side of fork, spear, put in mouth, chew with mouth closed. Pick up bread from bread plate. If not already in bread plate, reach for it in middle of table, but offer it to Wolfje before taking any yourself. Pull off piece of bread. Don't hold it against your chest. Use both hands. Sip wine. It tastes like *benzine*, says Wolfje. Keep conversation going. What conversation? Today we painted the studio, Wolfje offers. What color? I prompt. What color? says Joris. White, says Wolfje. Left hand in lap when not in use.

HIBISCUS

Jan brought them from his mother's garden, mauve and white, a copious bunch with abundant leaves. There seemed to be at the door, Grietje said, an hibiscus bush in full bloom on two skinny long brown legs, and with eyes in the leaves very like Jantje's, and with a voice trying to change. Found a Chinese vase, still unpacked, for them. Jan blushed to be thanked with a kiss from Grietje, as the little sex fiend was unzipping his pants, assuming in his calm way that his afternoon rendezvous with Hans at their space on my floor was custom neither noticed nor commented on.

SMERIG EN SEKSIE

All heart, those two: Sander's contented remark about the nasty britches. Just when we're getting Wolfje housebroken and with a taste for soap and elementary hygiene, these rats come along with joggling and slobbing *zaad* in and on pants they'll wear unwashed until they mildew and fall apart.

JORIS
What we ourselves are.

ZO IS HET
Well yes, Skeezix, says Joris, I'm one to come. By collusion of cock and an accurate imagination, by elision of reality and dream, the way all things happen. Lots? Jan asks. *Een melkfles dagelijks. Zo'n bok!*

HORDE ZEBRAMASTER AND BADGER CUBS
Sink as much peter as you can, lips tight around it, and roll your tongue around the knob, flicker the tip on the eyelet. Squeeze the root, tickle and palm balls. The hair on the back of your neck should be crawling, your knees rubbery, your hearts thumping with love. Sander at the Free Badger Port in bib overalls, a brush piratically in his teeth, Wolfgang on his shoulders. Jan out of his briefs, dancing his penis between two fingers. Hans had been padding about waiting for him with voluptuous impatience, wandering from bookcase to window with a floppy erection. When Jan romped upstairs and they'd pounded each other on the shoulders and rolled across the floor and back in a clatter of knees and heels, and stripped, here was Sander giving lessons. Sexy, says Wolfje, bending to kiss Sander on the nose. Because, says Sander, they're in love. Pukey, says Wolfje. Next they'll be holding hands. But I love you, says Sander. You love Grietje, Wolfje says, you'd fuck her all day if you didn't have to paint pictures. True, says Sander, but I only paint pictures so that I can have you close enough to hug when I want to. Me too, says Wolfgang. This house is different from other houses, isn't it? There is, says Sander, carrying Wolfgang back to his studio, no house anywhere else in the world with Adriaan and Grietje in it, or Sander and curly-haired Wolfgang. Outside, the politicians are sucking money and picking their ugly noses, but in here we're painting a zebra, white stripes by Wolfgang, black by Sander.

TECHNIEK
One pollywog, hair a thatch in tumult, vibrant charm in millicupids topping Mach One, scuddled out of bed smiling my way, hitched on slight blue briefs, nipped over to the fireplace, got hugged, and drank a glass of orange juice in two long swallows. *Yndig!* Shook his thatch at coffee, nodded *jo* to hot chocolate, marmalade, butter, bread. Fetched a sweater of Hans' and put it on him,

thanked by a kiss rich in crumbs. Munched together, looking each other over, by the fire. Found, unnerved and queasy, I could caress his thin brown legs, cuddle upruck of underpants, nuzzle nape. He nuzzled back, rippled candied fingers across my mouth, kept looking at me with calm eyes and utterly sweet smile. Olaf, God be thanked, woke, yawned sonorously, giving us a fine sight of long torso, abundant nests of hair in armpits and chest furrow, pitch of blond forelock over eyes, stupendous stretch of swimmer's arms, roll of shoulder. *Morgen*, he mumped. Is that breakfast? *Olympisch naakt*, warm from bed, smelling kindly of axial musk, horse, and sperm, padded over with an erection sturdy as a hammer handle. Billy he scrunched in a crushing hug, kissed mouth, nipples, navel, briefs pod, and, briefs plucked down, peter, all of it. Outside, foggy morning, to pee. Olaf praising my coffee, mouth full of marmalade and bread, Billy on his lap, asked how big the island was, how I ever got all these books out, could we see it all, now? Your phone call sent shivers through me. Explained Billy. He had to be brought, nobody to leave him with. He was a new scamp among the *ulveunger*, won't talk, mucky past.

UNGE HERRE BILLY

Vaeldig sjovt! was Olaf's yelp over the phone. Blunt, explicit, practical. *En sand nydelse*. No mention of frisky Billy, but there they were at the point, both sporting Frihedkamp shoulder patches on Danish blue camping jackets all zippered pockets and knotted white cords. *Maskot* on Billy's cap. Landed just before dusk, a walk around the island, supper by the fire, Billy hyperkinetic with it all: the only cabin on a small island miles from anywhere. And *unge herre* Billy, Olaf said undoing Billy's sneakers while butting his crotch with his forehead, nudging tummy with nose, is as much with friends as at the wolfden. But after he has been loved into idiocy, he's going to get to sleep awhile in this wild *slaapzak* by the fire, *jo*, and then in the bed. Undressing him to an elvish nakedness, Olaf said of Billy in English: an enlightened woman caseworker had given the wolfden kids before, especially boys beaten blue and needing massive doses of affection. Nosebleed all over his clothes when Olaf first saw him at the *familievejleder* office, bruised butt and shoulders, undernourished, practically catatonic. Held him in his arms for two hours before he could get any response, tharn as a trapped rabbit. Took him home, bathed him, dolled him up in the jersey Olaf had been wearing all day for a nightgown, the way you put shorts with your smell on them in with a new puppy its first night alone, got him to eat cream and bananas over *Scotsk* oatmeal, hugged him all night. When the caseworker looked in next morning, Billy was having none of leaving Olaf. They've been bonded since, inseparable. Can't belong to the

wolfden, but in some sense as Olaf's adopted cub he's there with Olaf, a kind
of mascot, with all the _ulveunger_ under orders to treat him as if he were Olaf
himself. Wears the blue briefs of full membership (white for beginners, orange
for intermediates).

PANISKOS
Snuggled into Olaf's open thighs and crossed ankles, watching now the fire
with dreamy eyes, now Olaf, now me, calmly inquisitive, Master Billy played
his stapple, idly some, seriously some, Olaf generously spelling his hand with
milker's fingering. As we talked, kisses for Billy's ears, nice big ears somewhere
under the mop, shoulders, naked armpits, making him squeal. Kneading fingers around nipples, down his ribs, on his round rubbery _pung_. This makes
him purr, said Olaf lifting him and heaving him over to my lap. Just till I get
my clothes off, Billikins. If, I said, I give him back. Olaf, Sander with a gymnast's overwrought body, made smart work of stacking his every stitch in a
neat pack at his feet, and stood easy, aware of his beauty by firelight, eying
critically, amused, my thrip and chug measure for jacking Billy.

ARCADY WITH BEES AND THYME
Billy a thumbsucker and crotch grappler. Total wiggler and flirt. Cool ears,
warm neck. Once Olaf was naked and sitting with his hands to the fire, Billy
skedaddled out of my arms to crawl in under and between his thighs. All
yours, Olaf said, until bedtime. Then we share, _jo?_ Then all yours again.

HYSSOP VIOLET
A broad tease in the frank question of his friendly smile and asking eyes, Olaf,
palming the hunch of his jeans fly, said brightly that midafternoon always
finds him goatish. He ticks off on his fingers, laughing, this dazzler Sander,
who paints, who will do everything with anybody, carries a stepladder in case
he meets an amorous giraffe (this snags Billy's attention), whom you hug and
kiss, and who hugs and kisses you, and then you go bashful and turn over in
bed, though both of you are making a baby on his sister, the three of you in the
same bed fucking her simple, time about, every afternoon and night, sometimes mornings as well, to give the lucky little bastard a half chance to miss
being an idiot with a tail (this causes Billy to flip his ears with his fingers), and
there's your nephew Hans and his mate Jan who snudge down together every
time they can winkle each other's nappies off (a complacent dip of Billy's
shoulders), and even our friend Comrade Joris with the docked black curls
and handsome eyes who drools over the likes of Billy here (_Not me!_ Billy yips),

and there's Strodekker, that good-looking devil, with his houseful of halfsized peterpullers. Is it because I'm hung like a pony? Don't answer. I'm overstepping. There are places in the heart which might have been gardens, or favorite quarters, around which we have built high walls, whose doors have been shut too long. A resolute indraft of breath, a long exhalation, and Olaf squared his shoulders, bounced on his toes, and clattered drumming slaps on his midriff: Billy's blushproof.

DAIMON
Stykke sukkeret here, frisky Billy, says Olaf, the bog goblin with his ears up pert and his britches off, will add his waggery to the doings, to keep us locker room chummy. Billy's goosy and hates mush. Makes me spuke, says Billy unhousing Olaf's rising whopper, stripping the foreskin back, flittering his tongue around the glans. Olaf, by way of Danish drollery, hoisted Billy and kissed him full on the mouth. To barf! says Billy heaving.

HET RETOUR
Done, *bedankt*. Bolted, unboggled, so wanton a charm Olaf wily as Eros had slid, gripped, licked, and kissed gullet deep into my besotted cock, his slick jolt of creamy pulp tasting of warm barley water baking soda sweetgrass sap, and the ladle tilt sloshed after it, and the crowded jumps and sopping spurts sequent. And he mine soon afterwards, as surging a gusher, and we hugged tighter for a while, and fell apart spent. *Dejlig*, Olaf said. And wow. *Hejsa!* there are tears in your eyes, *kammerat*. Billy climbed between us, and we pulled the blanket up snug and had a sweet nap. I was with Piet again, for a while, hugging beside our kayak, our brown bodies hot, our hearts confused, a great happiness in us and around us.

DIDYMOI
A clutch of goose eggs tight in a thick ganglion of vermicelli, the feel of Olaf's testicles plump in a thicket of bronzewire hair. Mushroom fleshy, the glans. Olive codfish kelp, the odor. Pliable bone, the shaft.

HERO
Poor funny Billy, Olaf teases, dressed for bed in Olaf's smelly undershirt because he's lost without it, and whose nubbin nose is very like a rabbit's and is the sexiest in all Denmark, and whose *pik* here is a baby carrot that will grow up to be a cucumber if he keeps it stiff. Like, says Billy, Frisk and Graeshoppe. *Til enhver tid.* Frisk and Graeshoppe, Olaf explains, are pals daffy about keep-

ing an erection going as permanently as they can engineer. They're Billy's heroes. They turn up bowlegged at the den and spring their cocks loose just inside the door rigid and bouncing, having improved them in the pissoir at the bus stop and kept them throughout the school day with, as Frisk says, mind pictures, furtive handwork in class, and honest handwork in the locker room.

A WALK

Billy into Olaf's arms with an effusive eft wiggle, a kiss on his chin, and up onto his shoulders, crowing. A walk around the island. Olaf reached and hugged me to him, shoulder to shoulder. You were looking for something, he said. A lost part of myself. A long easy silence, except for Billy's prattling, before Olaf stopped and searched my face.

PURK

What I like about out here, says Billy, is peeing out the door. And eating good things by the fire. I don't like being by myself in the *slaapzak*, but I understand. I like people who like Olaf. Your peter is as big as Olaf's and you have more hair all over than he does. That's *vidunderlig*. It's fun being out here. Olaf and I are the same person in two bodies. I'm me, of course, and he's Olaf, but I'm Olaf too, and he's me, Billy. We read a big book every night. Olaf puts me in his undershirt he's worn all day, and then we get in one sweater, except that my arms are not in the sleeves, his are, and in the same sweatpants, with all our legs in, and we read some about Mister Toad and his car, or about Nina Pytt And, and then we read a long book with towns in it built in trees in a jungle, and some Icelanders who go to the middle of the world. And sometimes we read about things, like giraffes and whales, and kinds of trees. And then we drink chocolate milk out of the same glass. We're not eating out of the same plate here with you, because Olaf says you might think us funny. I'll bet you wouldn't.

ISLAND QUIET

Olaf talking about his body, the workouts that keep it hard and trim, his sense of its beauty, how he's going to shape Billy's. Might even marry, so Billy can have a mother. There must be some girl, somewhere, who would understand. How could Billy's parents have treated him so, battering him, beastly drunk and fighting? Squalid, shitty stupid, and squalid. Billy meanwhile looking at art books, inspecting the barometer, maps. It's like a school, he says. School, Olaf sighs.

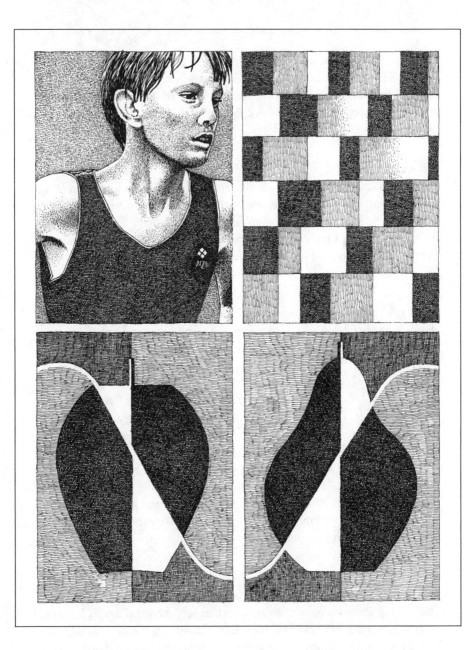

L'IMMONDICITÉ SPÉCULATIVE

Les caleçons immondes are not, Joris says, from Jan's erotic imagination but from *Kouros*, photographs of a Düsseldorf and Bonn DSAP outing, healthy summerbrown teenagers in snug white, or once white, little pants so drenched across the front with deliberate sperm and adventitious urine as to be splotched a dapple of ochre and yellow-grey, spare crotches golden sienna, cock bulge a dark silvery leafmold brown. Joris intrigued: it's like his briefs. The adorable rascals Jan and Hans had indeed studied (such was their word) that number of *Kouros* at Joris'. Sat on my hands the whole time, he said, and his eyes scrunched in their smile. A good talk with him over coffee about Fourier's *l'immondicité spéculative*, the little hordes, Harmonian clarities. When we rose to leave he patted his bust of Lenin on the head.

TOLVÅRIG

Danish film at the Nederlandse Verenigingen van Sexuele Hervorming on the Blauburgwal to which Grietje and I took Hans and Jan, who easily convinced us that we wanted to see it. The voice-over, clear as rung glass, is that of the twelve-year-old boy smiling amiably at the beginning. Long blond hair covering forehead and back of neck. Merry eyes shift sideways with delight, dimples tuck deep. Cabin porch in a deep sunny wood of Norway pines. Hans and Jan, arms over each other's shoulders between me and Grietje, had been as solemn as in church during the talk by a frizzle-haired earnest Mexican-hand-craft-braceleted woman. They sat up and forward as the camera receded, the *12jaar* pulled his shirt off, unzipped and dropped his jeans, and stepped out of his small briefs. This is their first erotically explicit film. Hans gives me a quick look of surprise. Camera moves in to fill screen with fingers twiddling penis stiff before slipping back the foreskin. *Whee*, Hans said, and got shushed from two rows back. Jan rolled his shoulders. Full length again, the boy stood gilded by greengold forest light. Looks up from penis into camera with a good-humored obligingness. This is me, Emil, he says, and this is my friend Sven. Camera finds a second boy, full clump of pubic hair, well-hung, a ripe fullness of glans and scrotum rounded tight, hair a tumult of brown curls, lips still pudgy with baby fat, chest muscles in rich definition. He's fourteen, says Emil, and we love each other a lot. The two fritz at each other, sparring, before they lock into an embrace. Back home afterwards, Hans observed that they didn't ever kiss, except of course their peters. Everybody, Jan said, does everything in the style of their culture. Grietje said she was ruined and depraved, having no notion two boys could have such wild fun. Their eyes! Their hands! And little Emil's well-mannered voice talking about how jolly his weewee feels when he masturbates. They'd jacked each other time about, the one sitting between the other's legs, thigh over thigh, free hand chucking balls, golden smiles abandoned only for gapes of pleasure, before covering one another *zestig en negen* in a pulsing wriggle with rolling backs. Discussion after the film. Flat Heels in a Bun talked about affection, trust, and deep neural feeling. Hans looked like a mouse who has heard the cat. Jan gave him an assuring hug. Bald Sandals and Socks said we must love everybody every way we can, especially children, must cherish all affection as a precious commodity in a violent and corrosive world. Grietje asked me with her eyes if we could go. We could. Jan grabbed Hans and kissed him as soon as we stood, getting stares and sentimental approval. Outside, a fit of giggles. Golly, Hans said, neat kids. Jan asked us to see the slope of his fly. Sander and Wolfgang painting when we got home. Hans described the film in detail. Yes, said Sander, but those Vlamingen need to see me and *de onverzadelijk* Wolfje here jellying our brains. Skeets two drops and a driblet, does Wolfje, but with full zing peashooter force, but being part billy goat he keeps right on once he's squirted his two drops and a driblet, over and over, bruising his peter blue, whereas I, having come a stout creamy pearly half liter five or six times, have to lie down dead doggy and be primed. So what did the spadgers look like in the film?

A SQUARE IN PARIS

This pleasure, Grietje dear, which you've already seen with your girl's X-ray eyes, that everything Adriaan does is deliberate, in his own style, like nobody else. Other people bump through the world. Adriaan looks for things, finds them, knows them. I have been with him in Paris. He goes to a place and sits there putting it inside himself, atom by atom, smell by smell. Of course, in some wonderful way he brought the place with him, out of books, out of history and poems. He makes the place be. That's where Proust's grandmother had her heart attack, he says, here Gertrude Stein walked with her Alice. Here in the Netherlands he has taken me with him to a house. Just a Dutch house, some trees around it, cars parked in the street in front of it. We sat at a bus shelter across from it. Take in the feel of it, Sander. Put it into your imagination. This is the house where the Nazis kept Huizinga under arrest. There. Remember it.

PEUTER WITH BRIGHT HAIR

The small (Eros, Holland, children, kittens) have a mischievous flexibility, curiosity, venturesomeness, that's lost in the large. Extension makes for dullness. Hence the genius of Fourier's self-contained estates.

ILLYRIAN HORNBEAM, WITH OWL

Swedenborg's integral presence of thing and angel. A flower garden, a familiar tree, is angelic in that meaning has drenched them. That is, they are congenial to daimons. Saartje smiling in a happy squinch and squeak of delight becomes a quaggamaster before our eyes. Quagga, nickering recognition, judders his nostrils, and rounds his big black knowing eyes.

CAMPARI AND BLUE FIGS

Let's drive Sander crazy, Grietje says. You take that end and I'll take this. You scritch his head and I'll tickle his toes. Don't you dare, Sander bellows, tickle the bottom of my feet! Knead his scalp and underjaw, rumple his nose, creep fingers along his shoulders and hook into his armpits and scrounge.

TETRADRACHMA WITH ARETHUSA AND DOLPHINS

Their room with its high square windows, low bookcases that make a running shelf around two walls, friendly space, framed *collages* (enlarged photographs of Greek coins, floral prints, birds, moths, cave paintings), the Danish flag, becomes our sweet place for talking and making the Nipper.

COMPOSITE LOGARITHMIC GOLD

Sander babbling, Grietje kissing her way up his legs, I knead his chest, roll thumbs on teats, skim fingertips over ribs, shybold Billy in overimage my stay boasting astraddle my lap what a mess of *sædvæske* Olaf comes, oodles in jumping blobs. Grietje whiffles up inside thighs, kittling scrotum with finger ruffle, bobbling his glans unsheathed under own power. With a nimble torsion his cock rights on its axis as it rears. Oho, says Grietje, Sander sandering. I love you two forever, Sander. Push my hand flat on abdomen from sliddering over navel to grasp haft, Grietje swallowing cap and neck deep enough to gag. Piet's, leafmeal in the slick of the grip, Bruno's in Greek light salt with the Aegean and satyrlasting Athenian afternoons shutterslat August sun in comb-teeth stripes fine on our nakedness, time about, Sander's younger, Olaf's out of restive curiosity and green lust. Shoulders flinching, she slides hands under his butt and persists. Sander coos. Her head lifts and sinks. I hitch an easy grip and pull with a squeeze. *Grootscheeps!* hollers Sander. Brain melting down spine into balls, he reports in a flat voice. Love you both. Don't dare stop. *Allo nu*, the loveliest and best-loved of all sisters is about to be choked and drowned. Balls snuggled into my scrummaging handful, he yipes and chitters, Grietje recklessly shoving onto all but a finger's length. Cock kicks, gushes throbbing, kicks again. Grietje gives up snurfling, eyes watered. Feel thirteen again, she says, swallowing hard, and like I've been playing with myself for two hours nonstop and with no intention of ever quitting. Nor now. Mounted her. *Osculi hians altero tanto lascivior.* With long slow sliding strokes we deepened the richness until we were both sighing with the animal sweetness of it, as if my riding plunges were blent with those of the old nemoral godling Pothos, the uncivilized Eros, charge of the archaic Hermes, of Priapos, the Satyrs, of ballockproud bullocks and longhung asses, smelling of beebalm and allium, adept at perilepsis, the deer-eyed stripling with heron shoulders, rusty knees, sound thighs, and a sprung foreskin bruised lilac. She came bucking and thrashing. Sander, when I looked, had fetched Wolfgang, whom he was undressing, with some difficulty, as he kept him in his arms as he was doing it, so that when he plopped him between us on the bed, Wolfgang still wore a sock and briefs. I took care of the sock, Grietje the briefs. Sander put a blanket over us and made spoons with Grietje, including Wolfje in his hug. You big gorillas have been fucking on Grietje, Wolfgang said. And did she love it, said Grietje. Does it feel good? Not as good, all things considered, as having Wolfje all warm and naked to hold.

MUSK ROBIN AND HOLLAND RUSSET

Grietje, who'd snuggled with Saartje and Jenny at Kaatje's after taking them to the Rijksmuseum and tea, and said when she came home, a tight hug for Sander and me and Wolfje, that she was still having shuddery quivers, was into her whatevereth orgasm, knees wide and trembling, toes curled, both hands busy, when Sander knocked off work for quiet hour. Rascally girls, she said, they come and come with such sweet squeals and sighs. They've got me feeling thirteen again. Unfair, said Sander, giving me only a batting smile of eye, when I began, wholly out of the order of things, to undress him, raising his arms for jersey to be pulled off, hoisting and making an armload of Wolfje as I took off his sneakers and jeans. An *oho!* for a kiss on the cock through his briefs, and a breathed *ja!* for a kiss on the mouth, across Wolfje, whose clothes Sander was peeling away to smooch kisses on every newly bared part, and *at long fucking sweet last!* Naked Wolfje he hoisted across his shoulders, raising me for a crunching hug, both of us laughing hilariously. They've gone mad, Grietje said, as if talking in her sleep. An orgasm by Beethoven, and the Nipper's daddies suit up as Napoleon. Inconsiderate. Undressed, Sander, having parked Wolfgang across Grietje, hindering with inept help, laughing fit to kill, returning my extravagant kiss root deep while I was still hobbled by my trousers shin and ankle. We piled together on the bed, Grietje saying *Is it real? I think I believe what I'm seeing.* Wolfgang: *Jiminy goeie grutten!* Sander, frantic with it all, eyes shining, disengaged, took Grietje, bellowed *idiot!* and withdrew. I took his place, Sander trying to hug us both. Came with an elemental, clear joy. Then Sander. O boy, said Wolfje, are things ever all mixing up together.

NUBBLE-HORNED, FRISK-TAILED PAN

Walk along the canal to the park, Wolfje on Sander's shoulders. Grietje asks pointed questions about Strodekker, Olaf, Joris. Apropos *de bosgod* vay oh ell eff yay ay. That's me! Wolfgang chirped, but not *Bosgod*, my name's something else. His silence about which, Grietje says, is simply that he doesn't know. He's bright, is learning to read, shows promise as a painter, can make a bed, wash dishes, tie his own shoes, fetch and carry. Grietje has bravely satisfied herself that he understands it's back to the streets, the reformatory, the orphanage, or us, and that he has opted for us. He goes blank when parents are mentioned. We'll do it this way, Grietje says, pushing a finger on Wolfje's nose. Amadeus here (Wolfje loves it that he and Mozart are namesakes) is to get his sugar where he wants to. Inside our outlaw family, with Sinaasappels and Keirinckxen only, however. Understood? I understand, Wolfje said, as if we were talking about brushed teeth and combed hair.

AKVARELL

Jan in his new white pants, a pale stain to the left of the crotch seam.

TUSCAN FARM WITH GOATS AND PINES

Child doesn't know one painter from another! Sander whoofs. I thought I was ignorant of history, but this little bugger doesn't know what century he's in, or what country. A large map to teach Wolfgang the continents and oceans. Grietje begins a series of large cards with people and things on them, for what she calls stage-costume recognition: Roman senator, Greek soldier, Egyptian, Chinese, and so on. When I ran him through a batch, he identified Nefertiti as the Queen of England, George Washington as Julius Caesar, Picasso as Mijnheer Halvehout the grocer, Albert Schweitzer as God, and Van Gogh as Tutankhamen.

BOY WITH FENNEC

Sander, sitting to consider his painting, deigns to notice the *lichtgeel* dot on Hans' white denim pants.

ANIS DE FLAVIGNY

Time and Eros, both wavilinear, both a medium in which all else is suspended, or benevolence would not come from a flower's beauty, or time seem a gift rather than a burden.

GEMINI

Foreplay, says Hans, thighs wide and unhampered, strutting a snooty erection, contentedly jacking it, a halfwitted grin of drunken glee for my wink as I came back from the kitchen with coffee. Working up a happy feeling. *Heilig slagroom*, does it ever throb with love! *Bons bons! Ten volle!* Talk about loving kindness. Give me a sip of your vile coffee, he said, and as he took the cup I sat crosslegged between his knees and courteously took over his warmhearted play. Sweet, he said, with an even sillier smile. Slow and tight's the beat. A scrunchy scuddling in my balls, putting a pleasant enough look on my face to make Hans prod my nose with a toe and rub his heel in my hair. You're funny, he said. How can you drink this boiled barge bilge? Papa says I don't jack off nearly enough. Other day, when I'd got in from school, Jantje the stinker at his music lesson, and shucked my britches and whacked off some in Papa's office and some in my room, and Saartje came in with ideas in her eyes and milked me again, and good, Papa put on his leg-pulling voice and called me a slacker and a baby. Said when he was my age he couldn't remember leaving his dick unjacked for more than an hour. He was still at it when I met him some years later, I could witness. Anyway, said Hans with a puff for Bruno's busy childhood and a three-noted whistle of praise for my dexterity, I bragged that I was only building up tone until Jan was free, and Papa said *oho well then!* and bet me *een vijfje* I couldn't jack a steady rhythm without coming until Jan turned up, or went crosseyed for life, whichever happened first. Saartje, sweetie that she is, jollied me frisky again, a truly chummy stiff dick that felt friendly toward the whole world, and Papa the thug kept meddling by saying I should nip along at a faster trot. I kept at it, watching the clock, ten minutes, fifteen, half an hour, steady but slow. Everytime Papa looked in I crossed my eyes. Then the phone rang, Jan calling to say he was going to be late. The hero's fate, said Papa, thumbs up. Don't stop, don't come. So I was a happy moron when Jan, who said he was the first person to play Bach's *Sheep May Safely while Their Shepherd* three times over with a hard on all the way through, turned up.

BACK AND FORTH GEESE

Kafka on his uncle's farm in Moravia, sunbathing naked by the pond, geese and goats under willows, cows and horses staring at the meadow fence. Walt Whitman in his head, the shores of New Jersey as wide and white as the one Crusoe paced with umbrella and blunderbuss, his parrot on his shoulder. His prose has the elemental substantiality of Rousseau's painting, a primitive conciseness innocent of rhetoric. It was written at three in the morning. In it, for all its anguish, one can feel his noontimes on Heligoland, bright mornings on Czech farms, the blue sky at Riva.

NAAPER

Het kikkert je op, says a smiling Jan of Joris' *bronsgeel* spermsodden briefs, sniffing.

DE NAAKHEID VAN EROS

Everything, in any case, Kaatje says, comes down to character. What happens to you depends on what you are. In making children a third sex because of their sexlessness, as he supposed, your Fourier was true to that peculiarly nasty Catholic assumption that all wickedness is *au fond* sexual. Such reasoning depends on the myth of the Fall, a shameful transition before an accuser from unknowing virginity to procreative impulses. Finding all sex an embarrassment, the proper middle class kept the facts of life from their young for as long as possible, as they do now. The middle class, on which, when in doubt, blame everything. Do they ever deserve it. The evil of moral emptiness comes to nothing upon innocence, as it comes to nothing on people who care, who are just and fair, who are reluctant to hurt. Evil is always basically disregard, carelessness, numbness. When Joris came over the time he took Hansje and Jan to the island, I sat him down and said: they are not ignorant, or in the world's eyes innocent. They have a very imaginative and idiotically impractical idea of affection. I like what he said: that he was perfectly happy just to be in their company. And, he added, in yours.

THE NEWS FROM DENMARK
Card from Olaf, who's planning a long film. Billy says tell me he has a new bicycle cap, telescope, star map, and long corduroy trousers, and that he's reading (meaning we're reading) *The Little Prince*.

PHILOSOPHER
Wittgenstein on the Irish coast, sparrows feeding from his hands.

HANS WARREN
In de spiegel week een deur open.
Man zag daardoor een zaal, en daarin
wegschrijdend de gestalte van een jongen.
Even waren het glanzend haar,
de schouderbladen in het strakke shirt
en 't zomers dons over de lange benen
vrijelijk zichtbaar. Even. Hij verdween
snel en diep in de spiegel op een bladerrijk terras.
Kaváfis, huiverend voor die nu lege zaal
keek recht en zag zichself, een oude griek
met beheerste open handen en met ogen
mooi van verlangen en herinnering.

CHARACTER
Fourier equipped the utopian imagination with resources it had never had in such abundance or with such articulateness. He did not want us to think of the Harmony as a utopia but as human advantages being successful, after a history of confusion and defeat. The severity of the defeat keeps us from seeing what he meant. Character, for instance. Once the structure of classes was rescaled according to income, neither the poor nor the rich raised their young to have character. This maintains, except that the middle has been lost also, and character has become an eccentricity, a benign abnormality tolerated as a kind of weakmindedness. All consciences are outlaws to the state. In Spengler's closing pages he argues that the decline of the West is inherent in the

displacement of manners by money. The power to collect taxes and to invest them in weaponry (the fattest return of invested capital) can recognize no scruples in the taxpayer and no freedom that varies the sameness of a state's citizens. Character is the ground of the Harmony, as it was for Shakers, Mennonites, and other pioneer harmonian communities. Hence the distribution of care to all events. Quaggas, tamed by imprinting, can only be ridden by their spadger mates, unlendable and unstealable. Duty and loyalties are structures inside affection.

GAMME

Goede morgen! sang Jantje britchesless in socks and jersey at the door, Wolfgang and I by as agreed to take Hans and Jan along to the gym for ten lengths of the pool before breakfast and for Wolfje's swimming lesson. Jealous, Wolfje had remarked of their wanting to come with us. But I like them, he added. Ready in a jiffy, Jan said, at least I think so. He then kicked an imaginary soccer ball across the sunroom, over my head, took the crowd's applause, stood like a swimmer poised to dive, tried for diffidence, asked if I wanted some coffee from the kitchen, and when I said no, sitting, *onjantjelijk* straddled my lap, a perplexed smile in his eyes. Wolfgang, thumb in mouth, came and stared at him. Tell all, I said. Well, Jan said, I think there's going to be a Keirinckx Family Hearing in a few minutes. You'll see. Fact is, we all sort of slept together last night, and things got out of hand, like we played too far, I think. Whereupon Kaatje came in, with Jenny, sexy sprite, in a crumpled nightgown. Followed by Bruno with Hans by the hand. Saartje (skimpy panties, glass of milk, worried look) straggled behind. What a sweetheart, said Bruno, rather out of the drift of the matter. Bruno, Kaatje said, they were at it all night according to what I've got out of Jenny and Saartje, an amateurish junior orgy of masturbation into fits, *negenenzestig* Hans with Saartje, Saartje with Jan, Hans with Jenny, Jenny with Saartje, Hans with Jan, Jan with Jenny, and plain everyday exogamous and incestuous fucking. Jenny wept, Jan looked like a Stan Laurel who'd wet his pants, Saartje hid in a hug from Kaatje, and Hans tried out a pleading glance on me. Four bare butts, said Bruno, and we'll have a public execution. Witnessed for good measure by Adriaan and Mijnheer Wolfgang there. Jan took his five loud hard whacks with Spartan unconcern, though there were tears in his eyes when I gave him a wink of solidarity. Hans tried to emulate his courage, but yelped once. Jenny bit her lip, blubbering. Bruno spanked her as hard as he did the boys. Saartje wailed outright but got no mercy. Kaatje, impassive throughout, nipped away and brought back hand lotion which she smeared on red behinds while Bruno delivered his lecture. You wretches! You have extraordinary freedoms and the most broad-minded parents in all Amsterdam. The punishment applied to your backsides is for being sneaky and furtive, never mind irresponsible, rebellious, and dim-witted.

BOUNCE

Zwembad. Hans and Jan untalkative for the longest. Wolfgang more embarrassed than they. His improving scissors kick and sidestroke got him twice halfway across the pool. To Jan, sitting winded on the pool's edge, I said that it was his feelings which hurt more than his butt. *Ja,* he sighed. Outside on the street, Hans said to nobody in particular that fucking is terrific, and Jan hugged him wonderfully, and hugged Wolfgang and some astonished citizen's large dog that was passing.

PHILOSOPHER AS HELDENTENOR

What status, Grietje asks, Miss Pollywiggle Saartje on her lap, has Fourier's philosophy among ideas that hope to save mankind from the mean fearful life it has evolved for itself? None, perhaps, except as critique. He argued that religion leaves our political life to us. *Reddite ergo quæ sunt Cæsaris Cæsari, et quæ sunt Dei Deo.* God has written how we are to live together in our passionate attractions, which Fourier understands to be unchanging. What's encoded in the genes of a wasp that makes it a wasp is as well encoded in ours, making us human. Our culture has had to express itself through culture after culture in symbols supplied by our imagination, warped by fear, superstition, and pedantry, salvaged by reason, art, and manners. The way to the Harmony is open only through corridors not yet blocked by fear and meanness. Via Erewhon, or not at all. But who can still the dynamos, scatter the voltaic piles? Not this generation, says Grietje. Prize idiots and blob heads.

NAUTILUS SHELL, ARYBALLOS, ACORNS

Flowery nightgowned Saartje sipping orange juice at breakfast, smug, Grietje combing her hair. Wolfgang, shy minor prophet, looks at her with suspicion. Yawns all around, Sander tremendously, with an unbelieving stare at Wolfje. Where (to me) did he go to? In with me and Saartje, says Grietje. We put him to bed after crackers and milk, Sander says, Adriaan and I, and we were having Greekish friendship when here the imp was, in with us, rooting around. He's queer for all the hair on Adriaan. Needs a bear to sleep with. Abandoned us. I was expecting him, says Grietje.

THE SILENCE OF TIME

Duke Amadeo d'Aosta on his bronze horse in the Giardino Publico of Turin, most metaphysical of cities, and Duke Ferdinand of Genoa, on his fallen horse in the Piazza Micca, and Vincente Gioberti, philosopher, before the Museum of Natural History, and Duke Victor Amadeus near the Dioscuri at the Palazzo Reale, and Massimo d'Azeglio, statesman and poet, in the Piazza Carlo Felice, and Marochetti's General Emmanuel Filiberto in the Piazza San Carlo, all with their long late-summer shadows. Between the clock on the turret of the railway station and Nietzsche's large silver pocket watch the disagreement was negligible compared to other differences. Nietzsche's watch was in July, the railway clock in September. As when Apollinaire later asked to be remembered because he lived in the sad silent time of the fall of kingdoms, a time of tripled courage and threefold grief, and described a fine September in Paris, every evening a vineyard whose musty light ripened at dawn into a red vintage of stars plundered by the silly finches of his delight, and a walk in Auteuil along melancholy docks, hearing a song go silent, to be taken up by other voices bright as bells up and down the Seine, so Nietzsche knew that this clean Torinese light upon the statues in the garden was the last light that Europe would ever see.

STERRENREGEN

Angels of the Rainer Maria Rilkeluchtvaartlijn refueling in midair.

A PEAR TREE IN THEOPHRASTOS

Jenny, demure as a girl by Whistler, improbably the daughter of Hilda Sinaasappel, at Kaatje's when I dropped by, sitting on the sunroom lounge in dancing-school togs. Hate dancing school, she said, wimps the lot of them, but Mummy's all for it, says I'll see the good of it later. Jantje's cool, goes through the motions with his mind a thousand kilometers away. Even in the Pestalozzi the sweet devil behaved perfectly, attentive to everything, but I knew by the look in his eyes he wasn't even there. He was at the museum with Daddy, or at the beach, or walking around a blue lake in Sweden, naming trees and birds. Hansje, though, is always where he is. His imagination lives on what he's doing. For God's sake, explain, said Kaatje. Yes, do, said I. I can't, she said. I could never explain anything.

LA SALINE D'ARC ET SENANS

Erewhonian time must flow backward that Harmonian time go forward. Back before the apple, to advance upon the pear. Time, the medium of redemption, will be of no matter in the Harmony. Day will round with day, season with season.

A WALK WITH JORIS

Canalside, edgewise between trees and cyclists, Mohican file through old folk on benches, hopscotch games, nimbly out of the way of cars. Capitalism invented the state, because it is an organization that must be financed by banks and because it can, through taxes, enlist millions of citizens in its massive and unpayable debt. The capitalist banker then has perpetual and compounding interest, which he lives on grandly by doing no more than tightening his shoelaces as his day's work. War is the state's most profitable business, war being a consumer in constant need. The Soviet Union is just another capitalist monolithic state that has enslaved rather than beguiled its citizens. The twentieth century has betrayed every ideal of the nineteenth. The machine, inhuman by definition, has been given a fate opposite to that planned for it. These fucking automobiles, for instance. They are wasting rather than supplementing human life. The people in them were much better off grubbing potatoes in Dutch mud.

DAT LAAT ZICH HOREN!

Transformations happen when attention's perfected. Culture is a transformation. Wolfje chews with his mouth closed, thanks Grietje for meals, rises when you enter the room he's in. Nice crazy people, he says. For God's sake, Grietje says, tell us your last name! Don't have one, he says. Elfnose Parsnippeter, says Sander, is your name. Coldtoe Bedhopper.

CHART OF THE FAEROES

Wolfje in, crack of dawn, to scuddle under the covers, flopping hair in my face to rub noses and turn me out for our morning swim. Grietje already out, running. Brisk walk, Wolfje skipping at all the zebras. Joris waiting for us outside the *zwemclub*. His Lenin's cap transferred to Wolfgang, rolled towel captured, snatched back, recaptured. As long as they make pants that small for boys as nifty as Wolfgang, Joris says, and with a fit that neat, capitalism's not wholly rotten. What's capitalism? All those bores who confuse money with living well. We get a lecture on banks, usury, and the armaments game, with an interlude for Joris' new briefs, citron and with a wolfcub pawprint in a white circle under the waistband near the left hip. *Padvinder welp!* Having made it breaststroke twice across the shallow end, Joris beside him, Wolfje asked to have a pair. Give you mine, said Joris, but they'd fall off you. Would

Grietje know where to get him dog footprint underbritches? Joris will tell her. Coffee and rolls afterwards, which Joris insisted on buying us. From the pocket of his jeans jacket a Radical Socialist Party button, with hammer and sickle, for Wolfje, and pinned it on his jersey. *Wel bedankt!* And as Wolfje was reading the round of words on his button as Radio Clubhouse Orange Slice, from his other pocket Joris took a *cellofaan* packet lettered *Signe de Piste*, a Wolfgang-sized wolfprint *slipje*. Round eyes, wide grin, and a kiss on the cheek for Joris. You're my friend, Wolfje said. I like you.

BRAMBLE WITH BUCK HARE
Grietje has great fun chasing Wolfje all over the house, up and down stairs, finding him in closets, pulling him by the ankle from under beds, Sander pleading with her to leave him alone. Wolfgang calm and unflustered: he runs on the theory that if he can escape each and every opportunity, never giving in, he and not Grietje will win this tussle, and he will not have to touch a girl. Kaatje's idea, that the Sensitivity Classes she takes Saartje and Hans to should be installed at Florishuis, on a regular basis. Grietje checked them out and came back enthusiastic. Very *fourieriste*, she says. What you mean, Sander offered, was that you and Kaatje and Saartje piled into bed together. *O ja*, wonderful, but we all need it. Show us, said Sander. Wolfje and I will then decide if we can stand it. So a suspicious but game Wolfje, skeptical Sander, eager Grietje, and I undergo Lesson One. We don't need this part, Grietje says, but maybe we'll find out we do. Everybody hugs everybody else, Wolfgang giggling. Next, in the buff, we feel each other all over with fingertips. Grietje and Wolfje a sight. Takes three tries before he can bring himself to run his fingers in her pubic hair, and reflexes double him when she gets to his genitalia. Top of hair to toes, touching everywhere. Sander has an erection like a pump handle before I'm a third of the way down his body. Wolfje and I, Grietje and Sander, Sander and Wolfje, achieving a laughing fit, Grietje and I. We were all in a fine mood to work at the Blue-Eyed Nipper, with suitable diversions time about for Wolfje, when Grietje, inspired and bouncing, called Kaatje, said we'd had, were still having, a wildly successful session: come over, all of them.

GEVOELIGHEID
Grietje brings in Wolfgang the way one carries a large dog, arms and legs dangling. Joris, gaping, tips coffee onto his sweater. Off with it, says Grietje, and let me run cold water on the spill, it's the only way. His one upper garment, the Fair Isles sweater, goes to the kitchen sink, leaving him curly hirsute, nipples brown in swirls of black hair on his hard chest. Grietje, back with more

coffee, says *woef!* you're as furry, Joris, as Adriaan, and as beautiful as a Thorvaldsen. Thank you, says Joris. You really don't like girls, not at all? Dear tactless Grietje. No, he said, not to love. He looked miserable. O God, what an awful thing to say, he whispered. To say you don't intend to love anything is a hateful attitude, isn't it? No, Grietje says brightly, we can't love everybody, or everything. Here, she says, taking Wolfje from my lap and putting him in Joris', hug this scamp while your sweater dries. It's good for him, and he likes it. Take your thumb out of your mouth, imp, long enough to say hello to Joris. Out pops thumb. Hallo you, says Wolfje, batting his lashes, bobbing his heels. Grietje describes the sensitivity sessions, praising Wolfgang's gift for affection, his clarity in giving it and receiving. As Grietje describes our sessions, Joris becomes a keenly curious but incredulous listener. *Ja*, says Wolfje, but I don't see why I have to put my fingers all over Saartje and Jenny, it's creepy crawly, but I suppose it's in the game. But I've kissed Grietje all over, that gave me a good tingle. Like this? Joris asks, running fingertips over Wolfgang's chin and nose. Like this, Wolfje says, gliding spread fingers through the hair on Joris' chest. Do it, says Grietje, you two. *Ja!* says Wolfje, get naked. He squirmed loose, rolled onto the floor, untied his shoes lying on his back, sprang up, and had all his clothes off before Joris could command the *here?* he eventually gulped. I can't, he says, I simply can't. Why not? asks Wolfje.

VAGROM KABOUTER

Wolfgang into my bed sometime before midnight. Hugged his warm, bony, cold-toed body against me. He's soon asleep. Perfectly comfortable with him beside me. Grietje says she's unaware of his coming and going in their bed, so easily does he adapt to shapes and hollows. His sensuality is as yet distributed all over his body. He naps with Grietje, unmoved by her delicious beauty, bonded to her in affection and friendliness. Sander he finds sexy, and adores him. Sander knows exactly the nuances of the erotic in Wolfje's imagination, thoroughly priapic yet a game of alert comedy, a foolishness in it all. Grietje for love, Sander for fun, me for security. Adriaan found me, he says. I didn't even know I was an orphan.

THIS IS NOT A PIPE

You can't be all of yourself at any one time, or the self you want to be all the time. Some people are never themselves.

ONTMOETING

Through, this afternoon, the little triangular park fenced by low hedges and an Art Deco railing, benches with nannies and *Volkskrant* readers, toddlers stomping, skateboarders sliding among them. A beautiful child in a warm-up jacket, hood down his back like folded wings, front open to within two centimeters of being unzipped, and white cotton *cache-sexe*, undercord in the crack of his bare brown butt. Fists in jacket pockets, a gesture for talking with buddies, three of them, all in knee pants. Nodding of heads, guffaws, punching of friendly shoulders, spontaneous heel dances. Nils Strodekker! Whose precocious pubic hair showed dark through the thin *cache-sexe*. Horde members, his fellows, in a playground full of bandlings, one of whom I recognize as Tobias Strodekker, who recognizes me. Blue briefs more off than on, he grins hello and bounces over on his toes. Papa's over there, he points, with Rasmus, reading or something, and puts a damp gritty hand inside mine to be taken. Godfried on a park bench outside the playground (jeans, sweater, cap) was writing in a notebook on his knee. Erasmus beside him, head on arm on Godfried's shoulder, was following the writing. Small white pants, barefoot, orange bill cap cockily on back of head, naked torso. Ah! says Godfried, golden luck. Come have coffee with us in this splendid weather in our garden. Erasmus, inward eye giving his smile a tricky illegibility, rose and kissed the corner of my mouth, saying he's read my essays on *zinnelijkheid*. Godfried had said he must, and he has questions to ask. But first, Nils, for whom he trotted off, and who took farewell of his buddies with a whisper in an ear, flicking fingers, kicking toes, and kneeing knees. His arm around Erasmus' waist coming to the Renault.

PIETER BLEEKER
Jurassic ganoid labyrinthodont bugeyed blenny.

WOONKAMER PASTORAAL
Big Sander and Little Wolfje (as they've taken to calling each other) working on a large square canvas of two Hordelings on a quagga, both painting, neither getting in the other's way, ducking an elbow here, reaching an arm across an arm there, Sander keeping an eye on Wolfgang's every stroke. The brush is a blade, bite in and draw back. A line is like the tune in music. Color's the ground. That persimmon loves that grape and fryingpan iron grey, they make each other's eyes go soft and silly, they want to snuggle and swap spit, but it's the lines around them that make them sing. Home from library, a tedious lunch with Paulus, walk, swim, tea with Kaatje, brought Saartje and Hans with me to Florishuis for Quiet Hour. *Met toestemming van de ouders?* Adriaan is a *voorstander* for the law. *Gewillig*, said Kaatje, but with whoever has the stomach for it checking on you, no matter what Hilda Sinaasappel says

about privacy. Grietje agrees with me. Jan on his way over from his music lesson, we began Quiet Hour in the conversation area of the studio, watching the painters paint. Saartje stood chummily for Grietje to wrench down her jeans, and, panties removed on the way, take her into her lap. She's already, Hans said kneeing room for himself between my legs, unbuckling his belt, slick and wet. Shoulder shrug from Wolfgang. Hans with a speculative bat of eyelashes and a goblin grin thumbed his underpants off in two high stomping steps. You people, Sander said looking over his shoulder, handsome frown, persimmon smudge on his nose, are pretty friendly for an establishment that specializes in pumping nippers into Grietje and an afternoon encampment for everready Boy Scouts. Saartje, after a whistle of praise for Grietje's cunning fingers, bragged that, safe for a good five days, she was getting fucked by Jantje and Hansje both. And Wolfje too, Grietje said by way of surprise. Sander, seeing (bless his heart) Wolfgang's panic into misery, grabbed him into a sweet hug, kissing his hair and ears. No, he said, Wolfje's mine. Fat hot tears melted down Wolfje's cheeks. Sander, a stormy look for us all, carried him out of the studio.

COMPOTE OF PEARS

Hans, brightly amused and hair ruffled, looked around our door, got invited in and sent away to bring Campari, glasses, and Perrier. Cough medicine, he said, back. Jantje's fucking himself goofy, he reported, and Saartje's having fits. He looked hard at Wolfje hugged in Sander's arms and legs. Grietje fetchingly half-dressed in my shirt handed drinks, and Hans joined our circle in the bed, all very jolly and convivial. How, Grietje said, would one who has not known Sander all these years believe him? He really doesn't exist, because there isn't anybody who can make love with Wolfje, then with me, with Wolfje again, and again with me, and I may have to share him with Wolfje tonight. Keeps things harmonized, Sander said. Adriaan's benippering Grietje, taking his blithering sweet time, Grietje's bleating that it's to her satisfaction, so I have Thumper here to squeeze, snuggle, pull, sip, and wabble. He squeezes back.

THE BAND AT GIVERNY

Sander translates Monet's charcoal drawing of Michel Monet, age six, and Jean-Pierre Hoschedé, age eight, into his style, keeping the charm. Done in 1884, on canvas. Haystack or row of poplars along the Epte or dripping willows over water lilies intervened. And now, a century later, Sander completes it. Monet, who bought his first Japanese prints in the Netherlands, and whose daimon was Hiroshige, could not disapprove, even though the lines are now from De Stijl, the colors Sander's (brown sweater, red cap, slate pants for Michel, blue sweater, brown pants for Jean-Pierre).

PALE YELLOW PEAR
From hard green, bright with rain, to a blush beneath the yellow, freckles over.

EVERYTHING COULD BE OTHERWISE
His mother Camille pinning up her hair behind him among flowering shrubs in the garden at Argenteuil, his kitten stalking a butterfly on the mock orange in a Japanese urn, little Jean Monet, age six, has thrown himself down in a ragdoll flop, playing *Aargh! I'm deaded.* In two more steps his mother, who was soon to be married to his father when this wonderful painting was done, the June of 1870 (France about to commit the idiotic imprudence of declaring war on Prussia), will pretend to find him, pick him up, and kiss him. Of course Monet is clean off the board here, Sander says. That happens every time you observe rather than copycat. Point out that the picture is iconographically a Moses in the bulrushes. Or, says Grietje, a Piero della Francesca Jezus laid out on the ground in an epiphany. So Sander does a Wolfgang lying on the floor looking out of the side of his eyes at Grietje reading, trying to magic her into looking at him. A quick drawing of Wolfje, hands behind head, bored, ankle on knee, beside Sander fucking Grietje. Laugh, pouts Wolfje, but I won't be bored when the Nipper comes. He'll be my brother. Don't ever tell him I'm not his brother. I'll talk with him while Grietje and Sander and Adriaan are busy with their things. We'll start talking as soon as he's borned.

Design by David Bullen
Typeset in Mergenthaler Sabon
by Wilsted & Taylor
Printed by Maple-Vail
on acid-free paper